MAFIA VIRGIN

THE KINGS OF ITALY
BOOK 5

MILA FINELLI

MAFIA VIRGIN
Copyright © 2023 by Mila Finelli

Cover: Letitia Hasser, RBA Designs

Editing: Jennifer Prokop

FOREWORD

Amici!

Some of you may be familiar with this world, so you know what to expect. But in case you've stumbled on this title, please know this is *dark* mafia romance. Brace yourselves!

Here is a list of content warnings for this book, so we're all on the same page:

- Breeding Kink
- Genital piercing
- Spanking
- Murder and torture
- Cancer/Terminal illness of a parent

It's also worth mentioning that you will find many Italian and Sicilian words in here. I've only italicized the first usage of each word/phrase.

Sicilian is an Italian dialect, but I tried to keep the Italian to those phrases and words that most of my readers are familiar with from previous books. So while Giacomo is Sicilian, he still uses the same dirty words we all know and love. (Along with some new favorites lol!)

I'm so proud of how this series turned out. Remember, join my newsletter at milafinelli.com for bonus content, links to merch, and more!

— Mila

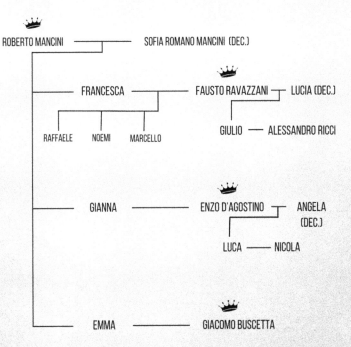

ROBERTO MANCINI ———— SOFIA ROMANO MANCINI (DEC.)

FRANCESCA ———— FAUSTO RAVAZZANI —— LUCIA (DEC.)

RAFFAELE   NOEMI   MARCELLO

GIULIO —— ALESSANDRO RICCI

GIANNA ———— ENZO D'AGOSTINO —— ANGELA (DEC.)

LUCA —— NICOLA

EMMA ———— GIACOMO BUSCETTA

THE KINGS OF ITALY

"It's not whether you get knocked down, it's whether you get up."

— VINCE LOMBARDI

PROLOGUE

Giacomo

October
An undisclosed address in Calabria, Italy

The meeting was bullshit.

I had a thousand more important things to do than to sit down with these fucks. But apparently, taking over as the boss now meant doing a lot of shit I hated.

So I was here. But I had news for them—if they hoped to make peace between our clans, they were wasting their time. My plans to take back what was owed to me were already in motion.

Across the table sat three Ravazzanis: Fausto, the oldest and head of the vast criminal empire; his consigliere and cousin, Marco; and the heir, Giulio. Two other men were with them, and I assumed by the way the tall one hovered by Giulio's side that it was his lover, the famous sniper Alessandro Ricci. He was every bit as impressive as the rumors made him out to be.

I should hate those two, seeing as how Giulio and Alessandro killed my brother and my father only four months ago.

Instead, I wanted to shake both their hands.

I loathed my father and brother. Always had. I hoped they were both being ass fucked dry in Hell. Repeatedly.

No, my problem with Ravazzani was business, not personal.

Impatient, I tapped my fingers on the table. Bernardo Virga, the head of the Sicilian Cosa Nostra, *il capo di tutti capi*, glared at me as if chastising me to stop. Fuck that. He demanded that I attend this, not that I play nice. I motioned with my hand for him to get started.

Introductions first. I shook hands and tried to appear relaxed. This was the part of the job I disliked—meetings and more meetings, talking for hours. I wasn't a diplomat; I was a fighter. I'd rather settle an argument with my fists.

But Virga demanded my presence here, so I had little choice in the matter. Everyone was worried I would retaliate for the murder of my family, and they hoped to pacify me enough to drop the need for revenge.

Like I said, a wasted effort.

I announced the names of my three men quickly, ending with my closest confidant. "This is Francesco Zaniolo, my right hand." I'd known Zani forever, and he was more like a brother to me than my own brother had been.

When it was Ravazzani's turn, he pointed at his son. "And this is my oldest son, Giulio. He runs our *'ndrina* in Málaga now."

I nodded, unimpressed, then looked at Ricci. "And this is your *ragazzo*, no? The famous sniper."

The tall man gave no reaction, just continued to stare at me. His eyes were flat, calm. A soldier ready for battle. I could appreciate this.

It was Giulio who answered. "Yes."

"I am a big fan of your work," I said to Ricci, who merely dipped his head in acknowledgement.

Ravazzani launched in, saying, "My condolences on the death of your father and brother."

Smart to mention this right away. The reminder of my murdered family would've irritated me if I gave a shit about either one of them. I folded my hands on the table. "They were both pricks. I hated them."

The room fell silent. Not getting the reaction he'd obviously hoped for, Ravazzani gestured to Pasquale Borghese, *capocrimine* and head of the Calabrian 'Ndrangheta. "Let us get started."

Borghese smiled like a kindly grandfather surveying naughty grandchildren. "The ugliness between your families has dragged on far too long. We are here today to settle it."

"Ugliness?" Ravazzani sneered. "You mean how the late Don Buscetta pretended to be my ally while working with Mommo and D'Agostino to take me down? Or how Nino Buscetta sent men around Europe to hunt and kill my son like a dog? Is this the ugliness of which you speak?"

Was he truly acting the martyr? Treating me like a *coglione*? I didn't always agree with my late father and brother—far from it—but Ravazzani was not blameless.

I hardened my voice. "You have repeatedly cut down our profits from the product coming in from the south. And your men killed my father and my brother."

Don Ravazzani's expression remained unchanged. "This does not make us even. At all."

Virga cleared his throat. "We must settle this discord because it is bad for business."

"We can't have more dead bodies in the streets," Borghese agreed. "Car bombs and shootings. This brings unwanted attention to everyone. The police are agitated over these murders, making arrests. Looking for people to blame."

"That is a shame," Ravazzani said, not sounding sympathetic in the least. His consigliere smirked and I longed to punch each of them in the face.

"It makes problems for me," I said. "Which in turn could make problems for you."

The amusement instantly disappeared on the other side of the table. Don Ravazzani asked softly, "Is this a threat?"

Was he fucking serious? Of course it was a threat. Unlike my late father and brother, I never said anything I didn't mean.

"*Signori*," Borghese said. "Let us remain calm."

Calm? Did he honestly think this meeting was a good idea? "Why are we here? This is a waste of everyone's time."

"We must settle this," Virga said. "Make peace. Otherwise, we are in the newspapers with the Guardia di Finanza crawling up all our asses."

"And what do you propose?" Ravazzani leaned back in his chair. "Because I am not changing the way I do business."

Meaning he wouldn't cut me into his drug trade, the *pezzo di merda*. Ravazzani took what used to be a Sicilian staple and made it his own. The Cosa Nostra still controlled the gun trade, but I wanted both. I intended to take everything back.

"Don Virga and I have discussed this," Borghese said. "We would like to join the two families in marriage."

"Fuck no," and "Absolutely not," Ravazzani and I answered at the same time.

At least we agreed on this.

"We are not asking," Borghese said, his voice as brittle as ice. "It is our job to see it settled and this is what we have decided. Neither of you have a choice. There will be a wedding between your two families." He sat back, a slick grin on his face. "And we have just the bride in mind."

Bride . . . Was *I* the groom? *Che cazzo?* I didn't want to marry anyone, no matter who gave the order. Fuck heirs, fuck the traditions. I never intended on having a family of my own. I would serve as the boss on my terms, not anyone else's.

"You carry too much anger, Giacomo."

My mother's words when I was a young boy still haunted me, but they were true. A further example of why I'd never carry on the Buscetta line. One of my brother's many bastards could have the crown when I died.

Ravazzani spoke first. "There is no female in my household, save my two-year-old daughter. Since you can't possibly mean her, then I don't know who you are proposing."

"Your wife has two sisters, no?" Virga said. "Unmarried and of age, I believe."

Almost everyone in the room froze. The Mancini twins, younger sisters of Francesca Ravazzani, were well known in our circles. Their mother had been a famous Italian model who married a Canadian mob boss. That sort of thing wasn't easily forgotten by men like us.

But marry a Mancini? *Ma dai*. "You mean the one shacked up with D'Agostino since last summer?" I asked with a derisive snort. "Fairly certain he won't like it if you marry her off to someone else."

"No," Borghese said. "The other sister. Emma."

"That is off the table," Ravazzani said calmly. "I won't allow it."

Virga continued like Ravazzani hadn't spoken. "Buscetta will marry the Mancini girl and receive some of the Toronto business. Then you will all act like one big happy fucking family, *capisce?*"

Toronto business? After Ravazzani stole the Colombians from us? Ma dai, what a goddamn insult.

I kept my tone steady, unyielding, as I folded my hands on the table. "I'm not marrying anyone—no matter who gives the order and what business I gain. Ravazzani and I will settle this shit between ourselves, without the need for a wedding."

Borghese and Virga traded a glance, but I couldn't decipher it.

"Finally, some sense." Ravazzani stood and buttoned his suit jacket. "I assume we're finished here. I need to return to Siderno."

I rose, as well. "And I must get back to Palermo."

"We expect this marriage to happen," Borghese said. "Do not disappoint me, Ravazzani."

"The same goes for you, Buscetta." Virga glared at me, his narrow-set eyes like black orbs.

"You ask the impossible," Ravazzani said. "And Buscetta and I both agree this is not happening."

The two old men appeared as if they wanted to say something, but how could they complain? Ravazzani brought in most of the 'Ndrangheta's money and me most of the Cosa Nostra's wealth. We weren't men you could easily push around or threaten, not if you wished to keep your big houses, fancy cars and expensive mistresses.

I walked out first, not wanting to give Ravazzani the satisfaction. Zani and the others trailed me into the hot Calabrian sunshine. "Let's get the fuck out of here," I said as I climbed into our car.

CHAPTER ONE

Emma

January
Toronto, Canada

For as long as I could remember, I wanted to be a doctor.

That dream seemed far away at the moment, though. I was struggling just to keep up in my second year of university. After this came years of medical school and residency.

I wasn't quitting, though. Someday this would all be worth it.

I waved to the guards as I passed through the front gate of my home. Toronto was bitterly cold this time of year, and I always felt bad for my father's men who were stuck outside. I guided my electric car up the drive and into the four-car garage. My father's two cars—a big gas-guzzling SUV and a sleek sports car—were idle, as they had been for months.

After plugging my car in to charge, I grabbed my bags and headed inside. I needed to eat something and then finish my mound of homework. But all of that had to wait until after I checked in on Papà.

I dropped my things in the kitchen, then strode through the quiet house. The once-vibrant home was now an eerie collection of empty rooms. The loneliness used to bother me, but I was too busy these days to notice.

Everything changed in the past four years. Not only were my two sisters living on the other side of the globe, happily partnered, but my father revealed four months ago that he has Stage 4 cancer. It started in his prostate, but quickly spread throughout his whole body. The only reason he told me was because he needed to have radiation and chemotherapy to attack the tumor. Because we lived together, he knew he couldn't hide it from me.

He made me swear, however, not to tell my sisters. Frankie and Gia had complicated relationships with my father, so I tried not to feel guilty about keeping this from them. It wasn't like either of them had been home to visit recently. Neither one of them even called him on the phone these days.

The soft sounds of a television reached my ears as I climbed the stairs. Papà must be watching another old movie. Maybe he'd feel up to playing chess today. Unfortunately his last round of chemo had really sapped his energy. It would take a few weeks for him to regain his strength.

Gloria, his live-in nurse, was in his room, reading in a chair. My father was asleep, his body completely still except for the rise of his chest. Medical equipment cluttered the large space around the bed. We kept his treatment here, a secret from the rest of the world.

Gloria held a finger up to her lips and gestured for me to follow her into the hall.

"Hi," I said as she closed his door. "How is he today?"

"Good. He ate some soup and complained about the lack of salt."

"Of course he did. Has he been sleeping long?"

"About fifteen minutes."

The doorbell rang, the unusual sound startling me.

Gloria and I exchanged a look. It couldn't be a visitor, not with the guards outside. They would never let a stranger come to the door. Had Uncle Reggie lost his key? He was the only other family member who knew of my father's illness, and that was because Uncle Reggie needed to oversee the business until my father was back on his feet.

"I'll go down," I told the nurse. "Be back in a few."

"No need." Gloria patted my shoulder. "You must be hungry and have work to do. I'll sit with your father a little longer."

"Thank you. That would be very helpful."

The bell clanged again. Jeez, impatient much?

I hurried to the ground floor. By the time I reached the front door I was breathing hard. I swung it open and found three well dressed men staring at me. "May I help you?"

The strangers moved forward, pushing past me to enter the house. I stepped back, out of reach, as a sense of foreboding crawled over my skin. "Who are you? What are you doing here?"

"Signorina Mancini," the older one said, his Italian accent thick. "May we sit?"

Thanks to my upbringing, I recognized dangerous men when I saw them. And these three definitely qualified. Blank flat stares? Check. Guns bulging under their suit coats? Check. A lack of respect for personal space? Check.

I fought to stay calm. "Tell me who you are first."

He ignored me. Instead, he strode into the formal sitting room and lowered himself into a chair. The other two men followed, standing behind the man now seated. They appeared bored, but I knew better. These were killers.

The guards let them through. The guards would never let a threat near the house.

This eased my worries somewhat, until I thought about my father upstairs. I had to get rid of these men before they discovered our secret. If word got out that Papà was sick, everything we had would be stripped away by his enemies. This house, the cars. The protection and money. We'd have nothing—and we'd never be able to afford Papà's care.

I took the seat farthest away from the one in the chair. He wore a fancy gold watch and had the straightest, whitest teeth I'd ever seen. Dark hair was slicked off his large forehead. Early to mid-fifties, if I had to guess.

"We're sitting," I said. "Now, please answer my questions."

"My name is Bernardo Virga. Have you heard of me?"

Swallowing, I shook my head.

He frowned, as if this answer disappointed him. "Your family has done you a disservice, then, Signorina Mancini."

"Why? What are you talking about? And how did you get past the guards outside?"

"Do you know anything about a meeting three months ago between your brother-in-law and Don Buscetta?"

Did he mean Fausto? Why on earth would this man think I knew anything about the Ravazzani empire? I wiped my sweaty hands on my jeans. "No."

"You see, signorina, I am responsible for the whole of Sicily. *Capisce?* And Don Buscetta is the head of one of my most important *cosche*." He waved his fingers. "Clans. "

I knew how the mafia worked. If what Virga said was true, then he was *il capo dei capi*. The boss of all bosses.

And he was sitting here in Toronto. In my living room.

This was a very bad sign.

"You see, Don Ravazzani and Don Buscetta are at odds. It's a long string of disagreements, the nature of which I will not bore you with. However, these things need to be settled amicably. The way it is going now is very bad for all of us. Too public. Too dangerous."

"And you wish to speak with my father about this?" It was the only logical conclusion.

"No. I am here to see you."

My stomach collapsed in on itself like a popped balloon. This couldn't be good. "Me?"

"Sì, signorina. You see, a simple solution to the bad blood has been decided. Yet neither side has moved to accept it. I am here to get the process started."

That sounded ominous. But I had no idea what Fausto's disagreement with this Buscetta person had to do with me. "By doing what?"

"By collecting you. I suggest you go and pack a bag, signorina."

"Pack a—"

Oh. The words collided in my brain and the puzzle began to solve itself. *Sicily . . . bad blood . . . solution . . . pack.*

Holy smokes.

I knew how things worked in the Old Country. They intended to join the two families in marriage to settle a business dispute between Fausto and this other man, Buscetta. *I* was the solution.

"No," I blurted.

Virga cocked his head. "Perdonami?"

Though it was likely unwise, I tried to explain. "You hope to marry me to this Don Buscetta person, but I'm not part of that world. I'm in my second year at university. I plan to become a doctor."

"You are Emma, Roberto Mancini's youngest daughter. You are part of our world whether you like it or not."

I rubbed my forehead and tried to think it through. No way Frankie had agreed to this. Which explained why no one told me— Fausto had no intention of marrying me off to a total stranger.

Looking up, I said with total conviction, "My brother-in-law will not allow this."

"Your brother-in-law does not have a choice. We serve a greater good, which is the brotherhood. Whether it's in Sicily or Calabria, the 'Ndrangheta or the Cosa Nostra, it's all the same."

I didn't believe him. Fausto answered to no one, save my sister. "My answer remains no. You'll need to make peace some other way."

"There is no other way, signorina. And this has already been decided."

I pulled my phone out from my back pocket and unlocked it. If this man wouldn't listen to me, I would ring Fausto.

"I wouldn't do that," Virga said. "It would end very badly for your sick father."

I paused, my finger hovering over the glass. "What did you say?"

"Your sick father, upstairs. Did you think we were unaware? Your father is dying, signorina, and if you do not come with me today, I will send my men upstairs to kill him. Is this what you want?"

My blood turned to ice in my veins and I sucked in a sharp breath. "You wouldn't."

But deep down I knew he would.

Virga's smile was filled with menace. "If you wish for your father to live, then you will not involve Ravazzani. You will pack a bag and come with me to Sicily."

I thought of Papà, weak but still very much full of life. Could I save myself and allow him to be murdered? I knew I couldn't do it. This was my father, the man who'd hugged me and helped me with homework. Bought me lemon cheesecake when I was feeling down. Taught me chess. Allowed me to pursue a career as a doctor.

"And we will shoot his aide, as well."

Horror rolled through me. Gloria didn't deserve to die any more than my father did. I couldn't live with myself if either of them were hurt because of me.

Did this mean I was agreeing to marry a Sicilian mafia don?

No, no, no. Please, no. I didn't want a life of violence and blood, death and destruction. My sisters might not mind it, but I needed to help people. To heal and comfort. To give back.

I couldn't become a mafia wife.

Lightheaded, I gripped the chair's armrests. Air refused to enter my lungs, my body seized in dyspnea. "This can't be happening," I wheezed.

"I'm afraid it is very much happening, signorina. If it doesn't, then not only will you cause the deaths of those two upstairs, you will cause a war between Buscetta and Ravazzani. Is this what you wish, to risk your sisters and their families?"

I knew how mafia wars ended, with carnage and loss. There were no winners. Fausto's first wife died in his last war, after all. I couldn't risk Frankie or my niece and nephews.

My eyes grew hot, but I wasn't a crier. I had to be strong for myself and for my family.

I had to be the responsible one.

I pushed my emotions down and tried to think logically. "This Don Buscetta, does he want to marry me?"

Virga's lips thinned, the lines around his mouth deepening. "It does not matter. He will do as he is told, as will you."

Ah. So, Buscetta didn't wish to do this, either. Good. It meant he and I could come up with a solution to this problem.

I forced myself to my feet. "I'll go pack."

"Va bene." Virga didn't move, but one of his men started toward me. "Sandro will come with you. And so you know, my men will stay behind here until the wedding in Sicily. Just in case."

Here? Near my father? "You can't do that. It will upset him."

"All you need to do is marry as I've instructed and they will leave Toronto."

I glared at him, feeling my life and future slip through my fingers like sand. I wasn't prone to dramatics and tantrums—that was more Gia's style—but I was close to starting right now. Maybe I should scream for the guards outside.

Virga spread his coat wide to show off the pistol he wore in a holster. His tone was as cold as Lake Ontario in February. "If you are hoping for a rescue from the men outside, I hate to disappoint you."

"What did you do to them?" I choked out.

"That shouldn't concern you at the moment."

I'd known most of these men my entire life. Were they injured? Dead? "Are they hurt?"

"I would focus on your own well-being, signorina, rather than anyone else's."

More threats? "If you hurt me, I can't come with you."

"You very much underestimate me, then. There are plenty of ways I can hurt you, Miss Mancini." He let that statement sit for a minute, and I could feel sweat building up at the nape of my neck. Then he said, "I suggest you start packing and we can avoid any further violence."

What choice did I have? I'd rather suffer at the hands of this man than see Gloria or my father harmed.

Buscetta didn't want this union either.

That gave me a tiny sliver of hope.

Shoving aside my panic, I started for the stairs. I had to speak to Buscetta as quickly as possible. We needed to come to a practical agreement—one that would save my family, while also avoiding a life-long commitment between a pair of strangers.

Then I would return to Toronto and my father's bedside, war and marriage avoided.

Don Buscetta, whoever he was, would certainly be reasonable about this.

CHAPTER TWO

Giacomo

"Be reasonable! *Vi prego*, Don Buscetta," the man gurgled.

I hit his face again and blood spurted from his mouth. "Reasonable?" I snarled. "Reasonable when you are stealing from the family? Reasonable when you are so disrespectful? Ma dai." I punched him in the stomach. "Why should I be reasonable after such grave offenses?"

I let him fall to the ground, where he crumpled into a little ball. He was one of my brother's men, a high-level soldier who handled transactions with the Russians. He thought I was stupid, that I wouldn't know what he'd done.

People underestimated me because of my large size and rough appearance. They believed me stupid, nothing more than a thug. This included my dead brother and father.

Except I liked math. I was good at it. Math was easy, straightforward, and it never changed, never lied. Which is how I was certain this *coglione* had stolen from me.

Whimpering, he said, "I'm not stealing from you, Don Buscetta."

"*Cazzata*." I spat into the dirt next to his head. "You are undercutting my profits, skimming from the top."

Slowly, he tried to crawl away, a denial on his traitorous lips. "No, I swear it."

Advancing, I kicked him in the ribs with the toe of my boot. "You sold them eight-hundred-and-fifty-thousand worth of guns, *stronzo*. Except I only have seven-hundred-and-fifty-thousand Euros to show for it. You are short one-hundred-thousand. If I had to guess, it's either up your nose or in some random pussy."

He didn't talk much after that. We dumped his body where it wouldn't be found by the *carabinieri*. Word of his disappearance would soon get around amongst my men and serve as a deterrent to others. I wouldn't tolerate anyone stealing from the family.

After we cleaned up, I climbed into my car and started the engine. Zani dropped into the passenger seat and pulled out his mobile. "Virga insists on meeting today," Zani said. "I have five messages from his people."

"Tell him no."

"You can't refuse him, Mo."

"I can do whatever the fuck I want," I corrected. "And I don't want to see that coglione ever again."

Since the Ravazzani meeting a few months back, Virga had hounded me. He thought he had the right to tell me what to do, but I didn't take orders from old men. Not anymore. I had enough of that to last a lifetime.

"Virga has come to Palermo to see you. He's here. And he's the boss."

"I know what he wants to discuss. The subject is closed."

Zani exhaled heavily and tapped the side of his phone against his leg. "You're being stubborn and it's bad for business. He could have you killed. Replace you with one of his men."

"He could, but he won't. Virga tries to replace me, he has chaos on his hands." While my father's men hated my brother, they liked me. Maybe because I treated them like human beings, instead of dogs, as my brother had. And I controlled too much money to get rid of based solely on a whim.

Zani's phone buzzed. "Virga's man again. You want me to ignore it?"

"Fuck this." I reached over, grabbed the phone out of Zani's hand, and answered it. "Buscetta."

"Don Buscetta. How kind of you to pick up."

The sarcasm was not lost on me. I put it on speaker so Zani could hear. "This is Buscetta. Who's this?"

Some shuffling in the background, then Don Virga's voice filled my car. "I expect to see you standing in front of me within the next fifteen minutes."

I scowled at the phone. "Why?"

"Because I am telling you to."

Che cazzo? "Today is not good. Maybe I can make time tomorrow."

"Giacomo, this is not a request."

"And if I say no?"

Zani dropped his head into his hands, but I ignored him. I rolled over for no man, even one as powerful as Virga.

Il capo dei capi grew quiet, then spoke softly. "Do you think I have no leverage over you, that I have come here with nothing? Eh, *cretino*? Ma dai, you think I don't know about Mirabella and who is living there?"

Instantly, my muscles locked up. I heard Zani hiss through his teeth, but I kept my attention on the phone as my fingers strangled the steering wheel. I'd busted my ass to protect this secret, so how had Virga learned of it?

My jaw ached from how hard I was grinding my teeth together. I didn't like being backed into a corner.

"Where?" I snapped.

He rattled off an address. We weren't far. Without saying another word, I hung up on Virga and tossed the phone back to Zani.

"Mo—" Zani started.

"Don't say it." I couldn't handle this conversation, not right now. As the only person I trusted, Zani knew that my sister, Viviana, was still alive. I had her well protected at Mirabella, a facility on the outskirts of the city. So how had Virga discovered this information? The entire world, including my late father and brother, believed Viviana dead. I'd purposely arranged it that way.

Zani spoke up anyway. "It wasn't me. You know I would never tell."

I did know this. Even under torture, Zani wouldn't share my secrets. But that didn't mean I wasn't pissed off, that I didn't want to wrap my hands around Virga's throat and squeeze the life out of him.

We rode in tense silence. Virga wanted to meet about the wedding. Again. So I would walk in, tell him to fuck off, and then demand he forget all he'd discovered about me.

"Call Mirabella," I said as I punched the gas pedal. "Check that Viviana is okay. Virga could have a man there. I want to make sure she's safe."

Zani dialed and spoke to the guard outside Viv's room. He reported that my sister was fine, everything perfectly normal. After warning the guard to be on alert, Zani hung up as I parked at the address we'd been given.

It was an old hotel, the kind that had passed its prime decades earlier. Exactly the sort of place I'd expect Virga to patronize, the outdated fuck. His man approached us in the lobby and we were quickly hustled into the elevator.

Zani and I didn't speak on the way up. In our world there were eyes and ears everywhere, and I wouldn't put it past Virga to be listening in.

When the doors opened we arrived at a large suite with plenty of windows and a balcony. The furniture looked cheap, the kind you self-assembled. I would probably break the sofa if I tried to sit on it.

A group was gathered on the balcony. Virga was surrounded by several men, everyone looking very serious. But that wasn't the disturbing part.

A priest was with them.

Che cazzo?

"Mo," Zani asked quietly over his shoulder. "What the hell is happening?"

Virga came toward us. I counted the number of men with him. Eight in total. Not great odds, but I was confident I could give them all a fair beating before they subdued me.

"Don Buscetta" Virga called cheerfully as he approached. "Thank you for coming."

"Don Virga. What is this about?"

He grabbed me and kissed my cheeks like we were family. "I would think it obvious, even to a man such as yourself."

Stupid, in other words. Though the old insult stung like salt in a wound, I didn't react. Out of necessity, I'd learned to hide my emotions at a very early age. Virga couldn't rattle me. "Maybe you should explain it."

"You thought you could ignore me." Virga moved in closer and put a bony hand on my shoulder, squeezing. "You thought you didn't need to do as you're told, that you are more important than the brotherhood. But you are not more important than me or the Cosa Nostra. And you will do what you are told, starting today. Capisce?"

I met his smug gaze with steady calm. He was talking in riddles and I needed answers. "How did you learn of her?" We both knew who I meant.

"I have friends everywhere, Don Buscetta. You would be wise to heed this moving forward." He dug his fingers into the muscle of my shoulder. "And should you try to move her, I will find out where. You can't escape me, *ragazzetto*."

Little boy.

Outside, I wore a mask of indifference. But inside I was a storm, raging with anger and resentment. He dared to threaten my sister? My pulse pounded with the need for violence, a burning desire to maim and destroy. I could almost taste Virga's blood on my tongue.

"Va bene," he said and patted my shoulder. Then he called the group on the balcony. "Let us proceed."

"What is happening?" I snapped at Virga. "Why is a priest here?"

A door opened in the rear of the suite and one of Virga's men emerged with a young woman—very young, probably late teens or early twenties. She was pretty, with dark hair and big brown eyes. No makeup, which meant she wasn't a mistress or wife. Someone's sister, maybe.

I watched her gaze bounce around until it landed on me, and the uneasiness and fear I saw there sent a sliver of trepidation through me. Who was—?

Understanding struck like a lightning bolt. No. It couldn't be. She was in Toronto, well guarded by her father's men.

Except my eyes didn't lie. This was Emma Mancini.

I stepped backward.

"Take your place, Giacomo," Virga ordered. "Right the fuck now."

"You can't do this."

"I am the boss, so I may do whatever I like. At my request, you will marry her today. You will consummate this marriage after the ceremony. And you will get her pregnant in six month's time—or else I will burn everything and *everyone* you love down to the ground."

My body recoiled, everything inside me screaming to run, to fight. There was one person I loved, just one, and Virga had somehow learned of her existence. And he was using her to force me into a marriage I didn't want.

Emma couldn't want this, either. I had done some digging into her after the meeting with Ravazzani three months ago. She was only twenty, far too young for me. Not to mention studious and smart, on her way to becoming a doctor. She wasn't interested in the role of a mafia wife. Everyone knew it, including her family.

I had to reason with Virga. "What of her father? Her brothers-in-law? As of three months ago, her family didn't want this."

"They will do as they are told, just as you will." Merciless dark eyes stared back at me. "Don Borghese will keep Ravazzani and Mancini in line, just as I am doing with you. In this we are in agreement."

Leaning in, he continued more quietly. "You stupid fuck. Think of the leverage this marriage gives you over both of those men. You can get our drug business back from the 'Ndrangheta. Marry her, ragazzetto. Get her pregnant. Do your duty to the brotherhood or your sister pays the price."

I didn't move. I let him see all the hatred boiling inside me at that moment. But I was cornered—and we both knew it. I wouldn't risk Viviana's life. I'd survived a family full of vipers for thirty-two years just to keep her safe.

I could survive this, as well.

Drawing in a deep breath, I edged around the old man and headed for the priest.

CHAPTER THREE

Emma

Hope soared in my chest as Don Virga argued with another man across the room. This had to be Don Buscetta, who appeared about two seconds away from ripping Virga's head clean off his shoulders.

What I learned about my prospective groom earlier today didn't ease my worries, either.

"Obey him," Don Virga had advised. *"Don Buscetta used to fight professionally. He once beat a man to death in the ring. What do you think he will do to a woman who defies him?"*

Beat me, too? I didn't want a violent husband. I didn't want a husband at all. I needed to finish school and help care for my father. The End.

But I couldn't back out. Don Virga's men were in Toronto, waiting in hiding to kill Papà if I didn't go through with this.

My only hope was that Don Buscetta had a way to avoid a marriage between us.

Please let him refuse.

Buscetta started in my direction, his chin set with determination, and my heart sank. Oh, no. Please, no. I shivered, even though I was sweating in my day-old clothes.

Holy smokes. This couldn't be happening.

I tried to take a step back, but the man on my right tightened his hold on my arm, preventing my escape.

Buscetta snapped at the priest, his deep voice reverberating with anger. I understood Italian, but not the Sicilian dialect. So I couldn't catch each of Buscetta's rapid words, but I noticed that the priest visibly paled as he started the service.

The service. As in, my wedding.

A high-pitched ringing filled my ears, my mind reeling. Was I actually being married off to this man? Things like this weren't supposed to happen in the western world anymore. This was the twenty-first century.

"You know the mafia has different rules than everyone else."

How many times had Frankie said this to Gia and me growing up? An ache settled in my chest. I missed my sisters so much.

Never had I felt more alone. Taken from my home by a group of murderers and brought to a run-down hotel in a strange country. Now I was standing next to a stranger, repeating words against my will in a room full of men with guns. Not a single member of my family was in attendance, not even my twin. No maid of honor, no bridesmaids. My father wasn't here to give me away. The backs of my eyes burned with unshed tears. This was a nightmare and I couldn't wake up no matter how hard I tried.

I'd get an annulment. No one was required to stay married anymore. My family—my two brothers-in-law, to be exact—would never let this marriage stand. I needed to go through the motions today and Virga would withdraw his men from Toronto. Then my father would be safe and I'd dissolve this marriage.

It would be like it never happened.

"Lo voglio," Buscetta growled from behind clenched teeth. *I do.*

The priest turned to me and rattled off a quick stream of Italian. When he paused, I knew what was required. Except I couldn't force the words out. My tongue felt thick and awkward in my mouth.

Once I said the words I was married.

Annulment, annulment, annulment.

Everyone stared at me. Yet I still couldn't do it.

"Speak," Buscetta hissed at me under his breath.

"Lo voglio," I choked.

The priest made the sign of the cross with his hand and offered up a final blessing. Before I could prepare myself, Buscetta was turning toward me. My *husband*. It was absolutely surreal.

He sighed heavily, leaned down, and briefly kissed my forehead.

Relief poured through me. I definitely didn't want to kiss him on the mouth.

"*Evviva gli sposi!*" everyone yelled and suddenly bits of wheat rained down on us like confetti.

"*Basta!*" Buscetta barked.

I could see the fury he was barely containing, the rage that simmered underneath his bulging muscles. *He beat a man to death in the ring.* I slowly edged out of his reach.

"Let us celebrate the happy couple," Virga declared and clapped his hands twice.

I looked around at the room full of strangers. Celebrate? Were they crazy?

As if on cue, waiters emerged carrying glasses of champagne that were quickly distributed to Virga and his men.

Virga lifted his glass. "*Auguri e figli maschi!*"

Congratulations and may you have male children. Ugh.

The man at my side said nothing and I stared at my hands, a refrain of *WTF* looping through my mind. How was this happening?

Buscetta held a delicate champagne flute and I stared at his hand. It was large with thick fingers, his knuckles scraped and raw. Had he beat someone to death today?

No one offered me champagne. This was for the best. Doubtful I could've kept it down anyway. My stomach was tied in knots.

In the oppressive silence, Buscetta and Virga engaged in a mafioso stare down. Why on earth had Buscetta agreed to this? What secrets did Virga hold over on Buscetta to force a marriage between us?

I studied him out of the corner of my eye. Buscetta was big and thick, with muscles bulging under his clothes. His nasal bone had been broken once or twice, judging by the bump on the ridge, which made sense if he'd been a boxer. Dark brown eyes rested beneath heavy eyebrows, and full lips framed a wide mouth, with the lower portion of his face covered in stubble. His hair was cut short, almost buzzed, with slightly more length on the top than on the sides.

He wore a white dress shirt with the sleeves rolled up to the elbows, which revealed a myriad of tattoos covering his olive skin. Dark jeans stretched across strong, thick thighs, and his brown boots were spattered with—my god, was that *blood?*

And it looked fresh.

I tore my gaze away, only to discover that the men in the room were watching me as they finished their champagne. What were they waiting for? Well, I wouldn't cower or cry in front of them. These Sicilian mobsters didn't scare me. I'd once been kidnapped by Russian sex traffickers. Now *that* had been terrifying.

I set my glass down and walked over to Don Virga. "Signore, a word?"

He ignored me and sipped his champagne. It was like I wasn't standing there at all.

I tried again. "Signore, I did as you required. Now please, your men—"

Buscetta was suddenly at my side. "We are finished here. Zani, *amunì sprigati!*" When he reached for my wrist, I did my best not to recoil. Except then he began towing me toward the exit.

"Wait," I said to the large man dragging me away. "I need to speak with Don Virga. He made me a promise."

"Giacomo," Virga said behind us, his voice cool. "You are forgetting the most important part."

Buscetta stopped but didn't let go of my wrist. "We said the vows, old man. We did as you ordered. As I said, we are through here."

Virga strolled toward us. "You are not finished, ragazzetto. You have only performed one of the three tasks I have given you."

Buscetta's neck flushed with anger, but his grip on my wrist remained gentle. "I will take care of those things in my own time," he growled.

Virga didn't care for that answer. He stepped closer, the lines around his mouth deepening. "That is not how this works, Giacomo. And refusing me is disrespectful. Shall I place a call to Mirabella?"

Mirabella? Who was that?

The man at my side grew even bigger, his muscles swelling as he glared at Don Virga. I could read the violent intent written on his face. Buscetta would make Virga pay one day very soon.

"Where?" Buscetta asked harshly.

"There is a bedroom in the back. I'll be waiting for proof."

Bedroom . . . proof.

That could only mean one thing. And I was not about to do that one thing, not with this man. Fear flooded my system and I struggled to free myself from Buscetta's grip. "Absolutely not."

Buscetta looked down at me, surprised, like he couldn't believe I was capable of speaking. "Quiet."

"I will not be quiet." Then I glared at Don Virga. "Proof of a torn hymen is unnecessary, barbaric, and highly improbable. I'm twenty years old, after all."

Virga squinted at me, then addressed my husband. "Do your duty. And teach your new wife better manners."

My jaw fell open.

Buscetta exchanged a brief glance with the man he'd arrived with earlier. Then, despite my protests, he tugged me across the room, past the leering stares of Virga's men. Shivers shot down my spine. No one here would help me.

"Don't do this," I said, trying to pull free, but he was stronger. I wasn't above begging, though. "Please, signore. Don Buscetta, *vi prego.* You don't want to do this."

Ignoring me, he kept going, taking me to the back bedroom.

Please don't let my first time be here, in a hotel, with a complete stranger.

Yes, I was a virgin. I knew it was silly. But it wasn't like I was waiting for marriage. That perpetuated an arcane patriarchal view of a woman's body and her rights.

No, I was waiting for a man I loved and one who loved me back. I wanted a man who looked at me like Fausto looked at Frankie, or Enzo with Gia. I hadn't found a man like that yet. In fact, most men thought

I was too studious, too serious. Too quiet and boring. Too *everything*, except what they wanted.

It wasn't a big deal. And I was too busy these days to even think about it. Who needed a partner anyway? I was very handy with a vibrator.

When Buscetta closed the bedroom door, he released me, and I raced to the other side of the room. If he tried anything, he would have a fight on his hands.

Except Buscetta didn't come after me. Instead, he sagged against the door and rubbed his hands over his face.

Huh. I hadn't expected that.

Still, I wasn't about to roll over and let this violent man hurt me. I darted to the single window and jerked open the curtains. Bars covered the glass, making escape impossible. My hands slapped against the glass in a futile display of frustration.

"A smart idea," Buscetta said. "But Virga will have thought of this already."

Spinning, I glared at him. "I don't want to be married to you."

"I don't want to be married to you, either." His eyes raked me up and down. "They say you are twenty, but you look like a little girl."

Okay, that was uncalled for. I knew I wasn't gorgeous and sophisticated like my older sisters, but I was happiest with no makeup and a messy bun. "*You* are insulting *me*? You're covered in blood, obviously straight from fighting with someone."

"Hardly a fight. An hour ago I beat the shit out of a man, then killed him."

Revulsion slithered over my skin. He *murdered* someone today. Minutes ago. My god.

I tried for reason. "Look, we're married. We did it. Now I'll go back to Canada and we'll pretend this never happened."

"Virga doesn't care only about the marriage. And he—" He slammed his lips closed and shook his head.

"He, what?" When Buscetta didn't answer, I kept talking. "Why are you agreeing to this? What dirt does he have on you to force you into this marriage?"

"There is no *dirt*. And what is between Virga and me is none of your business."

Did he think I hadn't been paying attention out there? "Who is Mirabella? Your girlfriend? Your relative?"

His jaw tightened and fury twisted the lines of his face. "Never say that name to me again, little girl. Capisce?"

I pinched the bridge of my nose between my thumb and forefinger. "You are making a huge mistake. Do you know who I'm related to?"

"Fausto Ravazanni," he said, but the tone held no deference, no respect.

"And Enzo D'Agostino."

"You are not related to D'Agostino. Your twin and he are not married."

"A formality, believe me. They are as committed as two people can possibly be without a piece of paper. And both of my brothers-in-law will skin you alive for this."

"Me? I'm not the one who forced you into this marriage. And Ravazzani can do nothing to help us. This is Sicily, not Siderno."

I rubbed my forehead, a migraine forming between my temples. "I have to get back to Toronto as quickly as possible." To my father.

There was no bend in his harsh expression, no understanding or mercy. "You will stay."

"What are you saying?"

"I must follow Don Virga's orders. As must you."

I couldn't believe this. "You aren't going to fight? You're going to let him win?"

He reacted as if I'd insulted his mother. His olive skin turned nearly purple, loathing burning in his eyes as he stared me down. "Let's get this over with."

CHAPTER FOUR

Emma

Oh, heck no. This was absolutely not happening.

I moved to the opposite wall and crossed my arms over my chest. "No way. This marriage will remain unconsummated."

He frowned and blew out a long breath, his expression exasperated, like I was a toddler who wouldn't listen to reason. But I wouldn't budge.

Without warning, Buscetta spun and punched the wall. Twice.

My hand flew up to cover my mouth. What in the world . . . ?

Blood ran down his fingers, the cuts on his knuckles from earlier now openly bleeding. Without explanation he strode to the bed and yanked the top cover off. Then he sized me up head to toe, examining me. I took a step back.

Bending, he rubbed his bloody knuckles into the fitted bedsheet. A tiny smear of red was left behind.

Oh. That was actually pretty smart. Would that be enough to fool—

Then Buscetta's hands went to his belt. The buckle jangled as he unfastened it and tore open his jeans. I croaked, "W-what are you doing?"

"I am doing what needs to be done. Unless you'd like to help me?"

He reached inside his briefs and pulled out a very thick penis. I saw a flash of silver before quickly averting my eyes. "Oh, my god! Warn a girl first."

He muttered in Italian and I heard his clothing rustle. I didn't look. It felt like an invasion of privacy. Was he . . . ?

Then he grunted softly, a soft erotic sound.

Holy smokes, yes he was. He was masturbating in the room with me. What in the world? Why? How was he even aroused?

Questions bombarded my brain at a rapid-fire pace. Gia always said I was too curious for my own good, but I was a proud science nerd. Curiosity came with the territory.

Then I thought about that smear of blood on the sheet. Buscetta was adding semen to the deception to make it believable. Doing what needed to be done, as he said, so Virga would think the marriage had been consummated.

Wow, that was actually pretty smart.

Another grunt sounded behind me. I'd seen men masturbate in videos before. I knew what it looked like, the stroking up and down, strong fingers swiping over the sensitive glans. Most Italian men weren't circumcised, which meant Giacomo's foreskin would offer a small amount of natural lubrication.

And now I was thinking about his foreskin. What was wrong with me? I should be repulsed. I should be running out of the room.

Instead, my skin was growing hot. I could hear his heavy breathing, the sound of skin rhythmically sliding on skin. His belt buckle jangled with the force of his movements, his fist tugging hard on his shaft. I could sense his arousal climbing, his pace increasing, and my mouth dried out. Were his muscles taut? His forearm veins popping?

I couldn't help it. I peeked.

His heavy lidded eyes were locked on me. Not on my chest or my ass, but on my face. Like he knew I would sneak a glance at some point and he was waiting to catch me.

His lips curved in satisfaction, softening his features, and I felt an answering tug in my lower belly. Oh, this was wrong on so many levels.

I spun toward the wall, an apology stuck in my throat.

The mattress springs creaked, then his breath hitched. I didn't move, didn't blink, as the moment stretched, but I imagined what was happening. I pictured the semen leaving his shaft, his head thrown back in ecstasy, muscles clenched as he ejaculated. Hormones, organs and nerves all working together to produce the greatest high humans could ever experience.

My whole body tingled.

"You can turn around now."

I spun slowly and found Buscetta buckling his belt. I wasn't sure what to say. Good job?

With one hand, he ripped the stained bottom sheet off the bed. "Let's go." He started for the door, not waiting to see if I followed.

I hurried after him. I didn't know where we were going, but no way was I staying in this hotel room. Besides, I had no phone, no money. I'd take my chances on the Palermo streets with Buscetta.

At the door he paused and looked me over. The displeasure in his expression made it clear I'd disappointed him somehow. "Try to look as if you've just had the fucking of a lifetime."

"What does that mean?" I stared down at myself. What was I supposed to look like after sleeping with him? "Should I mess up my hair?"

He heaved yet another sigh, shook his head, and yanked open the door. Once we entered the other room, Buscetta tossed the sheet at Virga's feet. "There's your proof."

Virga poked at the sheet with his toe. "That was fast. Too bad for your wife, eh, Don Buscetta?"

A stamina joke. Awesome. I guess we were checking all of the clichéd misogynist boxes today.

Buscetta and his man were already out the door, but I didn't move. To Virga, I said softly, "You made me a promise. I expect you to honor it by bringing your men home from Toronto."

"I don't negotiate with wives," Virga sneered, not even bothering to look at me. "You may bring this issue to your husband and he will discuss it with me. As is customary."

I heard the elevator ding in the hall. Shoot. I needed to get out of this hotel room, away from this nightmare. "This conversation isn't over."

When I reached the hall the elevator doors were just closing. "Wait!" I sprinted down the hall. A hand shot out to keep the metal doors open and I dashed inside. The other man who came with Buscetta was holding the door. "Thank you," I told him as the doors closed.

"Prego," he said with a deferential nod. "Signora Buscetta, a pleasure to meet you. I am Francesco Zaniolo, your husband's incredibly handsome friend and right-hand man."

Buscetta snarled something in Italian, but the only word I caught was *pig*.

I shook Francesco's hand. "Nice to meet you, Signore Zaniolo."

"Please, call me Zani."

"Then you must call me Emma."

Don Buscetta grunted. I frowned at him, even though he ignored me. Not a big talker, this man.

Awkward silence filled the car as the elevator descended until I blurted, "I'm going back to Toronto."

"You are not leaving until it's safe," Buscetta said through clenched teeth. "And that is the last I want to hear about it, capisce?"

Then the doors opened and he bolted through them, walking briskly into the lobby. Zani put a hand at the small of my back and led me out through the front entrance.

"Get in," Zani instructed, gesturing to a sedan parked on the street. I could see Buscetta's bulk in the driver's seat.

"That's not necessary. I'll find a hotel." Shoot, I didn't have any money. Could I get my sisters to reserve a room for me without explaining why I was in Palermo?

Ugh. Probably not.

"You have nowhere to go." Zani gently guided me toward the car. "And it isn't safe for you to be alone here. Come, Emma. Let's, the three of us, figure this out together."

I didn't see the point in arguing. I hadn't slept in more than twenty-four hours and all I had to eat today was an orange. At least Zani was coming with me. He seemed more friendly and reasonable than Buscetta. "Fine, but this is only because I'm too exhausted to fight you."

Zani opened the back door of the car for me and I slid inside. Buscetta stared straight ahead, his fingers tapping impatiently on the steering wheel. His knuckles were still bleeding. I stared at his large hands, remembering what he did upstairs. I didn't think I'd ever forget it.

When Zani got in and shut the door, Buscetta hit the gas and the car shot away from the curb. I quickly buckled myself in, then gripped the leather seat underneath me as the car swerved and jerked in the Palermo traffic. "Can you slow down, please? More than a million people die each year in traffic accidents."

Buscetta said nothing, but Zani spoke up. "You have to deal with this, Mo. Are you willing to lose everything? Are you willing to start a war? Lose your life? Her life?"

Buscetta merely changed lanes, so I answered for us both. "I don't need to stay here. We're married. That's enough."

"I heard what Virga said," Zani said. "It's not enough—and you both know it."

A baby.

I swallowed the panic threatening in my chest. Then I remembered who I was, who I was related to. "Listen, you only need to involve my brothers-in-law. They'll put a stop to this and set Virga straight."

Buscetta didn't answer, but his shoulders remained tight as he maneuvered the car through traffic.

Zani's response was patient, but firm. "Signora, both Ravazzani and D'Agostino—as well as your father—answer to Don Borghese, who is in agreement with Virga. Unless we want a full-scale war, we must abide by the decisions of our leaders."

This was what Virga said back in Toronto. That, and that he would kill my father.

"*Minchia!*" Buscetta shouted and slapped the steering wheel with his palm. Then he took a sharp turn, throwing all of us sideways.

"It won't be so bad," Zani said.

Buscetta snarled something in Sicilian, and I only caught the words "scared" and "my dick." Was he talking about me? Was he saying I would be scared of his dick? I really needed to learn the dialect down here.

I knew I wasn't sexy or desirable. Men never noticed me like they noticed my sisters. And I was fine with that. I wasn't trying to impress anyone. Getting into a good medical school and completing my residency required all of my focus.

That, and taking care of my dying father. Which was why I needed to be in Toronto, not here.

"Please, Don Buscetta," I said. "It's important that I get back to Toronto. Just drive me to the airport."

"I'm not taking you to the airport." His voice was rough gravel.

"Why not?"

"You know why."

"No, I really don't. This makes no sense. You're acting as if we don't have a choice in what's happening."

"Because we don't. Not at the moment anyway."

"Mo, whatever you are thinking," Zani warned in the front seat, "don't do it. Accept this and don't fight him."

I caught the flash of a grim smile on Buscetta's face. "But I love a good fight."

CHAPTER FIVE

Giacomo

I couldn't ever remember being so angry in my life. I wanted to hit something. Someone. Anything.

My skin buzzed with the need for violence, like it did right before I stepped into the ring. Virga thought he had me beat. He actually believed that I would use an outsider—an innocent woman in every way—as leverage in a business dispute. Only a coward would do such a thing.

My father would have done such a thing. My brother, as well.

That wasn't me. I would win this battle my way. I would end this marriage quickly *and* get the drug trade from Ravazzani. If that meant killing Virga and taking on the entire Cosa Nostra, so be it.

I just needed to ensure Viviana's safety first.

I pulled my car into the drive and motioned to the guards. They opened the heavy gate and I continued on toward the garage.

A heavy feeling settled in my stomach. I hated this place. It never felt like my home. The specter of my father loomed everywhere here, with ghostly remnants of his terrorizing reign around every corner, right down to the floorboards he used to make me kneel upon.

"Stay there until you are ready to show your respect, Giacomo."

Once I knelt for twelve hours, pissing myself in proud defiance. But I broke long before he did, unable to take the agonizing pain in my eleven-year-old body any longer. I had begged for his forgiveness, like he knew I would.

In response he slapped my face and called me a dog. Then he made me clean the piss off the floor with my shirt.

But I had endured. I suffered everything the old man had dished out because if Papà was focused on me, then he wasn't paying attention to my baby sister, Viviana.

I got out of the car and headed toward the door. Let Zani deal with Emma. He was better with people, anyway.

First I needed to call my sister. A sweet and gentle soul, she hadn't been strong enough to withstand our father's cruelty. At eight years old she started suffering panic attacks and night terrors. When she was twelve they grew worse and my father talked about marrying her off at thirteen years old. I couldn't allow that to happen, so I faked her death and moved her to a secret facility in the Italian countryside. For years everyone believed her dead.

And somehow Virga discovered my greatest secret.

Inside the kitchen I found Sal kneading bread. The smell, rosemary and garlic, was familiar and calming. "Don Buscetta," the older man said, looking up. "Zani didn't inform me you were on your way."

Sal has been around for as long as I could remember. He used to be my father's soldier, until he lost an eye and a gunshot practically destroyed his knee. Soon after he became a handyman, doing odd jobs around the estate without complaint. As a boy I spent a lot of time with him to avoid my father and brother, so it only made sense to bring Sal inside as my housekeeper when I took over as don.

It turned out to be a good decision. He was a decent cook and easy to be around, as well as unquestionably loyal.

"We were too busy to ring you," I said. "Fair warning, my new wife is on the way inside."

Sal's hands froze in the dough, his lips parting in surprise. "Did you say . . . wife?"

"Temporary, Sal. Capisce? Don't get attached."

At that instant, the back door opened and Zani ushered Emma inside. That was my cue to leave. "Let me know when dinner is ready," I called on my way into the house.

I went to my sparse office and closed the heavy door. The liquor bottles were lined up, waiting patiently to provide solace. First, I had to wash the bad taste of the last hour out of my mouth. I was fucking married—and to a woman I didn't know. I still couldn't believe it.

I threw back a mouthful of Irish whisky, the burn ripping through my chest and settling in my stomach. My father and brother had hated the stuff, which was probably why I ordered cases of it. Taking another glass, I went to the desk and picked up the phone. I dialed Viviana's room.

She answered on the third ring. "Ciao, Mo. *Come stai?*"

The sound of her voice soothed something inside me. Vivi was safe. And I would do anything to ensure that it stayed that way.

I found myself smiling despite my shitty day. "Ciao, *sorellina*. I wanted to check on you."

"Except you checked on me yesterday. And now there's an extra guard outside my room. Should I be worried?"

I could hear the anxiety creeping into her words and it gutted me. I'd spent my whole life trying to keep her safe, protecting her from the demons in my world. "No, absolutely not. Everything is fine."

"You would say that even if it weren't true."

"We agreed, no? I told you I'd be honest if you had something to fear. You don't." *As long as I follow Virga's orders.*

"Are you sure?"

"Sì, certo."

"I don't want to lose you, Mo."

"Basta," I said gently. "You won't lose me."

"You're my only family left, Mo. If there's something I need to know, then tell me."

"There is nothing to worry over," I lied.

She sighed into the phone. "I hate this for you. I know you never wanted to be don."

"Dai, it's meetings and more meetings, Vivi," I said. "A thousand questions every day that must be answered. So much thinking and talking."

This made my sister laugh. "Be grateful for the meetings. It's better than people shooting at you."

We chatted for a few more minutes, but I didn't tell her about my marriage. It would only upset her and raise her anxiety. If she grew too agitated, the attendants would drug her and I knew how much she hated that.

After we rang off I strolled toward the kitchen, ready for dinner. I felt better after speaking with Viv, but it didn't mean she was safe. I hated to move her to another facility and force her to leave her friends and nurses. The last time we did, Viv couldn't sleep and lost a considerable amount of weight. She was frightened that my father would discover she was alive.

When he died I begged Viv to come live at home with me, but she refused. She said the house had too many bad memories. It did for me, too, but I had no choice in the matter. I was Don Buscetta now and my security was apparently more important than my peace of mind.

Laughter drifted out from the kitchen and I scowled. What did anyone have to be so fucking happy about? When I walked in, Zani and Emma were at the bar, drinking wine, while Sal chopped herbs on the island. The cozy scene set my teeth on edge.

The laughter immediately died at my presence, and I felt like an outsider in my own home. Again.

Resentment scraped across my nerves like talons, digging up my childhood insecurities, and anger bubbled up in my chest. I wasn't supposed to feel like this. *She* was supposed to feel like an interloper. Unwanted and unloved.

My skin was suddenly too tight, too hot. I couldn't think straight. In a split second, I made a decision. "I'm going out."

Zani frowned, while Emma avoided looking at me altogether. Sal put down his knife and wiped his hands. "I made your favorite, aubergine caponata."

"Mo," Zani said, a hint of disapproval in his tone. "Do you think it's wise, tonight of all nights?"

Meaning he wanted me to sit and babysit Emma. Have some sort of wedding night. Fuck that. I would get my dick wet, but with someone who actually wanted it.

"I have plans," I lied, plucking an olive off the island and tossing it in my mouth.

"With who?" Zani asked.

"Theresa."

Emma looked at me, clearly understanding the rapidly spoken Italian. Good. I wanted her to know I wouldn't ever beg her for sex. There were plenty of women in Palermo gagging for a taste of my cock.

Not that I had plans with Theresa, but she usually made time for me when I needed it.

"You are married, Giacomo." Sal's tone dripped with disapproval. "You stood before God and made vows."

I snorted. "Under duress. And tell me, did my father or brother ever honor their wedding vows?"

No one had an answer for that, because we all knew the truth. They hadn't.

"Who are you taking with you?" Zani demanded. "You can't go out alone. You need guards."

"The only danger to me is blue balls. Don't wait up."

I went out the kitchen door, the late-day sun warming my skin. Zani caught up to me as I slid into the driver's seat of my sedan. I tried to shut the door on him, but he got a hand in to stop me. I glared up at him. "Che cazzo?"

"It's her first night here, Mo. Strange country, strange house. Strange husband. You fucked her in a hotel an hour ago. Shouldn't you stay and try to . . ." He rolled his hand as he searched for the right word. "She's innocent in all this. At least be nice to her."

Nice? I couldn't have been any nicer to her today. "I didn't fuck her in that hotel. I just staged it to make it seem like I had. And Virga wants me to use her as leverage against her family. Believe me, I'm doing her a favor by ignoring her."

"*Sciatiri e matri!* He actually said that?"

"Yes, and until I find out what game Virga is playing at, I'm not going anywhere near her."

"I thought the point was to make peace."

I shook my head. "I don't think Virga has any interest in true peace. He wants to use me and my wife as pawns to gain more power for himself, which I won't allow."

"You could confide in Ravazzani, ask for his help with Virga. We could move Viv—"

I cut him off. "I'm not Ravazzani's friend or confidant. And I don't need his help. That stronzo stole our business and I intend to get it back."

Zani considered this for a second. "What if Emma calls her family to rescue her? She has access to phones and the internet inside the house."

The answer was simple. "Virga has something on Mancini, something that forced him to send his daughter to marry a stranger. I'm not worried that she'll leave. Her father can't allow it."

"Yes, but she kept saying Virga made her a promise. Maybe he threatened her boyfriend to gain her cooperation?"

The scene in the bedroom earlier reverberated in my head. She'd been shocked, yes, but not repulsed. I caught her peeking at my dick, her chest heaving as she watched me jerk off, hard nipples poking through her shirt and bra. Hearing me had turned her on. "Possibly," I allowed. "But isn't this supposed to be the good sister? I don't see her flouting her father's rules with a boyfriend."

"Actually, I don't either. She's very close to her father."

"How do you know that?"

Zani didn't bother to hide his exasperation. "Because I bothered to talk to her."

"I fucking hate talking." I shoved him back, then slammed the door shut. "Besides, that's what I have you for. See you in the morning."

CHAPTER SIX

Emma

Relief poured through me as Buscetta left the house. I didn't care if he was meeting up with Theresa or Mirabella. Or both women at the same time. He could attend an orgy tonight and I would throw my hands up and cheer.

It wasn't fair that I couldn't return to Toronto. I had a very good reason to leave, one that actually mattered.

And now I am stuck here. *Married*. Ugh.

"He's a good man." Sal added the herbs he'd been chopping to the pan on the stove. "A kind soul."

Were we talking about the same man? The one who'd murdered a man today?

I sipped my wine and switched topics. "How long have you been on the estate?"

"Dai, I know what you are doing." He shook his wooden spoon at me playfully. "Fine. We won't talk about him. I've been here over thirty-six years, ever since I lost my eye." He pointed at his left eye, which was clearly glass. I'd noticed it earlier.

"How did you lose it?"

"This is a gruesome tale, not fit for a lady's ears."

"Sal, I intend to go to medical school. I've been studying science and anatomy for years. You can't gross me out."

"It was a baseball bat, signora."

Considering the world we both lived in, I assumed this injury didn't occur during a baseball game. "An orbital fracture?"

"Yes, and my retina detached. Cheekbone shattered, too. I had several surgeries, but they couldn't save my eye."

That must've been incredibly painful. "Well, your glass eye looks very natural. They did a good job matching it to your other one."

"This eye is new. Had it put in four months ago. Giacomo—Don Buscetta—bought it for me because the old one didn't fit right."

Just then Zani came back in, his mouth curved in a smile that didn't reach his eyes, as I heard a car drive away from the house. "When is dinner, Sal? I'm starving." He dropped onto the stool next to me.

He didn't need to put on a show for my benefit. "You don't have to stay and babysit me. I'm sure you have a lot more interesting things to do."

"I have nothing more exciting than this, signora. Good food, good company . . . it is every Italian man's dream."

Sal served a fantastic eggplant dish. I ate two helpings while Zani kept up a stream of lively conversation.

Before he left, Zani promised to come check on me tomorrow. "*Buona notte*, Emma. It will get better, I swear."

I doubted it, but didn't argue.

After Zani left, Sal took off his apron and folded it neatly. "Let's get you settled. Giacomo didn't say whether to put you in his room or—"

"Different room. Please." I didn't care if I slept in a broom closet, but I wasn't sleeping in Buscetta's bed.

"This is no problem, signora. We have plenty of unused bedrooms here."

Sal had mentioned that Buscetta's father and brother were dead. As we started through the house, I wondered what happened to Buscetta's mother. Was she dead, too? I knew next to nothing about this family— my *husband's* family.

Tacky was the only way to describe the house's decor. There was gold filigree and big ornate furniture, flanked with heavy drapery, tall mirrors, and white marble. It was like a French baroque king threw up everywhere in here. We continued down the long corridor and started up the steps. Sal went slow, his leg mobility affected by an old injury, and I matched his pace.

Once we arrived on the second floor, he pointed left. "Giacomo sleeps in his childhood bedroom down there."

I drifted to the right, eager to put as much distance between Buscetta's bedroom and myself. "What's down this way?"

"The bigger bedrooms. Those belonging to the late Don Buscetta and his son."

"What about Don Buscetta's wife?"

"No one has slept in the late Signora Buscetta's rooms since she passed away."

"How long ago was that?"

"More than twenty years now."

Yiiiikes. Her room had been empty for two decades? Talk about creepy.

I didn't believe in ghosts. But I had respect for the dead, the memories they left behind. "I'll sleep in the late Don Buscetta's room, then."

"Va bene." Sal led me to the end of the hall where double gold doors awaited. "Through there. The staff keeps it clean, just in case."

I turned the knob and went in. If I thought I'd find a tasteful, masculine room, I was thoroughly disappointed. The bedroom was every bit as gaudy as the rest of the house. Maybe more so. The bed was huge, with a gilded headboard adorned with cherubs. Mounds of gold and purple pillows rested on a gold silk duvet. A chandelier hung over the bed, crystals dripping like tear drops, while a divan rested against the wall. More heavy silk framed the top of the windows, with lace curtains hanging below.

Holy smokes.

"Someone really likes gold," I muttered as I took it all in.

"Cosa?"

"Nothing. How long ago did Don Buscetta die?"

"Don Gero went into hiding years ago. He let his older son, Nino, take over the day-to-day operations of the business. Nino was killed first, then Don Gero at his farm in the hills a few weeks later." He gave me a strange look. "I'm surprised you don't know this."

"Why would I?"

"Because your sister's stepson was the one responsible."

The news hit me like a douse of cold water. "Giulio Ravazzani?" At Sal's nod, I blinked several times. "Oh, goodness."

No wonder Buscetta hated me. My sister's family had killed Buscetta's father and brother. Was he planning on exacting revenge for it?

Of course he is, dummy! This was the mafia we were talking about. No slight could go unpunished.

All the more reason for me to find a way out of this marriage as quickly as possible.

The chime of the doorbell startled us both.

Frowning, Sal pulled out his mobile and read a text message. "There has been a delivery for you, signora."

"Me?"

"The guards brought it to the front door."

No one knew that I was in Palermo. Who would've sent me something? "I'll go down."

"No, you wait here," Sal said. "I'll go."

His leg must hurt all the time. There was no reason for him to go up and down the stairs on my account. "Sal, I don't mind," I called as he started down the hall. "You should head to bed."

"My bedroom is on the ground floor. I have to go down anyway."

"Then I'll come along and save you a trip back up here."

His smile was kind as we started walking together. "You are a sweet girl, signora. I think you will be good for Giacomo."

My lips pressed tight. No, thank you. I didn't want to be anything for Buscetta, good or bad.

The descent was slow, but I pretended not to notice. He paused to rest on the bottom step, so I went to the front door. "Signora," Sal called, "you should really allow me—"

"Nonsense. I have it." I yanked open the door and found a man standing there, a rectangular-shaped box in his hands.

"Signora Buscetta," the guard said, not directly meeting my eyes. "This has been delivered for you."

"Has it been checked, Dino?" Sal asked behind me.

"Sì, certo. It's safe, Sal." Then he dipped his chin and hurried away, boots crunching on gravel as he disappeared into the night.

Sal shut the door as I lifted the lid off the box. Scraps of delicate silk and lace met my eyes. Garters, a thong, a bustier . . . Oh, my god.

I slammed the lid shut.

Sal looked as horrified as I felt. His skin turned red and he cleared his throat awkwardly. "I suppose that makes sense. It is your wedding night."

"Well, I won't be needing this." I tried to give him the box, but he wouldn't take it.

"No, signora." He backed away quicker than should've been possible, considering his leg. "You take that upstairs with you. I need to finish up in the kitchen. Buona notte."

He left, so I had no choice but to take the box upstairs. Who were they from? Certainly not Buscetta. Zani? But when would he have had time to shop for these?

It made no sense.

Once I was back in Versailles, I sat on the bed and placed the box next to me. I stared at it, hesitating. Then I chastised myself at how ridiculous I was being. This was lingerie, not a snake. Actually, I didn't find snakes all that scary. Spiders, yes, but not snakes.

You're rambling, Emma.

Okay, I was braver than this. Last summer I attended a camp at a body farm studying decomposing human and animal bodies. All the other campers puked at least once, but I never did.

Inhaling a deep lungful of air, I flipped the lid off the box. The garments were arranged carefully, with lots of ribbons and bows on display. Everything was white, naturally. Had to keep that virgin vibe going, I guess.

A note was on the inside of the lid.

Signora Buscetta—

You will be pregnant with Giacomo's child within six months' time.

If you are not, then you know what happens in Toronto.

Your phone is enclosed. Notice the security application installed. It is connected to a camera in your father's bedroom.

Just remember, you are not the only one watching.

It was signed with a large "V."

My stomach clenched, the eggplant pasta threatening to reemerge. Virga had sent this to me. Why was this happening? I hadn't hurt anyone. My whole life I'd followed the rules and never stepped out of line. My two older sisters had been wild enough for all of us, always causing trouble and aggravating our poor father.

And what was my reward for doing the right thing? A marriage I didn't want to a man who couldn't be more wrong for me. Stuck in a place where I knew no one.

Ugh. I had to find a way out of this.

Digging through the box, I found my phone and pulled up the new security app. My father's bedroom appeared on the screen. Gloria and my father were there, watching television together. I touched the screen, wishing I could be with him. A lump rose in my throat, but I swallowed it. There was no time for pity or regrets now.

Clicking on my contacts, I pressed the button to call.

Gloria answered for him on the first ring. "Hello?"

"Hi," I forced out, trying to sound as natural as possible. "It's me."

"Oh, Emma." Worry coated her voice. "Is everything okay?"

I hadn't told her much about my leaving, only that I'd be away for a few days and not to mention anything to my father. "I'm fine, I swear. Can I talk to him?"

"Sure, hold on."

Some scuffling, then my father came on the line. "Hello, baby girl. Where are you? At school?"

I hated this. I hated lying, especially to my father, but I had to do it. My story needed to sound convincing so he wouldn't worry about me, and I couldn't risk involving my sisters. True, they never talked to our father, but lies involving other people always went badly.

Much better to tell a story that would fool my entire family.

"Hi, Papà. I'm away on a last minute research trip with school. I should be home in a couple of days."

"Are you studying dead bodies again?" His chuckle was weak, but genuine. "Who knew my sweetest daughter would be so fond of death?"

He liked to tease me about this. "I'm fond of saving lives, Papà. Not death. How are you feeling?"

"The same. Don't worry about me. Enjoy your trip and call us when you can."

"I will. Rest up and don't overdo it when I'm not there."

"Always nagging me," he complained affectionately. "What would I do without you?"

My heart constricted, the organ squeezing painfully in my chest. With any luck, he'd never have to find out. "Love you, Papà. Speak soon."

"Ti amo. Ciao, baby girl."

We hung up. To distract myself from the lump in my throat, I checked on my texts. The group chat with my sisters was as active as ever. Everyday boring stuff, like what Frankie's kids were doing and a drawing by Gia's stepdaughter. They chatted about what they were streaming and asked for movie recommendations. Perfectly normal conversations between the two of them, and they hadn't noticed my absence. I wasn't sure whether to be relieved or annoyed.

The whole world was carrying on as usual, I supposed. It was only my life that had been turned completely upside down.

As Gia would say, FML.

CHAPTER SEVEN

Giacomo

I purposely came home late.

My mood was only slightly improved by a fantastic lay tonight. Theresa had been energetic, to say the least. We fucked for a long time and no doubt I reeked of pussy.

It had helped, but not much. The day's events lurked in the back of my mind the whole time, distracting me while I emptied my balls.

A marriage I didn't want.

A bride who didn't want me.

A boss I needed to kill.

A sister to protect.

I couldn't escape any of it, not even despite a mind-numbing orgasm.

The kitchen was dark when I came in. I hadn't eaten tonight and I was ravenous. Like a mind reader, Sal left a note on the counter with instructions on how to reheat the caponata in the refrigerator.

As the microwave buzzed, I pulled out my phone and checked my messages. There wasn't much. My men reported everything verbally. This was out of necessity. My father had been careless with his words and wallet, allowing the Guardia di Finanza to build a case against him. He'd gone into hiding and spent the last six years of his life on a farm, living in the mountains like a peasant.

That would not be me.

I'd rather die than go to prison and sit like a rat in a cage. I lived simply. Quietly. Intelligently. There would be no flashy purchases, like expensive watches or custom-made suits. Those government bastards would have to work hard to find dirt on me.

Surprising that I hadn't heard from Mancini or Ravazzani yet. Hadn't Roberto Mancini informed the family of the marriage? Emma might be temporarily stuck here with me, but I still expected a few useless threats from Toronto or Siderno.

Something to look forward to, I guess.

I carried my food to the kitchen island and poured a glass of wine, rolling the tension out of my neck. Then I found a football match on my phone and began to eat.

"You're home."

The feminine voice startled me. Emma stood in the doorway, still dressed in the clothes from earlier even though it was the middle of the night. Her brown hair was loose and soft, hanging around her shoulders. She looked tired and fragile, completely out of place in my world.

I returned my attention to my food. "Hoping to give me a heart attack? Then you could become a wife and a widow in one day, no?"

Her feet whispered over the tile as she padded over to the island and lowered herself onto the stool next to me. "I've been waiting for you to return. We need to—" She sniffed the air. "You smell . . . " Her voice trailed off, as if she wasn't quite sure.

"Like pussy? That's because I was just eating and fucking one." She recoiled, as if this news upset her. I sighed heavily and muted the game on my phone. "Would you rather I fucked and ate yours?"

"Of course not!" She shifted on the stool. "Jeez. I wasn't expecting you to admit it, I guess."

This proved she knew nothing about me, because I didn't lie. Unless it was to the government, of course. "Dai, this is not a real marriage or a love match. It's an inconvenience we must endure until I can find a way to end it."

"Until *we* find a way to end it. I'm just as stuck as you are."

She reached for a glass and filled it with wine from the open bottle on the counter. I snorted. "Are you old enough, little girl?"

"Yes, considering the legal drinking age here is eighteen." She took a long drink. "I'll be twenty-one next month, by the way."

Madre di dio. Twenty years old. So fucking young.

Theresa was twenty-three, but she seemed much older, more womanly, than the girl at my side. "Good for you," I mumbled.

"This is the part where you tell me how old *you* are."

"Thirty-two."

"Huh. I thought you were older."

I shook my head. *Young people.* They had no concept of age. It was what made them reckless and stupid. "I thought you were supposed to be the smart one."

"If you're referring to my sisters, they're both very smart."

Considering their choices in men, I doubted this. I watched it my whole life with Nino—women drawn to money and power. They didn't care if he was a stronzo, a coke head. The man treated women like shit, never faithful, and they came running back for more.

I put down my fork. "Why are you here in Palermo? Why did your father agree to marry you off to me?"

Her lips pressed tight as she stared at her wine. When she didn't answer, it became clear. She wasn't going to tell me. She didn't trust me.

Honestly, I didn't blame her. I had secrets, as well.

I returned to the football match and my food.

"You have to let me leave," she said. "We'll lie and tell Virga I'm pregnant. Then I'll go back to Toronto and—"

"He will want proof. How are you going to fake a blood test?"

"We find a doctor willing to lie."

I cast her a side glance. "I thought you wanted to be a doctor. Yet you are so quick to disregard the ethics when it suits your purposes. I'm impressed. A true mafioso, Emma."

"Shut up. This is for the greater good, Buscetta."

"No one calls me that." I finished off the rest of the food and pushed the plate away. "Call me Giacomo. Or Mo, if you like."

"Giacomo is a pretty name. Mo sounds like a cartoon character."

I was too tired to make sense of this conversation. I needed sleep, because tomorrow I had to figure a way out of this mess. "There is no lying to Virga. He will insist on using his own doctor for the test."

"Okay, so we aren't faking a blood test," she said. "What other options do we have?"

Just one: Removing Virga.

But Zani and I needed to discuss the potential repercussions first.

"I'm working on it," I told Emma. "Don't worry."

"Well, I am worried. This is my life we're talking about."

"And also mine. You're not the only one affected by this."

"You're right," she said calmly. "I'm sorry."

Any other woman I knew would be yelling and cursing me, ordering me to fix this. Emma was collected and polite, even though her life had been turned upside down.

Not to mention I'd admitted to infidelity, as well as insulted and dismissed her. In response? She hadn't even raised her voice.

I didn't know if I was impressed or disappointed.

It didn't matter. Her meekness was proof of how wrong she was for me, for this life. To stand at my side a woman had to be strong and able to hold her own. Emma was too sweet, too inexperienced. My world would crush her and break her spirit, if she had any.

God knew my mother hadn't lasted. My father ground her down to nothing before she died. He'd tried to do the same to my sister. Thankfully, I'd been able to save Viv from most of his cruelty. But it hadn't been easy and she still suffered.

As did I. There were nights I woke up in a full sweat, certain I was locked in the cellar again. Trapped in the musty darkness with no hope of escape. Waiting for my father to forgive whatever transgression I committed and let me out.

Sweet and soft had no place in the Cosa Nostra or in the Buscetta family. It never had.

I cast her a glance out of the side of my eye. "Why didn't your father fight Virga on this?"

"I suspect he had his reasons. But the arrangement was only for a wedding, not a baby."

"I will find a way to fix it. Give me time."

"How long?"

The back of my neck tightened and I couldn't hold the irritation out of my voice. "Soon. I can't be more specific, Emma. This is bigger than you and me, capisce?"

"I know. Don't get upset. I just . . . People are depending on me there."

I remembered Zani's theory about a boyfriend. "A man?"

"No!"

It was said with such disdain that I wondered about her past. Had Mancini kept her pure for a future husband? "Have you had sex before?"

Her skin turned the color of a ripe tomato and she focused her gaze on her wine glass. "I suppose you think it's your right to ask because we're married, but that information is personal."

Mamma mia, a virgin. Even more reason to stay away from her. "You don't need to worry. I won't try to have sex with you."

"Yes, you made that perfectly clear in the hotel room. And it seems you already have someone to help with that, so . . . ."

"So you are off the hook, no?"

"Yes, except for this baby Don Virga expects us to create."

"I'll find a way out of this mess long before it comes to that." Six months was an eternity. Without a doubt I could devise an escape before then.

We drank in silence for a few minutes. It should've annoyed me to have a strange woman in the house, especially one so young, but Emma wasn't on her phone. She wasn't carrying on an endless conversation or trying to impress me. She was merely . . . here.

I didn't hate it.

"Your father," I started. "He gave his consent for this marriage. What will he do if you don't honor the agreement with Virga?"

"My father will understand."

Cryptic, but her father wasn't my only problem. I couldn't have Ravazzani and D'Agostino causing trouble that would endanger

Viviana. "What of your sisters? What have they said about the marriage?"

She traced the edge of her wine glass with a fingertip. "They don't know I'm here."

"Won't they find out?"

"No. My father won't say anything and I told them I accepted a short internship with a vaccine research company. They think I'm in Peru."

"You contacted them. How?"

"With this." She pulled a mobile out of her back pocket. "Virga returned my phone."

The delivery she'd received earlier. The men had notified me as soon as the box arrived. "You lied to your sisters instead of telling them the truth. Why?"

"Because they know I don't want this life and they'll be furious that it happened. So until we figure a way out of this mess, I don't need them—or their husbands—causing trouble."

Trouble? Emma's family, including Ravazzani and D'Agostino, must abide by Mancini's wishes. As Emma's father, he made the decisions regarding her life. "I don't understand."

"You don't need to understand." Standing, she cradled her wineglass and started toward the hall. "All you need to know is that this is our mess. And we'd better find a way to fix it—fast—without starting a war."

CHAPTER EIGHT

Emma

There were a flurry of text messages waiting on my phone the next morning. Questions about what I was doing and who with and for how long.

> FRANKIE
>
> The more I think about this Peru trip Em... is it a good idea
>
> GIGI
>
> Yeah fr
>
> Do we know it's safe?
>
> FRANKIE
>
> Can you give us the number of someone to reach in case we don't hear from you?
>
> GIGI
>
> Em you turned location off on your phone!!!
>
> wtfffffff

> FRANKIE
>
> Shit I hadn't checked
>
> GIGI
>
> Em if you've been kidnapped by Russian
> traffickers again ISTFG
>
> FRANKIE
>
> Facts
>
> Now I'm worried. Em, check in ok?
>
> GIGI
>
> If I don't hear from you in the next four hours
> I'm sicking my man's hackers on tracking
> you down

I rubbed my eyes. Peru had been a stupid choice. At this time of year it was an hour behind Toronto, which meant seven hours behind Italy. Technically I should still be asleep. I should've picked a country in the same time zone as my sisters.

I stared around at the Buscetta golden bedroom and thought about whether to respond yet. Doctors kept odd hours, so hopefully my sisters wouldn't be too concerned about the time.

I decided to text them back.

> I'm okay! I'm okay!
>
> Calm down, both of you

The response was instant.

> GIGI
>
> Turn on location services!!

I couldn't. They would know I was lying.

> The company asks us to keep them off for
> security purposes.

Ugh, I hated this.

> FRANKIE
>
> That is bullshit
>
> GIGI
>
> Fuck that!

>> You don't need to worry. It's very safe. Lots of people here.

> FRANKIE
>
> Sounds sus Em

>> It's not! I promise. I'm fine.

>> It's a great opportunity and I'm going to learn a lot.

> GIGI
>
> This happened way too quickly
>
> FRANKIE
>
> Yeah why didn't you tell us you applied for it

God, my sisters were so nosy. I understood why they were so protective of me, but I wasn't completely incompetent. I was smart, and I'd been looking after Papà ever since they both left home.

I looked down at my phone.

>> I can't answer any more questions. I have to sleep now. I'm exhausted.

> GIGI
>
> Ugh. Text us when you're up
>
> FRANKIE
>
> I'm going to need regular updates sis

>> Of course! Love you both. Talk to you tomorrow.

. . .

Never mind that it was already tomorrow here.

I stretched my arms and tried to put my sisters out of my head. I couldn't involve them in this mess. Giacomo and I would figure something out.

Giacomo. My husband.

It was an absolutely wild thought.

At least he wasn't a liar. I guess that was one good quality. He told me where he went last night, what he'd been doing. I couldn't complain—it wasn't like this was a true marriage—and he'd been honest about it.

He seemed like that kind of person, someone who told the truth whether other people wanted to hear it or not. My twin was the same way. She always said it was better to offend someone with the truth than to coddle them with lies.

I opened my phone again and checked the security app in my father's room. He was sleeping, the room dark and still. Gloria kept a monitor near her bedside in the guest room so she could hear if he needed anything.

The rise and fall of his blankets soothed some of my worries. Papà was alive and safe. For now.

Unfortunately, Virga's men were watching, as well. God, I hated that.

I forced myself out of bed. My life wasn't going to un-fuck itself if I slept all day. After breakfast I needed to deal with my classwork. The term had just started and I couldn't fall behind, otherwise my grades would never recover.

I got dressed and went downstairs. I wasn't a coffee drinker, unless it came frozen with caramel and whipped cream. I much preferred to wake up with a mug of hot tea. Boring juice, as Gia called it.

The kitchen was empty, the morning light streaming through the windows. It was just after eight o'clock. I normally got up around six thirty, so this was late for me. I wondered what time Giacomo usually woke up.

After searching through cabinets and drawers, I found a mug and a box of old tea bags. Sal limped into the kitchen. "Buongiorno, signora." He looked disheveled and his t-shirt was on backwards.

Clearly I'd woken him up.

"Allora," he said, coming over to the microwave. "Let me do that for you."

"Thank you, but I've got it. Why don't you sit down?" I took his arm and gently led him to the island. "Then you can talk to me as I make tea."

"I apologize for not getting up sooner, signora. Giacomo isn't usually awake until ten or eleven, so we aren't big on mornings here."

I practically forced him onto a stool. "I don't expect you to wait on me, Sal. I'm not a great cook, but I can make tea."

"But—"

"Don't argue with me. Besides, I like having things to do. What can I get you? Tea? Caffè?"

"You shouldn't wait on me, signora. That wouldn't be right."

I started heating the water in the microwave. "I'm not waiting on you. I'm offering."

His shoulders relaxed and he gave me a small smile. "You are very stubborn for such a tiny thing."

"So I've been told. Now, what would you like?"

"I haven't had tea in a long time. If you are willing, I'd like a cup."

I readied another mug and teabag. "Of course. Do you take milk and sugar?"

"Milk, per favore." He leaned forward to peek at my phone. "You have a bunch of messages, signora."

"Probably my sisters. Just ignore them."

"Are you close, the three of you?"

"Very." No, this wasn't true. "Well, we used to be. Before they moved away and found their partners."

"Your oldest sister is married to Don Ravazzani, no?"

"Yes. And my twin is with Don D'Agostino. He's in Naples."

"I know of Don D'Agostino," Sal said. "As well as Don Ravazzani. Your sisters have aligned themselves with very powerful men."

"They fell in love. And the men love them back, which is all I care about." I switched the mugs in the microwave. "Were you ever married?"

"I was engaged once, before I lost my eye. After that, she decided not to marry me."

I glanced over at him. "She broke it off after you were injured? That's terrible."

He shrugged, but I could see the hurt in his expression. "Many people want perfection. They are embarrassed by anything less."

"You're better off, then." I dropped a tea bag in the water to let it steep. "I find it's the imperfections that make people interesting."

"You are in the minority, I am sad to say."

I walked the mug over and placed it in front of him. Then I went to get the milk. "Tell me about the Buscettas."

"What would you like to know?"

"Start with the father. What was he like?"

"Don Gero." Sal added the milk to his tea and stirred. "He was a hard man. Tough. A good leader."

"Good to his wife? His kids?"

He grimaced. "It isn't my place to say, signora."

"Sal, please. I'm trapped with a bunch of strangers, married to a man I don't know. Help me understand."

"The people who want perfection?" When I nodded, he said, "This was Don Gero. He tolerated only the best. There was no room for failure."

"Do you mean with the business?"

His solemn gaze met mine. "I mean with everything."

That was impossible with kids. Expecting perfection only set up unrealistic expectations and often led to higher anxiety in some children. Failure was an important part of learning. At least that's what I'd learned in my psych classes.

"Nino was his favorite child. The oldest, you see." Sal sipped his tea. "So Don Gero molded Nino into a younger version of himself."

"And Giacomo?"

"He resisted such molding."

Ah. That made sense. Giacomo didn't seem like the type of man to easily bend or break. The fights must've been epic. "So not a happy childhood?"

"There was no happiness here, not for anyone."

I thought about this. While my own father had been kind, I'd heard stories of other mafia homes. Violence often wasn't contained to the streets. Sometimes it ended up inside the house, as well. "Was Don Gero abusive?"

"What do you consider abusive?"

I paused, the mug halfway to my mouth. A sick feeling bloomed in the pit of my stomach. "Did he hit his wife or children?"

"No." My shoulders relaxed a bit until Sal said, "But there are other ways to hurt someone without using your fists."

Yikes.

I had to ask it, even if I was terrified of the answer. "And his wife? How did she die?"

"She died when Giacomo was twelve. She was very sick for a number of years, too weak to even get out of bed. Eventually her body gave up on her."

Giacomo's childhood sounded awful. Raised by an abusive father, with no mother to intervene or show affection of any kind? Truly horrifying. Our mother had died when I was little, but we had Frankie. My older sister always made sure we were looked after and loved.

"Do not feel sorry for me."

I nearly jumped out of my skin at the sound of Giacomo's deep voice as he strode into the kitchen, a blue t-shirt pulled tight across his muscular chest. His short hair was wet, like he'd just stepped out of the shower, and he wore no shoes. He looked strong and fierce. And annoyed.

I focused on my tea and tried not to stare at his impressive arms. "I don't feel sorry for you."

"Good." He went to the espresso machine. "My father? A stronzo. My brother? Another stronzo. And I barely remember my mother. I'm better off without all of them."

I didn't know what to say.

There was only silence as the soft whir of the machine filled the kitchen. When it finished brewing, Giacomo lifted the tiny cup in his large hand and downed the hot liquid in a few gulps. Then he put his cup in the sink and started for the door.

I gaped at his back, watching the trap muscles shift as he moved. "Wait, is that it?"

"Is what it?"

He bent over to slide on his boots and the perfect globes of his buttocks drew my attention. Wow, he was in good shape. Tearing my gaze away, I reached for my tea. "You're leaving? Just like that?"

"Emma, I have shit to do. If you need something, spit it out."

I actually did have something I wanted. I wasn't sure if he'd allow it, though. "I need a laptop. To finish my classes."

"There's one in the office somewhere. Sal can show you where it is."

"And what if I want to go out?"

His forehead wrinkled. "Where would you go?"

"I don't know. But I don't want to be a prisoner here."

"Then go." He waved his hand toward the door. "There are cars in the garage. Take one and explore Palermo. Get drunk. Go to the clubs. Sal will send guards with you. Just don't leave town."

"I won't. I mean, I wouldn't even if I could. I don't have any money or ID."

Dark eyebrows shot up. "You brought nothing with you when you left Toronto?"

"I did, but Virga kept my bag."

A muscle jumped in his jaw as he found his car keys. "I will get it for you." The words held all kinds of menace, like he was relishing the encounter. I almost felt sorry for Virga.

"Thank you."

He nodded once and started to leave, then paused. Reaching into the pocket of his jeans, he withdrew a large stack of Euros and began counting them. Muttering to himself, he dipped his hand into a different pocket. A black card landed onto the island with a thunk. Was it made of metal? "Go, use it. Buy yourself whatever you need, capisce?"

I stared at it warily. Taking his credit card felt too . . . couple-y. Like I was his kept woman. Or his wife.

I waved my hand for him to take it back. "That's okay. All I need is my bag."

"Dai, Emma." He put his hands together and shook them at me. "Take the card, go buy the things that will make you happy and comfortable here until we solve this mess. Buy some other shit, as well. Nails and hair, whatever the fuck. Okay?"

Now he was ordering me around? I put my mug down on the counter and tried to remain calm. "I don't like shopping, Giacomo. And I'm not going to the *spa*. This isn't a vacation. I just want my bag from Virga."

I thought he'd be pleased that I wasn't interested in spending his money. Instead, his eyes flashed with anger and his jaw went tight. "You turn your nose up at my generosity?"

Stay calm, don't panic. "I'm grateful for the offer. Really. But I'm jet lagged and tired, and I just need to catch up on my classes. So I'll shop another day."

His expression didn't change. "You are telling me what you think I want to hear."

Smart man. "Everything I need is in my bag."

He pointed at Sal. "Take her shopping. Make her buy shit that women need. Whatever she wants. And even shit she doesn't want."

This was ridiculous. "Giacomo, I—"

"Enough, Emma," he snapped, the sound reverberating off the tile. "Do it, or I will call Theresa and send her out to shop for you."

I nearly fell over, so I braced my palms on the island. "You're joking."

"I never joke, Emma. Ever. And you should know, Theresa's style is very different from yours. So unless you want high heels, short dresses and sexy as fuck lingerie, I would buy your own things."

He spun and disappeared out the door, slamming it behind him.

Sal nudged the credit card closer to me. "It looks as if we are spending the day together, signora."

CHAPTER NINE

Giacomo

Virga had checked out of the hotel.

No surprise, considering security was a nightmare there, but it meant I had to track him down and waste more time. Finally, Zani learned from one of our contacts that Virga was on his boat at San Vito lo Capo, a seaside town almost two-hours from Palermo.

Cazzo madre di dio. Could nothing go my way?

By the time we arrived at the slip where Virga's yacht was docked, I was thoroughly pissed off. Virga left town with my wife's things, knowing perfectly well I would want them back. This was a ploy to get me to chase him, to make me dance to his tune, and it only fueled my anger.

"Are you certain I can't kill him today?" I asked Zani quietly as we walked along the dock toward the yacht.

"Yes. Which is why I told you to leave the guns in the car."

"I don't need a gun to kill him." We both knew I could beat a man to death without breaking a sweat.

Once Zani and I were on deck, two of Virga's men patted us down for weapons. Then we were shown to the back of the yacht, where a shirtless Virga was relaxing on a lounge chair. He smoked a cigar, gold chains resting on his saggy skin, while he looked out at three young topless women sunbathing on the deck below.

It reminded me of the parties my father and brother used to hold on the Buscetta yacht. Booze, drugs, girls . . . anything to make them feel important. The yacht was one of the first things I got rid of when I took over as don.

"Don Virga." I dipped my chin in some semblance of respect, though it almost killed me.

"Buscetta," Virga said, not bothering to stand up and greet me. "I am surprised to see you. I would've thought your new wife was keeping you too busy for such long trips."

"You have something that belongs to her. I've come to get it."

He blew out a long plume of white smoke. "Oh? And what is that?"

As if he didn't know, the stronzo. "Her bag. The one she packed in Toronto."

He glanced over at his man. "Is this true? Are we still holding Signora Buscetta's bag?"

"It's down below," the man answered.

"Dai, then bring it up for Don Buscetta." He waved the man away, then turned toward me. "Perdonami, Giacomo. I have no idea how this could have happened."

I didn't believe him for a second.

"While we wait," he said, "have a seat. Enjoy the fantastic tits down there."

It wasn't a request, so I lowered my bulk into the lounger next to Virga, while Zani took off his sunglasses and leaned against the railing.

"Don't you miss it?" Virga asked. "The boxing and the pussy, I mean. Women must have thrown themselves at you after those bouts, no?"

They had, but only a fool let that go to his head. I started fighting because I was young and full of anger, not because I wanted girls. My father first dropped me off at a gym when I was ten, and I remember overhearing the owner saying to Don Gero, *"Giacomo, he has the maloc-chio."* The evil eye.

This told me what I'd always known. I was cursed.

I said tightly, "I don't miss the injuries or the concussions."

"Madre di dio, your generation. So soft." He puffed on his cigar. "Would you like a drink? Or a cigar?"

This wasn't social. I needed him to say whatever was on his mind so that I could get the fuck out of here. "No."

"The Serbians are asking for more weapons. Can I trust you to take care of it?"

"Sì, certo. No problem."

"Good, good. Tell me, how are you getting on with your new wife?"

"Fine."

"Va bene. I'm happy to hear it. She's a smart girl, your wife. The smartest of the three sisters, that's for certain. Still can't believe Ravazzani married the oldest instead of keeping her as a *mantenuta*." Virga chuckled. "Casual pussy always tastes better, no?"

"Yet you forced me to marry yesterday."

"I did. I expect you to do your duty and bring peace for our families." He paused and blew another stream of cigar smoke. "So explain to me why you were out with your whore last night instead of your wife. Is that doing your duty, Giacomo?"

My fingers strangled the metal armrests of the chair. "I took her virginity. Her body needs time to recover."

"Recover?" Virga dropped his voice. "I don't want you worrying over a bruised pussy or her goddamn feelings. I want you fucking her day and night until you put a baby in her belly. The sooner, the better. Am I clear?"

I said nothing. Fury had a stranglehold on my tongue.

Virga exhaled heavily. "I can see you are still resisting me. Three months, Giacomo."

"Three months for what?"

"To get her pregnant."

"You said six," I said slowly.

"I changed my mind." He rolled the cigar between his thick fingers. "I expect to have my own doctor verify that your wife is pregnant in three months' time. Otherwise I will kill your sister."

I reminded myself that Virga wouldn't be alive in three months' time. Zani and I would begin making plans today. I didn't care how many meetings I had to sit through, how many promises I had to hand out. I was going to kill this stronzo.

"Are we clear?" Virga asked. "Just so there are no misunderstandings later."

"Yes." I stared at the water, not really seeing it. I was tired of dangling on Virga's strings. If I learned what he was planning, I could use it against him. "Something occurred to me," I said. "Seems strange that I haven't heard from Ravazzani. Then I thought, maybe he doesn't know about the marriage yet."

Virga's eyes flashed and I knew I'd hit my mark.

"You haven't told anyone," I confirmed.

"It's too soon. I won't have this marriage annulled. When she's carrying your child, Ravazzani can't say shit—and that is when you are going to leverage her well-being for our Colombian contacts back."

So not only was my wife a pawn, but my child, too? Was Virga so stupid as to think I'd agree to that?

A man carried a rectangular blue suitcase out onto the deck. Virga pushed up off the lounger, so I did the same, and he clapped me on the shoulder affectionately, like a father to a son. "Allora, Giacomo. Give your wife my apologies for keeping it."

I started to move, but his fingers tightened on me, holding me in place. "One last thing. No more mantenuta until your wife is pregnant. We wouldn't want you wasting any of your seed."

My muscles clenched. "Does this mean I can't jerk off, either?"

"You think this is a joke, Giacomo?" The barrel of a gun suddenly dug into my side as he snarled in my ear, "You worthless piece of shit. You aren't fit to carry the Buscetta name. Your father and brother are rolling over in their graves right now."

He shoved the gun deeper, between my ribs, but I didn't react. He kept going, saying, "This is about loyalty and respect. Doing as you're told. And if you disobey me again, I'll put a fucking bullet between your sister's eyes."

I said nothing.

Finally, he pushed me away and put the pistol on a table. I went over to the suitcase and picked it up, ready to get the fuck out of there. As I started to leave, Virga's voice called out behind me.

"Incidentally, has she told you about her father?"

I exchanged a look with Zani, but my friend looked as confused as I felt. "No," I said. "Is there something I should know?"

He clamped his cigar in his teeth and rubbed his sagging chest with one hand. "I think I'll let her tell you. Run along, ragazzetto."

I led the way, Zani close behind me. Once we were off the yacht, I dragged the suitcase along, the wheels thumping on each plank of wood. Zani and I didn't speak.

I'd purposely parked out of sight of the yacht. So when we returned to the car I popped the trunk and opened Emma's suitcase on the ground. Going slowly, Zani and I took each piece of clothing out of the luggage, shook it, inspected it, then put the item inside the trunk. I even went through her panties—which were plain but surprisingly sexy —and her toiletries. I wasn't taking anything from Virga without making sure it wasn't bugged or bombed.

When the suitcase was empty, I closed the trunk and we got in the car. We left the suitcase in the parking lot and drove off.

I slammed my palm into the steering wheel. "Motherfucker!"

Zani began typing on his phone. A few minutes later, he said, "My contact in Toronto hasn't heard anything about Mancini dying. He said orders are still getting around, though they're coming through the brother, Reggie."

"Mancini must be ill, then. It would explain why she wants to be there so badly."

"It would also explain why Mancini didn't resist the marriage."

"Exactly. Because he couldn't."

"This complicates everything, Mo."

"No it doesn't, because Mancini isn't my problem. Viv is my concern. First we find the rat at Mirabella, then we'll get rid of Virga."

"You know we can't go against the capo without laying groundwork first."

That meant meetings with the other families, making deals and giving promises. "It's like a fucking spiderweb."

My father would hate that I was now don. Nino had been the precious heir, the son anointed to wear the crown since he was born. But fate had put me in control of the kingdom, a position I resented. I'd rather jump into the ring and settle things with my fists.

But there was no choice. The world believed me to be the last true Buscetta, the final link to generations of the past. And I would play that part until I died, just to ensure that no one ever discovered the truth. I couldn't let anyone find out one more Buscetta still existed, one that could be used to produce the next generation—whether she was willing or not.

I knew how our world worked. Women were used up and spit out, forgotten once their womb had done its duty. That would not happen to Viviana. My sister would not be subjected to more cruelty.

I wouldn't subject any woman to it, even one I barely knew.

"I think she's a virgin," I said to Zani.

His head shot up. "Are you serious?"

"She all but admitted it last night."

"I'm surprised, considering how the other two sisters ran wild before they settled down. Mancini certainly wasn't watching them." I could feel his eyes studying me before he said, "You like that she's a virgin."

I sent him a dark scowl. "*Va eccati!* Get the fuck out of here with that."

"I've known you a long time. I know the anger you carry over the attention Nino received as the first born, how you were treated by your father. Are you telling me you don't like the idea of—"

"Shut your fucking mouth. I'm not popping her cherry. It's what Virga wants."

But as silence descended in the car, a deep dark part of me worried that Zani might be right.

CHAPTER TEN

Emma

I found Giacomo in the cellar.

He'd requested my presence, apparently, but I wasn't thrilled about going to see him. I didn't like cellars. Never have. They're dark and musty, and full of creepy crawly things.

Blood and gore I could handle. Creatures with more than two or four legs? No, thank you. Hard pass.

It turned out the Buscetta cellar wasn't a cellar after all. Instead of cobwebs and mold, I stepped into a well-lit fully equipped gym.

Holy smokes.

Machines and weights were stationed in neat rows, while a full scale boxing ring sat in the back. Mirrors lined one entire wall, and American hip-hop music blared. I eyed the treadmill and made a mental note to ask Sal about using it.

Movement out of my eye caught my attention, and I froze, unable to process what I was seeing.

It was Giacomo and he was shirtless, covered only in long shorts and trainers, with his hands wrapped in white tape. Every inch of his olive skin glistened with sweat as he hit the bag with his fists over and over again. His movements sharp and well-practiced, I was mesmer-ized by the shift of his trapezius and deltoid muscles. Wide shoulders narrowed into a taut waist, and continued on to thick thighs.

Heat blossomed in my belly and rolled through my limbs. I felt like a voyeur, yet I couldn't tear my gaze away.

Goodness, his forearms. They were huge and covered in tattoos. The real star, however, were his glutes. There was no fat on this man. None whatsoever. I knew without seeing him from the front that his abs were shredded, his obliques forming a perfect v-cut that women drooled over. Including me, apparently.

As someone familiar with anatomy, I could appreciate his strength and physical fitness. Yes, *that* was the reason for the tingling sensation coursing through my veins. Nothing more than a physical response to the beauty of the male form.

Because I couldn't allow it to be anything else.

I must've shifted on my feet, because he abruptly stopped and glanced over his shoulder. Dark eyes pinned me to the spot.

I wasn't capable of speech at the moment, so I lifted my hand in greeting.

Chest heaving with the force of his breaths, he turned—and I felt my knees turn to water. Good God. If I thought his body was perfect from the back, it didn't compare to the front.

More tattoos. More taut olive skin. My gaze tripped over the ridges of his stomach muscles. I was right about the v-cut, which flanked a set of abs that belonged in a museum. I watched beads of sweat coast over his pectorals and resisted the urge to lick my lips.

My husband was ripped. *Temporary* husband, I amended.

The music suddenly cut off, leaving us in silence. "Are you done looking, little girl?" he asked.

I jerked my eyes up to meet his, my stomach twisting at his gruff tone. Except he hadn't sounded annoyed. He'd sounded . . . sinful. Seductive, even.

Which had to be my imagination. Right?

Pushing my shoulders back, I said, "You wanted to see me?"

He put his hands on his trim hips and stared me down. "What did you do today?"

"I went shopping with Sal. As instructed."

He grabbed a towel off a weight machine and began wiping himself off. With an effort worthy of a gold medal, I kept my gaze on his face. He lifted one dark eyebrow and said, "From what I understand you were out shopping *for* Sal. Not with."

Ah, so he'd heard. I shouldn't be surprised. I knew how mafia men gossiped. "Sal mentioned that he hadn't received a birthday or Christmas gift in years. I figured he was due."

"And what did you buy him?"

Was he worried about how much money I spent? "Not a lot. We got new sneakers that are highly rated for people with leg injuries. A smart watch so he doesn't need to fumble for his phone when he's cooking. Bath salts and some muscle creams. I wanted to buy him this motorized lounge chair for his bedroom that's easy to get in and out of, but he said it was too expensive—"

"Emma." He threw the towel to the ground. "I told you to buy things for yourself, not Sal. You deliberately ignored my orders. Do you know what I do to men who dare to defy me?"

The precariousness of my situation was not lost on me. I was in a cellar with an angry, violent husband who could probably do almost anything to me and get away with it.

But I thought of the man who could've taken me by force in that hotel room. Instead, he'd hurt himself and jerked off into the sheets.

I didn't cower or look away. "I assume you'd make them pay. But you aren't going to hurt me."

He blinked twice. "How are you so sure?"

"Because you gave Sal a job inside where it wasn't as physically taxing for him. Because you bought him a new eye when the old one didn't fit right. Because you could have forced me to have sex with you yesterday, but you didn't. You're a decent person."

My answer seemed to anger him, his body swelling as his jaw hardened into granite. I didn't understand. Did he want me to think he was mean? The moment stretched, but I couldn't tell what he was thinking.

Then he came toward me, his long legs eating up the distance between us. Heart pounding, I fought the urge to retreat. It was pointless anyway. Where could I go that he couldn't find me? I was trapped here in this city, in this house. There was no escape.

Still, he kept coming, advancing, an angry mountain of a man, and my self-preservation kicked in. I was brave, but not stupid.

I backpedaled until I hit the wall. Shoot. Now I really was trapped.

I edged sideways, but it was too late. He was there, directly in front of me, sweaty and mostly naked. I held my breath as he put his hands on the wall on either side of my head, caging me in. I could feel the panic creeping in. Had I misjudged him? Had I let a day of hearing Sal tell charming stories of a young Giacomo color my opinion of this man?

Heat poured off his frame as he loomed over me, his eyes bottomless pools of rich coffee. A sneer curled his top full lip. "I beat and killed a man yesterday. He begged for his life just before I slit his throat. Then I married you while his blood dried on my hands and clothing." He eased closer, nearly touching me. "Still believe I am *decent*, piccola bambina?"

Little girl.

The reminder of his recent murder caused me to press into the wall, desperately trying to put distance between us. My autonomic system went into overdrive and the spike of adrenaline heightened every sensation. I was hyper-focused on this man, my blood rushing my ears.

His hips met mine, and I could feel the heft of his groin against my pelvis. Then that heft began to grow and take shape and I sucked in a sharp breath. Was he becoming erect?

"Do you know what I learned today?" His mouth drew closer to my ear. "Don Virga has moved up his timeline. We have only three months to either get out of this marriage or for me to give you a baby."

Three months! My lips parted in surprise. That was an aggressive time frame by any standard.

Giacomo was now hard, his erection digging into my stomach. He rocked his hips once and I swallowed. He surrounded me, the room blocked by his shoulders, and I felt his hot breath on my skin as he said, "Feel that? A decent man would not get hard thinking of being the first cock inside your cunt. A decent man would not get hard thinking of all the ways he could defile your virgin pussy, or of giving you your first taste of come."

Another thrust. My limbs were heavy and loose, uncoordinated, while a steady throb pulsed between my legs. I hadn't experienced desire this strongly before. It was as if I had no control over what was happening, and I found the sensation both thrilling and disconcerting.

"A decent man," he continued in my ear, "would not get hard thinking about shooting inside you, *breeding* you."

Oh . . . god.

Why was he saying these things? I didn't want to find them arousing. Except I did. The combination of his proximity, his body rutting into mine, and the low rumble of his voice was more powerful than my common sense.

Closing my eyes, I inhaled deeply through my nose, but that only sent more of his scent—sweat and some citrus soap—flooding through my head. I melted, my knees no longer capable of supporting me.

All that held me up was the wall behind me and the mountain in front of me.

When I lifted my eyelids I found him looking at me strangely. "You like that idea, no? I can see the truth written all over your face."

"Don't be ridiculous," I croaked. "Get off me."

The words held no force, probably because I didn't really want him to move. If I were being honest, I wanted to examine what was happening, to better understand why I suddenly had no control over my body. Then maybe I could better prepare for next time.

Next time?

Without warning he ground his erection into me once more—and we both gasped. Moisture pooled between my thighs, my sex organs swelling with desire. I longed to rub my clitoris against him, to seek relief for the ache building in that tiny bundle of nerves. Would it feel better with another person than when I used a vibrator or my fingers?

"That's it," he crooned. "Eager for your first taste of cock, wife? All you have to do is ask for it."

Wait, what? Was he implying . . . .?

No, no, no. This was all wrong.

Somehow I gathered enough strength to shove him away. He

stepped back and I hurried toward the stairs, my knees not steady in the least.

It had been a mistake coming down here. I never should've let him—

"Emma," he snapped as I darted up the steps. I didn't break stride, just kept going, focusing on my escape. His voice carried up to follow me. "Do not disobey me again. Because if you do, I won't let it go. I will punish you for it."

I had no idea what kind of punishment he had in mind, but I wasn't about to stick around to find out.

———

I didn't see Giacomo again for the next few days.

Not that I went looking for him. The less time we spent together, the better. Especially after what happened in the cellar.

I wasn't a regular masturbator, though I knew it was a perfectly healthy and normal bodily function. While in Toronto, I gave myself orgasms maybe once a week or every other week. My libido had been almost non-existent, with the pressures of school and my father's illness.

Now? After the cellar?

I was obsessed. I masturbated at least twice a day, sometimes more. It was like Giacomo's body and words had unleashed the sexual side of my brain, a torrent of insatiable lust. I craved satisfaction, yet no amount of self-gratification fully satisfied the itch.

I tried to keep busy and distract myself from these feelings. With my virtual classes in full swing, I had plenty of work to do. I made sure to run for forty-five minutes every day down in the gym. I texted with my sisters and chatted with Sal as he cooked dinner.

Even with all this, though, I couldn't stop thinking of the three month deadline.

"A decent man would not get hard thinking about shooting inside you, breeding you."

Heat washed through me and I punched the buttons on the tread-mill, increasing my speed. My feet pounded on the belt as I berated myself. Why, why, why couldn't I forget these words and the way he'd said them?

I should be repulsed. Horrified. I should be forced to listen to Ted Talks on the dangers of misogyny on a loop for a full year.

So why this morning had I pulled up a browser and typed *breeding kink romance books* into the search bar?

At the other end of the gym, feet appeared on the stairs. More feet followed. A stream of men began descending the steps. What in the world?

Giacomo was first to the bottom landing and his dark gaze found me instantly. He did a long sweep of my body as I ran, and it was full of such blazing intensity that I feared I might trip.

Then I saw the men behind him, the prone body being carried into the cellar by several hands. Even from here I could see the blood on the man's shirt.

I hit the stop button and began slowing down.

"Emma, go upstairs," Giacomo barked.

Zani moved around him and led the group into a side room. Everyone ignored me, except my husband. He pointed to the stairs. "Move, woman. This does not concern you."

I stepped off the treadmill and grabbed my water bottle. "Wait, is someone hurt? I can help."

"The doctor is on the way. I do not need you involved."

"Giacomo, please." I came toward him. "I can be useful, I promise. I shadowed a Toronto trauma doctor for four months and I volunteered at the hospital." He looked unimpressed, so I continued my rambling. "And I watch a lot of surgeries online. Blood won't freak me out."

Sal started down the stairs, a tray of supplies in his hands. He was moving slowly, and Giacomo turned to climb the steps to take the tray from the housekeeper's hands.

See? Decent man.

I didn't wait. I hurried into the side room, which was more like a mini clinic. The injured man had been laid out on a table, and all the soldiers were standing around, like they didn't know what to do.

I pressed through the large bodies to get closer to the table, suspicious gazes tracking my movements. I ignored them and assessed the patient. His complexion was pale and his teeth were chattering slightly. I knew what this meant, but I wasn't exactly qualified to start giving orders. Especially not to this crowd.

With men, I sometimes found it best to let them think an idea was theirs, not mine.

"Is he in shock?" I asked Zani. "Should we cover him with a blanket?"

"I'll fetch one, signora." Zani hurried from the room.

"Emma!" Giacomo barked, slamming the tray of supplies down on the end of the table.

Frowning, I shook off his disapproval. He might not want me here, but that didn't mean I would leave.

The injured man was holding a cloth—an old shirt?— loosely on the wound. It was soaked through, so moving around the table, I went to Sal's tray of supplies. I pulled on latex gloves first, then started opening heavy gauze bandages, the kind for deep wounds. Sal was well stocked, so this emergency care must be a regular occurrence. That was an issue to consider later on.

I went to the head of the table and held up the scissors and gauze in my hands. "Here," I said quietly to the injured man. "Let me help you."

He glanced over my head—at Giacomo, no doubt—then lifted his hand so I could remove the soaked cloth. Then I cut away the man's shirt to reveal the wound. The gash was deep, but not ragged. I immediately pressed fresh gauze on it to stem the bleeding, and the man winced. "Hang in there," I told him. "You're doing great."

Sal was suddenly by my side, also wearing gloves and holding gauze packets. Between the two of us, we kept pressure on the wound, while the injured man fell in and out of consciousness. I talked to him softly in an effort to keep him calm whenever he was lucid.

A man in his late fifties or early sixties pushed in, edging me out of the way. I assumed he was the doctor when he placed a black medical bag on the floor. Was he chewing *gum?*

He withdrew a pair of gloves from his coat pocket. "Who is this woman, Don Buscetta?"

"Someone who shouldn't be in here," was Buscetta's gruff answer.

Really? That was all he was going to say? "I am Signora Buscetta," I said loudly. "And who are you?"

The doctor's eyebrows climbed up his forehead before he turned to focus on Giacomo again. "I hadn't heard. My congratulations, Don Buscetta."

"There is a man bleeding here," I pointed out.

The look on the doctor's face said he didn't care for my stating the obvious. He addressed Giacomo like I wasn't in the room. "I cannot work with a woman here, Don Buscetta. You understand, no? They grow hysterical and distract from the procedure."

Giacomo nodded, as if this made sense. Which it absolutely did not.

"Emma," he growled, waving his fingers for me to come over to him.

I stayed put. "You can't be serious," I said to them both. "I will not *grow hysterical*. And your misogynist opinions are an insult to female medical professionals everywhere."

"We need calm and quiet, Don Buscetta. This is no place for young girls."

I hadn't even raised my voice. This was ridiculous.

"Now, Emma," Giacomo snapped as I opened my mouth to argue once more. "Leave the doctor to his work."

Rarely did I get angry. But I could feel the fury, the frustration rising in my chest, strangling me. I didn't like being dismissed or belittled. Right now my husband and this doctor were doing both.

And I did not want to give in.

I put my hands on my hips. "I can help. I know what I'm doing."

The words had barely left my mouth when Giacomo darted toward me. There was no time to prepare myself before I was lifted off the ground like a sack of potatoes, then thrown over my husband's shoulder. I hung, limp, as he carried me out of the room.

CHAPTER ELEVEN

Giacomo

Madre di dio, this girl. She was raised in this life, so she should know better. Women have their place in our world—and it isn't playing doctor to injured soldati.

Clearly, her father hadn't prepared Emma for her role as the wife of a mafioso. Mancini coddled her, indulging her fantasy of becoming a doctor and living outside the mafia.

It was ridiculous, considering her last name. No one left this world alive.

And now she was my problem.

Everything about her pissed me off at the moment—her immaturity, the disrespect. The fact that we'd been forced to marry in the first place.

Her ass in these skin-tight workout pants.

Every single one of my men had been staring at her barely covered, taut body in that room.

Who knew she'd been hiding such luscious curves under her clothes?

Once upstairs, I kicked open my father's old bedroom door, strode to the bed, and tossed her on top of it.

I put my hands on my hips and stared down at her. I tried to convince myself she was completely unimpressive as a woman. No polish on her fingernails, no makeup or jewelry. Her hair was pulled up into a ponytail, causing her to look even younger.

Yet I couldn't make myself believe it. Emma was pretty without even trying, sexy in an unassuming way. Her tits were pushed high and together in a sports tank, her legs long and lean. The sight of her running, sweaty and breathing hard on the treadmill? Mamma mia.

Her sports tank had ridden up, revealing a flat belly . . . . And I was suddenly reminded of what I'd been ordered to do.

Three months.

I dragged my eyes away as she tugged down her shirt and sat up. "Was it really necessary to carry me out of there?"

"You have no business helping treat one of my soldiers who was stupid enough to get stabbed."

"You knew that I could help. You let that doctor treat me like a child."

"You *are* a child."

"Hardly," she returned calmly. "I'm twenty years old, twenty-one next month. A fact you're aware of, because I told you a few days ago."

This meant nothing to me. What had she done in that time, taken a few exams? I felt ancient just staring at her. "A sheltered mafia princess. Hardly someone with any life experience."

She pinched the bridge of her nose between her thumb and forefinger. "I've seen blood and injuries before. I may not be a doctor yet, but I'm not ignorant of what's involved."

"It's not appropriate for you to be in there, Emma. Do you think your sister is in Ravazzani's face every time one of his men is injured?"

"Frankie is not a pre-med student with practical knowledge about trauma patients."

She was purposely not seeing my point. "It's not how things are done here. You may have more freedom in Toronto with your father, but I can't allow it. You are a Sicilian wife now, not a college student."

She came up on her knees and I tried not to stare at the way the fabric cupped her mound. Fuck, those leggings were indecent.

"Wrong. I *am* a college student, *not* a Sicilian wife. This marriage is not real."

"My men don't know that! No one knows the true circumstances but you, me, Sal and Zani."

"You have no right to yell at me, because I did nothing wrong. I will not perpetuate a backwards society where I'm supposed to be lesser than you just because I'm a woman."

I threw up my hands. "*Porca di puttana!* You are in my *backwards society* whether you like it or not. And you will abide by its rules while you are here."

"Or else? Is that what you were about to say?"

I didn't like how oblivious she was being. Did she not understand the importance of appearances here? Did she not understand how her actions reflected on me? My father and brother were barely cold in the ground and I had a mountain of problems to deal with right now. The last thing I needed was this woman making things worse.

I thought about trying to explain this to her, but what was the point? I wasn't great with words and Emma wouldn't care. She would leave for Toronto the first chance she got, return to her perfect little world. I would have to deal with the aftermath.

I pointed at her. "Stay the fuck here. Do not dare leave this room until I come and get you, capisce?"

Her jaw fell open as her eyes went wide. "You are locking me in?"

Words from my childhood flooded my brain. *"Don't lock the door! I'll go crazy in here! Please, Don Gero!"*

Never "marito" or "amore." Not even his first name, Calogero. My mother had called him Don Gero, no doubt at the old bastard's insistence.

Then months and years passed and she stopped complaining, long having accepted her fate in our personal hell.

I wasn't that man. I didn't want to *ever* be that man.

But I needed Emma to keep out of my way.

I tried to put a fair amount of intimidation in my voice. "Are you planning to disobey me?" Emma's lips flattened, like she was holding back. I knew she didn't like it, but she needed to learn. "Are we clear, Emma?"

"Yes." Just as I turned to the door, she added, "But I wish you would reconsider. It's unreasonable."

I ground my molars together until pain shot through my jaw. "My word is law in this house. I decide what is reasonable and unreasonable. You will do as you are told."

"We'll discuss this later."

"No, we fucking won't!" My roar echoed off the walls. "This is not a negotiation. I don't care about your opinions or thoughts. I don't care whether you are happy here or not. You are nothing to me. An annoyance, a problem I must solve. And as soon as I deal with Virga, you're gone."

I couldn't read her expression, but she kept quiet. I almost wished she'd show some backbone, a little fire. Tell me to go fuck myself or throw something at me.

Then I wouldn't feel like such a bastard for yelling at her.

But she stared at me with those big doe eyes, like I was the one who was being unreasonable. I couldn't take anymore, so I left the room and slammed the door behind me. My boots stomped on the carpet as I made my way downstairs and I contemplated a drink. Cazzo, this girl.

The sooner she was back in Toronto, the better.

———

I leaned against the cellar wall and watched the doctor sew up my soldato. How the fuck had this happened?

It had been an attack in broad daylight at one of our warehouses outside the city, which was practically unheard of. My clan had a stronghold in Sicily, and not many would openly defy it.

I knew in my bones Virga was behind it. It would be smart to come after my businesses, as well as my personal life. A war on all fronts. Nothing disruptive, but enough to make me look weak in front of the other families. Just in case.

Zani came over, his face pulled into a deep scowl. "You think this is Virga?"

"Of course. Who else would dare?"

Over the last few days Zani and I had secretly met with some other bosses. We needed to find out who might be convinced to back us against Virga when the time came. I could take the capo out myself, but I didn't want any retribution for it.

Had one of the families reported back to Virga? Everyone we spoke with hated him more than we did, but it was dangerous, going against *il capo di tutti capi*. Maybe someone has cold feet?

"I'm going upstairs," I said, pushing off the wall. "Pay the doc when he's finished and then come join me."

"Wait. I want to talk to you."

I wasn't in the mood. Ignoring him, I left the room, but was annoyed to find him trailing me up the stairs. "What do you want?"

"I want to know what happened when you carried Emma upstairs. You seem on edge."

I pushed through the cellar door and went into the house. "How is that your fucking business?"

"Sal says you've been spending more and more time in the cellar. How are your knuckles?"

"You're pissing me off. Don't we have other things to talk about that are more important than my home life? What have you learned about Mancini?"

Zani showed me his palms, signaling peace, as we reached my office. "Still no direct answer from Mancini. His brother, Reggie, is still passing on information. And more bad news: Virga is in the wind. No one knows where."

"Cazzo madre di dio!" I pounded the wooden desk with my fist, then pointed angrily at Zani. "I thought we were tracking him. I paid a fuck ton of Euros to get a tracker on that boat before it left port."

"Someone must've found it. All I know is that we lost the signal. Virga's on the open water."

That motherfucker. He planned to stay hidden until the deadline so I couldn't kill him.

Zani's voice penetrated my dark thoughts. "Does your wife know the timeline has been pushed to three months?"

"It doesn't matter." I went to get a drink. This day had been shit from start to finish. "Whether it's a year or a month I'm not fucking her."

"Mo, you might not have a choice."

"There are always choices. And sleeping with a twenty-year-old child is not happening."

"She isn't a child. She's a woman. An *attractive* woman."

Ignoring that comment, I said, "So, we can't find Virga or speak to Mancini."

"Correct."

There were too many unknowns. I needed to strategize.

When I failed to impregnate Emma there was one person Virga would come after. One innocent person who would suffer unless I took drastic measures. I had to protect my sister, even if she didn't like it. "We need to move Viv here."

Zani shook his head like he was hard of hearing. "Sorry, did you say move your sister here?"

"It's the only way to keep her safe when shit goes sideways."

"She won't like it. The change may set her back."

Why was he telling me things I already knew?

Viviana hadn't lived in our house for years. It held only terrible memories for her, as it did for all of us. But miserable and still alive was better than happy and dead. "There is no choice. I'll bring her nurse, too. I'll move her whole fucking room here, if that's what it takes."

"The right thing to do is to fuck your wife and give her a baby. You'd rather ruin your sister's life?"

"And tie myself to this woman—and Mancini and Ravazanni and D'Agostino—for the rest of time? Fuck no."

"You could do worse for in-laws. And the two of you are already married. No one can say shit about her getting pregnant. Most people would expect it."

I didn't want a wife, especially a quiet Canadian pre-med student. And I really didn't want a child. What did I know about fathers and having a family, except suffering and mind games? I was cursed, an evil seed. *Malocchio*. It was what made me unrelenting and ruthless in the ring. A blunt object of destruction pain.

I intended to rule Palermo in exactly the same way.

"Mo, the whole world learns of Viviana's existence if you bring her here," Zani said quietly. "You've kept her a secret for this long. Don't let your selfishness put her at risk."

My heart squeezed painfully. The sound in the room was suddenly too loud, the sunlight too bright. I wanted to howl and scream. I wanted to hit someone, kill someone with my bare hands. I hated this. I hated the helplessness, the uncertainty.

Mostly I hated Virga for manipulating me.

I couldn't believe I was contemplating going through with it, but Zani was right. Better to ruin my life than Viv's.

And it was nothing new. Protecting her was how I'd endured my father's cruelty for years, the words a loop in my head. *Better me than her, better me than her.* How could I abandon that now?

I couldn't.

I propped my hands on the desk and leaned over, my muscles like lead. Stupidly, I thought everything would be easy once the old man died. But my father was still fucking up my life from beyond the grave. He must be loving this from his special place in Hell.

"Bring the fucking doctor in here," I snarled. "I have questions."

While Zani was gone, I downed another full glass of whisky. The liquor burned all the way to my stomach, dulling some of the pain twisting me in knots. I tried to tell myself it didn't matter, that a wife and child didn't matter. Men in my position married for political reasons all the time. This would be no different. God knew my parents hadn't been happily married.

It was a duty. A burden. Nothing more.

Emma would have the child, then return to Toronto after a speedy divorce. I would hire nannies or whatever the fuck, and the child would carry on the Buscetta line when I died.

Virga would suffer, however. The first chance I had I would kill that stronzo. Slowly. Painfully.

Zani came back with Dr. Mazzola. I pointed to the chair in front of the desk. "Sit down."

Mazzola put his black bag on the floor, then lowered himself warily into the chair. "Yes, Don Buscetta?"

I folded my hands on the desk and leaned in. "First, if you repeat a word of this conversation, I'll pull your intestines out through your asshole. Capisce?"

Mazzola paled, but nodded. "Of course."

"I need to get my wife pregnant in a very short amount of time. I want to understand the process, the timetable, so it can happen as efficiently as possible."

If the question surprised him, Mazzola gave no indication of it. Then again, he was old school. Likely it wasn't the first time he'd had this particular chat with a Sicilian mobster.

"Do you have a calendar or a planner handy?" Mazzola waved his hand at my desk.

My upper lip curled. "Not many office supplies around here. Just get to the fucking point."

"Here." Zani put his phone on the desk and I saw the calendar app was open. "Use this."

"Thank you," Mazzola said, leaning in to see the display. "What is your timeframe?"

"Three months."

"Three months from seven days ago," Zani qualified.

Has it already been a week? Dio, that was depressing.

The doctor's eyebrows shot up. "That is ambitious."

I scowled at him. This was hard enough, considering I didn't like asking others for help. I liked solving my own problems, but we didn't have the time in this particular case. "Just explain when all this happens. The egg and sperm shit."

"When was her last menstrual period?"

"No idea."

"Allora, let's just cover the basics." He pointed to the third month. "For her to get pregnant by this date, she would need to miss her period in this month. In a normal cycle, ovulation occurs roughly two weeks after a woman's last period. The egg is viable for eighteen to twenty-four hours."

My jaw fell open as Zani cursed softly. "That's it?" I asked.

Mazzola nodded. "Sì, but sperm can live inside a woman for up to five days."

Thank fuck. Hardy little assholes.

"Her best chance at conceiving is between days eleven and fourteen," the doctor continued. "So regular vaginal sex during this time is best. How old is she?"

"Twenty."

"That's good. She's at her most fertile in her twenties. Do you have any sexually transmitted diseases?"

"I've always used condoms."

"Doesn't matter. If you haven't been tested, we should do that right away. There are certain diseases that can impede conception for a man."

I sighed. "Fine. What do you need to test me?"

"Only blood." The doctor reached into his bag and took out some supplies. "We should test her, as well. To be sure."

"That's not necessary. She's a virgin."

Mazzola's expression didn't change at this revelation. "Of course, she is your wife, after all. I meant no disrespect, Don Buscetta." He cleared his throat. "We should be thorough, however."

"I said it's unnecessary."

Mazzola paled at my menacing tone. "If you're sure, then we'll just test you." Standing, he came around to my side of the desk. "Hold out your arm."

He tied a band around my biceps, then swabbed the inside of my elbow with a wipe. When it was over, I waved him away. "Let me know the results as quickly as possible."

"I should have them tomorrow. In the meantime, I suggest you try and learn your wife's cycle. It will make the process easier on both of you."

I didn't care if this was easy or not; I just needed it done. "So fuck during ovulation, then she should be pregnant two weeks later. Is that all I need to know?"

Mazzola put the vial of blood in a plastic bag and sealed it. "If you want to be certain, ejaculate inside her every day during those two weeks. That will increase your chances. But her cycle may be irregular, in which case she'll need to take her temperature to determine the ovulation window."

Fuck me. Why was this so complicated? "Anything else?"

"Both of you should avoid smoking or cannabis use and eat a diet rich in nutrients. I can prescribe prenatal vitamins now. She should begin taking them, even before conception."

"Leave the prescription. I'll have it filled. You're excused."

Mazzola straightened and extended his hand. "I wish you the best of luck, Don Buscetta."

I didn't move, ignoring the outstretched palm across the desk. "I expect a call tomorrow with those results, doctor."

After he promised I would hear from him, Mazzola left with Zani. Alone, I stared at the wall and thought about how I planned to fuck a baby into my wife.

CHAPTER TWELVE

Emma

The next morning I was up early, chatting with Sal in the kitchen, when Giacomo came in.

I surreptitiously watched his broad back as he stood at the espresso machine. We hadn't spoken much after he yelled at me and ordered me to stay in my room.

"I don't care whether you are happy here or not. You are nothing to me. An annoyance . . . ."

I told myself I didn't care but the words hurt. No one had treated me so callously before. Yes, I realized how privileged that made me sound. But it was true.

Giacomo legitimately hated me—and I didn't blame him. I'd been forced on him.

But did he think this was a picnic for me? My entire life had been disrupted! He was still in his family home, surrounded by friends. I was struggling to lie to my sisters, keep up with my online classes, and check in with my ill father.

My husband turned around with a demitasse cup cradled in his large hand. "When do you need your woman's things?"

I blinked several times. "My what?"

"Pads. Tampons. For bleeding."

What the hell? I couldn't answer for a long beat, surprise freezing my tongue. First he wanted to know if I was a virgin. Now he was asking about my period. Had I lost all right to privacy after repeating marriage vows? "You're asking about my period?"

"Yes."

"Why?"

"Just answer the fucking question."

"Giacomo," Sal said sternly from the stove. He spoke too quickly for me to translate, but I could tell he was displeased with my husband.

Giacomo paid Sal no attention. He remained entirely focused on me. I resisted the urge to squirm like a bug pinned under his dark stare. It was far too intense.

"Emma," he said. "Answer me."

This was all so bizarre. But I wasn't ashamed. Every person with a functioning uterus bled each month. "My period ended right before I left Toronto. I'm not due for another two weeks. But don't worry—I have enough supplies."

Giacomo exhaled heavily, clearly disappointed in my answer. "Cazzo," he muttered, then downed his caffè in one shot.

"Why do you care?"

"I don't."

I didn't believe him for a second. Would I ever understand this man?

He put his cup in the sink, then faced Sal. "Find somewhere else to be tonight."

Find somewhere . . . . Whoa. Hold up. This wasn't about supplies or stocking my favorite chocolate gelato in the fridge. This was about *conception*.

Virga's mandate.

"Stop right there," I said when Giacomo started to leave. "Whatever you think is happening tonight is not happening."

He paused near the doorway, his shoulders slumping. I imagined he was heaving another annoyed sigh. "Sal," he called. "The room, per favore."

Sal gave me a quick nod before leaving the room. I chewed on the inside of my cheek and waited. I immediately missed having the buffer of a third person. Giacomo—and my reaction to Giacomo—made me anxious.

He came toward me, his lips flattened into a determined line. His biceps popped with each step, and his jeans clung to his thigh muscles. He was all hot-blooded Sicilian male. I'd never met a man so intense or intimidating—and that was saying something, considering my brothers-in-law.

Giacomo propped his hands on the marble island next to me and leaned in. "You will do as you are told, Emma. Whatever I say is happening tonight will happen. Capisce?"

I was growing tired of this same refrain. When would he learn that I had a mind of my own? "We are not having sex tonight."

His top lip curled into a sneer. "You think to refuse your husband, little girl? Your body is mine by right."

"Not according to the law."

He threw his head back and laughed, the tendons in his thick neck shifting as the sound continued. "The law does not apply to me, even less so to you."

"What of Fausto and Enzo's laws? Because they will learn of this one day."

"I can't worry about your brothers-in-law. And none of this changes our responsibilities at the moment."

"And what are our responsibilities?"

"To get pregnant in three months' time. I don't like it, either, but we are left with no choice."

"There are always choices. You need to talk some sense into Don Virga."

He leaned closer, and I could smell the clean scent of his citrus soap, see the whiskers on his jaw. Each long lash that rimmed his eyes. His expression was anything but patient as he explained, "Don Virga has disappeared. He is on his yacht in the middle of the ocean. I can't find him. No doubt he plans to stay hidden until the deadline to remain alive."

"You were going to kill him?"

"I *am* going to kill him. The first chance I get—and I promise it will be painful."

A shiver worked its way along my spine at the softly spoken vow. I didn't doubt him for a second.

I stared at the black marble countertop. How long would I be stranded here? I thought of my father lying in bed, wasting away as cancer ate away at his body. I wanted to spend time with him, soak up all the minutes and seconds before it was too late. Whatever it took, I had to get back to Toronto as quickly as possible.

But I didn't want to have a baby with this man.

I concentrated on my breathing in an effort to stay calm. There had to be another way out of this. We needed more time. Virga would show up eventually. Like, he'd need to gas up the yacht in port somewhere, right? Then Giacomo would find him and kill him.

This was so messed up. Was I really hoping for the death of another human being? It went against everything I believed, everything I was working toward.

But what choice did I have?

This was spiraling too quickly. I closed my eyes to avoid my husband's too-intense gaze. I wasn't ready to have sex with anyone today, let alone with a stranger. I wanted a man who cared about me, who loved me, to be my first. Not someone doing it out of obligation.

I looked up, resolved to tell him no, but the words died on my tongue. He did not appear in the mood for a rational conversation, not with his wild eyes and intimidating posture.

So I went with a lie instead.

"I'm on the pill."

The lines around his mouth deepened as he frowned. "You are on birth control."

"Yes."

"You? A virgin? Why would you be on birth control?"

"First, I've admitted to nothing in regards to my sexual experience. Second, many women take the pill for reasons unrelated to preventing pregnancy." I didn't, but I knew this to be true.

"What does this mean?"

"It means I can't conceive until I stop taking it."

"So stop taking it."

"Even if I do, you'll still have to wait until I ovulate after my next cycle."

He pushed off the counter and jammed his hands into his pockets. "And how long will that take?"

"Two to four weeks for my cycle, then another two for ovulation." This wasn't always true. Some women became fertile within days, others longer, after stopping birth control. But Giacomo didn't know that. Besides, none of that mattered because I wasn't on the pill.

And we weren't having sex.

Head shaking, Giacomo stared at the floor. I could see his lips moving as he cursed quietly in Italian. "Stop taking them today, Emma. No more pills. And if I find out you are lying to me, I will punish you."

He wouldn't find out. Not to mention that I would do everything in my power to string it out as long as possible, too.

"Okay," I agreed.

"Prepare yourself, wife. I'm giving you three weeks. If we haven't arrived at another solution to our problem by then we will have sex every day for a month. Your only job will be to milk every drop of come from my balls with your tight pussy."

He made it sound like a threat. "Whether I like it or not? Was that what you were about to say?"

He walked around to my side of the bar and came to stand behind me. I started to turn, but he pressed close, his front sealing tight to my back. The heat from him sank into my skin through my clothes as his strong body surrounded me. My skin crawled with awareness, a rush of desire settling between my legs.

"Piccola bambina innocente." *Little innocent girl.* His lips rested above my ear, his gruff voice penetrating deep into my bones. "When I fuck you, you will like it. Every. Single. Time. *Te lo prometto.*"

Then he was gone.

His footsteps retreated on the tile, then I heard the door slam. I gripped the marble counter, my fingertips clutching the polished stone like a lifeline. The only sound in the kitchen were my rapid exhalations as I tried to recover from whatever just happened.

The Italian, the endearment, the way his voice sounded like smoke and sex . . . .

Whew. I fanned my face with my hand. I wasn't certain I could resist this version of Giacomo. The feeling of him against me, like I was both in danger and completely safe at the same time, thrilled some deep dark part of my animal brain. It was every naughty fantasy, every filthy desire brought to life.

Even now, after he left, my heart was racing and I craved more. I couldn't escape these thoughts, these erotic feelings he elicited no matter how hard I tried. There was no hope for it.

Taking my phone, I left my cup on the island and crept out of the kitchen. I didn't want Sal to know I was turned on and going upstairs to masturbate. Breakfast could wait.

At the top of the stairs, I paused. Hmm. I should head toward my wing, opposite from where my *husband* slept, but I hadn't ventured into his space yet. I was curious. What did his bedroom look like? Would it smell like him? Was he neat? All the rooms in my wing were huge with ornate fixtures and loads of light. Somehow I couldn't picture gold curtains in Giacomo's room.

Screw it. I had to find out.

———

The opposite wing was much different than my end of the house. There were no ornate details or fixtures here. The cream-colored walls were dirty and bare, with the paint peeling in places. Old and frayed carpets. It was like the decorator hadn't bothered to continue along this section of the house during the remodel. This vibe was utilitarian, more like a hospital room. A far cry from the Las Vegas strip I was sleeping in.

A single door stood open at the end of the hallway. Was this his bedroom?

I started forward, then paused. There might be cameras. Both of my brothers-in-law had security in almost every nook and cranny of their homes. So, was someone watching me snoop? I did a quick search of the ceiling and walls, but didn't see any devices.

I was willing to risk it.

Besides, this was just a peek. I didn't plan on stealing anything.

With a fingertip, I pushed the door wider to reveal a small bedroom. Straightaway I knew this was Giacomo's domain. The scent of him—like wood and oranges—hung in the air. My eyes drifted to the bed immediately.

"When I fuck you, you will like it. Every. Single. Time."

The bed was smaller than I expected, not even queen-sized. How was he comfortable in it? My bed was twice the size of this one, which made no sense.

On top rested a dark blue bedspread with matching sheets and a few pillows. Nothing fancy and perfectly made. He clearly wasn't the type to leave it messy. In fact, the entire room was neat, with no clothes on the floor or discarded shoes. I hadn't expected that. Most men, from what I gathered online, weren't very tidy.

Maybe his bathroom was a mess.

Wrong. It was just as organized, just as sparse, as the bedroom. A toothbrush in a holder and hand soap—that was it. Two bottles were lined up perfectly in the shower, and a folded towel rested on the rack. The air was still humid from his morning shower.

As far as revelations went this was a big let down. If someone hoped to learn more about Giacomo Buscetta, it wouldn't be here.

But I wasn't one to give up, so I went to his closet.

It was empty. Bare, with not a shirt or a tie or a pair of trousers in sight. I almost didn't believe it. I'd seen Fausto's closet once and it was filled with designer suits and custom-made shirts. My father's was a close second. I guess Giacomo never dressed up?

There was one narrow dresser and the contents of each drawer were neatly organized. Folded t-shirts, jeans, and shorts, like you'd see in a store. This had to be Sal's doing. I couldn't imagine Giacomo folding laundry.

A small nightstand sat by the bed, a lamp on top. There was one drawer and I wondered if this might be the place where I'd finally learn more about Giacomo. Sitting on the mattress, I eased the drawer open. An eyeglass case. Condoms. Lube. A book on military history.

Interesting. The pages looked well-read and worn, so I eased the book out of the drawer.

I flipped through it, marveling at a mafia don who studied his craft, when a photo popped out from the pages. Oh, *hello*. This was the first personal item I'd found. I only felt a smidge of guilt as I flipped the photo over to look at it.

A young boy and girl stared at the camera, his arm wrapped around her shoulders. The girl couldn't have been more than eight or nine. The boy was older, maybe fourteen or fifteen, and there was no mistaking this was Giacomo. I'd seen this same unhappy full mouth and intense dark stare.

So, who was this girl? Don Gero had only Giacomo and Nino, so was this a neighbor? A cousin? She had dark hair and similar eyes—

"Signora!"

Startled, I dropped the photo onto the pages of the book. "Sal, my goodness. You scared me." I hurried to straighten everything and put the book away. I closed the drawer and stood, trying my best to appear like I hadn't been caught snooping.

Sal placed a stack of not-so-neatly folded laundry on Giacomo's bed. Wow, had I been wrong about Giacomo's folding skills, as well?

"You shouldn't be in here," Sal said. "Don Buscetta wouldn't like you going through his things."

"I know. I'm sorry." I moved toward the door. "I was just curious and the room was so bare."

He gestured for me to leave, then closed the door behind us. Disapproval radiated off the older man and my stomach knotted. I suddenly felt like my father caught me cheating on a test—not that I would ever do such a thing.

"Giacomo is very private," Sal said as we started down the hall together.

Giacomo might be private, but I was curious by nature. I couldn't help it. My inquisitiveness was what drew me toward the sciences. I'm an analytical thinker; I like to find answers to any problems I encounter.

I asked, "There was a girl in the photo. She looks a lot like him. Do you know who she is? A cousin, maybe?"

"Signora." Sal sighed. "You should not be asking questions. Leave it alone."

"I'm trying to understand him better. I've been dropped into this house, this country, and married to a man I don't know. You can hardly blame me for trying to make sense of all of this. And it's not like he's Mr. Talkative."

Sal stopped and put a hand on my shoulder. His smile was kind, but firm. "*Cara*, there are some questions that are better left unanswered, capisce? You do not want to turn over this rock, te lo prometto."

"Why? I won't tell him you told me. I'm great at keeping secrets."

Sal released me and began walking again. "You must ask your husband these questions. It isn't my place to share. Per favore, signora. Don't put me in this position."

I immediately backed off. This wasn't Sal's responsibility. And I didn't want Giacomo to get pissed at this sweet older man. "You're right. I'm sorry."

We stopped at the top of the stairs. He gave me a soft smile. "You're a good girl, signora. I am glad you are here."

"Thank you, Sal. I don't know what I would do without you." And I meant it. He gave me someone to talk to, someone to eat with. I didn't feel so lonely with him in the house.

"I must return to my bread before it deflates." He grabbed the bannister and began going slowly down each step.

"Have you considered getting a lift for the stairs?"

"A lift? Does this mean someone carries me?"

"Sort of. It's a chair that attaches to the wall and goes up and down."

He waved his free hand. "Dai, I don't need such things. I go slow, but I manage."

I wasn't so sure. Maybe I could talk to Giacomo about putting in an elevator or a chair lift. I watched Sal's progress, ready to help if he needed it. So that Sal wouldn't think I was hovering, I called, "Giacomo folds his own laundry."

"Sì, signora. He is very particular that way. I have tried, but he says I can't do it correctly."

"Why doesn't he have any suits?"

Sal's laugh was dry. "This boy, I have never seen him wear a suit in his entire life. I think he'd rather take a punch to the mouth than wear a tie."

"I thought a don needed to look professional. Like a businessman."

Sal reached the bottom of the stairs and looked up at me. "Don Buscetta does not care what others do or say. He answers only to himself."

He limped away, leaving me to think over these words.

CHAPTER THIRTEEN

Giacomo

The phone rang in the car. Zani and I both looked at the display. *Theresa.*

Pushing a button, I declined the call and kept driving.

"Let me guess?" Zani said. "You haven't told her."

"She is a fuck buddy. I owe her no explanations."

And I had bigger problems than Theresa.

Since my conversation with Emma yesterday morning about her pills, I couldn't stop thinking about her. Specifically, I couldn't stop thinking about fucking her, taking her virginity. Pumping her small body full of its first dose of come. I wanted to dirty her up. Be the one to turn her into a filthy girl.

In my entire life I couldn't remember being first for anything. Nino got everything growing up—my father's attention and respect, then girls, cars, money. Everything had been given to my brother with nothing left over for me. I'd fought hard for scraps merely to survive.

But Emma Mancini? She was mine, no one else's. She hadn't fucked my brother or any other man. I would be her first.

She would also be the first woman I fucked raw. The first woman to carry my child.

There was something primal about it that appealed to me. My father said I was barbaric and unsophisticated, and maybe this proved him right. I didn't care. All I knew was that I couldn't wait to stick my dick inside her sweet, tight *virgin* pussy.

Beside me, Zani wouldn't drop it. "You have no idea how to handle women, Mo."

"Neither do you, coglione."

He chuckled. "Dai, I get five times the pussy you do."

I took a corner and turned into the gravel lot of our destination. "I have a wife. That is the only woman I am concerned with at the moment."

"And how is that going? Did she stop taking her pills yesterday?"

"I assume so. I didn't check."

"Don't you think you should?" When I didn't say anything, Zani shook his head, like a teacher disappointed in his student. "Your wife has a mind of her own. In my experience, the only way to make a woman like that do what you want is by making her come. Eat her out a few times and she's like putty in your hands. You'd be surprised how many men don't do it right."

I pulled behind the abandoned building and shut off the car. "I don't need your advice to deal with her."

Zani must've realized I was serious, because he said nothing more as we got out of the car. I started toward the back door. This was one of the many secluded places we used from time to time to work someone over. It would give me a chance to expel some of the frustration coiled in my muscles.

We went in and found a man hanging by his wrists on a hook. He was limp, unconscious, and from the blood on his clothes it looked like he'd struggled before my men got him subdued.

A hammer, pliers, and gardening shears rested on a table in the middle of the room.

Franco and Dino, two of my men, were leaning against the wall, waiting. They straightened when they saw me. I went over and shook their hands. I made it a habit to know the men who worked for me, to know their families. I treated them with civility, with gratitude, something my father never did. "This is him?"

"Sì, Don Buscetta," Franco answered. "He's the manager."

"Va bene. You've done well." I slapped Franco's shoulder. "You can both go now. Zani and I will handle it from here."

"Of course," Dino said. "Want us to stay nearby for clean up?"

"That would be helpful," Zani said, ushering the two men out the door. "I'll ring when we're ready."

I paid them no attention. I was already picking up the hammer.

"Wake him up," I told Zani when we were alone. "Let's get this started."

As I waited for Zani, I twirled the hammer in my fingers. How many times had I done this over the years? Countless. Usually with Zani, but sometimes alone.

I learned cruelty at an early age. It was all I'd ever known, thanks to my father and brother. This was my place—receiving and inflicting pain. A soldier to follow orders and fall in line.

And I never failed.

The man on the hook was Mirabella's director, Silvio Dimarco. My second cousin. He was the only one who knew Viviana's true last name. I'd trusted him to keep our secret safe. I put Viv's care in his hands. A stupid decision on my part. Even family turned against each other under the right circumstances. Didn't I know that better than almost anyone?

Silvio disappeared on the day of my impromptu wedding, but my men tracked him down and found him hiding in a small apartment in Partanna. He wouldn't leave here alive.

Zani held the smelling salts under the man's nose and Silvio jerked against the bonds, his head arching away from the strong smell. His eyes fluttered, and I saw awareness creep in with the subtlety of a sledgehammer.

"Ciao, *cugino*," I said casually. "It's good to see you again."

He licked his lips, nervously looking at me and Zani. "What is this about? Your men took me from my holiday, brought me here and strung me up like meat. What the fuck!"

Holiday? Like hiding out in a shit hole in Partanna was a holiday. "You know what this is about, Silvio."

"My shoulders are killing me, Giacomo. Let me down."

"Who did you tell?"

"What are you talking about?"

I drew closer, thumping the hammer against my palm. *Tick, tick, tick* . . . . "I want to hear who you told. I want to hear how much he paid you to betray me and put my sister's life at risk."

He swallowed hard, the muscles in his throat working. "I've kept your sister safe. I would never betray you."

Lies. "Cut his clothes off."

Zani didn't hesitate. Taking a switchblade, he removed Silvio's clothes efficiently. When my cousin was nude, I said, "Now, explain to me how Don Virga learned of her existence after all these years. After all the effort I've gone to just to keep her hidden. How did that happen, Silvio?"

"I don't know what you're—"

I drew my arm back and swung. The flat head of the hammer smacked into his ribs. Silvio howled, the sound echoing off the cement walls.

"Hold him still," I told Zani. Then I hit Silvio again on the opposite side. The noise he made wasn't as loud this time, but it was hard to scream with two broken ribs.

"I want to hear it from your own mouth," I said. "I want to hear what he offered you, what was worth betraying your own family."

"I . . . didn't," he wheezed through labored breaths.

I shattered his knee cap next. He yelled as best he could, panting as he struggled against the pain. I walked around to his other side. "Should I break the other one, or are you ready to tell me?"

In the end Silvio held out much longer than I anticipated.

The story emerged when I switched to the gardening shears. It turned out that Virga leaned on several of my second cousins for any secret to use against me, but Silvio was the only one who cracked. Instead of coming to me for protection, Silvio told Virga that Viviana was still alive. For that, I had no sympathy or mercy for Silvio.

I killed my cousin slowly, painfully. He was a bloody, broken heap when I finished.

I walked to my car and put on the clothes I'd stored in the trunk. Adrenaline was surging in my blood, a buzz under my skin that I experienced after a fight or a kill. It was like a high where everything was too intense, too fast. Sharp and unrelenting. In the past I would've called Theresa, gone to her and fucked this out of my system. But that was no longer an option, thanks to Silvio and Virga.

Merda. Having a wife was inconvenient for so many reasons, but this had to be one of the worst.

Except . . . maybe Zani was right.

Maybe it was time to exploit her building attraction for me—use it against her to gain her complacency.

Maybe it was time to bring her to heel.

————

I found Sal waiting for me in the kitchen. I went to the refrigerator and pulled out a sparkling water. "Why are you still awake?"

"To speak with you."

I could feel the heaviness, the weariness pulling me under. Would this day never end?

Sighing, I opened the bottle in my hand. "And?"

"I caught her looking around your room earlier. She found a photo of you and your sister."

Cazzo! It was the only photo I had of the two of us, and I kept it tucked in a boring military book. Sal had been around long enough to remember Viviana, and after my father's death I'd confided in him that she was still alive. "I hope you didn't say anything."

"Of course I didn't. She asked who was in the photo with you and I told her it wasn't my place to share."

I leaned against the counter and sipped my water. I didn't like this. Emma shouldn't be in my room, looking through my things. Fuck her for snooping in there.

I set the bottle on the marble counter with a snap. "I will start locking my door."

"I don't believe that's necessary." Sal shook his head. "She is desperate to help make sense of you, of this." He gestured to the room. "She's in a strange country, married to a stranger. If you helped her, talked to her, then she wouldn't need to sneak around and look through your things."

"Oh, so this is my fault? Che cazzo?"

"Yes, in some ways. You left her here and ignored her for more than a week. You've made no effort to get to know her or to make her feel comfortable."

I didn't like the sliver of guilt that worked its way under my ribs like a blade. I wasn't here to babysit Emma. I had an empire to run, and Virga to hunt and kill.

Sal's voice gentled. "If you're going to have a baby, a family, with this woman, she needs to like you."

"Why? The sperm and the egg don't give a shit whether or not we like each other."

"My nonna, she used to say that my father was so mean because she and Nonno hated each other. She always said you have to make love to make a loving and healthy child."

Minchia, what nonsense. "You can't really believe such things, old man."

He shrugged. "It can't hurt. They say if the woman enjoys herself, it helps conception."

"Another wives' tale."

"No, it's true. And would you want for your wife to not enjoy it? Dai, Giacomo. You're not that cruel."

Zani's words echoed in my head. *"Eat them out a few times and they're like putty in your hands."*

And Zani wasn't wrong. I knew this from experience. Theresa often said good sex wasn't easy to find, and that's why our arrangement had suited her perfectly. She put up with my moods and odd hours just for an excellent fucking.

I stared at the worn kitchen tile and thought about Emma. I couldn't have her looking through my things, causing trouble. I needed her to do as she was told. I needed her docile, placated. Willing to get knocked up and disappear back to Canada. Out of my life.

All that mattered was keeping Viv safe.

My eyes swung toward the doorway leading to the main stairs. She was up there. Emma. My *wife*. Her unused pussy was just waiting for me to show it some attention.

Blood rushed to my groin. It was fucked up, getting hard at the idea of taking a woman so young.

First. I can be first.

Dio mio, I had to stop thinking like that. It wasn't helpful. This wasn't about my issues. This was about ensuring that she followed my orders. That she stayed out of my room.

Fuck it.

I finished my water and placed the empty bottle on the counter. "I'll see you in the morning."

"Don Buscetta," he called when I'd almost left the room.

I paused, but didn't turn around. He almost never called me by my honorific. He knew I hated it because it reminded me of my father.

He continued, "Be gentle with her. Ha un gran cuore, sai?" *She has a big heart, you know?*

I cast him a harsh glare over my shoulder. "You insult me by insinuating that I would do otherwise. Don't forget your place, old man."

"I would fail you both if I said nothing." He lifted his chin, not insulted by my response in the least. "She has no one here, no father or family member to speak up for her, so I must do it."

Once upon a time Sal was a tough soldier. What had happened to make him so soft? "Don't get too attached. She will return to Toronto soon."

"Don't be so sure, ragazzo. Fate has a funny way of giving us what we need when we least expect it."

I sighed and rubbed my face. Emma was not what I needed. Not now, not ever. "I will punch you in your good eye, if you do not shut up."

I didn't give him the chance to offer up any more sage advice. I walked through the dark house and went upstairs.

Usually, I would turn toward my wing. Tonight I went the opposite direction.

I strode along my father's side of the house, the end with terrible memories. The fights, the hitting. My mother's screams. It hadn't bothered Nino, but I moved into the empty wing when I was five. And when Mamma died I took Viviana out of here and stashed her in the room beside mine.

It gave me a perverse sense of pleasure that Emma took my father's bedroom as her own. Not even Nino, the golden child, had dared to do so. A small smile twisted my lips. My father would've hated knowing that a Mancini, an 'Ndrangheta family member, was staying in his room.

I reached the door. I could knock, but what was the point? She wouldn't refuse me entrance, and she'd already invaded my personal space today. Wasn't it only fair to return the favor?

I twisted the knob and threw open the door. Emma was on the bed, under the covers, with her hair in a messy knot atop her head. She wore no makeup and was scrolling on her phone, a pair of eyeglasses on her face. She looked sexy and smart, like a young librarian.

At the sight of me, her eyes rounded and she jerked the covers up to her chin. "Giacomo! What the heck?"

Emma rarely cursed, I'd noticed. It made me want to dirty her up even more.

I closed the door and folded my arms. "You were busy today, no?"

Her slim throat worked as she swallowed. "He told you." At my nod, she hurried to explain. "It was wrong and I'm sorry. I was just curious about you and couldn't help myself. Really, I'm very sorry."

"What were you hoping to learn? What brand of briefs I wear?"

"No, of course not. Though your folding skills are impressive. My drawers aren't half as neat as yours."

"Emma," I snapped. "Why the fuck were you in my room?"

"I wanted to learn more about you and your life, like artwork or photos. What colors you like, what kind of toothpaste you use. I literally know nothing about you."

"You know enough." I started toward the bed. "You know that I never wanted to be don, I used to box, and I need to get my wife pregnant in the next three months. There's nothing else you need to know."

She clutched the covers tighter at my approach, her fingers turning white. "That can't be true. I-I found that photo. Of you and that girl. Who is she?"

My muscles tightened, fear sinking deep into my bones. Emma could tell one of her brothers-in-law about that photo, about my sister, and my life would never be the same. It was bad enough that Virga knew about Viviana. I couldn't let Emma discover my sister's existence, as well. "You don't need to worry about her. She doesn't concern you."

"Is she your cousin?"

Fuck this. We weren't having this conversation.

I bent and grabbed the covers in one fist and pulled hard. The cloth slipped out of Emma's grip and fluttered onto the floor. Her small body was revealed, covered in a blue pajama set. The cotton shorts accented her toned legs, and the loose top hinted at her tits. I usually liked enticing lingerie, the kind with lace and satin, but this almost-masculine getup was so Emma that I found it charming. And somewhat sexy.

"Take off your shorts."

"W-what?" She scrambled to sit up and hugged her legs. "Giacomo, get out of here. I was almost asleep."

"Cazzata, you were on your phone. Take off your fucking shorts, Emma."

"Why?"

"You know why."

"No, I don't. I told you, I'm on the pill. We can't have sex."

"We're not having sex. But we are going to do other things."

She pushed a strand of long brown hair behind her ear. "Sex isn't just vaginal penetration. That's a very misogynistic way of looking at—"

I put one knee on the bed and placed my hands on her legs. She shut up immediately, her wary gaze going wide. But she appeared a heartbeat away from kicking me in the face.

"I'm not going to hurt you," I said, trying to quiet my voice. "I want to make you feel good."

"How?"

"Just trust me. You will like it."

Her expression didn't change in the least. "I want to know exactly what you plan to do. I need to give consent, Giacomo."

Most women eagerly spread their legs for me. Lucky me, I married the one woman in all of Sicily who didn't want my tongue or my cock.

Sighing, I yanked her legs apart and wedged my body between them. I wished Emma would relax and let me do as I like. But I was coming to know her well. Something told me nothing less than a full explanation would do.

"First, I will strip off both these shorts and your panties. Then I will bend down and lick your pussy until you come."

Plump lips parted on a swift intake of breath. She looked incapable of words, so I grabbed the waistband of her shorts.

"Wait!" She covered my hands with hers, stopping me. "I'm not sure I want you to do that right now. It feels, I don't know, sudden."

"Trust me, wife. If you had only ten minutes to live, you'd beg me to suck on your clit and make you come. It's going to be the best thing that's ever happened to you."

She nibbled her lip, like she might be considering it. I rubbed my palms over her smooth skin to convince her. She didn't pull away, which I found encouraging. "Ready?"

"No," she said. "Even though we're married, I don't want to start trading sexual favors."

"Emma, I'm not doing this to get something in return."

That caused her to roll her eyes. "All men do this to get something in return."

I didn't like that. Especially because she wasn't altogether wrong. I was doing this to gain her obedience, her cooperation. But this was no hardship. I loved pussy. And something told me Emma's would be superlative. "I don't want a blow job, if that's what you're worried about."

"You don't?" Her eyes crinkled around the edges as she narrowed her gaze on me. "You don't want me to perform oral sex on you?"

I shrugged. "If you want to, I won't turn it down. But that's not why I'm offering to eat you out."

"Then why are you?"

This was why I couldn't give up, why I had to insist on putting my face between her legs. If any woman desperately needed an orgasm at the moment, it was Emma. She was too tightly wound.

I threw my head back and shouted at the ceiling, "Minchia! Just let me fuck your pussy with my tongue, woman."

She tried to pull away from me. "No. I'm sorry. I'm not Theresa or some other woman who lets you do whatever you want to them. I barely know you and you're asking to do something very intimate with me."

Dai, now I understood.

I knew she was a virgin, but most women her age had some experience, such as kissing and fingering and tongues. But Emma had even less experience than I expected. She had no idea of what was involved, which made her nervous.

No other man had tasted her, given her this intense pleasure before. This meant that I would be the first to lick her slit and tongue her clit. The first to taste her sweetness. Cazzo, the idea of it . . . .

Ignoring the rush of lust inside me, I stroked her legs once more. "I know no one has done this to you before. Let me try. I'll go slow. And if you hate it, I'll stop after a few seconds. Okay?"

"You'll stop if I ask?"

"Of course. I'm not going to do anything you don't like. Te lo prometto."

Her eyes darted to my mouth. "I admit, I am curious. My sisters talk about it like it's better than chocolate."

I stretched out on my stomach, my shoulders pushing her thighs wide. I pressed my lips to the soft flesh of her upper leg. "Oh, piccola bambina innocente. Chocolate cannot compare to what I am about to do to you."

CHAPTER FOURTEEN

Emma

I couldn't believe this was happening.

I was lying in bed, checking the security feed in my father's room, when Giacomo stormed in to insist on performing cunnilingus on me. It made no sense.

But there was something about it, something about this big, rough man being eager to *service* me that got me hot all over.

And he was so matter of fact about it that I wasn't as nervous with him. His blunt, straight-forward approach appealed to the scientist in me. If he'd tried romance or seduction, I never would've believed it.

But this was the perfect scenario for me, a way to experience oral sex without any messy emotions clouding my brain. This would be purely physical, nothing more.

I could be brave. *For science.*

He arranged himself on his stomach between my legs. Large fingers reached for the waistband of my pajama bottoms. "Off," he ordered, his dark eyes glittering in the low light.

I helped him take off the shorts, but left my panties on. He stared directly at my crotch, his lips curling into a slight smile. "Mamma mia, look at that wet spot."

His words made me defensive. "I can't control the amount of arousal my body produces."

"If you think it displeases me, you could not be more wrong." Leaning in, he pressed his nose close to the fabric and inhaled. "Mmmm," the sound rumbled deep in his chest. "So sweet."

More blood rushed to my center and my heart pumped madly behind my sternum. I had the sudden urge to drag my fingers through his thick brown hair, to hold him tight to my body.

Madness. Pure madness. I needed to get a grip on myself.

I started to take off my glasses. Quick as a whip, Giacomo grabbed my wrist, holding me still. "No, bambina. Leave them on."

He was so close that his breath warmed my skin and sent goose bumps all over me. "Why?" I asked.

"You look adorable in them."

In my glasses? Was he crazy? I always thought I looked a bit like Zooey Deschanel, but Gigi said I looked like a nerdy mushroom with my glasses on. Granted, she was high on edibles at the time, but now I couldn't look at a morel in quite the same way.

I had no chance to argue, though, because Giacomo was sliding my panties off. I tensed, but didn't stop him. Instead, I lifted my hips and let him remove the last barrier between him and me. With a deep breath, I kicked the cotton panties off my ankle and onto the floor.

He studied me for what felt like the longest five seconds of my life. "You don't wax," he said. "I like it."

"My sisters were always trying to get me to go with them to get waxed but—"

I bit off the rest of the words as he dragged his nose through my labia, nuzzling me, rubbing his nose and mouth against me. Coating himself in me. It was primal and dirty, and a bolt of lust arrowed to my clitoris. "Oh, god," I breathed.

He growled, an animalistic sound of pleasure emerging from his throat. Then he shoved my thighs wider and went lower, exploring my entrance. "Minchia," he whispered. "So wet."

He flicked with the tip of his tongue—and I jolted. He did it again, and I realized he was trying to capture my wetness in his mouth.

"Perfetto," he mumbled. "Some day I will fuck you with my tongue."

I blinked at the ceiling. I'd read about that in books, but thought it was hyperbole. A fantasy women created. Was it really possible? Would I enjoy it?

He moved higher, parting my labia with his thumbs until I was spread wide. "Look at how gorgeous you are. I can't wait to devour you."

Our eyes met over the length of my half-naked body. He didn't look away as he stuck out his tongue and dragged it over my clitoris. It was like every nerve ending my body was centered there and Giacomo brought each of them to life. The shock of it startled me—and I sucked a sharp breath.

He did it again.

Warm, slick heat stroked over my flesh, so much better than a silicone toy or my own fingers. I could feel myself growing wetter, more swollen, my body responding to the intimate touch. We'd hardly begun and already I was close to begging for more.

Long eyelashes fluttered as he shut his eyes and licked me. I couldn't look away, mesmerized by how he used his lips, teeth and tongue to stimulate my clit. The feeling was indescribable. Pleasure radiated from that one spot in waves, each lick and suck sending me higher, higher, higher until I was panting and trembling.

Then he backed off, gentling his movements, teasing me with light kisses.

My body sagged into the mattress, frustration clawing at my insides. It was like being sent up to climb half a mountain. The payoff remained just out of reach.

"Now, you beg me to finish you off," he said quietly between kisses.

"What?" I could barely understand him over the sound of my heavy breathing.

"Beg me, Emma."

"Why?"

"Because it's sexy. I like it." Another kiss. "And I won't let you come until you beg."

I'd read about this in some of my books. "Is this a dom/sub thing?"

"This is a *me* thing," he said, now sounding annoyed. "Now, fucking beg me to lick this pussy."

My toes curled at his raw and filthy words. "Please," I said softly.

His dark gaze met mine. I could see my slickness glistening on his lips as he gave me a sinister smile. "Not even close. You must do a lot better." Then he blew on my swollen flesh and I shivered.

"Please!" My voice was noticeably louder this time.

He chuckled in response.

With his finger he traced each side of my clitoris. It wasn't what I needed. I twisted my hips to try and get him closer.

He pulled back. "Say, 'Please fucking lick my pussy, Mo.'"

No way could I say that. "You're trying to embarrass me."

"No, I want to teach you."

The cool air was torture on my overheated flesh. My heart was pounding in my ears. Could I do this?

As if to convince me, he gave me one long swipe of his tongue from my entrance to my clit. I threw my head back, the bliss echoing in every cell, every pore.

But nothing followed.

I huffed, aggravated. "You suck."

"Do it, piccola bambina innocente." Then he began whispering in Sicilian, while kissing the insides of my thighs. I closed my eyes, floating on the incredible sensations, listening to his mostly dirty words and encouragement.

It was too much. I couldn't hold out any longer.

"Please, Mo." I dragged in a deep breath. "Please, lick me."

"Say it all together."

He flicked the tip of his tongue across my clit, and I shouted, "Please lick my pussy, Mo."

"You forgot one word."

God, why did it matter? He needed to hear me curse so badly? "Please fucking lick my pussy, Mo."

"Va bene," he crooned, then drew my clitoris into his mouth and sucked. It was like being plugged into an electric outlet. My back bowed, the muscles in my thighs quaking, and I let out a long moan as I instantly shot toward the peak.

His tongue lashed across my flesh in his mouth. It was too much. I held my breath and clutched at him, my fingers threading through his hair. My hips rocked upward, but Giacomo's strong hands held onto my hips to keep me still. I didn't hate the feeling. I was his to control, his to pleasure.

I was his.

"Oh, god!" I went over the edge, shaking, muscles contracting as the climax sent me flying. It was so, so good, a thousand times stronger than any orgasm I'd given myself. And it went on and on, his tongue and lips working me over, like he was wringing every drop of pleasure from my body.

It finally ebbed and my body sagged into the mattress, spent. I panted as I tried to catch my breath, my skin covered in sweat. I couldn't move if I tried.

Giacomo didn't have the same problem, apparently. Eyes locked on my naked crotch, he shot up to his knees and reached for his belt buckle. Before I could ask what he was doing, he reached inside his briefs and took out his very hard penis.

I was now staring directly at his erection. It was larger and thicker than I expected. I hadn't seen many erections, but this seemed a prime example.

And it was impossible to miss the silver beads along the top and bottom of the head.

A piercing. He was *pierced*.

On his penis.

He ran his fingers lightly over the piercing, then began stroking his cock. I couldn't look away. I had so many questions—about his piercing, about masturbating. But this was no time to ask. He gripped himself tightly, much tighter than I would've dared, and pumped feverishly with his fist.

"Innocente," he mumbled, still looking at my exposed flesh. "Ero primo." *I was first.*

With a grunt, he began orgasming and ropes of thick white liquid shot onto my thighs. It was warm and wet, and showed no sign of slowing down as the jets kept coming and coming. It coated his shaft and piercing, and ran down into his briefs. All the while his massive body twitched and shook, his large chest heaving as he sucked in air.

Wow, performing oral sex on me had really turned him on. I hadn't expected a partner to enjoy it, too. I stared at his dick as he touched himself. Would I like having that in my mouth?

Finally, his shoulders relaxed and he let go of his shaft. It hung there, not fully erect but not soft, the skin coated in the same sticky fluid that was covering me. The room smelled like both of us, the air humid with bad decisions and irrevocable choices.

I pushed my glasses up on my nose to better see him. "You have a piercing."

He blinked before reaching for the bedsheet. "An apadravya, sì." Grabbing the silky fabric, he wiped his shaft, then his hands. He tucked himself into his briefs and refastened his jeans. "You will like it, don't worry."

His piercing? I knew some provided pleasure for a partner, but I found them intimidating. And I wasn't having penetrative sex with him, so I would never feel it. "Did it hurt?"

"Not really." He bent and started cleaning me off with the same bedsheet. "I've endured worse."

What did that mean? Did he have other piercings? "How long have you had it?"

"I was twenty, so a long time."

"What does it feel like?"

He eased off the end of the bed and straightened. "Now? I hardly notice it unless I'm having sex or in a car with the bass turned up."

Oh, the vibrations. That made sense.

Raising up on my elbows, I closed my legs. "Can you urinate normally?"

"Of course." He shook his head like I was exasperating him. "Dai, Emma. I just ate your pussy for the first time. Wouldn't you rather discuss that?"

His piercing was far more fascinating, but I could see his point. "I suppose. Thank you, by the way."

"You don't need to thank me. I enjoyed it as much as you did." Closing his eyes, he inhaled deeply. "Cazzo, that's nice. I'm going to sleep like a fucking baby with you dried all over my face."

He wasn't going to clean up? The tips of my toes tingled, my veins alive. Why was that so hot?

I sat up and edged toward the end of the mattress. "Well, I'm going to shower. So, good night."

"See you in the morning, wife." He crossed the room and disappeared into the hall, closing the door softly behind him.

I stared at the messy bed, the stained bedsheet. Between my legs was sticky and swollen, but I didn't mind. I was relaxed, full of endorphins and dopamine. I should be embarrassed over begging him earlier. Maybe tomorrow the embarrassment would set in.

But right now I kind of wished he'd stayed. It would've been nice to feel his strong arms around me, if only for a few minutes.

Which was silly. We weren't lovers or even friends. I was an annoyance, something he had to endure.

Except he hadn't seemed too annoyed with me a moment ago.

Hmm. Maybe Giacomo wasn't as difficult to understand as I feared.

———

What sort of man needed four cars?

I stared at the options in the Buscetta garage. There were two Ferraris—one red and one black—and a Maserati convertible. Giacomo's sedan sat at the end, the only car I'd known him to drive.

The sedan was sensible, sure, but why drive a boring car when these flashier, faster models were available? This went against everything I knew of mafia men. They liked to show off their wealth and power, usually through luxury purchases.

I should take the sedan, as it was the most practical. But I didn't want to drive his car. It felt too personal, even after last night. And me, in a Ferrari? I couldn't see it. Gia would leap at the chance to drive a car like that, but it wasn't really my thing.

That left the Maserati convertible.

I peeked into the interior. A manual stick shift, which I could handle. The fob sat in the cup holder between the two front seats. Perfect.

I needed to hurry. I had an errand to run before the household awoke.

I slid into the car's buttery leather seat, then I adjusted it so I could reach the pedals. A few button presses later and I got the garage door open. The engine started smoothly and I dragged in a deep breath for courage as I backed out of the garage.

Something occurred to me last night. If my father moved to a safe house, a place Virga couldn't reach, then I wouldn't need to stay in Sicily. I wouldn't need to stay married to Giacomo.

I wouldn't experience any more nights like last night.

But I knew my father. He wouldn't agree to go on his own and I couldn't tell him why I was asking. That meant involving my Uncle Reggie. He could tell Papà there was an active threat and the safe house was non-negotiable. But I couldn't contact my uncle with my own mobile, which Virga probably bugged before returning to me. Nor did I trust the phones in the Buscetta household. Anyone could be listening there.

This meant getting my hands on a burner phone.

I hadn't used one before, but I was confident I could figure it out. I just had to buy one first, which meant going into the city without Sal or Giacomo finding out.

To be fair Giacomo did tell me to take a car and explore Palermo. I was merely taking him up on his generous offer. Before anyone else was awake.

I slipped the car into first gear and eased off the clutch—and saw Sal emerge through the kitchen door. My heart sank, but I gave him a cheery wave. I wasn't doing anything wrong.

Sal looked tired as he limped toward the car, blocking me, concern etched in his brow. "Buongiorno, signora," he said, his good eye inspecting me as he leaned on the edge of the driver's door. "You are up early. Where are you going?"

"To get some pastries," I lied. "I thought I'd explore the city a bit."

"Ah, I understand. I'll have one of the guards come with you."

"No, that's not—"

"Dai." He patted the roof of the car. "We must keep you safe, signora. Unless you'd like me to wake your husband and have him join you instead?"

"No!" I said loudly. Too loudly. "You don't need to do that. I mean, back home I'm allowed to go where I please without protection."

Sal waved this away. "Foolish of your father. And Palermo is not Toronto. Drive up to the gate and wait. One of the boys will jump in with you."

Shoot.

I swallowed my arguments. They were futile. I'd have to find another way to get a pay-as-you-go phone today.

I put the car in drive, waved to Sal and left. The gate was closed when I came to the bottom of the property. Two men were there, smoking, and I could see the obvious bulges under their jackets. Their faces registered their unhappiness.

One of the men started for the car, so I sighed and unlocked the doors.

The smell of stale cigarette smoke hit me like a brick when he got in. "Signora," he said respectfully.

I lowered my window for fresh air. "Buongiorno. What is your name?"

"Rafael."

"Nice to meet you. I'm Emma." The gate began to swing open. "How do I get to downtown Palermo?"

"Turn right. I'll direct you from there. Any place in particular?"

"A bakery, please. A popular one," I amended.

"Pasticceria Oscar." He leaned forward and started punching buttons into the car's GPS system. "But a long wait at this hour."

The directions loaded and I started off. Any attempt to engage Rafael in conversation was met with a one-word answer, so I finally gave up and concentrated on my driving.

Palermo was a fascinating mix of old and new, with a lot of Arabic-inspired architecture. It was hot and dry here, the land surrounded by mountains on one side and the Mediterranean on the other. There were no skyscrapers, no congestion. The air held the tang of the ocean and not a single cloud marred the blue sky. It was beautiful.

We found the bakery, which was directly off a busy thoroughfare. Things were looking up.

I began searching for parking. "Che cosa?" Rafael asked, his head swiveling. "You drove right by it."

"I'm looking for somewhere to park."

He snorted. "A Buscetta doesn't need to find parking. Pull right to the front. No one will say a word."

Was he serious? "I can't do that."

"Yes, you can." He pointed across the street. "Those yellow lines over there? Park there."

"The ones with a wheelchair painted on the ground? Those spots are for disabled drivers."

"Dai, it doesn't matter. The police won't care."

"*I* care. I can't park there. It isn't right."

Rafael huffed and stared out the window as I continued around the block. Soon I found a place to park on the next street. When I got out, I said, "You can wait here, if you want. I'll only be a few minutes."

Rafael shut his door and straightened his jacket. "I must come with you."

As we walked toward the pasticceria, I scanned the names of the shops along the street. Would one of these places carry a burner phone? I spotted a tabacchi shop, which I knew sold SIM cards. Would they have a phone, too?

There was a long line at the bakery. I insisted on waiting, not skipping to the front as Rafael suggested. This caused a lot of heavy sighs and chain smoking on his part. I ignored him and worked on my plan.

At the counter I ordered a wide selection of pastries. The woman working there took one look at Rafael and waved away my attempt to pay. I couldn't have that, so I shoved money in the tip jar by the register and thanked her.

Instead of leaving, I thrust the box in Rafael's arms. "I need to use the bathroom. I'll meet you out front."

He pressed his lips together, but didn't argue. He took the box from me and went toward the exit.

I headed in the opposite direction. A closed exit door was near the bathrooms. When I peeked out I saw the alley. Relieved, I slipped out and hurried toward the street.

The tabacchi shop was off to my right. Keeping my head down, I walked fast. I had to make it back before Rafael grew suspicious.

Inside, there were a few other people milling about. I quickly looked around for cheap phones. There were plenty of SIM cards and cigarettes, as well as candy and lottery tickets. Maybe the phones were behind the counter?

Just as I turned to ask for help, the shop door flew open. A large figure blocked most of the light, huge shoulders filling the tiny space. Those shoulders . . . .

The hairs on the nape of my neck stood up and I instinctively took a step back. Was that . . .?

No, it couldn't be.

The man came in and let the door swing shut behind him. As the light from the shop filled in his rough features, I felt my knees wobble.

Giacomo.

How . . .? My stomach twisted into a knot. I couldn't believe what I was seeing.

Relax. He doesn't know what I'm doing here.

His gaze zeroed in on me. I knew his eyes were brown, but right then they looked like twin pools of midnight, merciless and unforgiving. His flat expression didn't change a bit as he started walking toward the place where I stood, and each thump of his boot on the wood floor nearly caused me to jump.

I attempted a small smile. "Giacomo. What are you doing here?"

"I didn't realize you smoked," he said. "Or maybe you've decided to start? I can recommend a good brand."

"Signore Buscetta." This was the shop worker, who stood a few feet away. "How may I assist you today?"

Giacomo didn't look away from me. "Do you need assistance, wife?"

I didn't care for the growl in his tone. It made me defensive. "Yes. Obviously. Why else would I be here?"

"*Wife?*" The tabacchi employee nearly choked on the word. "Signora Buscetta, it is an honor."

I was staring at Giacomo, but the tabacchi worker sounded like he was sweating. Calmly, I said, "Grazie, signore."

Giacomo moved closer to me. "What are you buying, Emma?"

"Stamps," I blurted.

"Stamps for what?"

"Letters."

"Interesting, then, that I saw you near the SIM cards."

"Only because I was looking at the candy."

His mouth curled into a knowing smile. "Oh? Pastries and candy this morning?"

I didn't say anything. I was a terrible liar, but it was too late to back out now.

"Signore," he called loudly to the tabacchi man. "Get my wife some stamps."

The man cleared his throat. "Of course, Don Buscetta. What kind? Postcard, letter—"

"Whatever the fuck you have. All of it" Turning his full scowl onto the worker, he waved his hand. "Anything she wants."

"Postcard, per favore," I called as the worker sprinted to get the stamps. "There's no need to be rude," I whispered to Giacomo. "You're scaring him."

"He is not the one who should be scared."

Though my insides were crumbling to terrified dust, I faced him bravely. I hadn't done anything wrong. I went out to buy stamps, the end.

"Here you are, signora." With a shaking hand, the man placed a sheet of postcard stamps on the counter.

"Grazie." I opened my wallet. "How much?"

"Nothing." Giacomo grabbed the stamps with one hand and my wrist with the other. He started towing me away from the counter.

I wrenched out of his grip. "I need to pay for those stamps."

"No, you don't."

"I do." I angled toward the counter, opening my wallet. "How much, signore?"

Before the man could answer, Giacomo tossed a fat stack of Euros onto the counter. "There. Now stop fucking arguing with me and get moving."

Keep the peace. Don't complain. Don't make trouble.

It was what I used to say growing up, the by-product of having two rebellious older sisters. But I wasn't in Toronto any longer, and Giacomo wasn't Gia or Frankie.

I couldn't let him push me around.

Once we were outside, I stopped on the sidewalk. "I did nothing wrong. You said I could explore Palermo."

Giacomo came toward me, his face taut with anger. He pointed at his sedan, which was parked illegally at the curb. "Get in the fucking car, Emma."

CHAPTER FIFTEEN

Giacomo

I thought she'd been running away.

When the men told me she'd driven off in my Maserati, I instantly knew this excursion wasn't about pastries. Emma had something up her sleeve.

Except she was shit at subterfuge. The woman was the worst liar I'd ever met.

Rafael confirmed it. He texted me while they were waiting in line for pastries, saying she seemed jumpy and nervous.

By that point I was already halfway to downtown Palermo. From then on I drove like a madman, convinced she was trying to escape me.

But the panic quickly became confusion when Rafael trailed her to a tabacchi shop. Why sneak out to go there? She didn't smoke. Stamps or lottery tickets? I doubted it.

Then it hit me as soon as I saw her lingering near the SIM cards. She was trying to call someone without being traced. Who? Her family? Had she changed her mind about seeing this through?

Too fucking bad. I had no choice in this marriage. So until I figured out a way around Virga, Emma would stay here in Palermo, married to me.

In the passenger seat, she opened the pastry box and pulled out a cornetto. "Would you like something? I bought all kinds."

"What I would like is for you to explain yourself."

"I don't see what the big deal is," she said around a bite of flaky pastry. "You told me I could explore Palermo."

"We both know you weren't exploring this morning. You went to find a burner phone. Tell me why."

She sighed heavily and dusted the crumbs from her hands. "Because I don't want Virga tracing my calls and texts."

"What makes you think he is?"

"I don't, but it seems probable. He had my phone for a long time. Who knows what he's capable of?"

Smart girl. No one in our world was to be trusted. Even me. But if Virga was tracking her phone, maybe there was a way to use it to lure him out.

I slid her a glance. "Who do you need to call?"

"None of your business."

"Everything about you is my business, wife."

"Stop calling me that. This is not a real marriage and you have no right to control where I go and who I talk to."

I couldn't take it. She was wrong on so many levels and I needed to set her straight.

Jerking the wheel, I angled the car to the curb and came to an abrupt halt. Emma slammed her hand on the dashboard and clutched the pastry box. I threw the car in park and shifted to glare at her. "I will control whatever the fuck I want when it comes to you, bambina. Where you go, who you talk to. When you eat, when you sleep. This is a real marriage until I say it isn't."

"Do you hear yourself? You sound like a narcissistic sociopath."

"Keep calling me names and I'll lock you in your bedroom."

Her mouth dropped open, as if the precariousness of her situation had just dawned on her. "You wouldn't dare."

Oh, I would. She had no idea how much the idea of her locked away, tied to a bed and waiting for me to pleasure her, appealed to me. After last night all I could think about was tasting her pussy again.

Dropping my voice, I moved close enough that I could see the dusting of freckles on her nose and cheeks. "You belong to me, Emma Buscetta. Your mouth, your tits, your pussy—all of it. Mine to lick and fuck and finger. So you'd better obey me."

"I'm not a dog."

I smirked at her, not bothering to hide my amusement. "Dai, bambina. You were howling for me last night."

"Stop." Looking away, she shifted in her seat. "I don't want to talk about it."

So innocent. So adorable. But she'd stood up to me, which meant she might be stronger than I credited her for.

Good. She'd need strength to endure the next three months.

I restarted the car and put it in drive. As we pulled into traffic, I said, "We can help each other or I can be your worst enemy, Emma. It's up to you."

"Oh, you're willing to trust me with your secrets now?"

"No, of course not."

"So why would I tell you mine?"

Gritting my teeth, I turned a corner sharply. "You are not allowed to have secrets from me." I don't know why I felt this way, but I did.

"Exactly what I'd expect a narcissistic sociopath to say."

I fought a smile. How was this girl only twenty? She was intelligent and sassy, articulate and bold. I both wanted to ask her advice and turn her over my knee. "Who do you want to call on the burner phone? Ravazzani? Your twin?"

"I won't tell you, so stop asking."

"Then you are eager to have my baby, no? Because if you don't trust me, that's what will happen."

"No one is getting pregnant. We're going to find a way out of this before it comes to that."

The only way out was to end Virga's miserable life.

But that was no easy feat, which meant I needed to keep her close. I couldn't have her escaping or calling for help. It would ruin everything.

Clearly I'd been too lax with her. Today was proof of that.

I needed to step up my efforts to gain her obedience.

A call came in as I was driving. Zani. I pushed a button on the steering wheel. "Cosa?"

"I hear you are in Palermo chasing your wife. Che cazzo?"

"I have her in the car and I'm bringing her back to the estate."

"Ah, good. Ciao, Emma."

"Ciao, Zani," my wife said.

"I hope he's not too angry with you," my friend said.

"He's not," Emma replied, sounding pleased with herself.

"He is," I snapped. "And I'm hanging up on you."

"Wait!" Zani rushed out. "We have that thing today. Are you meeting me after you drop her off at home?"

We were scheduled to go out into the hills to meet with one of Ravazzani's suppliers. The idea was to lure them away from the 'Ndrangtheta and get the money back in Sicily where it belonged. "Give me a few hours."

"He won't be happy if we cancel."

"No one is canceling. I'll be ready by one o'clock."

"Okay. Call me when you're on the way."

I pressed a button to hang up. I didn't need Zani to remind me of my responsibilities. I knew them all too well.

Emma opened the pastry box and rummaged inside. She lifted out a *bombolone* filled with crema. "Sounds like you have a busy day planned."

I watched her take a bite, the crema oozing all over her mouth. *Fuck me.* I struggled to focus on the road ahead of me as her tongue quickly lapped at the thick liquid. I wanted to lick the sugar from her lips. Then spread it all over her body and lick it off from there, too.

I stepped on the gas. "Not too busy to teach you a lesson, *mia moglie innocente.*"

———

I followed her inside the house.

Emma set the box of pastries on the counter. "Sal, I bought a good selection for us. Eat whatever you want."

Sal looked pointedly at me and I could see the warning there. He was beginning to grate on my nerves. Had he forgotten who he worked for?

"She stays on the estate," I told him. "If she leaves, it's with me."

"That is ridiculous." She finished washing her hands and began drying them on a cloth. "We already discussed this. You can't turn me into a prisoner here."

"Get upstairs." I pointed to the doorway. "I want to talk to you."

Emma carefully folded the cloth and placed it on the marble countertop. "I think we're done talking, Giacomo."

"You're right. So would you like me to say in front of Sal why I really want you upstairs? Or would you rather continue the pretense that we are going up there to talk?"

Her mouth fell open as her skin turned crimson. "Neither. I want you to leave."

"Then you will be disappointed." I pointed to the archway that led inside the house. "Go—or I'll carry you, if I have to."

"I choose pretense, then," she mumbled and started walking.

"Va bene, bambina. That is the right answer."

We didn't speak as we climbed the stairs. It was so quiet in the house that I heard the whir of the ceiling fan overhead. I was reminded of kneeling as a boy, the hours of terrified silence while awaiting my father's punishments.

Malocchio.

I shoved those memories aside. The old man was rotting in the ground, his precious legacy in the hands of his most hated child. I would have the last laugh.

I followed her through the door to my father's garish bedroom. "How can you stand sleeping in here?" I asked, looking around at the gold decor. "It's hideous."

She put her phone and wallet onto the bedside table. "It's sort of growing on me. Why didn't you or your brother move in here after your father went into hiding?"

I snorted. "Nino always believed our father would return. And I'd rather cut off my dick than sleep in this end of the house."

"Why? Do you really like that tiny room better than these?"

I didn't want to talk about my family or my father. "Strip and get on the bed."

"What?" She paled, her eyes darting around dramatically. "You can't be serious."

"I am very serious. Take off your clothes and lie down."

"But . . . it's still light out! And Sal will know what we're doing. It's too weird. And besides, we already did this last night."

I held up a hand to stop the stream of words falling out of her mouth. "I don't give a fuck about Sal or the time of day. And you should be prepared for me to lick your pussy every day for the next two months."

"Every day? No way."

"Every day that you aren't bleeding. And even some of those."

She pinched the bridge of her nose under her glasses. "This is insane."

"I don't have time to waste convincing you." I folded my arms across my chest. "We already know you love it. Stop pretending."

"I'm not pretending. And that's not the point. You're catching me off guard. I'm not even turned on."

"Cazzata." I took a step closer to her. Then another. I kept closing in until we were less than an arm's length apart. One more step and her tits would brush my chest. "I can't stop thinking about your sweet pussy. I want to rub you all over my mouth again and taste you for days."

She wobbled slightly on her feet, and her palm flattened on my chest as if to help steady herself. "How can you say those things? You're the bluntest person I've ever met."

"I'm not the man who will give you pretty words and mixed signals. But I am the man who will let you grind your pussy on his face anytime you please."

"Giacomo," she breathed, and I liked the sound of my name on her lips. "What are we doing?"

I couldn't tell her why I was insisting on doing this every day.

"We're married. Would you rather I did this with another woman?" I wouldn't, but Emma wouldn't know that.

"No!" Her fingers tightened in my shirt, like she was holding onto me. "But haven't you heard of foreplay?"

I nearly laughed. "I don't have time for candles and making out in the back seat of a car. If I want to fuck, I fuck. And right now, I want to fuck your pussy with my tongue." I slapped her ass, hard. "Get on the bed, wife."

She closed her eyes and bit her lip. It was clear she was wavering. I decided to give her a push.

Leaning down, I said near her ear, "After you come, I'll jerk off and let you watch again."

A shaky breath escaped her mouth. Without saying anything she stepped back and unbuttoned her shorts. My dick gave a twitch, my balls already pulling tight. Madre di dio, this girl. I loved nothing more than corrupting her. Convincing her to ignore all her prim and proper instincts to do what I wanted.

Her shorts fell to the ground and she kicked them off. When she started to get on the bed, I said, "Panties, too."

She paused, but only for a second. In a quick motion she tugged her panties off, leaving her naked from the waist down. Cazzo, she was hot. Creamy skin with a hint of olive. Dark public hair covering her mound. Smooth legs. A high, tight ass.

I suddenly wanted to see all of her.

"Take off your shirt and bra."

She flopped onto her back. "Why?"

Dai, the constant questions. I crawled onto the bed and settled between her thighs. Her pussy was glistening, the swollen lips peeking out and begging for my tongue. "Because I told you to."

"It feels weird to be naked when you're fully clothed."

I whipped off my t-shirt and threw it onto the ground. "Better?"

She peeled off her shirt and bra, her gaze locked on my chest the entire time. Did she like tattoos? My body was covered in them. There was a time when I spent more days around an ink gun than real guns.

"You're beautiful," she said.

"I love your tits," I said, angling to take one hard nipple into my mouth. I sucked hard, and her fingers threaded through my hair. If I didn't have a meeting today, I would spend the next twelve hours exploring every inch of her.

Pulling back, I stretched out on my stomach between her thighs. "Lie back."

"But don't you want—?"

I shut her up with a long lick along her folds. Fuck, yes. That was what I wanted, her smell in my nose and in my head. I dipped my tongue lower to get more. She was tangy and sweet and so fucking wet already. Why did she pretend like she didn't want this?

I ate her out like a man possessed. I licked and sucked, and relished every little gasp and noise she made. When I felt her getting too close, I eased off, dragging it out as long as possible. My dick was pressing against my zipper, the skin stretched so taut it hurt. I thrust my hips into the mattress, the ball of my piercing digging into the head. It was the best kind of torture.

"Oh, god. Giacomo, please." Her hand fell onto the back of my head to hold me in place. "I can't take any more."

I grunted and sucked her clit into my mouth, my lips drawing on the flesh. She let out a strangled moan.

"Use a finger!" she cried. "Please. I need it."

I could hardly believe my ears. My bold little virgin, begging for a finger in her cunt?

Still, I hesitated. Had she inserted anything in there before? I didn't want to hurt her.

"It's okay," she panted, clearly sensing my hesitation. "I've used vibrators there before."

My cock weeped at the idea of it. Minchia, how I'd love to see her pussy stretched around a silicone dick.

I eased off her clit and slid my pinky finger through her wetness. I coated my skin to ease the way inside. Then I put the tip of my littlest finger at her entrance. "Ready?"

Emma's eyes were glazed, wild, as she looked down at me. "Yes, please."

I pushed in slowly, watching as tight heat enveloped my finger.

Slick velvet walls pulled me inside, walls that no man had felt before. Minchia! I was going to come if I didn't stop thinking about it.

Emma. Concentrate on Emma.

I shifted my gaze to her instead. Her eyelids fluttered closed, her mouth slack with pleasure. "That's it," I crooned. "You like that full-ness, no? You need to feel stretched. Don't worry, I am going to fill you up, bambina."

"Oh, god. I'm so close." Her back bowed, muscles tightening. "Don't stop."

I kept going, gently breaching her. Even with my smallest finger, it was a tight fit. I couldn't imagine this snug pussy squeezing my cock. I would probably die from pure bliss. I pumped my hand, sinking deeper each time, until my pinky was fully seated. "There you go. You like that, no?"

"Yes, yes, yes." She thrashed her head on the pillow, her fingers gripping the gold bedspread as her hips rocked into my hand. It was like she was fucking herself with my littlest finger.

"You are so fucking hot. Keep going. Work that needy pussy on my hand. Make yourself come."

"No, I need clitoral stimulation, too. Please."

I hadn't expected a virgin to be so confident and demanding in bed, but Emma continued to surprise me.

"You get what I give you when I give it." I slid my finger out of her and started to get up. "And you need to learn to follow directions."

"No!" Leaning forward, she grabbed me. "Don't go. Please."

I propped myself on my elbows, my face near her pussy but not giving her any stimulation. "Will you try to escape me again?"

She blinked and some of the lust cleared from her expression. "I wasn't trying to escape."

"You ditched your guard." I bent and gently nipped her clit with my teeth. She arched and moaned. "You could've been killed."

"But I wasn't!"

I kissed the edges of her folds, avoiding where she wanted me most. "Who were you trying to call, Emma?"

"Oh, you're a stronzo."

"Now, that isn't very nice." I teased her entrance with my finger. "Tell me who and I'll give you what you need."

"I can give myself what I need."

She reached between her legs, but I was faster. I caught her wrist just before she could stroke her clit. "I'll keep you here all day, edging you, until you tell me what I want to know."

"Eventually I'll orgasm without stimulation."

"I'll make sure you don't."

She bucked her hips. "Get off me. We're done."

"Not even close, mia moglie innocente." I blew directly on her clit. "Tell me who you need to call."

"Oh, god." Her voice was small and miserable. "*Please.*"

"I'll let you come, if you do. It will be the best orgasm of your life." I kissed the inside of her thigh and pressed the very tip of my pinky inside her pussy, teasing her. "Just tell me who."

Her lids were closed tightly and a sheen of sweat coated her skin. "Shit. Damn it."

"I love hearing those words from your lips, *sporcacciona.*" Dirty girl.

"You're the worst. I hate you."

I lightly kissed her clit and rimmed her entrance with my pinky. She rocked her hips, but I moved away. "No, you don't. I'm your husband, the first man to make you come with his mouth. Soon I will be the first man to fuck you and make you come on his dick."

She panted and covered her face with her hands. "Jesus, will you stop talking already?"

I licked her again, more forcefully this time. I needed to keep her desperate, on the precipice of orgasm, to get what I wanted. I pushed my pinky inside her pussy and sucked on her clit.

"Yes, yes, yes," she chanted, her muscles locking.

Then I stopped.

"No! God, you jerk!"

"Tell me." I drew her clit into my mouth then let go. "Tell me, Emma." I wiggled my finger inside her, but it wasn't enough to give her proper stimulation. "Say it. Tell me who you were trying to call."

"My uncle!" she shouted. "I was trying to call my uncle."

I didn't waste any time. I shoved my finger in deep and lashed her clit with my tongue, back and forth, back and forth. Her walls clamped down on me and her clit swelled. Then she screamed, her fingers tearing at my hair as her hips rocked furiously.

I helped her ride it out, but lost control in the process. My own orgasm rushed up from my toes and tingles raced all over my body. My balls drew up as come shot out of my dick in strong pulses. I groaned into her flesh, humping the mattress, as the hot jets coated the inside of my jeans.

Minchia! I hadn't done that since I was a teenager.

When she finally quieted, I flopped onto my back and tried to catch my breath. I needed to shower and change, but my limbs weren't functional just yet.

"Don't you need to . . .?"

Her hesitant question made me wince. "No. I came already."

"You did? But you were going to let me watch."

I opened one eye to peer at her. "Emma, I didn't come on purpose. It just happened."

"Oh." She looked at the front of my jeans. "I think that's normal. Because of the friction."

Mamma mia. I drew a hand down my face. "I'm aware how my dick works, but yes. That happens sometimes."

"Can I touch it?"

Both my eyes flew open this time. "My dick?"

She rose up on one elbow. "Your piercing."

Only Emma would be more curious about a bar of steel than my actual cock. I nodded, stood up, and stripped off my jeans and briefs. She scooted closer, her bare legs folding under her as she sat. Carefully, she lifted my dick in her palm and brought the tip closer to her face. With her other hand, she touched the metal ball at one end of my piercing and moved it around. "I can't believe this didn't hurt."

Dio, her small hand on my dick, playing with my piercing? Fuck, that was nice. "I never said it didn't hurt. I said I've endured worse."

"What gauge is this?"

Someone had done her research. "Six."

She studied the underside and moved the metal around there.

"You're uncircumcised, so how does your foreskin impact the piercing?"

"It doesn't. My foreskin isn't tight and it rolls into place like normal."

"Does the piercing feel good?"

"Yes, especially when my innocent wife plays with it."

Emma's eyes met mine. "Is that why you're staying erect?"

More blood filled my dick. Soon I would be ready to go again. "Your curiosity is turning me on."

"Oh." Her cheeks turned the most adorable shade of pink. "Oh," she repeated.

I took pity on her. As much as I'd like to spend all day corrupting her, I had things to do. "Tonight, when I get home? You may call your uncle."

"Why not now?" She wrapped her arms around her legs, like she was trying to get as small as possible. "He's probably awake."

"Because I want to be there when you talk to him and I don't have time right now." I motioned to the bed. "Lie back."

"Why? I thought we were done."

"You don't ask why, wife. You do as I say when I say it. Now, lie back." Reluctantly, she relaxed onto the mattress. "Spread your legs."

"Giacomo," she whined.

"Do it, bambina."

With a heavy sigh she shifted to open her legs. Fuck, that was nice. Her pussy, swollen and wet, was spread out before me. I grabbed my phone out of my jeans pocket.

"No way. You are not taking photos of me."

She twisted and tried to get away, so I clamped my hand on her ankle, holding her still. "They are only for me. No one else will ever see them. Te lo prometto, moglie."

"Hard pass. Your phone could get hacked. Someone else could see them."

I threw my head back and laughed. "You think someone can hack my phone? Do you believe I am so stupid as to leave myself vulnerable like that? And if someone is hacking my phone, they are not looking for dirty photos."

"I don't care. They could be used to blackmail me or my family."

My fingers tightened on her skin at the idea. "No one will dare blackmail you. If someone tries, I will chop him into tiny pieces and let the sharks have them. Now, lean back and let me take photos of your pussy."

"Why?"

"Because it gets me hard to see that virgin cunt after I make you come. I want to look at it later when I'm jerking off."

"Oh, my god." Dropping her head, she rubbed her forehead against her arms. "I can't believe that's something you want."

Was she serious? Did she not know? "Sei bellissima, mia piccola innocente."

"Stop." She didn't appear pleased by the compliment. Did she not believe me? Emma didn't try to be sexy, she just was.

Then I became distracted because she unfolded her arms, leaned back on the bed, and opened herself up to me again. I could barely breathe, it was so hot.

"There," she said. "And do *not* get my face in the photos."

In case she changed her mind, I moved quickly. I opened my camera app and took the photos I wanted. By the time I finished I was fully hard again. Merda, this woman. I needed to fuck her soon. "I'm done."

"Thank goodness." Flicking a glance at my erection, Emma hopped off the bed and hurried toward the bathroom. "See you later," she called right before closing the door.

If I didn't know better, I'd think she was running scared. The idea of it caused something unusual to happen, something that had rarely ever happened in this house: A wide grin split my face.

CHAPTER SIXTEEN

Emma

The texts came in just as I finished catching up on my statistics classwork that afternoon.

GIGI

Emmie!

I need a favor

Gia was supposed to be readying her newest collection to show in November. I had no idea what she needed, but I knew it wasn't good. When my twin called me "Emmie," I knew to be wary.

I picked up my phone.

Hi! What's up?

GIGI

remember that white jacket u got on that trip to LA

the one from Fred Segal

Yes, I remembered. The jacket was currently hanging in my closet back in Toronto.

> The one you wore to a party and got beer on?

GIGI

the beer didn't stain, ffs

but yes that's the one

I need it. Can you ask Papà to overnight it to me

I stared hard at my screen. That was going to be difficult to manage, considering I was in Sicily and she thought I was in Peru. And our father wasn't exactly capable of overnighting anything.

But I hated this for another reason. My sisters always put me in the middle. Instead of dealing with our father and their issues themselves, they made me deal with it.

"Emma, tell Papà I'm studying with a friend."

"Don't tell Papà where I really went, Em."

"I'm taking this bottle of whiskey. If Papà asks, you don't know what happened to it."

Constant covering and lying for them. I knew my sisters had valid reasons to be upset with Papà, but it wasn't fair to always rely on me to maintain their relationship. If they knew he was dying, would they rush to repair it? Or would they feel regret? Sorrow? Happiness? I honestly didn't know.

I looked down at my phone as my twin texted again.

GIGI

Hello?

> Why?

GIGI

it's not worth explaining

long story involving a seamstress that can't understand the way a jacket hangs

I nibbled on my fingernail, then typed,

> Just get a jacket there.

GIGI

would if I could but I need this **exact one**

pleeeease? I know I'm a pain in the ass but I'll owe you one

> You owe me a million already.

GIGI

true! lol

She sent a smiling devil emoji that was entirely on brand for my sister.

GIGI

I'll ship it back as soon as I'm done with it

My twin was relentless when she wanted something. She wouldn't give up, no matter how much I pushed back. I had to stall her.

> I have a really busy day ahead. I'm not sure I'll have time

GIGI

just call Papà. He can have one of the men do it. Please????

u talk to him every day right? What's the big deal

> I'm not sure I know where it is. I might have donated it.

GIGI

no way you donated that jacket

you said you wanted to be buried in it

True. I looked darn good in that jacket, except I had no place to wear it. School, the lab at school, and home were the only places I went to in Toronto. I usually wore leggings, a hoodie, and no makeup.

I texted:

> I spend most of my time in class or the lab. I felt like someone else could get more use out of it.

GIGI

> omg, Em. You're dead to me if you gave that away without checking w me first

God, she was so dramatic.

> Let me ask Papà to look for it and I'll text you later. Gotta run. Love you!

I turned off my phone and put it on the table. My stomach churned with the stress of lying to everyone, the misery of being away from home. The weariness of having sisters who were estranged from our father.

Not to mention the uncertainty of what was happening with Giacomo. Twice he'd given me an orgasm, and he seemed extremely possessive for a man forced into marriage. I'd expected animosity, but instead he was dragging me to bed and teasing me until I told him everything he wanted to know.

I needed to remain strong. It wasn't fair that I was revealing my secrets and he wasn't reciprocating.

And I definitely wasn't making that phone call while Giacomo could hear me. I didn't care how angry that made him. I deserved some privacy while living here.

Sal was in the kitchen, kneading dough, when I walked in. I went to the refrigerator to get a sparkling water. "Hey, Sal."

"Ciao, signora. How were your classes today?"

"Statistics sucks. Other than that they were good."

"Would you like some wine? And maybe fruit to go with it?"

I looked down at the bottle of plain sparkling water in my hand. After today, I deserved a treat. "Yes, actually. I would."

Sal poured us both glasses of white wine. We touched glasses. "*Saluti!*" Sal said. "I think you'll like this. It's a Catarratto."

I did like it. The wine was dry and crisp, sort of like a pinot grigio. "This is nice."

"It is the most popular grape in Sicily. Sort of like the Calabrian Gaglioppo your brother-in-law uses."

I didn't know anything about the Ravazzani wine. I only knew Fausto and Frankie slept out in the vineyards sometimes, which was both romantic and weird. "Have you tried his wines?"

"No, I haven't. You?"

"Yes, when I go to visit. They're very good."

"Your sister and Ravazzani, they are very much in love, no?"

"Yes." We drank in silence for a moment. "Has there ever been another woman in your life after your fiancée?"

"Sì, certo," he said with a laugh. "Dai, do you think an Italian man could remain celibate all these years?"

"I didn't mean for those reasons. I meant someone you loved."

A sly smile broke out on his face. "There is someone now."

"What? Who?" This was fascinating. Propping my chin in my hands, I leaned on the counter. "Tell me everything."

"I never kiss and tell. But she is *mia anima gemella*."

Twin soul. "That's beautiful. Why don't you marry her or have her live here with you?"

"We see each other enough." He refilled our wine glasses. "Do not worry."

"But I never see you leave—" I paused, realization dawning. "It's someone here. On the estate. Oh, my gosh. Who? You have to tell me."

Before Sal could answer, the back door opened. Giacomo strode inside, his gaze finding mine immediately. He took his time studying me where I sat at the bar. My skin grew hot under his stare and I suddenly felt naked, like he could see straight through me. Had he looked at those photos today? I was a fool for letting him take them.

I glanced away, watching Sal's hands as he worked the soft dough on the counter. Giacomo edged up next to me, his body nearly touching my elbow. I tried to ignore him, but it was like my cells were electrified, the mitochondria humming with energy. I both wanted to throw myself at him and run away.

He plucked the glass from my hand. "Drinking wine, wife?"

I spun toward him. "Hey! Give that back. I wasn't done."

With a smirk, my husband lifted the glass to his mouth and drained the little bit of wine that was left, his throat working as he swallowed. I stared at his soft lips, surrounded by rough whiskers. I realized that we hadn't ever kissed. What would it feel like? Was he a good kisser? We were close enough that if I angled in slightly, I could discover the answer for myself.

He swept his knuckles back and forth along my jaw. I shivered, the simple touch racing all the way to my toes to curl them. "How many glasses have you had, bambina?" he asked softly.

I pushed my eyeglasses higher on my nose. "Almost two. Why?"

"Are you drunk?"

"Of course not. No one gets drunk on less than two glasses of wine."

"Except people who don't drink."

"I drink." I mean, I didn't . . . but I didn't want him to know that.

He nodded, though his expression said he didn't believe me. "Your phone call. Do you want to do it now?"

"Yes!" I tried to get off the bar chair, but my feet tangled up and I nearly fell. Giacomo caught me, his strong hands wrapping around my ribs. Then I was upside down, over his shoulder and being carried out of the kitchen.

"Stop. Put me down!" I grabbed the back of his shirt. "Giacomo!"

He ignored me. His boots thumped on the tile as he strode through the house. I thought he would go up the stairs, but he surprised me by taking me into his office. Sal said Giacomo hardly ever used it, that he wasn't the type of leader who sat behind a desk. It made sense. He reminded me more of my father, a hands-on boss who was out with the men all day.

I flipped again and my butt hit wood. I straightened my glasses and let the dizziness pass. He had me on the desk facing his chair, which he was now sitting in. In a locked drawer he found a plastic package and took it out. It was a disposable mobile phone. The package was already open, so he slid the phone out. "It's charged, with an untraceable SIM card." He handed it to me. "There."

I took the small phone and turned on the power. "Thank you. I'll call after you leave."

Giacomo leaned back in his chair and placed his hands behind his head. I was momentarily distracted by the biceps bulging in his arms. Did he lift weights every day?

"I'm not leaving," he said. "So, dial."

I frowned. I didn't want him listening to this conversation. "This is a private call."

"Dai, there's no such thing. And do you think I would be so stupid as to give you a phone without knowing what you say?"

I heard the edge in his voice, so I rushed to explain. "I'm not telling my uncle where I am. This is not a rescue call." Not really. It was the first step in a rescue plan, but Giacomo didn't need to know that.

"Call now before I change my mind."

I tried to think of a way around it. I didn't want to talk to Uncle Reggie with Giacomo listening in. How could I discuss my father's illness and moving him to another location without tipping Giacomo off? I couldn't.

Uncle Reggie and I weren't close. I hardly ever spoke to him or his son, Dante. My phone call would only confuse him unless I could explain myself.

Gloria, though . . . .

My father's caregiver and I had spent more time together over the four months than anyone else. We practically finished each other's sentences. That's what happened when you were in the trenches together, so to speak, every single day. She'd be able to read between the lines—and I knew she had my father's best interests at heart.

I began dialing.

"Put it on speaker," Giacomo snapped.

The phone began to ring, so I pushed the speaker button. I tried to ignore the hulk of a man sitting mere centimeters away.

"Hello?" Gloria's voice crackled from the tiny phone.

"Oh, Aunt Gloria, hi. It's Emma. I was trying to reach Uncle Reggie."

I heard some shuffling, like maybe she was moving someplace private. "Hello, dear! Good to hear from you. How are you?"

"I'm fine. Peru is beautiful and the hours are brutal, but I'm learning a lot. I miss Toronto, though. How is everything there? Is Uncle Reggie giving you a hard time?"

Gloria didn't miss a beat. "He's the same. Your father, too. Nothing new to report here with the family."

That was good. "I need two favors. First, I need my bed and medical equipment moved into my new apartment by the university. Maybe you could ask Uncle Reggie to do it?"

Gloria paused but only for a split second. "Sure. Is it time dependent?"

"Yes, very. I'm sorry. I know you have a lot on your plate."

"No problem. We'll take care of it. What's the other favor?"

"Can you look in my closet for a short white jacket? It has this drape-y neckline and crosses over the front. Gia needs it sent to Milan. I know she won't give up until I have someone there send it."

"Sure, I can do that."

"Thank you, Aunt Gloria. You're the very best."

"Aw, shucks. We miss you. I hope Peru is treating you well." I'd told her the same lie about my location. It was easier that way.

"It's not easy, but I'm adjusting." I darted a glance at my husband, who was watching me very closely.

"I'm glad to hear it. Call again when you can."

"I will. Love you!"

"Love you, too. And don't worry about anything here. It's all being handled."

Giacomo disconnected the call. We sat there for a long moment. I was waiting to see if he was going to catch me in my lie or not.

He pushed back from the desk. When he looked up at me, his mouth curved into a seductive smile. "Allora, I let you place your call, bambina. How will you show me your gratitude?"

CHAPTER SEVENTEEN

Giacomo

She was very smart, my wife.

But she wasn't smarter than me. Reggie Mancini's wife's name was Carla, not Gloria. And there was no apartment over by the university. Emma lived at home with her father—her very ill father. No way would she leave him in such a state.

This meant Gloria was probably a nurse or aide who helped with the father's care.

Emma was trying to get her father moved out of their house. Why? It had to be the same reason I'd considered moving Viviana—for protection from Virga.

Clever, clever bambina.

If Mancini was safe, Virga had no leverage over Emma. No leverage meant there was no reason for Emma to stay in this marriage. That left my sister as the sole target of Virga's ire. I could not allow it.

I needed to speak with Zani. We had to figure out what we were going to do.

But first, this.

I slid my chair away from the desk. "Allora, I let you place your call, bambina. How will you show me your gratitude?"

"What do you mean?" She pushed her glasses higher on her nose, a habit I found both adorable and sexy.

"I mean, what are you going to do for me now that I helped you?"

"You want oral sex."

"I wouldn't turn down a blow job, but I don't think you are ready for that."

A crease formed between her brows. "Why not?"

Was she disappointed? "Because touching my piercing is one thing. Sucking it on it is another."

"Will it hurt me?"

"The piercing? Not unless you try to deep throat it without practice."

Her eyes drifted to my crotch. I could see her thinking, wondering. That was the thing about my wife: she was curious about everything, especially when it related to the human body.

That curiosity was making my dick hard.

Blood pooled in my groin and I began thickening in my jeans. She sucked in a breath. "Are you . . . ?"

"Getting hard? Yes. When a beautiful woman stares at my dick that is generally what happens."

"Can I watch?"

She didn't need to ask twice. I grabbed the end of my belt and unbuckled, then unzipped my jeans. Instead of just pulling my cock out, I shoved my jeans and briefs lower on my hips, exposing my cock and balls to my wife's innocent gaze. I was only half-hard, my dick resting on my thigh, but it was growing thicker by the second.

"Wow, that is amazing. You're getting harder. What does it feel like?"

I licked my lips. "Amazing. Like I need to fuck."

"I'm serious. Tell me what it's like."

"It's throbbing and tingling. More and more pressure. Like I need to fuck."

"I get it," she said with a laugh—and the sound sank into my bones. This girl, she was curious and happy and bold. A wave of contentment went through me, something I hadn't experienced in this house for ages.

This girl, she was dangerous.

My wife sank to her knees on the floor. "Can I touch you?"

"Are you still drunk?"

"I was never drunk. Slightly buzzed, maybe. But do you not want me to touch you?"

Of course I did. I craved it like a junkie craved a fix.

Except I was the one who was in control between us, keeping her complacent with orgasms. "Why don't you finger yourself on the desk while I jerk off?"

"Maybe later. I'd rather do this first."

"Wait—"

It was too late. Her small fist wrapped around my shaft and tugged. She stroked me up and down with a stronger grip than I would've thought a virgin capable of. Merda, that was nice.

I should've discouraged her, but what came out of my mouth was, "Va bene, bambina. Keep going."

"Like this?"

"Mmm, sì. È perfetto."

I rested my head on the back of the chair, but kept watching her hand. I was fully hard now, and her fingers were unable to meet around my girth. She was so sexy, kneeling at my feet and working my dick. She still wore her glasses and her hair was pulled up on top of her head. I reached and took out the hair band, freeing the long brown strands to drape over her shoulders.

"It's easier than I thought," she said. "Slippery almost. Because of your foreskin."

She sounded breathless, the words rushed. Was she turned on? Dio, I hoped so. "Play with the piercing. Drag your fingers over it as you stroke." Lightly, she brought her fingers up to the head and brushed the metal. "Again," I ordered.

She complied, squeezing the head more forcefully this time. The bar shifted in my skin as she moved it back and forth. "Does that feel good?"

"I like seeing you touch it. I've never had a woman so fascinated by it."

"Really?" Her head tilted up and she looked at me. "I find that hard to believe."

It was true. Most women just wanted to feel the metal against their g-spot during fucking. They weren't interested in the piercing beyond that.

Emma bent her head and flicked her tongue against the jewelry.

Pleasure arrowed through my shaft and down through my balls, and I hissed. "You ready to taste cock, *verginella?*"

She looked up at me with hooded, glazed eyes. "Little virgin?"

"Stop talking and suck me." I grabbed the base of my shaft and angled the head of my dick toward her mouth. "Let me be the first man inside those pretty lips."

Without breaking our stare she widened her mouth and lowered herself onto the crown. Heat surrounded me first, then I felt the warm, wet slide of her tongue as she closed her lips around me. "Minchia," I whispered. "That's it."

She hummed—and the sound reverberated through the metal. Waves of pleasure rolled through me. I would come too soon if she kept that up.

"Lick," I told her. "Let me see it."

She released me but kept me in her tight grip. Then she began giving my cock soft licks and little flicks of her tongue. She played with the ball of the piercing on each side. It was like she was exploring with her mouth, and the innocent journey was the most erotic thing I'd ever witnessed.

Then she moved lower, toward the base. She pressed my dick into my stomach so she could lick around the thickest part of my shaft.

And she kept going.

Her sweet tongue bathed my balls and it felt as though I'd died and gone to heaven. Most women didn't like balls. I didn't understand it, but I knew better than to argue. So they were usually left out during sex, ignored and lonely.

But Emma wasn't shying away from them in the least. She nuzzled and licked them eagerly . . . and suddenly, I worried that I might not be in control of this situation any longer.

"Do you like it? What do I taste like?" I whispered, smoothing her hair away from her face.

"Salt and hot skin. Soft." Another lick. "I like it. I especially like seeing your reaction."

"Oh? What am I doing?"

"Your eyes are dilated and you're breathing hard. I can see your carotid artery pulsing on the side of your neck. The involuntary twitching of your leg muscles. It's quite fascinating."

She was using me as a science experiment. I was both annoyed and aroused by the idea. But right now I wanted her to be an equal in this. I didn't want to suffer alone.

I helped her to her feet. "Take off your shorts and climb onto my lap. Now."

"But I wanted to—"

"Later." I popped the button on her shorts and let them fall down her legs. I left her silk panties on. "Right now I want you to grind your clit on my piercing. Come on, bambina."

I helped her straddle my lap, one of her knees on either side of me. Her ass, so perfectly round and tight, filled my palms.

"There isn't enough room for us in this chair," she complained as I settled us more comfortably.

Wrong. We had enough room for what we were going to do. "Start grinding. You're going to love it, te lo prometto."

Using my hands, I brought her hips down and rocked her sex over my dick. I knew the instant the ball on the end of the piercing hit her clit because her eyes went big. "Oh!"

"I told you. Keep going. Rub your pussy on my dick and make us both feel good."

She put her hands on my shoulders. "It doesn't hurt you?"

"No, but even if it did I would suffer the pain to make you come."

"That's . . . weirdly sweet." She stared down at where we were pressed together. "Like this?" Her hips snapped forward.

"Slow." I showed her how to move. "Feel how hard I am for you? Now build up a rhythm and use me to get yourself off."

She sucked in a breath when the metal found the right spot. "God, that is so intense."

I hummed in agreement and lifted her shirt off. She didn't protest, her eyes closed as she concentrated on her movements. Her hard nipples poked through the light blue lace of her bra and I couldn't wait to get my mouth on them.

When I tried to unhook her bra, she moved my hands away. "Leave it on."

"Why?"

"What if someone walks in?"

This wasn't about being caught. No one would dare come into my office unannounced. "Let me see your tits, Emma."

I smoothed my hands up her back and unfastened the bra. After I tossed the lace onto the floor, I bent her back so that I could reach her with my mouth. I licked the hard tip of her breast, teasing her, before drawing her nipple into my mouth and sucking hard.

"Oh," she breathed, like the pleasure surprised her. "Oh, wow. That's amazing."

She threaded her fingers through my hair, holding on as her hips rocked more forcefully. I sucked with my mouth and lashed with my tongue, not letting up as the sounds coming from her mouth increased in volume. Eventually I switched to her other tit. She dug her nails into my skull, and the sting of pain made my balls tighten. Fuck, I could come at any second.

She needed to hurry up. I wanted to watch her come on my dick, even if I wasn't inside her. Yet.

Releasing her breast, I sat back. "Emma, you have to—"

In a blink she smashed her mouth against mine, kissing me, and I paused for a beat. I hadn't expected this, even though that was foolish. Most of the women I slept with weren't interested in kissing on the mouth, but Emma surprised me again and again. Her glasses were pressed into the bridge of my nose, but she didn't seem to mind, her lips working mine with an exuberant lack of finesse.

I grabbed the sides of her face. "Wait."

"Oh, sorry." She didn't meet my eyes. "I got caught up in the moment. I should've checked with you first."

As she talked, I removed her glasses and set them on the desk. Then I cupped the back of her neck and brought her closer. "Now fucking kiss me and make yourself come, bambina."

Slowly, she edged forward and gently sealed her lips to mine. I let her explore for a few seconds before I took over, angling her head so I could kiss her properly. I slid my lips over hers again and again. I told myself to go slow, but she was so sweet. So eager. Soon it wasn't enough.

I slipped my tongue in her mouth and she welcomed me, dragging her tongue against mine. Her hips moved quicker now, chasing, and I kept fucking her mouth with my tongue. I devoured her, kissing her again and again. It had been so long since I made out with a woman like this, with such desperation and aggression. Emma gave it right back to me, though. She *wasn't* a shy innocent, not when it came to this.

Cazzo, I liked that.

When she wobbled on my lap, losing her rhythm, I took her ass in my hands and helped her keep stroking herself on my dick. I broke off from her mouth, placing my lips near her ear as we both panted. "My dick is what you need, no? Are you curious what it will feel like inside your pussy? I will make you so full."

"Oh, god," she whispered.

"I know you are dying to find out. What about my piercing? What will it feel like against your g-spot?"

"Giacomo." Her voice was a whine, a plea. A prayer.

"You're a dirty girl, no? I can tell that you want your husband to fuck your virgin pussy. Soon, Emma. So very soon. I am going to be your first and your last, mia piccola innocente."

She threw her head back as her muscles locked into place. Her body spasmed right there in my hands, a blissful expression overtaking her, and I'd never seen anything so beautiful, so humbling in my life.

Mine. This woman was mine to control, to fuck. No one else's.

I let go then, and the orgasm crashed into me like a train. Every part of me jerked, my dick pulsing as I shot my load between our bodies. She kept moving, her hot pussy sliding and grinding, until I was lightheaded with pleasure, my balls empty.

Minchia, that was fucking fantastic.

The skin quickly grew too sensitive, so I held her hips to keep her still. She collapsed onto me, her small body heaving with the force of her breaths, and I could feel her soaked panties on my stomach.

We sat there, time stretching as I rubbed the smooth skin of her back with my rough fingertips. She rested her head on the curve of my neck and curled into me like a cat. My mind emptied. There was nothing and no one that mattered right now, only this. I had no desire to move, no desire to do anything at all but hold her.

But awareness eventually returned, and with it my responsibilities. I was the boss. I had to protect my family and my business. Becoming starry-eyed over a woman was foolish, a sure way to lose everything.

"Did you stop taking your pills?" I asked.

She stiffened against me and seemed to be holding her breath. "Yes, of course. I told you I would."

I'd come to know this woman very well, and it was obvious she was lying. I could hear it in her tone, as if she forced the words out, unnatural and wooden.

This meant either she was still taking the birth control pills . . . or there were no pills to begin with.

Had she lied because she thought I was too stupid to figure it out?

"You are dumber than a dog, Giacomo."

My father and brother had said this often over the years, even though my marks in school were higher than Nino's. It hadn't mattered. They were only interested in keeping me in my place.

Well, Emma was about to learn that I wasn't as dumb as everyone thought.

I lifted her off my lap and set her on her feet. She wobbled slightly, her small tits bouncing. Her panties were wet and clinging to her swollen flesh, my come drying on the scrap of silk. Satisfaction ballooned in my chest. I loved getting her dirty.

Hitching up my pants, I tucked my dick away and fastened my jeans. I could clean up later. Emma reached for the waistband of her panties and started to pull them off. I grabbed her wrist. "Leave them on."

She plucked her glasses off the desk and slipped them on her face. "They're sticky and uncomfortable."

I gave her a dark smile, one full of possession. "Exactly. I want you to feel me between your legs for the rest of the day."

"That's extremely unhygienic."

"But hot." Rising, I cupped her face in my palms. "I have shit to do. But before I go, I need one thing from you."

"What is it?"

"Bring me your pills."

CHAPTER EIGHTEEN

Emma

I blinked up at him, my mind whirling. Giacomo was demanding the pills—pills I'd invented to buy time. What was I going to say?

His hard stare, implacable and confident, burned into mine. There wasn't the tiniest hint that he'd back down on this.

I tried to appear confidently annoyed at the request. "Why?"

He took forever answering me. When he did his tone was all mafia boss, a man who intimidated for a living. "Because, mia innocente, I don't believe there are any pills."

My stomach fell to the floor, but I tried to put on a brave face. "You think I'm lying."

"Do not sound so offended." His thumbs caressed my jaw, the touch almost tender. Loving. "I learned long ago not to trust anyone. You shouldn't take it personally. Allora, go upstairs and bring me down your pills."

I licked my lips. I could still taste him, feel the press of his mouth against mine. My crotch was wet and sticky, the proof of our dry humping clinging to my skin. After an orgasm like that, he should be blissed out and sleepy. Instead, he'd discovered my lie.

"I threw them out," I blurted.

His lips curved into a rare wide smile. It softened his features and made him even more handsome. Flutters erupted behind my sternum —and it had nothing to do with fear.

"Bambina, you are going to learn not to lie to me. Either tell me the truth, or I'm turning you over my knee right now."

Turning me over his . . . . ? "Meaning you'll spank me?"

"Sì, certo. What will it be, the truth or a spanking?"

No one had ever hit me in my entire life. "You want to hurt me."

"I will never hurt you, Emma. But I will make you understand that you can't lie to me."

"By hitting me."

A look of annoyed disbelief crossed his face. "You can't be so innocent as to think a spanking is the same thing as hitting you."

"It is if you're doing it as punishment instead of in a sexual manner."

"Maybe it's both."

"I can't see how that's possible."

He pulled my mostly naked body against him, his hands sweeping down to cup my ass. I shivered as his lips trailed across my shoulder and neck, feather-light sweeps of his mouth that warmed me all over. Giacomo had really nice lips. I really liked kissing him.

When his face was near my ear, he whispered, "You have been a very bad girl." A crack sounded just before fire exploded on my buttock.

I sucked in a breath and tried to move away, but he held me tight. "Feel that heat?" Another smack on the same spot. I jerked and let out a grunt. Then he said, "Wait. The pain will go away and leave only the best kind of burn."

And flood my body with dopamine. I knew how this worked. Even if I wasn't a pre-med student, I'd read enough sexy books to understand it.

But he was right. The sting eased and my skin felt *alive*. Tingling and bright. Wait, did I like it?

In a blink he sat and pulled me face down onto his lap. I stared at the floor and tried to regain my equilibrium. "What are you—?"

His palm connected with my flesh and another jolt of pain went through me. He was spanking me. On his lap. And my silk panties offered no protection at all against his palm. "Stop," I said weakly, trying to get up.

He held me firm with one hand pressed into the middle of my back. I felt his fingers sweep near the crease of my thigh. Then he lifted the edge of my panties and settled the fabric in the crack of my ass. Then he did the same with the other side, exposing both my cheeks. "My good girl has been very bad," he purred. "Do you deserve to be punished, bad girl?"

Arousal flooded between my legs at his words. Or maybe it was because of his low and seductive tone. Or maybe it was the anticipation of when he might spank me again.

My head was spinning and I was breathing hard. Still, I had to stick to my story. "I'm telling you the truth."

He just laughed, and I felt a rush of air before his palm slapped my butt again. "I don't like lies. Maybe if I punish you I will learn the truth."

Before I could say anything, he gave me a series of spanks that stole the air from my lungs. Pain exploded in every cell, and I could do nothing but hang there and take it. There was no escape, no mercy from my husband.

When he finally stopped I exhaled in relief. It was over.

Warmth spread all through me. Then I felt his fingers probing between my legs. He rubbed me over the wet panties that were coated in both of us from before. Between the rubbing and the way my skin was glowing, I couldn't hold back the moan that fell from my lips.

"That's it, *ragazzaccia*."

Bad girl.

I wasn't a bad girl. I wasn't like my sisters—but sometimes I wanted to be. Sometimes I wanted to be naughty and irresponsible, rude and dirty. "Please," I whispered.

He dragged the tips of his fingers over my clit. "Are you ready to tell me the truth?"

"I did."

Three smacks right in a row caused me to cry out. Then my sex swelled even more, slickness gathering between my legs. I closed my eyes against the rush of arousal. Was he going to edge the truth out of me again? I wasn't sure I could take it.

In a single sweep he removed my panties. Then he was touching my bare flesh, sliding his fingers through my folds. "So wet. My sweet virgin likes to be spanked."

"No, I don't," I said, but it came out weak.

"More lies." He gave me two more spanks. "Let's see if I can get you to tell me the truth."

I expected to feel another strike, but he surprised me with gentle, insistent fingers between my legs. He parted my thighs slightly and circled my entrance once. Then again. And again. He stirred and pressed a little deeper each time, a slow maddening breach of my body. It felt good, but it wasn't enough. I tilted my hips, silently begging for more.

He withdrew, not giving me what I craved. I huffed in frustration. "Mo, please."

"So now it is Mo." He slapped my butt cheek. Hard. "When you don't want something from me, I get Giacomo. When you want something it's Mo."

"That's not true."

"Lies. When will you start telling me what is really going through your head?"

His fingers played along my folds, the pads swiping over my clit. I nearly jumped out of my skin. "Oh, right there!"

He pulled away to resume teasing my entrance. "How many fingers can this virgin pussy take, I wonder?" His thick digit pushed halfway inside, stretching me. My back bowed as pleasure arrowed through me.

"Oh, god," I murmured.

"So tight. So hot. I could come just from watching you take me inside."

He fumbled in his jeans and I wondered what he was doing. I shoved my hair out of my face and twisted to see him opening his phone.

"What are you doing?" He was aiming his camera at my crotch. I tried to close my legs and get away, but he held me fast. "Giacomo, no!"

"Basta, ragazzaccia. Let me take a photo of this."

Humiliated, I quit struggling. There was no way he'd let me go. "Why?"

"Because you are beautiful. Tilt your hips higher." I obeyed, and his finger pushed deeper inside my channel. "Look at you, sucking me in. I never want to forget this sight."

It felt so good, like a necessary fullness. He pumped his finger a few times, then more pressure as he began to add a second. "That's it," he crooned. "Take another. Let me stretch you for my cock."

I tensed up. Was he thinking we were going to have sex here? Right now? "Wait, I'm not sure—"

"Calm down, little virgin. I won't fuck you here. But soon I will make this mine." He worked his fingers in deeper, humming in approval as I relaxed and allowed him in.

I heard his phone thump as it landed on the desk. With his free hand he smacked both of my butt cheeks, one right after another, and I moaned, my walls clenching around his fingers. He pushed in, sawing in and out, and I could hear my wetness as he worked. Finally his hand met my skin, his fingers fully seated.

"Minchia," he rasped. "That is the hottest thing I have ever seen."

I hung there, panting, my body buzzing. Desperation clawed at my insides, the lust nearly unbearable. I was beyond fighting, more turned on than I imagined. The skin of my ass burned in the best way and all I wanted was for him to finish me off. "Oh, god. I'm dying. Please."

He withdrew his fingers and I nearly cried. The protest died on my lips, though, because he began rubbing my clit in slick circles. Then his thumb slid inside my pussy. It was an overload for my senses. I clutched his leg with one hand, my body climbing higher with each quick pass. I rocked and moaned, chasing the peak just out of reach.

I felt his other hand sliding between my crack, fingers seeking until they found the tight hole there. Nerve endings fired as he brushed the sensitive skin, and I soared higher, a mindless creature of pleasure. He surrounded me, my body completely under his command.

"A virgin here, too," he said softly. "I will be the first man to fuck your ass. Every part of you will belong to me."

The tip of his finger pushed inside my backside—and I shattered, my body trembling atop his, the euphoria rolling over me from head to toe. I cried out and clung to him, my walls convulsing around his thumb. It was even better than the last orgasm, which I hadn't believed possible.

When it was over I tried to catch my breath. His hands withdrew and gently helped me sit up onto his lap. I slumped against his chest, my muscles like wet noodles. I was sore everywhere, but it was the best kind of ache. Giacomo just held me, smoothing his palms over my skin and allowing me to recover.

This was nice. I liked his warmth and care, the strong arms that wrapped around me. I was usually the one looking after everyone else. It was nice to have someone do it for me for once.

But the issue of the pills hadn't been resolved.

"Are you done punishing me?" I asked, my face buried in the rough skin of his throat.

"For now, yes."

"So you believe me about the pills."

"No, mia piccola innocente, I do not. I know you have no pills upstairs and never did." He kissed the top of my head. "You are a terrible liar."

I bit my lip, grateful he couldn't see my face at the moment. I'm sure the truth was written all over it, now that my defenses were down. "I'm a great liar."

He chuckled, his broad chest rumbling beneath me. "You are terrible at it and I'm grateful. I don't want to be married to a woman who prefers deceit. I respect honesty, Emma."

"I'm not ready to have sex with you." I wasn't ready to have a baby. I wasn't ready for any of this.

"We don't have a choice. You must be pregnant in three months' time."

"Just let me go," I whispered. "We can think of a way out of this."

His chest rose and fell as he blew out a long breath. "I have tried to think of a solution. If there was any other way . . . ."

He trailed off, not finishing the thought. Because there was no other way. We both knew it.

"You said you were going to find Virga and . . . ." I couldn't say it.

"Kill him? He's still at sea. No doubt he's having us watched, however."

"Isn't there anyone he cares about? A family member we can use as leverage against him?"

"He has no wife and his son died eight years ago."

I could feel my eyes start to burn. I blinked rapidly, trying to stem the flood of emotion in my chest. What was the point in crying?

With a gentle finger under my chin he tilted my face up. "Do not worry, bambina. Making the babies is the fun part."

I couldn't help it—I laughed. "Sure. But there's a lot I want to accomplish before having children."

"I'll not pretend to want a child. I don't. But you don't need to give up your life for this. You can return to medical school and live in Toronto afterward, free of responsibilities."

The practicalities of bearing this man's child hadn't truly occurred to me before now. Maybe because I hadn't believed it would actually happen. But Giacomo was talking about a future where we had a child together . . . a child I was leaving behind in Sicily. "Do you honestly think I'd do that?"

He shrugged. "Why not? I have the money to hire caretakers. Nannies or whatever the fuck. Our child will want for nothing, Emma."

Except love. And someone to fight this misogynistic society on their behalf.

Getting off his lap, I started redressing. This was not a conversation best had while naked. "I won't leave a son behind in Sicily to become some cold and ruthless mafia kingpin—or worse, abandon a daughter to be bartered off to some mafia family. The baby goes where I go."

He clasped his hands together and rested his elbows on the armrests. "You're not making sense. First you don't want a baby, and now you are taking our baby away from me. Which you know I'd never allow."

"Now who isn't making sense? You don't want a baby, but if we happen to have one you're keeping it?"

"I'm the boss," he said in a gruff, raspy tone that held notes of danger. "I decide what makes sense."

Oh, god. Someone please spare me from testosterone-fueled logic.

I swiped my hand in a chopping motion. "No baby. We're not having sex and you're not getting me pregnant."

Slowly, he pushed out of his chair until he towered over me. Then in a flash he reached out and snagged my hair in his fist, twisting just short of the point of pain. His mouth hovered near the edge of my ear. "If we can't figure out a solution in the next two weeks, I am going to fuck a baby into you. I will fill that virgin pussy with so much come you'll choke on it. And I promise you'll love every second."

Releasing me, he grabbed his phone off the desk, then stomped out of the office.

CHAPTER NINETEEN

Giacomo

"Fratello!"

My sister waved at me from the bench at the edge of the pond. A dozen or so ducks were gathered around her feet as they waited for the bread she was tossing.

It had been almost a month since I visited in person, which was too long. So when Viviana called this morning to ask me to come, I didn't hesitate.

Thankfully, my sister looked well. Happy. Mirabella has been her home since she was eighteen years old. Before that, she stayed in a different in-patient facility, one that catered to children. It hadn't been easy, faking her death and keeping her existence a secret from my father and brother. Every bout I won, every Euro of prize money, had gone to Viviana's care. It was part of what had motivated me in the ring.

Now she was twenty-six, an adult. But she was well cared for. Safe.

And I would marry ten women and father a hundred babies to ensure it stayed that way.

I nodded at one of the three guards I personally paid to keep watch over her twenty-four hours a day, then approached the bench. "Sorel-lina, ciao." Bending, I kissed her cheeks. "Come stai?"

"Bene. But why do you look so serious today? Here, sit with the ducks. They'll cheer you up."

I dropped onto the seat next to her. "And if they bite me, they become dinner."

"Did you hear that, amici?" She threw the ducks more bread. "The powerful mafia don is threatening you."

I snorted and stretched my arms out on the back of the bench. "You couldn't wait to remind me."

"I can't help it. I never wanted this for you. And I know you never wanted it, either."

"It doesn't matter what I want. I'm a Buscetta. But it's not so bad, now that I am the one in charge."

"Without Papà and Nino, you mean. I can see that." She tossed the rest of her bread and dusted off her fingers. "It must feel as if a weight has been lifted, no?"

"The weight has been lifted for you, as well."

She shrugged, her long dark hair shifting with the movement. "I try not to think about them."

"But they can't hurt you any more, Vivi. No one will ever hurt you, not as long as I am breathing."

"You're a good brother, Mo. I always thank God that he gave you to me." We both knew I wasn't religious, so I didn't respond. She studied my face carefully. "You're happy? Being the one in charge, I mean."

"It has its benefits."

"Like money and women."

I smiled. "Yes, those are two I happen to like."

"You're not . . . you're not doing it for me, are you?"

This wasn't the first time she'd asked. And I still wanted to avoid the conversation. She didn't like hearing that everything I did, every single day, was for her. "Stop worrying about me. Tell me, why did you want to see me today?"

"You said things have changed now that Papà and Nino are dead. You said things are better."

Hope rose in my chest. Did she want to come home? That would solve everything with Virga. "Yes, things are better. You're safe, Vivi."

"Good." She smoothed her skirt, not meeting my eyes. "Because there is a man here, another patient. He's being released and the two of us would like—"

"Fuck no."

The nearby ducks scattered at my harsh tone, but I didn't look away from my sister's face. She frowned at me. "You don't even know what I was going to say."

"It doesn't matter. I won't allow you to put yourself in jeopardy."

"You said there was no jeopardy. You said I was safe and there was nothing to worry about."

"There is nothing to worry about," I lied.

"Then why can't I move in with Federico?"

Over my shoulder, I cast a hard stare at the guard I paid to watch over her. "What the *fuck?*"

He lifted his palms toward me. "I didn't know, I swear. Don Buscetta, she—"

"I'll deal with you later," I snarled, then faced my sister. "You are not moving in with some stronzo I don't even know."

"We want to get married, Mo. I want to have a life outside of here. A *normal* life. I'm twenty-six years old!"

"The last time you moved somewhere new was when you were eighteen and you came here. Do you remember what happened? Now you want to leave to marry a man I've never met? With no protection? No fucking chance."

She winced but remained calm. "That was eight years ago. And the doctor said my anxiety is better now that Papà has died. He said I could be released, if I wished."

"Then come home and live with me."

"No." She paled, swallowing hard. "I can't live there. I don't care if he's dead, I will see him around every corner. I can't."

"I'll keep you safe. I'll redecorate the entire fucking house, Viv. Or I'll burn it to the ground and build a new one. Come live with me."

Her chest began rising and falling more quickly, and she gestured wildly with her hands. "You are not listening to me. It won't matter. I'll remember every cruel thing he ever did to me. I won't be able to sleep there."

"Then you are staying here."

"I want to live somewhere else, a place of my own. Somewhere far away."

Impossible. It would make her a target at the worst possible time. Virga would find out and she'd be at risk. Unless she was willing to come live with me, then she had to stay here with the guards until I dealt with Virga. "No."

"Be reasonable, Mo. Talk to my doctors. They will tell you—"

"I don't give a shit what your doctors say. I'm your brother and you will do what I say. And you will stay here until I say otherwise."

Her expression lost all its warmth, all its affection. She looked at me as if we were strangers, not siblings, but I wouldn't back down. I had to make the hard decisions, even when she didn't like it.

"I never thought you were anything like him," she said quietly. "But I was wrong. When you say things like that, I can see him in you and that scares me more than anything else."

Rising, she hurried toward the facility, her long hair blowing behind her. My chest was burning, hurt strangling my lungs like a knot.

"Take care of your sister, Giacomo. She needs you. Be strong for her."

I was twelve when my mother died, Viviana only six. But my mother had been saying these words to me for far longer. For years she'd been too weak, too ill to look after us, so it had fallen on me to protect Viviana.

Every day had been a struggle, chased by the fear that I would fail and Viviana would suffer. As soon as I turned eighteen I was able to get her out of the house, move her into a facility without my father's knowledge. Then Zani and I staged an accident with a recently deceased young woman's body to fool my family.

I've spent my life keeping Viv safe.

And I wouldn't stop now, just because some stronzo named Federico was putting ideas in her head. Even if she hated me for it.

Shooting to my feet, I stalked toward the guard, who knew better than to leave before we chatted. My fists clenched at my sides as I closed the distance between us.

He put up his palms. "I swear, I had no idea. *Mi dispiace*, Don Buscetta!"

I grabbed the front of his shirt and shook him like a rag doll. "Idiota! How does this happen? You're supposed to be watching her. Now some puppy has gotten into her pants!"

"I'm not with her all the time. After she goes to bed, we walk the perimeter. We're not always by her side."

"Well, one of you had better stay by her side at all times from now on. I don't want her alone again." I shoved him away from me.

"We will."

"And find out who this Federico boy is. I want to know everything about him before the day is over." I pointed a finger in his face. "Fair warning. If I don't get answers by tonight, I'm coming back to beat the shit out of you. Capisce?"

I stomped toward the front of the facility, fury boiling in my veins. This was all Virga's fault.

CHAPTER TWENTY

Emma

I finished washing my face then patted it dry with a towel. I was exhausted. For three days I'd lodged argument after argument with my professors and my advisor, but they wouldn't budge on their decision: I was not allowed to complete my required lab work remotely. Apparently such exclusions were fine during a pandemic, but not for one student who'd been forced to marry a mafia don and live in Sicily.

Not that I told them any of that.

If I couldn't complete my lab work, I failed my classes. Failed. I'd never received any grade lower than a B+ before. What was I going to do?

I could quit school, then resume whenever this mess with Giacomo was finished. *If* this mess was ever finished.

That would push me back years before I could practice medicine. It wasn't fair. What was I going to do?

My phone buzzed, so I glanced down to see who was calling me. Unknown caller. That was weird.

I tapped the glass and lifted the phone to my ear. "Hello?"

"Ciao, Emma."

The deep male voice froze every muscle in my body. "Who is this?"

"You don't recognize my voice, Signora Buscetta? I am hurt."

Virga! Why in the world was he calling me? "What do you want, Signore Virga?"

"I want to know why you are not doing as I have instructed."

"Because it takes time," I lied. "We're trying."

His voice went scary soft. "Do you think I am a fool? Do you think I am not aware of what you and Giacomo are trying to do?"

"And what are we trying to do?"

"Do *not* lie to me, ragazza. You both think you are smarter than me, but you are wrong. If you don't believe me, turn on the video feed in your father's room."

Dread coiled like snakes in my belly. "What have you done?"

"Nothing yet, but I want you to see what will happen if you don't follow directions." Then he hung up.

Oh, shit. I fumbled with my phone, hastily opening the video app. When it loaded my heart squeezed painfully. Virga's man, the one who'd watched me pack in Toronto, was sitting in my father's room, right next to Papà's bed. Gloria was nowhere to be seen and the man was laughing with my father over something on the TV.

Virga's man tilted his face to the camera and it was like he was looking right at me. He winked.

God, no. This couldn't be happening. I didn't want Virga's men anywhere near my father. A lump settled in my throat. It would be so easy for that man to kill my father. I couldn't allow that to happen.

I couldn't take my eyes off the screen. Papà seemed happy to have a stranger in his room. How had Uncle Reggie allowed this? Where was Gloria?

Screw a burner phone. I didn't have time for that. I pulled up Gloria's contact and hit the button. Then I switched back to the video feed.

My heart was pounding, slamming against my ribs as I waited for her to pick up.

"Emma?" She spoke quietly.

"Gloria! Oh, my god. What is happening over there? Who is that man?"

"He said he's with someone named Borghese in Calabria? He's your father's personal protection as long as it's needed."

"And they believed him?"

"I have no idea. They must, though, because your uncle allowed this man into the house."

"Do not trust him, Gloria. He is a bad man."

"What?" I heard her exhale heavily. "I had no idea. He's been cozying up to your father, playing cards and watching television together. What should I do?"

I dragged my hand down my face, sick to my stomach. "Don't leave him alone in a room together. Stick close to my father."

"Okay. I'll get in there. I won't let him get hurt."

"Thank you, Gloria." I squeezed the phone in my hand. My head spun and it suddenly felt like the walls were closing in on me. "I'm so grateful for all you're doing."

"You're welcome. I care about your father and I don't want to see him hurt. But Emma, something weird is going on. I mentioned our conversation to your uncle, the one about moving your father to a safer location. He told me to mind my place and stay out of family business."

Didn't my uncle care about my father's safety? I watched the screen, Virga's man in close proximity to Papà. How had Reggie allowed this? "Don't worry. I'll figure something out."

"Good. Call me later." She disconnected and I watched on the livestream as she reentered my father's room. He smiled at her, then yawned. Gloria hustled the other man from the room so my father could nap, but I didn't miss the way the man looked at the camera. At me. He knew I was watching and he was taunting me.

Sweat broke out on the back of my neck, and air trickled in and out of my lungs. I bent over at the waist and tried to calm down. This was no time to start having panic attacks. I had to deal with this right now. Tonight.

My eyes darted to the door that led into the hall, toward my husband. Toward the possible future father of my child.

Oh, god.

It was an impossible choice. Unfair and cruel, as well as archaic.

This wasn't part of my plan. I'd wanted a big wedding, with white lilies and a huge lemon cake with vanilla bean frosting. I wanted a husband who loved me beyond reason, a man proud of his doctor wife. A home with laughter and respect and safety. A family of my own someday, when my schedule allowed for carpooling to sports practices and attending plays.

None of it was supposed to happen this way.

Suck it up, I told myself. *You know chaos theory. You should've known you'd never get what you wanted.*

And what did my objections matter when my father's life was at stake?

So, I would do as Virga ordered. Giacomo and I would solidify the arrangement between the two families with a child. Then Virga would back off, and my father could live out the rest of his life in peace, with me at his side.

Me and a baby, of course. Because no way was I leaving a child here, I didn't care what Giacomo said. And if he didn't like it, then he could talk to either of my brothers-in-law, who would no doubt take my side. Any child of mine would automatically have the protection of Enzo and Fausto.

I stared at the hall again. *It won't be so bad. People have babies in less than perfect circumstances all the time.* I would be a kick-ass single mom, too. Gia and Frankie could help until I finished medical school. Then Giacomo could mob boss his way across Palermo instead of raising a child. I didn't need him.

I could do this. My IQ was 161. I aced nearly every test I'd taken since primary school. I could figure out how to have a baby with a Sicilian mafia don, keep my father safe, and still follow my dreams.

Resolved, I went to my dresser and looked for something appropriate to wear. I had a husband to seduce.

CHAPTER TWENTY-ONE

Giacomo

I braced my hand on the shower tile and let the scalding hot water pound my back. Every muscle ached from my workout. Unfortunately, hitting the bag in the cellar hadn't eased my frustration or anger. I was still pissed off and resentful at Virga, my father. Myself. I hated the whole fucking world.

The shower door clicked open.

Che cazzo? Spinning, I braced myself for a fight.

Emma stood there. She wore a silk robe and her hair hung loose around her shoulders. She looked soft and sweet and so damn young.

I blinked and wiped the water off my face, not bothering to cover my naked dick. "Emma, what is it?"

Instead of answering, she stepped back and pulled on the ties of the robe. The sides parted and the thin fabric floated to the floor.

She was naked.

Sciatiri e matri! Holy shit. Lust punched the air from my lungs as I drank in the sight of her. Smooth pale skin and small, high breasts tipped with rosy nipples. A slightly rounded stomach that led to the juncture of her thighs. Dark hair covered her mound. I didn't know what to say, but my cock responded by thickening between my legs.

Her gaze darted to my crotch and I saw her swallow hard. Nervousness?

I reached to shut off the water. "What are you doing?"

"You know why I'm here."

Angling to face her, I braced my arms on the edges of the glass door. "I'm not very smart, Emma. Why don't you spell it out for me?"

"We need to do this."

"What, bambina?"

Her face had turned scarlet. "Have sex."

"We had sex already. Someone told me it isn't defined by putting a penis in a vagina."

"You know what I mean. It's time. Let's get it over with."

I pushed off the glass and walked out of the shower. She took several steps back, nearly tripping over her feet to keep distance between us, which told me all I needed to know. She wasn't here because she wanted this; she was here because something happened.

Something had pushed her over the edge.

I reached for a towel and wrapped it around my waist. "No offense, but I don't want to fuck a woman who says, 'let's get it over with.'"

"I didn't mean it that way. But you're acting like we have a choice—and we don't."

Hadn't I thought the same thing when I left Viviana today? Still, I recoiled at the idea of procreating under orders from Virga. "Emma," I said with a heavy sigh. "We shouldn't—"

"Yes, we should. Right now. Tonight."

"Why?" I narrowed my gaze on her when she didn't answer. "What changed your mind?"

With a lick of her lips she came toward me, her bare breasts bouncing slightly with each step. "Don't you want to?"

As she drew closer, my heart crashed inside my chest, a rhythmic pounding that echoed all over my body, sending more blood to my groin. My cock was now throbbing with need under the towel. "That has never been the issue," I croaked.

Her palm landed on my chest, directly over my racing heartbeat. "We're out of time, Giacomo."

I knew she was right, but I wasn't stupid. "What happened?"

Instead of answering, she dragged her fingers down my sternum. Pure fire trailed her touch south, her fingertips smoothing over my stomach, our eyes locked together. When her hand reached the towel she gave it a tug, and the cloth dropped to the ground. It left me naked, the heavy length of my cock pointing directly at her.

Warm pressure enveloped my cock as her hand wrapped around me, and she stroked once. My eyes slammed shut against the rush of pleasure that followed. "Cazzo!" I hissed.

Her other hand caressed my ribs. "You really do have the most perfect body."

I grabbed her wrist, the one connected to the hand on my dick, so I could stare at her. "If we do this, there is no going back."

"I know. But what choice do we have?"

I wasn't sure, but I wanted to fuck her more than I wanted my next breath. It was all I'd been thinking about since she rode my dick in my office chair.

My resistance crumbled. I wasn't capable of withstanding this much temptation, not when she was begging me for it.

Gently, I removed her hand from my shaft. Then I bent down, lifted her up, and wrapped her legs around my waist. I carried her out of the bathroom, but I didn't stop at my bed. I kept going, straight into the hall.

"Wait, where are you taking me?" Her arms tightened around my neck, like she was afraid of letting go.

"My bed isn't big enough for what I need to do to you."

"I'm pretty sure it is."

"No, bambina, it's not. Because I'm going to fuck you in every position I know how tonight."

She pressed her face into the side of my throat. "Should I be worried?"

"Verginella, from now on your pussy belongs to me. And one thing you should know is that I take care of my belongings."

I kicked open her bedroom door. For once I wasn't thinking about my father or the hideous gold decor.

I was only thinking about getting my cock deep inside this woman as quickly as possible.

After shutting the door, I carried her to the bed and set her on her feet. She didn't move. Her eyes were bright with lust, her breathing every bit as heavy as mine. I cupped her face in my hands and stared down at her. "Are you ready to feel my dick inside you, mia piccola innocente?"

"Sì, *mio grande marito*."

My big husband.

Fuck, I liked that.

Swooping down, I pressed our lips together and kissed her. I angled her head and deepened the kiss almost instantly, and she opened her mouth to accept my tongue. She was warm and wet and eager, and I didn't hold back. I fucked her mouth with my tongue and showed her how to take it, just like she was going to take my cock in a few minutes.

When her little whimpers grew desperate, I kissed my way down her jaw and along her throat. I felt drunk on her velvety skin, as if she were a drug I was inhaling. My teeth sank into the soft juncture where her neck met her shoulder, right above her collar bone. She gasped and clutched me tighter, but I didn't let go. I put my mark there, sucking hard and imprinting myself on her. Claiming her. I wanted this woman to feel me everywhere in the morning, let no millimeter of her skin go untouched.

"Giacomo," she breathed, trembling against me. Then her fingers found my erection between us and she clasped me firmly. Sparks ran along the backs of my thighs.

I bent to lick her nipple, my tongue swirling over the tight bead. "Get on the bed," I growled. "You want to fuck? Then it's time to fuck."

She released me and crawled onto the mattress. I tried to gather my wits as I watched her arrange herself on the bed, her legs together, arms at her side, waiting patiently. No, that wasn't what I wanted at all.

"Spread your legs and show me how wet you are." I fisted my cock and stroked, letting her see how much I needed her. "Show me how much that virgin pussy wants to be filled."

She parted her thighs slowly and soon every bit of her was revealed, the perfect pink heaven I would take as my own. Madre di dio, she was beautiful. And she was mine.

I crawled between her legs and pressed my face in her sweet heat, inhaling the scent of her arousal just before I tasted it. Fuck, there was a lot of it. She was soaked, every bit as turned on as I was.

I needed her ready. She may have inserted a dildo inside before, but that was different than taking the pounding I was about to give her. So I lashed her clit with my tongue and worked her relentlessly, giving her my lips and teeth, too. She writhed beneath me, but I held her hips still in my hands and kept going, driving her higher. She needed to come at least once before I fucked her.

One finger slid inside her easily. When I gave her two, her back bowed and her thighs began shaking. The third finger sent her over the edge, her body clamping down on me as she shouted to the ceiling. I loved those sounds and how she clutched at my head to pull me closer. She might be a virgin, but she wasn't shy. Innocent, yet naughty. And I was going to enjoy breaking her in.

First.

The thought made my dick jump and I had to take a few deep breaths to calm down. I wanted her to enjoy this, so I needed to be in complete control the entire time.

When she sagged on the bed I gave her clit a final kiss and propped up on one elbow. My fingers remained snugly inside her, though. The stretch was necessary for what came next.

Her dazed eyes searched my face. "What are you waiting for?"

"For you to beg me."

"Because you need my consent?"

I chuckled darkly. "Bambina, I had your consent when you stripped naked in my bathroom. I want you to beg me because it gets me hard. Capisce?"

"You're already hard."

"I can always be harder. And there is nothing sexier than a woman begging to be fucked." I bent to suck her swollen clit into my mouth, nearly smiling at the loud moan she gave. I released her with a slick pop. "So beg me to pop your cherry, wife. Beg me to give you your first cock."

"Please, Giacomo."

It was enough. I pushed up to my knees and looked down at where my fingers stretched her opening. She was so tight around me, so hot. I couldn't wait to feel her pussy strangling my dick.

Withdrawing my fingers, I reached for the drawer by the bed. She was wet, but I wanted to make sure I didn't hurt her, so I found the plastic bottle of lube I stashed there. I drizzled some of the liquid onto my shaft and rubbed it in, coating myself.

"I like to watch you do that," she whispered, her feverish gaze watching my hand.

"Yeah? You can watch me jerk off anytime." I gave my cock another stroke and then positioned myself between her legs. "But right now I'm too close to coming. Spread."

She parted her thighs and I grabbed the base of my dick. I placed the tip at her entrance, my eyes locked on her pussy as I slowly pushed inside. Her flesh parted in welcome, and I watched as she sucked me in, every centimeter disappearing into her body. Heat scalded my flesh, and it was the first time I'd ever been in a woman without a condom on. Fuck, that was intense.

It was so tight, with the walls squeezing the head around my piercing. My hips twitched and I sank deeper, causing her to gasp. "Oh, god!"

"Tell me, innocente. Tell me what I feel like inside you."

"Thick. Hot." She panted in short little bursts. "It's different from the toys. Better. I can feel the metal of your piercing."

My little scientist. She had her eyes closed, no doubt cataloguing all the sensations during her first fucking. But I wanted her feeling, not thinking right now. After making sure my thumb was slick, I began using it on her clit, making small circles. Emma's fingers fisted in the covers, her face slackening in bliss.

"That's it," I crooned as I kept up my slow invasion. "Take my cock, bambina. It's going to make you feel so good."

Her chest rose and fell with her heavy breaths. "Is it all the way in?"

I glanced down. We were halfway there. I gritted my teeth against the urge to come. "Not yet. Just relax."

She threw her head back. "It's so much pressure."

I lowered myself on top of her, keeping my weight on my elbows, my mouth at her ear. "You can take it. You were made for me and only me." I thrust once, giving her more. "I will be the first and the last man inside this pussy, Emma Buscetta."

Her arms wrapped around me and her fingernails dug into my back. "You like that idea, don't you?"

"Fuck yes, I do. You belong to me, mia piccola moglie."

She was squirming, her hips rocking against mine. "No one person . . . belongs to . . . anyone else."

My hips snapped forward, and I filled her completely in one thrust. *Fuck.* Pleasure shot up my spine and rolled down through my balls. I groaned into the soft skin of her throat. "Cazzata. You are mine until you draw your last breath on this earth, little girl."

"Holy . . . hell," she breathed. "Oh, god. It's . . . just wow."

"And you haven't even felt the best part." Coming up on my hands, I withdrew slightly, then rammed home again. She jolted, her eyelids flying open. I could see the surprise there, the realization that no toy could feel like I could. That even her scientific imaginings couldn't live up to reality.

"The piercing," she whispered. "It hits . . . ."

I gave her another taste, another sample to draw from. "Yes? Where does it hit?"

"My g-spot. It's so intense. Why didn't you warn me?"

Her eyes were glassy, her skin flushed. She was so fucking beautiful. "Because then I wouldn't have seen this look on your face." I bent to kiss her quickly. "Now hold on while I make you come on my cock."

I started thrusting then, short punches of my hips to keep as much stimulation on her g-spot as possible. I didn't usually think about my piercing this much during sex, because I fucked experienced women. But Emma wasn't experienced and she was my wife. I wanted her to love getting fucked by my dick as much as I loved fucking her.

Sweat built between us, the heat suffocating. Her cries grew louder, her muscles tensing, and I kept at it. The pressure in my groin was nearly unbearable and the urge to come burned under my skin like an inferno. I wouldn't be able to hold out much longer.

The bed rocked and the godawful headboard smacked against the wall with the force of my thrusts. "Fuck, bambina," I growled. "I need to come. I have so much stored up in my balls for you. I haven't jerked off in *days*, just to save it. You're going to take all of it like a good girl, no?"

Her back arched, the walls of her pussy gripping me. "Oh, god. Mo!"

A satisfied rumble echoed in my chest, pieces falling into place. She'd loved the things I said in the cellar the other night, too. My little scientist had a *filthy* side to her—and she never even knew it. Gesù, I loved it.

Rolling my hips, I made sure to hit the sweet spot inside her with each thrust as I kept talking. "I'm going to fill you up. As many times as it takes, and more after that. You'll let me give you a baby, won't you, sporcacciona?"

That did it. She froze, then started convulsing, her walls milking me. I held on by a very thin string. It was too good and I could feel my balls tingling as my orgasm rushed up.

My cock thickened, the inevitable happening, but at the last second I didn't think. I just pulled out.

"Minchia!" I shouted, my cock pulsing as I poured onto her stomach. White light exploded behind my eyes, my head spinning with the force of my orgasm. It kept going and going, jet after jet of hot fluid coating her. By the time I finished my arms were shaking and sweat dripped off my forehead onto her chest.

I dropped onto the mattress beside her, my muscles incapable of supporting my weight. "Mamma mia." My chest bellowed like I'd run a race. Still dizzy, I needed a lifeline, an anchor. Anything. *Her.*

I clutched her hand like a foolish, lovesick boy. *Only for a second.* "Are you okay?"

"Holy smokes." She was breathing hard as she angled to face me, and her legs tangled with mine. "I had no idea it would be like that."

It wasn't always like that. In fact, I'd never experienced anything even close, with the burning need to touch her and breathe her in.

Where her pleasure mattered more than mine. Like I was lost and she was the only light I had in this godforsaken world.

But I couldn't tell her any of that. I learned a long time ago to bury tenderness, to hide it away. Feelings were only used to hurt you in the end.

I released her hand and closed my eyes. "I think the words you are looking for are 'Grazie, Mo.'"

"Is that so?" She poked my arm. "I think you should be thanking me."

"And why would I do that?"

"Because I was awesome. Or were you not the one who shouted to the ceiling and nearly passed out during your orgasm a moment ago?"

We stared at each other, and I resisted the urge to smile. I didn't like the affection tugging at my gut. I couldn't allow myself to feel anything for her. This wasn't real; this was duty.

She folded her hands under her cheek. "Why didn't you come inside me? I thought the point was for us to get pregnant."

I dragged the back of my knuckles along the soft edge of her breast. "The point is for me to fuck you senseless."

"We both know that's not true. You need to come inside me."

Some deep part of me knew she was right, that we'd run out of time. But my body had rebelled at the last second, even if I wasn't consciously aware of why.

"I can see him in you and that scares me more than anything else."

Viviana knew me better than anyone. If she saw hints of my father in me, then I couldn't risk a child. Children deserve love. I was raised without it, trapped in a household of punishments and terror, so what did I know about being a father or having a family? My role model had been a monster.

Except I wasn't ready to have that conversation, so I pinched Emma's nipple and rolled it between my fingers. Her lips parted on a quick breath before she asked, "What about those things you said, you know, before? About filling me up and giving me a baby."

"You like the idea of it. I could see it on your face in the cellar. Did you search breeding kink on the internet? I bet you read articles on it."

She bit her bottom lip and I knew I was right. She lifted her chin defensively. "Psychologists claim it's partly the risk and partly the domination. Or it could be the deep-seated biological need to reproduce. It doesn't mean I really want to be a baby factory."

"I don't care about the reasons. If it makes you come all over my dick, then I'll keep talking about it."

I let my fingers travel south, over the streaks of come on her stomach, until I reached the juncture of her thighs. Wetness greeted my fingertips, the proof of her orgasm and mine. "Feel how slippery you are with me all over you. Now imagine it inside you. My *seed*."

"God," she whispered, her eyelids fluttering closed. "I think you have a breeding kink, too."

Did I? It did turn me on, but I wasn't sure if it was her reaction or the idea of leaving something of me inside her. "Only with you, mia piccola innocente."

She grabbed my hand and moved it away from her. "You have to stop."

"Why?"

"Because we need to talk first. I want to know what Virga has on you."

CHAPTER TWENTY-TWO

Emma

He pulled away instantly and cold air washed over me. I missed his warmth, and for a moment I regretted bringing up the topic. But this was a conversation we needed to have.

When he started to sit up, I reached out to grab his arm. "Wait. We need to talk about this."

"I don't want to talk about it."

"Listen, we have to trust each other. It's time."

"Time for what?"

"For us to work together." The unhappy crease in his brow didn't ease up in the least. I kept explaining because I had to convince him. "We aren't getting anywhere by ourselves. Maybe if we work together we'll have better luck."

"It isn't *luck*. It's Virga disappearing because he knows I'll kill him the second I have the chance."

"What if we can help one another? Because if we can remove the leverage Virga has over each of us, then—"

His top lip curled, his expression unforgiving, almost cruel, as he sat up. "If I help you, then what? You go back to Toronto and I'm still at risk."

He thought I would abandon him the first chance I got? Did he think so little of me? Maybe other people might, but I wouldn't. "Giacomo, I'm not going to leave you here to deal with this alone. I'll help you and you help me."

"There is no help for me, except Virga's death or a positive pregnancy test."

"You can't mean that." I propped myself up, uncaring of my sticky nakedness. "Tell me what Virga is blackmailing you with."

"You tell me first."

I stared at him, my mind whirling. Would he use this against me? I doubted it. What would it gain him? Not to mention he'd told me the truth at every turn. He'd protected me, shown me kindness. I had no reason to fear him.

And we just had sex. I let this man inside my *body*. If I didn't trust him, then what were we even doing?

Of course I trust him.

I drew in a deep breath and forced out the words. "My father is dying."

Giacomo didn't appear surprised. In fact, he gave no reaction whatsoever. Okay, weird.

I added, "Virga has men in Toronto, in the house itself. He said if I fail to produce an heir for you then he'll kill my father and his aide."

"You mean Gloria?"

My mouth fell open. During my untraceable call the other night, I pretended Gloria was my aunt. That obviously hadn't worked. "How did you know?"

"I've suspected about your father's condition for some time. And I know your aunt's name is Carla, not Gloria. Your call the other night was a dead giveaway."

"You suspected? How?"

"He hasn't been heard from directly or seen in quite some time, not even to speak to his favorite daughter's new husband when contacted. So either he's given up control of the family business or is too ill to run it himself. And you still live at home with him. The commute from your home to your classes is a long one, but you do it because you look after him. You want to take care of him."

He'd put all that together in such a short time? No one had questioned Papà's behavior in the six months, not even two of his own daughters. Yet this man who'd known me for a hot minute figured it out.

How was that possible?

Giacomo stood and held out his hand. "Come. Let's shower."

A shower was the last thing on my mind right now. "You contacted my father?"

"Of course. Except your uncle keeps saying he speaks for Don Mancini." He turned and walked to the bathroom. I was momentarily distracted by the absolute perfection of his glutes as he moved. Holy smokes, there was zero fat on this man. Narrow hips and a broad muscular back . . . .

"Emma!" he called as he disappeared into the bathroom. "Stop staring at me and get in here. I want you clean so I can dirty you up again."

I shook myself and heaved off the mattress. He'd already started the shower by the time I walked in. Steam billowed from the glass enclosure as he pulled open the door. "In."

"Wait."

His face twisted with impatience. "Stop arguing with me and get in the shower."

"I need to use the bathroom first. I'm not risking a UTI just because you're impatient."

He shook his head, but got into the shower without me. Thankfully the toilet was hidden behind a tile wall that divided the bathroom. After I finished I stepped into the shower and joined him. Heat enveloped me as the water cascaded over my head. My muscles sang with joy. I hadn't realized how sore I was until now.

I was no longer a virgin.

It was strange, but not strange. There was no pain other than a dull ache. That, and the memory of his body moving inside mine. The piercing had been a revelation. *Yum*.

He swept my wet hair to the side and pressed a soft kiss to my shoulder. Goosebumps raced up and down my body. I was quickly coming to learn that my husband was both tender and tough. Rough and gentle. Thoughtful and smart. He was a mix of many things, not only what he showed to the world, and I found it fascinating.

But we had things to discuss.

"Tell me what Virga has on you."

His whole body locked up and he moved away, starting to clean himself with brutal efficiency. It was obvious what he was doing. Sighing, I reached for the shampoo. "Why won't you trust me?"

"Because I don't trust anyone."

"Giacomo, we just had sex."

He did that lip curl thing that happened right before he was about to say something cruel. I was proven right when he snapped, "I don't need to trust a woman to stick my dick inside her."

Ouch. "What about to come inside her and have a baby with her?"

"I didn't come inside you."

"It's only a matter of time before you have to—unless you trust me to help you with whatever Virga is blackmailing you with."

"It doesn't matter. You can't help me, just like I can't help your father. Nothing can be done except eliminate Virga."

Uneasiness filled my chest as I searched his face. "Wrong. My father can be transferred someplace where Virga's men can't find him. Right now they're in his bedroom, playing cards and watching tv with him. It's terrifying."

Giacomo opened his mouth, then closed it, hesitating, and the uneasiness in my body compounded. "What?" I croaked. "Spit it out. What are you not wanting to tell me?"

"Emma," he said on an exhale. "You know how our world works. Virga's men can't get close to a man like your father unless . . ."

"Unless, what?"

"Unless your uncle allows it. Capisce?"

All the air left my lungs in a rush and I clutched at the wet tile. "No. You are saying . . . ? No. Absolutely not."

"Bambina, think about it. Your father has been protected this whole time, his brother running the business while no one suspects a thing. Now Virga finds out, takes you away and his men are allowed to be in the same room as Don Mancini. You know this doesn't happen without your uncle's involvement. It isn't possible."

"You're saying my uncle wants my father dead."

"Yes, but not immediately. Otherwise Roberto wouldn't still be breathing." Giacomo stepped under the spray to rinse, then said, "We deal in favors, Emma. Promises and alliances. Virga has made an arrangement of some kind with your uncle."

"Uncle Reggie and my father are close." I squirted some body wash into my hands and did a very quick rub down, then rinsed.

Giacomo held onto my shoulders, his thumbs tracing my collar bones. "Family can turn on each other, hurt each other, just as easily as anyone else. More so, sometimes."

"I know about your father and brother, but that's different."

"Don't be naive, Emma. There's no difference between our families except the last name. We all operate under the same code, which is only the strong survive."

Naive. That word scraped and raked across my chest to open old wounds. I was tired of people thinking I buried my head in the sand just because I saw the good in others. Just because I was *nice.*

And was he implying my father was weak?

"I don't want to talk about this. You don't want to trust me with your secret? Fine. But you don't get to make me feel worse about mine."

I edged around him and pushed the glass door open. I heard him shut off the water, but I was already grabbing a towel and leaving the room.

We were so done.

————

My microbiology classwork blurred in front of my eyes. I couldn't focus. For two days all I'd been thinking about was what Giacomo said in the shower.

"You know this doesn't happen without your uncle's involvement."

I nibbled my fingernail. Was he right? Was Uncle Reggie working with Virga? That would mean . . . .

It would mean that Uncle Reggie allowed Virga to take me to Sicily and marry me off to Giacomo. That Uncle Reggie allowed Virga's men on the property, in my father's bedroom.

And the worst part of all? It meant Uncle Reggie told Virga about my father's illness.

How could my uncle—my father's *brother*—do this? It was the worst kind of betrayal.

I couldn't believe it. I'd known Reggie my whole life. I played with his son, Dante, as a child. I tutored his daughter, Emelia, through trigonometry in high school. Family dinners, holidays, the lake house . . . a hundred memories of time spent together, proof of the affection between my father and his brother.

And this was how Uncle Reggie repaid him?

At first I thought there was no need for backstabbing, because my father would die soon. Uncle Reggie was the next Mancini in line, seeing as how my father has no heir.

But maybe Uncle Reggie wasn't the heir. Maybe this whole thing was about what happened when Papà died.

The logical choice to absorb the Toronto business was Fausto, my sister's husband. But I couldn't exactly call up Don Ravazzani and have a chat about things. *Hey, Fausto. I know we've never really had a one-on-one conversation, but how's it going?*

No, I had to go through my sister. Maybe she'd know if promises were made.

I glanced at my phone. Frankie had three small kids to deal with, including a two-month-old. I wasn't sure she'd have time for me.

It was worth a try. Besides, I was overdue to check in with her anyway.

I pulled up my older sister's contact, then hit the button. It rang twice before I heard her voice through the tiny speaker. There were kids yelling in the background. "Girl, you are so fucking lucky you called me today. I was about to send a small army into Peru to check up on you."

I rolled my eyes. "It's been three days, Frankie. Hardly worth invading a country over."

I heard her tell someone she'd be right back, then she said, "Emma, Let's switch to video. I want to see your cute little face."

I was sitting in Giacomo's office, the one he never used. It hardly looked like a medical tent in Peru. "My signal isn't strong enough for that," I lied. "And I only have a minute."

"Damn it. We need to get you better equipment out there. Maybe I'll ask Fausto to send a satellite truck there just for your own personal use."

"Yeah, that wouldn't be awkward at all," I said sarcastically. "How are you? How are the kids?"

"I'm exhausted, and the kids are living their best lives and being spoiled by their father. Basically, the usual."

Fausto did spoil Rafe and Noemi, which I knew was the source of many arguments in the Ravazzani household. "And the baby?"

"Marcello is fine," she said about their youngest son. "He's so chill. The exact opposite of Rafe in every way."

Gia and I had both gone to Siderno for the birth. Frankie had handled it like a pro. My sister was born to be a mother.

"But enough about my boring life," my sister said. "I want to hear about all the lives you're saving in Peru."

"It's research, nothing exciting. I spend most of my time in a lab." Lies, lies and more lies. I hated not telling the truth.

"Well, I'm very proud of you. I know it's exactly what you want to be doing."

God, that made the lying a thousand times worse. Tears sprung to my eyes, emotion overwhelming me. On top of the guilt weighing down my soul, my period started yesterday. Yes, my hormones were all over the place, but there was now a ticking clock counting down to a pregnancy I didn't want. I had to find a way out of this.

"Thank you," I forced out. "I hope Papà is doing okay in Toronto without me."

"I'm sure he's fine," she said tightly, the same borderline-angry tone she used whenever the topic of our father was broached. "You need to live your own life, Em."

"I know, but he's getting older and he has a lot on his plate."

"He's a grown man. He'll survive."

No, actually. He wouldn't. I swallowed the lump in my throat. I wished Papà had let me tell Frankie and Gia about his condition. At least then I wouldn't have to carry this grief alone. "Do you think he talks to Fausto about business?"

Frankie snorted. "I have no idea. Fausto knows Roberto Mancini is a subject best avoided in this house." She paused. "Why do you ask?"

"Just wondering. God forbid anything happens to Papà, I don't want to be forced out onto the street by whoever takes over."

"That will never happen, Em. We'll protect you. Jesus, where is this coming from? Are you in some kind of trouble that I don't know about?"

"Stop worrying. Everything's fine. Maybe because you've just had a second boy, it made me wonder about who will take over for Papà. Because we're not sons."

"It can all go to Reggie or Dante, for all I care. I want nothing to do with Roberto or his business."

She never called our father Papà anymore. Only Robert, or Roberto when she was feeling Italian. She was still resentful over how he handled everything surrounding our mother's death, then breaking his promise about letting her attend university. They had a complicated relationship that was completely different from the one he and I shared. "What about one of your sons?"

I could almost hear her frowning as the question lingered. "I don't want my boys moving to Toronto. I want them living here, with me. I'll be worried enough when they're out working for—" Biting off whatever she'd been about to say, she exhaled shakily and gave a strained chuckle. "I'm still breastfeeding and my hormones are all over the place. Fuck, just the thought of my babies moving away . . . I can't handle it."

Great, now I'd made her cry. "I'm sorry. I shouldn't have brought it up."

"No, it's okay. You wouldn't be Emma if you weren't being inquisitive."

My phone buzzed with an incoming call. Papà's oncologist. "Oh, Frankie, I'm sorry. I have to go. I'll check in soon, okay?"

"Of course! Ti amo, mia bella sorellina."

"Love you, too. Hug the family for me. Ciao!"

I hung up and answered the incoming call. "Dr. Morrissey. Hello."

"Miss Mancini, hi. I hope I haven't caught you at a bad time."

Because he thought I was still in Toronto. "No, not at all. What's up?"

"I just got off the phone with your father, and as his medical proxy I thought you also had a right to know what's going on."

My stomach clenched, my body bracing itself for bad news. It reminded me of when I learned Papà first had cancer. "Yes, what is it?"

"The numbers I'm seeing in your father's blood work are concerning. He's resistant to coming to the hospital, however. So, I'd like to meet with you both and discuss what our next strategies might be."

"Do you mean a hospital stay to run more tests or to keep him there for palliative care?"

"I don't want to speculate. That's part of what I'd like to discuss."

The lump in my throat grew larger. Dr. Morrissey obviously believed my father didn't have much time left. We both knew it was the only reason to admit him at this point. "You know why moving him is difficult." I had confided in Dr. Morrissey regarding my father's identity when the cancer was first diagnosed.

"Yes, I'm aware. But we must do what's best for his care, even if there are challenges. If you choose to keep him at home, that's your decision. But it's best if we talk through the pros and cons."

"I understand." I steadied myself with a few deep breaths. "I'm traveling right now, so maybe a video conference would be better."

"That works, though I'd prefer in person. But if we can't, I understand. It's best to have these conversations sooner rather than later."

I told him I'd speak to my father about a time, then I hung up. I stared at my phone for a long time, eyes blurry, feeling the weight of it all on my shoulders. I had no answers, no plan. Just the knowledge that I was alone.

CHAPTER TWENTY-THREE

Giacomo

I poured a large amount of whisky into a glass and sat on a stool at the kitchen counter. Cazzo, I was tired. Over the last few days Zani and I had been searching for any sign of Virga, but no one had seen him. Not along the coast, not in any of his usual haunts. I'd visited every place I could think of on the island, and talked to anyone connected to the capo. No trace of Don Virga existed anywhere.

Worse, the boy at Mirabella, the one fucking my sister? He wasn't just anyone. His name was Federico Chiellini, and he was the son of another powerful Cosa Nostra family. This meant I couldn't beat the shit out of him or kill him.

Fuck, fuck, fuck.

Federico's father had sent the boy to Mirabella eight months ago to get off heroin. Still, I wondered if Virga had nudged Federico in Viv's direction to seduce her and fill her head with nonsense. Anything was possible. I swallowed half the glass and let the liquor dull my irritation.

If that wasn't enough, I had other troubles. Emma and I had avoided each other since the night we fucked. She was probably still angry, but I wouldn't lie to her. There was no chance in hell her uncle would allow Virga's men to have run of the place without an ulterior motive. And this likely meant Reggie leaked the information about Mancini's condition to Virga in the first place.

That meant Reggie Mancini was my problem, too.

I finished my drink and went to pour another. Once I had a full glass I checked in the refrigerator to see what Sal left for me. Tagliatelle with bolognese was wrapped and waiting, so I took it out and reheated it.

As I ate, I checked football scores on my phone until it rang with an incoming call. *Theresa.* I didn't want to answer, but I owed her an explanation on why I had dodged her calls.

I answered. "Ciao, Theresa."

"Fucking finally. Why haven't you called me back?"

I wiped my mouth with a napkin. "Mi dispiace. I've been busy."

"Cazzata. That isn't how things work between us. We've always been honest with each other. Give me the truth."

"I . . ." She was right. I couldn't lie. It wasn't fair to her. "I am trying to sort things out with my wife."

The silence stretched frostily, and it was like the air cracked and froze between us. "You're *married?*"

"Yes."

"When?"

"Theresa—"

"When did you get married, Mo?"

"A few hours before the last time I saw you."

She inhaled sharply. "You cheated on your wife with me? You cheated—"

"No, Theresa," I tried to talk over her.

"—on your wife with me! Pezzo di merda!"

"Wait, calm down."

"No, I won't calm down. You know how I feel about cheating, how I avoid married men. You should have told me."

I dragged a hand down my face. She was right. I should have. But at the time I wanted nothing to do with Emma. "Our marriage wasn't like that. It was arranged. I didn't want it."

"It doesn't matter. You said words before God."

"You know I don't believe in that."

"But I do—and your wife probably does, too! I can't believe you did that to me. To *her*."

"Bella, listen—"

"No, I won't listen. Lose my number. Don't ever call me again. You and your big dick can find some other woman to suck on it, I don't care. All I know is that it won't be me."

She disconnected and I tossed my phone onto the counter. Cristo, what a mess.

"She didn't sound happy with you."

My head snapped up as Emma wandered into the kitchen, her frame clad in tiny sleep shorts and a tank top. I immediately zeroed in on her nipples, which were visible through the thin fabric. "Eavesdropping?"

"You weren't exactly trying to be quiet. Was that your mantenuta?"

Unsurprising that she knew the Italian word for mistress. After all, her older sister had been one until Ravazzani married her. "It was Theresa, but she isn't my mantenuta."

"Could've fooled me." She took a carton of chocolate gelato out of the freezer. Then she found a spoon. "You called her bella."

"Italian men call everyone bella. It means nothing."

"I'll be sure to remember that." Leaning against the far counter, she opened the carton and dug her spoon inside. "Are you still sleeping with her?"

I pushed the empty plate of food away and went for my whisky. "I haven't been with her since the night of our wedding."

"And I'm supposed to believe you?"

"I don't care what you believe, but it's true. Why do you think she was yelling at me?"

She slipped a spoonful of gelato in her mouth, her lips pulled across the metal in the most delicious way. "Are there other women?"

I tried to follow the thread of the conversation when all I wanted to do was taste the chocolate on her tongue. "No."

I watched her shoulders relax. Was she jealous? I threw back the rest of my drink and stood. "You seem relieved, *piccola vergine*."

"I'm not a virgin anymore, as you well know."

She looked adorable in her pajamas, rumpled hair, and plump kiss-able lips. Unable to resist her, I closed the distance between us. When I reached her I braced my hands on the cabinet above her head, caging her in. "There are other places you haven't taken me yet, places that I'm dying to claim."

"Those places will have to wait," she whispered, her cheeks turning pink. "Until after."

After I gave her a baby.

My cock began to thicken as dark primal thoughts swirled in my brain. Fucking Emma had been so much better than I expected. I'd been obsessed with memories of it the last few days, reliving the way she'd taken my cock inside her for the very first time. This woman was *mine*.

And coming inside her felt forbidden, something I longed to do but knew I shouldn't.

Which made it all the more appealing. My rebellious side, the one my father tried to beat out of me, rose up to whisper in her ear. "Are you eager for it? Are you ready for me to pump you full of come?"

Her mouth parted slightly as her eyelids fluttered closed. "Holy smokes, you are dirty."

"You like it. Now answer my question."

"You're the one who refused last time."

I ran my nose along her cheekbone, nuzzling her and letting her feel my breath on her skin. "Do you need it, ragazzaccia?"

I heard her swallow. "Not tonight. My period is just finishing."

Her period.

The news sank into my belly and a flurry of conflicting emotions went with it. We were out of time. We had to start trying for a baby in the next few days or else we might miss our chance for this month. And there was only this month and next month. Two attempts to get Virga away from my sister and Emma's father. Minchia!

I started to pull away, but Emma grabbed onto my shirt. "Giacomo, wait. I can't lose him. I have so little time left with my father and I need every second. If I get pregnant, then Virga will leave Papà alone and I can go be with him while he dies. Don't you understand? I can't waste any more time."

"What are you saying?"

She put her palm on my jaw and stroked the rough whiskers, sending little sparks into my blood. "I need to do this. I need to get back to Toronto."

"You think I'm right. About your uncle." I could see the truth in her steady brown gaze.

"I do. Which means I have a whole host of problems there that I need to deal with."

No, I would be the one to deal with Virga and both Mancini brothers. Did she honestly think I'd allow my pregnant wife to walk into that situation?

Pregnant wife. I stared into her wide, doe-like eyes. This woman was sacrificing her future, her body for her father. I was doing this for Viv, but it wasn't the same. Emma was bringing a child into the world, *our* child, and though I swore I never wanted a son or daughter, everything had now changed.

We were both pushed into a corner, but this wasn't finished. Boxing taught me that sometimes you took a punch in order to fight back even harder. So I would get Emma pregnant, then go on the offensive and take Virga down.

She ate another bite of gelato. "I also have to deal with the university. They're threatening to fail me."

I reared back, surprised. "Are your grades suffering?" I knew she'd been doing online learning to keep up. Was it not working?

"It's the labs. They're telling me I can't do them remotely, only in-person." She scooped up more gelato then set the carton on the counter. "It's nothing. I'll figure it out. But I need to do it soon."

I made a mental note about this as I rested my forehead against hers. "We are doing this, no?"

"I can't see how we have a choice."

"You are a good daughter, Emma Buscetta. I'm not sure your father deserves it."

She moved her hand between our bodies, lower and lower, until she palmed my cock through my jeans. "Some studies show that peak male fertility occurs after one or two days after not ejaculating. So . . ."

Lust spiked like a fever in my blood at her words, and my balls constricted. "You need me to save it up for you? Is that what you need, bambina?"

She bit her lip in that innocent, embarrassed way that always made my dick hard. "Will that be a problem?"

"Only if I'm around you. Or thinking about fucking you. Or smelling you in my house."

A soft chuckle escaped her lips. "You'll need to keep busy outside the house for a few days, then."

I rocked my semi into her hand. "Two. That's all you get." Even that would be a struggle. "But I suggest you prepare yourself. When I finally give you everything I've stored up, you'll be drowning in it."

I pushed off the cabinets, walked over to the counter, and adjusted myself in my jeans. This was going to be a long two fucking days.

"You don't have to leave now. You can stay and we'll watch a movie. Do you like gelato?"

Grabbing my phone and keys, I walked toward the back door. "I like pistachio, but Sal never buys it. And if I stay for a movie I'll fuck you, period or not."

"So where are you going?"

"To sleep at Zani's. See you in two days, wife."

———

"Minchia!" I slammed the phone down on the desk, frustration roiling inside me. We were in the back of Nino's auto dealership, trying to find Virga. The latest report of a sighting turned out to be another false lead.

Zani sat across from me. "Quit moping. We can still get him, but it'll take time."

Time was the one thing I didn't have. I stared at my hands, hating the powerlessness I felt. First my father, now Virga. Both had taken my choices away from me and I resented it.

I had to think of something different, something we've yet to try. Maybe it was time to use brains, not brawn.

"You're too dumb to be my consigliere," my brother had said. *"Just use your fists, Mo. That's what you're good for."*

Stronzo.

I might not be smart, but I knew how to keep fighting. And there was one avenue we hadn't tried yet. It was risky, possibly stupid, but I was desperate.

I focused on Zani. "What are the odds that Ravazzani told D'Agostino what happened in that meeting with Borghese and Virga?"

Zani's answer was instant. "Zero percent. The two hate each other. And D'Agostino would have told Gia Mancini. Didn't Emma say her sisters had no idea? No way her twin knew about the possibility of an arranged marriage and didn't warn Emma."

That was my assessment, as well. "Good. Let's ring D'Agostino. We'll ask for the help of his hackers."

To his credit, Zani didn't flinch. As a rule we didn't like working with the 'Ndrangheta. "You will owe him a favor in exchange. Are you sure you want to do this?"

"If anyone can locate Virga's yacht, it's him. There's no one we work with who has that kind of skill or resources. I'll gladly trade a favor for that. Place the call."

Zani took out one of our many burner phones. He looked up the contact for D'Agostino and dialed. A voice answered after the third ring. "Pronto."

"I am calling on behalf of Don Buscetta in Palermo," Zani said. "We need to speak with Don D'Agostino."

Silence.

Finally, a man said, "This is Vito D'Agostino. You can speak to me."

The oldest brother. But I didn't want the second-in-command. "Cut the shit and give me your brother," I snapped.

"Don Buscetta," a different voice said, a touch of amusement coloring the Neapolitan accent. "You are every bit as blunt as I've heard."

"Don D'Agostino, I assume?"

"You assume correctly. Now tell me why you are calling."

"I need someone found."

"Oh? And what does this have to do with me?"

"I would like to use your resources to do it."

"I see. Who is this person?"

Did he think I was so stupid? "I will tell you after you agree."

"That isn't how this works," he said calmly. "Palermo really is out of touch, eh, Vito?"

D'Agostino's brother chuckled and I gripped the edges of the desk and squeezed. The pain in my fingertips centered me, calmed me, and I let out a long breath. "Maybe I should call Siderno instead. Maybe your brother-in-law would be more amenable."

The reminder of Ravazzani worked. D'Agostino's voice turned hard. "You are the one who called me, Buscetta. I should hang up on your Sicilian ass and let you sort your own shit."

"I'm calling to ask for a favor. Which would mean I would owe a favor in return. If that means nothing to you . . . ."

"Is it true you once knocked out Clemente Russo?"

The abrupt change in topics caught me off guard, but then this was D'Agostino. He wasn't known for his stability. "Yes. We fought in Caserta when he was training for the Olympics. Seven rounds."

"Impressive. I used to go to his bouts. He was very good."

I was better, but had to stop fighting after my second concussion. And this was a pointless conversation. "So you will help me?"

"Find Virga, you mean?"

My eyes met Zani's, and I saw my own surprise reflected back at me. How had D'Agostino known? "I never said—"

"You never said it was him," he cut me off to say. "But there's only one reason you wouldn't go through your own people for this. It's because you can't."

"It's not only that. He's aboard his yacht, hiding on open water. You have some experience with this, no?" We all knew how he'd eluded Ravazzani all those years.

"And what makes you think I can find him?" D'Agostino asked.

"You have the best resources with satellites and shit. GPS, whatever the fuck. We've tried every other way I can think of and it's not working."

"Why would I help you?"

Because I'm married to your girlfriend's twin.

But I couldn't say that. D'Agostino and Ravazzani would try to take Emma from me, and I couldn't let that happen. "What do you want in exchange?"

"Not sure what you have, Buscetta. Siderno has taken everything of value from you."

The Sicilian drug trade. I would soon take it back, but for now it belonged to Ravazzani and the 'Ndrangheta. "Not everything."

"I have no interest in your guns."

"A favor to be determined, then?"

"Do I have your word?"

"You do."

"I'll think about it." He hung up.

Zani dropped the phone onto the ground and stepped on it, crushing it under the heel of his boot. "I hope we don't live to regret that."

So did I. "No matter what happens with my wife, I'm going to kill Virga as soon as we can find him."

His lips stretched into a wide grin. "You mean even if you get her pregnant and become a Papà?"

I shot him a dark look as I stood up. "Stop enjoying this, coglione."

"I can't help it. And if the roles were reversed, you'd be laughing your ass off at me."

Possibly, but I wouldn't let him off the hook by admitting it.

Pocketing my phone, I found my keys and started for the door. It was time to get my wife naked. My cock twitched in anticipation of the night ahead. "See you tomorrow."

"You know what I am looking forward to?" Zani called my back. "The birthday parties with D'Agostino and Ravazzani. Will you hire a clown and wear a tiny paper hat?"

"*Vaffanculo*, Francesco!"

I slammed the door on the sound of his laughter.

.

CHAPTER TWENTY-FOUR

Emma

"Sal, this is unbelievably good." I twirled the spaghetti on my fork. "And I usually don't like olives."

"Simple ingredients," he said, wiping his hands on a towel. "That is why Sicilian food is so good."

I didn't know if he was right, but I loved eating whatever Sal made. This pasta dish—sun-dried tomatoes, olives and capers, with bread-crumbs sprinkled on top—was to die for. "Have you always been able to cook?"

"I learned from my grandfather. He ran a restaurant near Teatro Massimo for years."

"I'm surprised you didn't take over." I took another bite and almost died from sheer happiness.

"My father had started working for the late Don Buscetta by that point. Don Gero, everyone called him. Anyway, life is too short for regrets. Wouldn't you say?"

Was he talking about my marriage and potential baby? "I'm not sure it's the same thing. I haven't had a choice in all this."

"Fate, signora, is a powerful force. Never underestimate it."

I didn't want to argue, but this wasn't fate. This was being forced to bring a child into the world with a man I hardly knew. It was terrifying to think about. "Will he be a good father?" I asked quietly.

Sal limped over, set his wine glass on the counter, and clasped my hand. "He is a good man, caring and compassionate. And he fights to protect those he loves. He will be an excellent father, bella, even if he did not have one himself."

Something eased inside my chest, a knot of anxiety I hadn't even known was there. "Thank you."

"But," Sal continued. "You should know that our world has rules and traditions. Not even Don Buscetta can skirt them."

"What do you—?"

The back door opened and Sal straightened, letting go of my hand. I looked over and watched as my husband stalked inside the kitchen. His hair was tousled, like he'd been running his hands through it, and his old t-shirt clung to the slopes and planes of his impressive chest and shoulders. Giacomo had a determined way of walking, all business in an effort to get from point A to point B, intent on the task at hand.

And right now that focus was squarely on me.

A rush of tingles broke out all over my body. He didn't spare a glance for Sal, just continued toward me, and I couldn't move. My heart thumped wildly in my chest, my breath stuck in my lungs. He was here.

And his intent was written all over his face. It was time.

He stopped beside me and put one hand on the back of my chair. The other came up to cradle my cheek. Energy poured off his frame to surround me, and he smelled like leather and the outdoors. "Have you finished your dinner, bambina?" he asked in a low rumble.

Swallowing, I nodded. The tiny lines around his eyes crinkled in amusement. "Va bene. You will need your strength for what I have planned for you."

Bending, he scooped me off the chair and lifted me into his arms. I exhaled in surprise, then threw my arms around his neck to hold on. I wanted to say I hated when he acted like a caveman, but I didn't. His displays of strength were super hot for reasons probably buried deep in my chromosomes.

Stupid genetics.

We went up the stairs. I expected him to take me to the gold bedroom where I'd been sleeping, but he went the other way. To the opposite wing of the big house. "Where are we going?"

"The first time I come inside you will be in my bed."

Between my legs swelled, arousal now throbbing in time with my heartbeat. Yep, genetics. There was no other explanation for why I liked the idea of it. But I did. I was so turned on that my skin felt both hot and cold, my body buzzing with anticipation.

"A decent man would not get hard thinking about shooting inside you, breeding *you."*

Had he been thinking about it the past two days? God knew I had. Almost every waking second.

We didn't speak as he pushed the door open and carried me inside. His room was small but neat, his bed made. I thought he'd put me on the bed, but he didn't. He set me on my feet in the middle of the floor, then went back to close the door.

I rubbed my arms, the need to fill the silence rising inside me. How was he so calm? I was a mess inside, arousal and nerves jumbled around in my muscles, so much that I couldn't stand still. "You know I'm probably not ovulating, right?" He turned and leaned against the closed door, but I kept talking. "It probably makes more sense for me to start taking my temperature and tracking any slight changes. That's how we'll know when I'm most fertile—"

"Emma."

"What?"

He reached down to unbuckle his belt. "Naked, now."

"Would that help to turn you on?"

"I've been hard for the last two days just thinking about fucking you. I don't need any help getting turned on." He yanked the leather free of the loops and dropped it on the floor. "What I need is to get my dick inside you as quickly as possible. So get fucking naked and help me out."

Oh.

Before I could comment, he whipped off his t-shirt and revealed all that glorious muscled, tattooed skin. Sweet Jesus, he was built. He was art come to life, the type of body that Michaelangelo would have sculpted. A warrior. A Greek god—

"Emma! Madonna, woman. Stop staring at me and get moving."

"I can't help it." I took off my tank top. "You're very distracting."

His eyes locked onto my breasts still encased in my bra as his fingers went to work on the buttons of his jeans. "Then let my dick distract your pussy, because I'm desperate."

"Is this because you didn't masturbate for two days?"

"No, mia piccola innocente." He shoved his jeans off his hips and stepped out of them. The bulge in his briefs was enormous, the thick ridge of his erection evident through the thin cloth. "This is because I can't stop thinking about fucking you again. Now, hurry up."

I unfastened my shorts and shimmied out of them. When I removed my bra Giacomo pushed off the door and came toward me. I didn't have the chance to do anything else before he was on me, pulling me toward him and slamming his mouth onto mine. His hands cupped my butt cheeks and pressed my pelvis against his shaft. It sent a wave of heat through me and I rolled my hips, seeking friction.

"Minchia!" he broke off to curse. "I can't wait."

He took my mouth again, his tongue finding mine, and I ran my hands all over his chest and ribs. Then I was up off my feet and being carried to the bed. My back met the mattress. Still kissing me, he settled his hips between my legs and rubbed his erection on my clit. My body softened under his, all my resistance relinquished, ready for what was to come.

Holy smokes, how I wanted it.

He ground down and we both moaned, two writhing animals caught in heat. I couldn't think straight, my hands clutching at him to bring him closer. His tongue flicked at mine, our breath turning the small space between our skin humid. There was no fear or trepidation in my head, only longing and desire.

His arm lowered between us and I felt him shove his briefs off. Hot skin met mine, and his piercing dug into my belly. He broke off to kiss my jaw, then down my throat. Rough words coasted over my skin, Italian pleas and curses, while his hips rocked back and forth. "Are you wet? Can I get inside you now?"

"Yes. Please, hurry."

He rose up on his knees. Spreading me wide, he grabbed my panties in both hands and tore them off my body. Just shredded the cloth like it was nothing, and I swear my nether region quivered in response. Then he fisted his cock and notched the head to my entrance. "This will be fast and hard, bambina. Then we'll go again and it will be better for you, I swear."

He shoved forward, breaching me, and I gasped at the immense pressure. He was thick and hard, the piercing sliding through my wetness, and I closed my eyes tightly. So good. So, so good. Now I knew why women lost their minds when they found a man like Giacomo. Good grief.

"You feel that?" He nudged forward, invading more. "Your pussy is welcoming me. It knows what is about to happen, that I am going to make her very, very happy."

He withdrew slightly, then slammed all the way in. I arched my back, both trying to get away and bring him deeper inside. It was so much, but not what I needed. "Oh, God."

Leaning forward, he covered my body with his, bracing himself on his elbows. His mouth was right by my ear, so I could feel every breath, every grunt, as he began thrusting inside me. "Fuck, you are so wet. So soft. I have thought of nothing else but fucking you for two days."

"Me, too," I breathed. "I masturbated twice thinking about it."

He groaned and his hips moved faster. "That is the hottest thing I've ever heard. Were you imagining all of the come I stored up for you? How I'm going to give you a baby in the next few days?"

"Yes," I breathed.

"I can't . . ." His cock sawed in and out of me, his movements growing frantic. "Cazzo, I need to . . . Madre di dio!"

He swelled inside me and his muscles clenched, his entire body going stiff. He pressed his face into my throat, like he was trying to burrow under my skin. I could feel him pulsing, coming, pouring himself into me. I held on, loving that I could make this strong and powerful man lose his control.

He slumped forward, his chest heaving like he'd run a race, but only for a few seconds. Then he began sliding back and forth inside me again, slowly, like he was testing the feeling. "I've never come inside a woman before," he murmured into my ear. "We are so slick together, a beautiful mess. Do you like it, bambina?"

I didn't know about the mess part, but I was really liking the way his piercing dragged across my g-spot. "Mmmm," I hummed. "Keep going."

"I will make you come, do not worry. I just want to feel the two of us around my cock for a little longer. Can you tell how much I gave you? It was liters, mia piccola moglie."

He was still mostly hard, the orgasm not really slowing him down in the least. I dragged my nails over his shoulders and up into his hair. He trembled under my touch, and I knew he wasn't immune to what was happening between us. He got off on the idea of it, too. Emboldened, I whispered, "I need every drop. Per favore, mia grande marito."

Hissing, he snapped his hips forward. I moaned loudly, which mixed with his shout of, "Minchia!"

He withdrew suddenly and crawled down between my legs. "I need to see it," he said as he settled between my thighs. "Then I'm going to taste it."

My clit throbbed at his filthy words, knowing exactly what he meant. He was so dirty, so raw, and it somehow flipped a switch inside me to turn me on like nothing else.

With his thumbs, he spread apart my labia and inspected me. "You are swollen and red. Fuck, that is hot." He bent and sucked my clit into his mouth. It was like he jolted me with electricity. I nearly levitated off the bed, the pleasure was so intense.

"My greedy wife," he crooned and kissed my clit gently, almost romantically. "She needs my tongue so badly."

"Yes, I do," I panted. "Please, don't tease me."

He hummed in the back of his throat and moved lower. "Look at this pussy. *Bedda matri!* I can see my come dripping out of it. You are drenched with me." He slid one finger, then another into my opening. "I want to push it all back inside you. Maybe I will buy a plug for you, so I can keep all my come inside this beautiful cunt."

The idea of walking around with a plug in my vagina, just to keep his come in there . . . I contracted around his fingers, my body squeezing reflexively.

"Oh, she likes that," he whispered darkly. "My woman likes that a lot."

Growling, he withdrew his fingers slowly. I wasn't ready for him to stop, so I grabbed his arm. "No, not yet. Please!"

"Calm down, ragazzaccio. I want to take a photo. Then I'll make you come."

He eased off the bed and walked over to his jeans. I couldn't help but watch his ass flex as he bent to find his phone. When he turned, I was mesmerized by the sight of his cock, hanging thickly between his legs, the shaft glistening with my juices, the piercing decorating his skin. How did he get anything done with something so magnificent to play with attached to his body? I bet every woman he'd ever slept with still fingered herself to the memories of him.

He climbed onto the mattress and unlocked his phone. "Spread, Emma. Now shift to the right so the light can catch all my come seeping out of your hole."

My mouth dried out, arousal spiking in my blood, and I did as he directed. He pressed the button, taking photos, but I didn't complain. I didn't even care if he captured my face in the shot, I was so out of my head with lust.

"Look." He held the phone up to my eyes. "Look at how fucking hot we are together."

I saw my entrance, wet with the two of us, and I had to admit that it was sexy. It was like we were made to fit together, and the result was our juices mixed on my skin. But I'd been wondering over the last few days if this was something he did all the time. "Do you have lots of photos of naked women on your phone?"

Dark eyes cut to mine sharply. "I only have photos of one naked woman on my phone—my innocent wife. Mia verginella."

"Really?"

He held out his phone for me to take. "Would you like to see for yourself?"

"No, I believe you. You tell the truth, even when people don't want to hear it."

He tossed his phone onto the floor. "That's right, Emma. For better or worse you are stuck with my honesty."

A reminder that we had taken vows. He was my husband at the moment, and we were going to have a child together.

It was like he didn't want to give me the chance to obsess over this thought, because he leaned forward and licked my entrance, swiping up the two of us with his tongue. "Cazzo, that's nice. Your pussy tastes even better with my come on it."

I arched my back, desperate for his touch. "Please, marito."

Another long drag of his tongue. "Don't worry, bambina. We are going to make sure you come a lot. It improves the chances of conception."

He wasn't wrong, but how had he stumbled across this information? "How do you know that?"

"You aren't the only one who does their research when it comes to anatomy."

A rush of wetness flooded my pussy. Goodness, the idea of him doing this kind of research was so flipping hot. I groped for his head, desperate to get his mouth where I needed it. "Stop teasing me. I'm too turned on to take it."

He chuckled and placed my hand on the back of his head. "Then tell me to eat you out, wife."

"Eat me out, husband."

Thank sweet baby Jesus, he didn't make me wait. He used his lips and mouth to create the perfect suction, his tongue lashing my clit. Large hands slid under my buttocks to lift up my hips, holding me to his mouth like a feast, and I knew this had the added bonus of forcing all his semen into my uterus. The knowledge wound me tighter, my pleasure spiraling like a corkscrew, and I wrapped my fingers around his hair to hold on.

His thumb slid into my pussy, stretching me, and I couldn't take it anymore. Sensation swallowed me, the orgasm like a freight train, and I shook uncontrollably on the bed until I finally crested. "My god," I wheezed. "I don't know how you do that to me."

He rose up in a blink and I caught a glimpse of his rock-hard erection before I felt him slide inside me once more. My nerve endings sang out in pure bliss, and I closed my eyes, swept away on the tide of euphoria.

"I don't know, either," he said, driving deep. "But I'm about to do it again."

————

It was sometime in the middle of the night when we took a break.

My husband went to the kitchen and brought back a whole tray of snacks. It included meats and cheeses, cold pasta, and Sal's florentine cookies that I loved. As I reached for the pasta, he poured us glasses of sparkling water. "Drink," he told me. "I need you to stay hydrated."

Me? He'd already come twice. "I think you're the one who needs to stay hydrated."

The edge of his mouth lifted in a satisfied smirk as he stretched his long legs on the tiny mattress. "Don't worry, Emmalina. I will always have enough come for you."

I blushed at this version of my name, a form of endearment with Italians. "Even when your prostate is enlarged in your later years?"

He shook his head and popped an olive into his mouth. "Only my wife would be worried about my prostate after I've fucked her all night."

"I didn't say I was worried," I hedged. "But I know the statistics. You shouldn't neglect your prostate."

"You can massage my prostate any time."

Now that surprised me. "Really?" I searched his face. "I would think a big, strong Italian man like you would be squeamish about backdoor play."

"No, I am not squeamish, as long as you don't call it 'backdoor play' ever again." He took a long drink of water. "If you want to finger or fuck my ass, it's yours, bambina."

Fuck his . . . . *Oh*. "Have you ever let someone do that?"

"Yes."

My eyes went big. I needed every detail. I wasn't jealous, only extremely curious. "When? How? What did it feel like? Was it a man or a woman?"

Groaning, he flopped back onto the bed and threw a forearm over his eyes. "I should have known better than to tell you this now. This is all you'll want to talk about for the rest of the night."

"You can't drop a bomb on me like that then expect me to forget it." I nudged his leg with my toe. "Start talking, babe."

He sighed heavily and dropped his arm. "It was when I was twenty-two and traveling in Spain. I was in a boxing competition there. I met an older woman and she took me home one night. It was a dildo, and yes, I loved it."

Fascinating. This man was like an onion. "And not since?"

"Theresa used a finger now and again."

According to the internet, not every man was thrilled about anal. Yet I'd met plenty of emergency room doctors, and they all told tales about heterosexual men sticking very inappropriate, sometimes dangerous, objects in their rectum. I presumed this was because society taught straight men to feel shame surrounding stimulating their prostate.

But Giacomo wasn't ashamed about liking it.

"You are different than what I expected," I admitted.

"You thought I was stupid, you mean." His voice had taken on an edge I didn't understand.

"No, I never thought you were stupid. You're very smart. But you're also caring and gentle, and into having your prostate massaged."

He laughed, the harsh lines of his face easing. "Fair enough." Then he sobered. "You're not what I expected, either."

"How so?"

"You're young, but mature beyond your years. Easy to talk to. Your sisters have reputations as ball-busters, but that's not you. You're calm and steady."

"Boring."

Rolling toward me, he propped up on one arm. "I didn't say that. You could've thrown a fit over being brought here and married against your will. But you didn't. You handled it like an adult. And I'm grateful that you did, because I don't like drama."

"Would you have sent me back to Toronto if I threw a fit?"

"No, I would've locked you in your room."

I didn't believe him for a second. The man who punched a wall and jerked off on a bedsheet to preserve my virginity would not have locked me away. "Sure you would have."

He smiled at me, an actual smile, and I could feel my chest expanding with emotion. Something dangerous was happening inside me, a depth of feeling, a tenderness I could not allow myself to possess. Not now, not this man.

I looked away and tried to rein in my stupid hormones.

He grabbed a few slices of prosciutto and rolled it around a chunk of parmesan. "Oh, I talked to your school. Doing your lab work remotely won't be a problem any longer."

I froze, mid-chew. Giacomo talked to my school? About my labs? "Wait, what?"

"You heard me. I took care of it."

"How?"

"By making a big fucking donation to the science department." The edge of his mouth kicked up. "They'll let you do whatever the fuck you want now."

I stared at him, my mind trying to wrap itself around this information. I never threw my father's name or money around on campus, instead preferring to get ahead on merit. But how could I complain about Giacomo's interference when his donation would fund research and improve facilities? Ultimately it would do a lot of good for many people.

"I don't know what to say. Thank you." Leaning over, I sealed my mouth to his and gave him a long, deep kiss.

"Prego," he whispered when we parted. "I can't solve all your problems, bambina, but I will do my best to make you happy."

Oh, boy. The giddiness currently dizzying my mind could not be good. But I couldn't deny the warmth settling into my bones as I stared at him, a sense of rightness I'd never experienced before. I wanted to curl up next to him and stay there forever.

He gazed back at me, but I couldn't read his thoughts. Was he as perplexed by what was happening between us as I was?

Finally, he pushed up, took the tray of food and set it on his dresser. "Time for bed."

"Okay." I scooted to the edge of the mattress and reached for my bra and t-shirt. Where were my shorts?

"What are you doing?"

"I'm going back to my room."

"Why?"

Hugging my clothing to my chest, I straightened. "Because you said it's time for bed. I assumed you wanted to sleep alone."

"I don't. I want to sleep with you. Allora," he said and motioned to the bed.

Another firework in my chest, another burst of giddiness, and I bit my lip to keep from grinning. "Is this in case you need your prostate massaged at some point in the night?"

He chuckled and rubbed his eyes. "Get in bed and shut up, moglie."

Dropping my bundle of clothing, I climbed into his bed and buried myself beneath the covers. It was going to be a tight squeeze but I didn't care. "I like your room," I told him as he crawled in next to me.

"You do?"

"I do. I can tell you're comfortable here."

He settled behind me and pulled my back to his front. He was better than a weighted blanket, surrounding me with heat and pressure. It was nice.

"My father didn't like this side of the house. That meant it was my favorite."

How sad. I wanted to know more about his childhood, his family. "I don't think I would've liked your father."

"He was a stronzo. No one liked him."

"Not even your brother?"

"My brother was an even bigger stronzo. They were like two beans in a pod."

"Peas."

"Cosa?"

"Two peas in a pod."

He kissed the back of my head. "So smart, my bambina."

The use of the word "my" wasn't lost on me, and I melted into the mattress. "Have you ever had a woman in your room before?"

"You are the first. Fitting, no?"

"Why? Because I'm your wife?"

His thick thigh wedged between my legs and he pressed closer. "Because I was the first man to touch your pussy, to lick it and fuck it." He sank his teeth into the back of my neck and rocked his hips against my backside. "I have laid claim to you."

I pressed my lips together, trying to contain the happiness I felt. I shouldn't find his barbarism so thrilling, but I did. "You make me sound like a castle, or something a knight would win in the spoils of a war."

He exhaled heavily into my hair, then found my free hand and threaded our fingers together. "You, Emma Buscetta, are my reward for the cruelty and misery I endured in this house. You are the only good thing to live under this roof for almost two decades."

I fell asleep with a sappy grin on my face.

CHAPTER TWENTY-FIVE

Giacomo

Steam filled the glass enclosure as the hot water pounded my back. I leaned against the tile and stretched out my sore muscles. Making babies was hard work. My body felt like I went eleven rounds last night.

I left Emma sleeping in my bed. She looked too peaceful there to wake up, even if my dick had demanded attention. Maybe I needed a bigger bed. Then Emma could sleep with me every night, instead of in my father's old room.

The glass door clicked and I turned to see my wife step into the shower. Her hair was loose around her shoulders, her breasts high and firm. The nipples were already furled into little points and it made me want them in my mouth.

"Hi," she said shyly. "I hope you don't mind if I get in, too."

"Ciao, bambina." I reached for her, my fingers sliding over the smooth soft skin of her hips. I kissed her mouth long and hard. "You look good enough to eat this morning."

She skimmed her hands over my biceps and shoulders. "So do you."

My cock grew heavy, thickening, at both her proximity and the idea of sliding into her mouth. "You like my muscles."

"Of course I do. If you ever posted workout videos online, you would have millions of followers."

"I don't care about followers, but you are more than welcome to watch me workout."

Her lips curled into a teasing smile, eyes twinkling playfully. "Can I record you? And before you say no, you have lots of photos of me. So it's only fair."

I chuckled and kissed her nose. "You can take all the photos and videos you want."

"Oh, good. They'll only be for me, I swear."

"I know. Tell me, will you watch them while you touch yourself?"

She bit her lip. "Maybe."

Dai, she was killing me.

She traced one of my nipples with her fingertip. "Will you teach me how to box?"

That wasn't what I was expecting her to say. "Why?"

"Because it's good exercise. I've been running in your gym, but I thought boxing together might be fun." She squeezed my biceps. "I'd get to see you sweat and your muscles flexing. Yum."

My groin tightened and I was so, so hard. Bracing my hands on the tile above her, I pushed my hips forward and let her feel me. "We are going to fuck in this shower."

"Are you sure?" She glanced around. "Is there enough room?"

"To fuck you? Bambina, have some faith in your man."

She moved her hand lower until she fisted my shaft. Her eyelids went hooded as she stroked me. "I don't want you to hurt yourself, marito."

This girl, *fuck*. I loved when she called me that. I held her close, one hand on her hip and the other around the side of her neck. Each sweet tug of her hand sent pleasure arrowing down to my toes. She pulled gently on the piercing, giving me a delicious bite of pain, and I dropped my forehead against hers and moaned. I couldn't take much more of this.

"I want in your mouth," I rasped. "Get on your knees and suck me, ragazzaccia."

"Okay, but don't, you know. In my mouth."

"Come?" I angled to block the water with my back. "Don't worry. I will give your pussy what it needs. Now, hurry."

She started to lower to her knees and I grabbed her arm to stop her. "Wait." Opening the glass door, I took the towel off the rack, then folded and dropped it onto the shower tile. "Kneel, mia verginella."

Gracefully, she lowered herself to the ground, placing her knees on the wet towel. The hot water stung my shoulders, but all I could see was Emma, clasping my dick and shuffling forward to get closer. She licked her lips then began pressing soft kisses to the crown. When her sweet tongue flicked the piercing my knees actually trembled. I braced my hands on the sides of the shower and angled my hips toward her face. "I will spank you if you keep teasing me."

Her lips curved, but she finally opened her mouth and drew me inside. *Fuck.* It was hot and tight, her tongue sliding over my skin to create slick pressure, and I had to tighten my muscles to keep from coming right then. "Sì, sì. *Ciucciami.*"

She understood, sucking harder, and my hips rocked until I bumped the back of her throat. I saw her wince, probably from the piercing, which made most blow jobs difficult. I withdrew slightly. "Just use your tongue everywhere."

Pulling off my dick, she said, "You don't need to be gentle with me."

"I don't need to hurt you to get off. I want you to love this as much as I do."

"I do. Don't worry."

She swallowed me again, this time taking me deep. She moved back and forth, the tight heat causing my muscles to coil as the feeling intensified. Her eyes never left mine and watching this sweet girl on her knees, her mouth full of my cock, lips stretched around my thickness, was something I'd never tire of.

I was becoming addicted to her.

She tortured me for another minute before I pulled out of her mouth. I lifted my cock up and jerked it slowly. "Now my balls. They need you."

The smirk she gave me twisted something inside my belly, a fierce emotion I'd never experienced before. I suddenly knew that I'd never refuse her anything. I would lay the world at this woman's feet, if she asked.

Her first and her last.

Plush lips kissed the delicate skin of my sac. Her eyes were closed now, and she moved over every millimeter of each orb, kissing them reverently.

"That's it," I crooned. "Dio, that feels good."

She switched to licking, little flicks of her tongue that swirled and massaged, and my hand moved faster on my cock, pumping harder as the pleasure built. I couldn't look away. She was so beautiful, so pure. I didn't deserve her, but I sure as fuck wasn't giving her up.

"Suck on them," I ordered, my voice barely audible over the rushing water.

Emma obliged, drawing each weight into her mouth and sliding her tongue over it. It was so incredibly sexy, her hair and skin wet, droplets running along her tits. She looked so young, yet she worked my balls like a seasoned pro. I couldn't take it any more.

I put my free hand on her head to stop her, but I kept her face in front of my groin. "Give each of my balls a final kiss, bambina. Thank them for all the come they're about to give you."

Leaning in, she pressed a kiss to each orb. "Grazie," she whispered reverently, and her compliance made my cock throb, desperate to get inside her.

"Stand up and turn around." I helped her to her feet. "This will be hard and fast. Hold onto the tile and present me with your pussy."

When she faced the wall, she tilted her hips up and put her ass out. "Like this?"

"So fucking perfect." I lined the head of my cock up at her entrance. Slick heat met my skin. "I hope you are wet, because I need to get inside you." I shoved in, and the clamp of her cunt around the head caused my vision to blur. "Minchia!"

"Oh god, Mo. Yes, more."

I hung my head, took deep breaths, and tried not to spill right then. When the urge to come receded, I eased in with little pulses of my hips. She was very wet, but her pussy had to be sore from last night. "Just relax. I'm going to give my cock to you."

Before I could stop her, she pushed back and fucked herself all the way onto my dick. Fire shot down my spine and along the backs of my thighs. "Fuck, Emma!" Then I couldn't stop for all the money in the world. My hips began to piston, my cock dragging in and out of her cunt, the slap of our wet skin echoing in the tiny space.

"It feels so good," she said over her shoulder. "Your piercing is hitting just the right spot. God! Don't stop."

Bracing my feet, I pumped faster, my hands wrapped around her hips. I panted, my body focused on one purpose, one goal. Nothing else. Each thrust was a jolt of pleasure, the grip of her body pure heaven. I belonged to her wholly and completely at that moment.

"Are you ready for me, bambina? Are you ready for more of my come inside you?"

"Oh, god. Please, Mo. Please." Her hands scratched at the tile, like she was barely hanging on.

Grabbing her hair, I pulled her upright so I could talk in her ear. "You're going to take my load like a good girl, no? And I'm going to put a baby inside you."

One hand found my leg and she dug her nails into my thigh. "Oh, shit."

She never cursed, so I knew she was getting close. "That's right. You like that idea. No condom, no birth control. Just me, coming inside you." She moaned almost pitifully, so I put my hand between her legs and stirred her clit with my fingers. "You like that I'm giving you my seed, that you have no choice but to make a baby for me. You are *mine*, Emma."

That did it. Her pussy clamped down, the walls strangling my cock, and then she was trembling and shaking in my arms. The pressure was too much and I started coming, my body emptying into hers, hot jets pulsing rhythmically inside her. Filling her.

"Cazzo," I hissed, my hands tightening on her breasts, squeezing, as I rode out the storm. I poured into her, jets shooting deep into her pussy. I wasn't thinking about family or babies or Virga—only the hot clasp of her, the way she felt in my arms. Her sweet moans and slick taste. How I wanted to drown myself in her until I never recovered.

It ended all too soon. I panted and tried to keep on my feet, all while holding her upright. Neither one of us moved for a long minute. "*Gesù cristu*," I wheezed, stirring my softening cock inside her. "That was good."

She slumped against the shower wall. "Holy smokes."

"Stay there." I turned off the water. Then I pulled out and dropped onto my haunches behind her. My come trickled out of her entrance, the perfect reminder that a part of me was inside her still. I used one finger to push the thick drops back in.

She arched her back, but didn't try to get away. "No, I'm too sensitive."

"Shhh, bambina. We don't want to waste any."

"God, it is literally so wrong how hot that is."

I pulled my finger free and stood up. "But you love it."

Without meeting my eyes, she reached to turn on the shower again. It was as if she didn't want to answer me, like she was embarrassed that I'd noticed this about her. When she reached for the soap, I grabbed her face and forced her to look at me. "It's not wrong to like what you like, even in bed. Capisce?"

"I just . . ." She blew out a long breath, her eyebrows drawing low. "Is everyone like this? Or is there something about me that craves this particular power dynamic? Why do I get so—?"

I shut her up by kissing her. I ate at her mouth and held her close, letting her feel my tongue and the reassurance of my touch. Sicilians didn't like a false face; we appreciated honesty in all things. So while I didn't have answers for her, I needed her to know that it didn't matter to me. We were good together, an equation that added up—and that was all that fucking mattered.

"Emmalina," I whispered as I dropped kisses along her cheek. "There isn't a thing in the world wrong with you. You're perfect."

"Thank you." She petted my shoulders and arms, running her hands over me, before shifting her body into the spray. "We should finish showering. There's a water crisis in many parts of the world."

CHAPTER TWENTY-SIX

Emma

He was already in the gym when I came downstairs, attacking the heavy bag like it had offended him. A t-shirt with no sleeves showed off his arms, and his calf muscles popped as he moved and punched. I remained perfectly still, enjoying the view, until he said, "Stop staring at me and get over here."

I walked over and set my towel and water bottle on the floor. "How did you know I was there?"

He stopped and turned toward me. A bead of sweat rolled down the column of his throat as he stripped off his gloves. "Bambina, I could practically hear you panting across the room."

Liar. I hadn't made any noise whatsoever. "Can you blame me? You're a legit thirst trap, marito."

Lifting his shirt, he wiped his face, which gave me a nice view of his spectacular abs. "I don't know what that means," he said, "but if it gets you wet, then I like it."

I bit my lip to hide my smile. I was always wet around this man, but he didn't need to know that.

He eyed my tight workout bra and leggings. "Do you run in that outfit?"

Glancing down at myself, I checked to see what he would have to complain about. "Yes. Why?"

"Next time you do, I want to watch. Your tits look fucking fantastic in that top."

"They do?"

He snagged me around the waist and brought me into the cradle of his large body, then gave me a hard kiss. "Fuck, yes. You're very sexy, bambina."

I was about to suggest we forget boxing when he released me. "First, you need to protect your hands. Come on."

He led me to the ring, where a pair of gloves and long wraps waited. "Let me see your hand." I held up my left hand and he took one of the wraps. He started around my wrists then began wrapping around my palm and fingers, working fast, like he'd done this hundreds of times. When he dropped my hand I examined the finished job. It was perfect.

"Comment?" he asked as I held up my other hand.

"No, I was thinking it was very impressive."

As he wrapped the other hand I stared at his fingers, so thick and strong, but gentle with me. A barrage of questions hovered on the tip of my tongue, my brain desperate for information when it came to this man. "How did you start boxing?"

"At school I got into too many fights. I was angry all the time. So when I was ten the school told my father I couldn't come back unless I stopped fighting. He dropped me off at a gym."

"And you loved it right away?"

"No, I fucking hated it. Those old men beat the shit out of me on a daily basis."

My eyebrows flew up. "That's terrible. They could've killed you."

He snorted. "They couldn't hurt me. What they did was nothing compared to what happened in this house."

His father, Don Gero. I was desperate to learn more. "Like what?"

"You don't want to hear those stories." He finished wrapping and reached for the boxing gloves.

"You're wrong. I definitely do."

He didn't say anything, just shoved the glove on my left hand and secured it. "How does that feel?"

"Good," I said. "Was your father an alcoholic?" Alcohol and abuse often were linked. Even still, I wasn't above making wild guesses if it prompted him to share.

"No." He slipped the other glove over my right hand. "Clear-eyed sober for every punishment."

"And he hit you and your brother?"

He stopped and stared at a point on the far wall. "Only me. Nino was perfect in my father's eyes. And it was never physical, not like that. It was a test of endurance, fucking mind games. Like locking me in the dark, or making me kneel for hours. Withheld food. He never left bruises or anything anyone else could see." He shrugged and started to step away. "Now you know why I hate him."

I snagged his arm with the thick gloves. "Baby, wait." He didn't look at me, like maybe he was ashamed or worried over my reaction, so I wrapped my arms around his waist and squeezed. "I'm sorry that happened to you. None of it was your fault, not one single thing. I hope you know that."

He let out a long breath, but didn't hug me back. I tried to pour all of my compassion and affection for him into this one-sided embrace. Was this why he didn't want to be a father?

The moment stretched until he finally patted my back. "That's enough," he said gruffly. "Let me show you how to punch things, bambina."

I reluctantly let him go.

For the next hour he instructed me on how to stand, how to shift my weight and throw a punch. There was a lot more to boxing than I'd realized. I thought it was two men in a ring beating the crap out of each other, but it was far more technical than that. It required power, yes, but also intelligence. You had to anticipate your opponent's next move, learn how to defend yourself. Attack where they didn't see it coming.

Mostly, boxing was about employing strategy to use your strengths against an opponent's weakness.

Panting, I slumped on the ropes in the ring and tried to catch my breath. It was annoying that my husband wasn't even breathing hard. "This is why you're a great don."

He looked at me like I'd lost my mind. "What are you talking about?"

"Because of boxing." I gestured to the ring. "I can see why you're good at both things. You're smart, calm, disciplined. This was good training to take over for your father."

"Most people would say stepping into a ring to get hit is the dumbest thing a person can do."

He'd obviously heard this a time or two. And to be fair, I might've said the same thing an hour ago. "It's not dumb. It's very brave. And if you weren't smart, you wouldn't have been so successful at it."

His brows lowered in confusion. "How do you know I was any good?"

"Sal has mentioned it. He said you were very impressive."

He leaned back on the ropes, hooking his elbows out to the side and showing off his impressive chest. "I did okay. I made a lot of money."

"Did you get one of those gaudy giant belts?"

A grin split his face and he laughed, a rare sight that I soaked up like a sponge. "Sì, I did get some of those gaudy giant belts."

"Can I see one?"

"Take off your top and I'll think about it."

"What?" I huffed in surprised amusement.

"You heard me. Show me your tits and I'll consider it."

He was serious, those intense eyes devouring me, and my belly tightened as desire raced through me. I licked my lips. "But I'm wearing these," I said in a shy voice, holding up my boxing gloves. "I'm helpless, mio grande marito."

Oh, that was the wrong—right?—thing to say. His lips curled into a predatory smile as he pushed off the ropes and began stalking toward me. I could see the thickening of his cock in his thin shorts. "Mia piccola innocente, you're about to get fucked in a boxing ring."

———

Yawning, I zoned out as my Physics 2 professor droned on about wave optics. I liked this class, but I was too tired to concentrate today. Someone was keeping me up late every night—and getting me up early —with lots of sex.

I wasn't complaining, though. Yes, sex was biologically designed to be pleasurable—it guaranteed the continuation of the human race, after all—but this was on another level. I felt drunk on Giacomo, a sex-crazed creature who was obsessed with my husband.

It didn't help that I was currently sitting in his office, surrounded by his smell, and using his laptop. No wonder I couldn't concentrate here.

The computer screen went black and I blinked away my brain fog. Whoops, class had ended a few minutes ago.

Just as I pushed to my feet, the old rotary phone on the giant desk rang. I froze. This phone hadn't made a noise before. I hadn't thought it even worked, to be honest.

The ringing continued and no one picked up. Was it sounding else-where in the house? Shouldn't Sal be the one to answer when Giacomo wasn't around?

The ringing stopped. Oh, well. That took care of that. I'd go to the kitchen and mention it to Sal.

As I walked to the door the phone started up again. After three rings, I decided to answer it. What was the worst that could happen? Maybe it was Giacomo trying to reach me.

"Pronto," I said into the receiver.

"Who's this?" It was a woman. She spoke in heavily accented Sicilian.

My stomach clenched as irrational jealousy swept through me. Why was a woman calling my husband? Was it Theresa?

Whoever she was, did she honestly think I was naive enough to give out unsolicited information on the phone? I was the daughter of a mafia don, raised in this secretive, violent world. I knew better than that. "Someone with the right to answer the phone. Who's this?"

"Are you Mo's wife?"

"No." The lie fell awkwardly off my tongue, so I followed it up with an accusation. "Are you?"

She started laughing. "Dai, absolutely not. The thought makes me want to vomit."

Not a mistress. A relative, then? This would explain the vehement reaction. For some reason the girl from the photo in his bedroom popped into my mind. They'd looked so much alike. Was this her? "Who are you? His cousin?"

"No, and you are definitely the wife. I can hear your jealousy. How long have you been married to my brother?"

Brother. What the hell?

It couldn't be true. Giacomo would've mentioned a sister. This woman had to be lying to get information from me.

"Listen," I said. "I'm not telling you anything until I talk to Giacomo."

The woman on the other end kept going. "I know Mo married a Canadian girl, the daughter of some important boss in Toronto. Everyone is talking about it."

"*Everyone?*" Was this true? I didn't want this news to get out. If word of the marriage reached Naples or Siderno, I was beyond screwed.

"Yes," she said, "so I wanted to call and reach you when he's out. I had to speak to the woman who stole my brother's heart."

I ignored that comment. "What's your name?"

"Viviana. I'm not surprised my brother hasn't told you about me. I'm a secret."

A secret? "Nice to meet you, Viviana. I'm Emma."

"Emma! I love that name. You sound very sweet, just what Mo needs."

"I'm neither confirming nor denying that I'm with him."

She exhaled heavily into my ear. "It's okay. He always tries to protect me, too. Tell me, are you in love with him?"

I stared at the wooden desk, tracing the grooves in the grain with my finger. I wasn't sure how to answer. Love? I liked him, sure. And I did get a fluttering, sick feeling in my stomach when I thought about him.

But love was something unquantifiable, a foundation of feeling that built over time as two people grew closer and shared their lives. Giacomo and I barely knew one another.

Ugh, why did I pick up the phone? Hesitantly, I said, "I'm very fond of him. But we're getting off topic. Who told you about the marriage?"

"You're *fond* of him? You make him sound like a puppy."

"Well, we haven't known each other very long. Please, Viviana. How did you learn of the marriage?"

"I have friends here. They talk to people from the outside and get news. I'm not completely isolated."

In here. From the outside. Was she in prison? In hiding?

"I just wish he would've told me," she continued. "We used to share everything."

Instantly, I felt terrible. My own sisters would be equally hurt when they learned of my marriage, so I rushed to explain. "It's not what you think. We were forced to marry." When she fell silent for a long minute, I thought maybe we'd disconnected. "Hello?"

"I don't understand," she said. "He didn't wish to marry you?"

"No, he definitely did not. Let's just say neither of us were given a choice."

"Does this lack of choice have to do with me?"

I inhaled sharply. The answer snapped into place like two puzzle pieces. The leverage Virga had over Giacomo? *Viviana* was that leverage. It had to be. He never mentioned his sister, yet they clearly got along. She said he always protected her. Marrying me to protect his sister fit with the man I knew, the man I cared about.

"It does, doesn't it?" She sounded worried, the rate of her breathing increasing. "Mamma mia, I have ruined his life—"

"Stop." I kept my tone gentle yet firm. "None of this is your fault. Take a deep breath. Everything is fine and your brother is handling it."

"No, everything *is* my fault. It's always my fault."

"It's not, I promise. Don't give it another thought. Your brother and I are making the best of our marriage. We're . . . happy."

It wasn't a lie. At the moment I didn't hate being here. Yes, I needed to get back to my father, but it wasn't torture being given the best orgasms of my life by a well-built man.

Viviana's voice trembled as she said, "You are only saying this to make me feel better. You're a good person, Emma."

"It's the truth, Viviana. I really hope we can meet in person soon."

"Impossible, but it would have been nice. I'm sure I would've liked you."

Why was she speaking in the past tense? "It's not impossible. Just tell me where you are and I'll come see you."

"Take care of my brother, Emma. He's a good man."

Then the line went dead.

I stared at the receiver, almost willing her to return, before I slowly hung up. Something about the last part of the exchange really bothered me. The things she said, the way she spoke in the past tense. She sounded on the verge of tears by the end, and I hated that I'd upset her.

Why hadn't Giacomo told her about the marriage? If he had, then Viviana wouldn't have drawn her own conclusions and been so upset by our exchange.

I had to tell him what happened. He needed to explain everything to his sister.

Stupidly, I realized I didn't have his contact in my phone. There hadn't been the need to call him before now.

Hurrying from the office, I raced to the kitchen, where Sal was frying something on the stove. "Sal!"

He turned and looked at me with his good eye. "Che cosa, signora?"

"I need to call Giacomo, but I don't have his number."

"Of course, of course." Sal turned the burner off as he pulled out his mobile. We met at the counter and Sal connected the call, then handed the phone to me.

"Pronto," a familiar deep voice said after one ring. "What is it, Sal?"

"It's me, not Sal."

"Hold on." I heard movement in the background, like Giacomo was going somewhere to speak privately. Biting my lip, I waited until he said quietly, "What is it, bambina? Are you okay?"

"The phone in your office rang and I picked it up." I saw Sal flinch, but I let that go for now. "It was your sister."

There was dead silence on the other end. If Giacomo was breathing, I couldn't tell. Finally, he said, "I'll be there in fifteen." Then he disconnected.

I gave the phone back to Sal. "He said he'll be home in a few minutes."

"He doesn't speak about business on the phone. He is like the older bosses in that way. You never know who could be listening."

"Oh." He set a glass of sparkling water in front of me and I took a long drink. "Did you know about her?"

"I've been on the estate a long time, signora. I know a great many things about the Buscettas."

"Will you tell me about her?"

Sal went back to the stove. "That is for your husband to decide. It wouldn't be right for me to share."

I rubbed my forehead. "I shouldn't have answered the phone, I know. But it kept ringing and I thought it might be Giacomo. I've never heard any of the phones in the house ring."

"He speaks only to her on that phone, no one else."

"I didn't know that."

The list of things I didn't know around here kept growing and growing. My stomach churned with dread. What was I doing? I didn't have a clue as to who Giacomo really was, or anything about his family history. For god's sake, this man has a sister he never told me about.

"Stop worrying, signora," Sal said gently. "It will all work out."

He placed a small bowl of frozen lemon granita in front of me. It was like the shaved lemon ice sold at the fair back home in Toronto, except smoother. I loved it and Sal always had it on hand.

"I wish I had your optimism," I said. "Can you at least tell me if there are more family members I don't know about? Then I won't be so surprised later on."

He patted my hand. "Viviana and Giacomo are the only two left. There is no one else." He gestured to my lower half. "At least, not yet."

We sat in silence until the sound of a car engine approached the back of the house. When Giacomo burst through the kitchen door, his brow was wrinkled with concern. It was on edge as I'd ever seen him.

He barked, "What did she say?"

"She heard that you married—"

"Who told her?"

"She said a friend who talks to people on the outside. I didn't know what that meant."

My husband exchanged a look with Zani, who was just walking in. "It has to be the boy. Try to call her again."

Zani dipped his chin then stepped outside. Giacomo motioned to me. "Tell me every word of the conversation, if you can."

I repeated as much of the exchange as I could recall. When I got to the part where Viviana speculated that her brother's marriage was her fault, Giacomo grimaced. "Minchia! What did she say next?"

"That I was only trying to make her feel better, and when I said I hoped to meet her in person one day, she said that was impossible. She told me to take care of you and rang off."

Propping his hands on the counter, he leaned over and stared hard at the marble. When he said nothing, I blurted, "She talked in past tense. It really worried me. Maybe I had trouble translating, though, because she talks really fast. I'm so sorry. I never should have answered the phone."

Zani walked in. "She's still not picking up. The guard says she's been in her room all day."

"Does he have eyes on her?"

"No, so I told him to check on her and ring me back."

"I swear to Christ, if he has—"

Zani's mobile rang and his olive skin paled as he listened. "Start looking!" he snapped into the phone. "We're on our way." When he disconnected, he said to Giacomo. "Her room is empty."

"Motherfucker!" Giacomo grabbed my empty granita bowl and hurled it against the wall. It smashed into a hundred tiny pieces and rained down on the tile. I jolted at the loud noise, both guilt and shock stunning me into silence.

Giacomo started toward the door, his attention on Zani. "Let's get over there. And while we're driving, get Don Chiellini on the phone. I want to know where this Federico piece of shit is."

"Wait, Giacomo!" I called before he disappeared. "Please, explain what's happening. Is she missing?"

My husband didn't turn around, instead speaking over his shoulder. "I don't have time right now, Emma. I'll be back later."

Then the two of them were gone, leaving just me, Sal and a pile of broken glass.

Leaning forward, I covered my face with my hands. I hated this feeling, not knowing what's going on yet feeling responsible.

"It's okay," Sal said gently. "He'll sort everything out."

"What is there to sort out? I'm lost."

Sal winced. "Your husband should explain—"

"Sal, please. I'm dying here." I wasn't used to causing trouble. I was the one who solved problems, not created them.

He studied my face for a long moment, then spoke quietly. "She suffered as a young girl. Her father . . . mamma mia, he was hard on her. He was hard on the boys, too, but they were different. Viviana wasn't built to take such cruelty. She was kind and sensitive, much like you, signora. But Don Gero tried to toughen her up." He sighed. "It took a toll on her. Giacomo tried to protect his sister, so he would take on more to spare her. Capisce?"

I swallowed and nodded. My sweet husband. He'd taken Viviana's punishments.

"You, Emma Buscetta, are my reward for the cruelty and misery I endured in this house."

"What happened?" I asked. "When did it stop?"

"Eventually, Giacomo got stronger, bigger. Became a fighter. Then Don Gero went into hiding and Nino took over the responsibilities of the business."

"So what happened to Viviana?"

Sal pushed off the counter and started to turn. "I should let your husband—"

"No, please." I grabbed his arm to keep him from leaving. My tone was desperate. "I won't tell him you said anything, but I have to know what happened."

"Giacomo faked his sister's death. It was the only way to get her away from Don Gero and this life. So he boxed to win prize money, which allowed him to afford her care in a facility where they treated troubled teens. When she grew older she moved to Mirabella, which is for adults. And now you understand. Giacomo would do anything to protect her."

Viviana's words from earlier echoed in my head. *"Everything is my fault. It's always my fault."* She was Giacomo's weakness, and Don Virga had used it against him. And now she was missing because I couldn't let a phone go unanswered.

Moaning, I leaned my head onto my folded arms on the counter. "God, I feel terrible."

"Do not worry, signora. Giacomo will find her. Even if he must turn Palermo upside down to do it."

CHAPTER TWENTY-SEVEN

Giacomo

Silently, I stripped out of my clothes. I was exhausted and angry, not to mention worried. Viviana was still missing, with no trace of her anywhere.

She was at risk outside of the facility. No guards, no phone. She didn't have money or even identification. What was she thinking, going off so recklessly?

One thing was certain: Federico Chiellini was a dead man.

I slipped into my wife's bed. I needed a few hours' sleep, but I also needed her. I was desperate to lose myself in her sweetness. When I rolled toward her my hands met soft, warm skin. *Naked* skin. Had she been waiting for me to get home and give her what she needed? Cazzo, that thought was so fucking hot.

My dick was already half hard as I cupped her tit and plucked at her nipple. Her breathing changed as she came awake, so I kissed her neck. She smelled like lemons and sugar. "It's me, bambina. Wake up for me. Wake up so I can fuck you."

Sighing, she pressed her ass into my crotch. I rolled my hips, sliding my cock between her cheeks. "You feel that?" I whispered. "I need you, mia piccola moglie."

One slim arm reached behind my neck to pull me closer. Her top leg eased over my thigh, spreading herself open, and my cock pulsed, thickening with each beat of my heart. "Then have me," she rasped.

God, this woman. I needed her like air.

Moving lower, I dragged my nails through the coarse hair on her mound, lower until I found her slit. Her pussy was hot and luscious, and I wanted her with a ferocity that almost scared me. I wasn't thinking about getting her pregnant. I just needed her body wrapped around mine, her sweet cries in my ear.

Being inside her was as close to heaven as I'd ever get, a baptism. A renewal. She pulled me apart and then put me back together each damn time.

I teased her clit with my fingertips. We'd done this a lot and I knew how to get her ready. I rolled her on her back. "Do you want my mouth?"

Her answer was instant. "Yes. God, yes. Please, Giacomo."

So eager. I loved that about her. I inhaled her scent before I licked her. So fucking good. I went back in for another taste, using my tongue to gather her wetness. Impatient, I ate at her with deep kisses and long sucks on her clit. She whimpered and grabbed my hair to pull me closer, unashamed to demand I keep going.

Everything melted away but this woman. She was perfect, her slick juices covering my mouth and chin. I held her ass in my hands and kept her spread wide for me as I feasted on her.

"Please, I need you, m'amore."

My love.

No woman had dared to speak those words to me before, but Emma's softly spoken Sicilian endearment did something to me. A part of my chest cracked open, emotion flooding me, and I was helpless to resist her. I would have handed over my fortune, my kingdom, my balls —anything she asked for—in that moment.

Surging up, I stretched out over her and covered her mouth with mine. Then I used my knees to spread her thighs. "Use me, bambina," I whispered. "Put me inside your pussy." Her small hand reached between us to grip my shaft. She shifted, trying to line me up. "Hurry, dusci." *Sweetheart.*

I heard her suck in a sharp breath, but I didn't have time to think about it because the head of my cock met scalding wet skin. I thrust forward and sank inside her, the walls of her cunt strangling my tip. "Fuck," I gasped.

She held onto my shoulders, her nails digging into my muscle. "More. God, please. Move, baby."

Our faces were close, only millimeters apart, as I pushed the rest of the way inside. Once we were joined, her ragged exhale coasted over my skin and I breathed her in. I didn't move, just let her adjust to the initial stretch while I tried not to come. It felt so unbelievably good.

"You don't need to be careful with me," she said. "I can take it."

I stroked her cheek with my thumb, tracing the fine lines of her face. "I don't want you to take it. I want you to love having my cock inside you so much that you weep every time I pull out."

"I do love it. But I'd love it a lot more at the moment if you fucked me."

Minchia—that dirty word on my good girl's lips. Lust spiked in my groin and my hips snapped forward in rapid succession, my body giving her what she demanded. Sparks danced along the backs of my thighs, pleasure racing to my toes. Emma threw her head back, and I sank my teeth into the column of her throat, like an animal needing to claim its mate. I sucked on her skin as I pounded into her, fucking her with abandon.

Soon she tipped over the edge, trembling and shaking, the walls of her pussy contracting around my cock, and I couldn't take it. I let go, giving her hard jabs of my hips, and the urge to come surged up from my balls, twisting and squeezing in my gut. I shoved deep and let the orgasm wash over me.

A thousand colors exploded behind my eyelids, and I could feel the come shooting out of me and into her body. I never wanted it to end. The high was better than anything I could imagine, and it was like I gave her a piece of myself each time. But she gave me something back in return, something I'd been missing for thirty-two long years.

"Mine," I growled as the last twitches quaked through me, my fingers tangled with hers.

"Yours," she returned with a quiet sigh.

Gesù, it was wrong how much I liked that. "Good. Now kiss me again, *bidduzza*."

"What does that mean in your dialect?" she asked, dragging her nails over my scalp.

"Beautiful."

She hummed and kissed me again, her mouth opening and letting my tongue find hers. There was no urgency in our kiss this time. It was a lazy tangling of tongues, and I let myself drift, stirring my hips slowly. I loved this. I didn't want to pull out. I wished I could stay here, deep in her bare pussy, forever.

I love her.

I hadn't believed it possible, hadn't believed that I was capable of the emotion for anyone other than Viviana, but it was true. Sometime in the last few days I realized that I was in love with my wife.

She smoothed her palms over my shoulders. "I like when you wake me up in the middle of the night for sex."

I pulled out and flopped onto my back beside her. "I will remember this, wife."

"Did you find your sister?"

The tightness in my chest came flooding back, my good mood instantly gone. "No."

"Do you have any clues? She couldn't have gone far, right?"

"The cameras were cut, and no one claims to have seen anything. She disappeared."

Though my eyes were closed, I could sense her staring at me in the dark. "I'm so sorry," she said. "I feel terrible."

"I can't stop looking until I find her—even if it means putting my hunt for Virga on hold."

"Oh. I hadn't thought of that." She eased down beside me and rested her head on my shoulder. "Why didn't you tell me about her?"

Was that accusation in her tone? Was she implying I was to blame somehow? "The world believes she is dead. It's too dangerous if people know."

"But I'm not people. I'm your wife."

"Temporary wife," I snapped before I could stop myself. But I wouldn't take it back. I was too worried and tired for a rational conversation. She was the one who started this, being so sweet and irresistible. Making me love her until I couldn't breathe.

And she's going to leave you.

Emma didn't want this life. She'd said it many times, and planned to take a child away from me. What was I doing, letting myself love a woman who would do that to me?

Malocchio. Cursed.

She sat up and I opened my eyes. My skin grew cold at her distance, but I still didn't reach for her. I stared at the ceiling.

"I see," she said calmly. "So I'm good enough to screw and bear your child, but that's it."

"What do you want from me? I'm letting you live here. I'm offering you protection and trying to find a way out of this marriage."

"You're *letting* me live here?" She sat up, her expression full of disbelief. "Are you for real right now?"

"Do you think I'm lying?"

"No, I think you're being cruel, but I have no idea why. I already apologized for telling your sister about us. But if you'd trusted me with that information in the first place, I wouldn't have been caught off guard today."

"So this is my fault that you have a big mouth?"

"I wouldn't put it like that, but yes."

I couldn't believe it. She was still trying to turn this on *me*. Moving sideways, I threw my legs over the edge of the mattress and stood. "You are the one who fucked up, Emma. But I haven't once accused you or yelled at you, have I? Instead I just gave you an orgasm."

"So I should be grateful? Is that it? Sex doesn't solve this, Giacomo. In fact, it makes it worse. You don't trust me enough to be a part of your life, even though we're married and sharing a bed."

The back of my neck grew hot. "None of this is a surprise. You knew Virga had leverage over me. You didn't have any problem with letting me fuck you then, still begging me to put a baby inside you. So what changed?"

"What changed is that I didn't think that leverage would call here and nearly start crying on the phone to me."

Vivi almost cried? Emma hadn't mentioned it before, and now I was even more worried. Did this Federico boy know of Viviana's history? Would he know what to do if she had a panic attack? "Fuck! Why didn't you tell me that?"

"Do you hear yourself? You want me to tell you everything, yet you tell me nothing. How is that possibly fair? Trust has to go both ways."

An inferno raged inside my chest, a storm of frustration and fear. I couldn't think straight. "Fair? This life isn't fair, little girl. I am the boss and *you* answer to *me*. And why should I trust you? You didn't want this marriage, either. You're trying to leave me the first chance you get. You said it yourself—all you care about is getting back to Toronto."

"My father is dying!" She stared at me like she'd never seen me before. "I need to be with him. Now, before it's too late."

"Why? You can't save him. Soon he will barely know you're there."

Her bottom lip trembled, but she lifted her chin. "True, but I still need to see him before he dies. He is the most important person in my life."

The words made me even angrier. My come was still dripping out of her pussy and all she could talk about was her precious father. I put my hands on my hips and snarled down at her. "My sister is the most important person in my life—and thanks to you she's in danger."

"She is twenty-six! Maybe she wants a life for herself, one where she isn't locked away. People can recover from childhood trauma to live healthy, full lives."

My heart stopped beating for a fraction of a second. How dare she say these things to me? The nerve of this woman to presume she knew anything about my family.

My muscles swelled and a red mist coated my brain. "You have no fucking idea what you are talking about. Childhood trauma? She was terrorized by our father for years, screamed at and told she was worthless. Locked in her room. At six, he forced her to watch him torture and murder a man. She woke up screaming every night, catatonic with fear. So do not talk to me like you are an expert ever again."

Speaking the horrors out loud threatened to send me to my knees, but I couldn't show weakness. Not even in front of Emma. So I strode over to the wall and punched it twice. The pain did little to dull the anger hammering in my head.

When I turned I found her watching me with disgust. Finally. Now she knew the kind of man she married, brutal and barbaric. Raised by a monster to rule over an army of monsters. If she thought that would change because she whispered a few sweet words in my ear, she was mistaken.

I would never be anything different. I was cursed from birth.

Her throat worked delicately as she swallowed. "You have no intention of trusting me, do you? You'll screw me, let me live here and give you an heir, but you don't respect me enough to treat me like an equal."

"Equal?" I sneered down at her. "It doesn't work like that here. Do you think Ravazzani treats your sister like an equal? Or D'Agostino with your twin? No fucking way. Even if we both wanted this marriage, which we don't, it wouldn't work like that."

"I know you're hurting over Viviana and so you're transferring your anger to me. But I don't deserve this, Giacomo."

She was so calm and it made my fury burn hotter. I was nearly shaking with it. "You don't know shit, Emma! You think you're smarter than everyone else, but you're a naive sheltered girl, raised to be a mafia trophy wife and coddled by your father. You know nothing of the real world."

Her eyes grew glassy, but I didn't budge. I wasn't wrong. She'd answered the phone today and put my sister in danger, all because she believed she knew best.

Then a tear slipped down my wife's cheek.

I stared at the single drop, my insides clenching in regret. At no time in the past month had I seen Emma cry. Not at being forced here, married at gunpoint to a stranger, away from everything she knew— not one tear. This woman had endured it all bravely until right now. Because of me.

"You're worse than a dog, Giacomo."

I couldn't block out my father's voice, not in this room. Not when I was so fucking tired and heartsick.

And now I was just like him, spouting cruelty at those I should be comforting and protecting. I should be working to win Emma over, reassure her and get her to stay with me, but I couldn't find those words, only accusations and venom. At this moment I hated myself every bit as much as I hated him.

"Minchia!" I shouted, slamming my fist into the wall once more.

At the sound Emma curled into a ball on the bed and covered her head with her hands. I couldn't hear her crying, but her shoulders were shaking as she quietly sobbed.

Like my mother.

The realization was a gut punch. My skin felt like it was going to split open at any second, spilling all the ugliness festering inside me onto the worn carpet. This house, this family was cursed.

I knew it would end like this. I could never make her happy.

One thing was crystal clear. I never should've grown close to Emma in the first place.

With ruthless efficiency, I began dressing. I didn't look over at her. I couldn't. I buckled my belt and dragged on my shirt. Then I grabbed my phone. I'd go work at the club and keep digging into my sister's disappearance. There had to be someone out there who knew something.

As I opened the door, I did the only thing I could think of.

I ended it.

"Go back to Toronto, Emma. There's no reason for you to stay here anymore."

CHAPTER TWENTY-EIGHT

Emma

"What the actual fuck?" a woman shouted at me.

I finished climbing into the lush private plane, a large figure trailing behind me. "Give her a minute, micina," Enzo D'Agostino said. "She doesn't need you yelling at her right away."

My twin arched a well-sculpted eyebrow at him. "I will yell if I fucking want, il pazzo. *She married a Sicilian mob boss without telling me!*"

Enzo moved toward her. When he drew close, he cupped Gia's face in his hands and bent to whisper in her ear. She practically melted at his touch, her eyelids falling shut, and she clung to his wrists like he was her lifeline. He always had this effect on her, and her on him, as if they shared a special language no one else understood. It was an intimate moment, one I had no business witnessing, so I turned away.

Instead, I found a seat and busied myself with the seat belt.

Things happened fast this morning once I'd called Enzo to come get me. A man of few words, he hadn't said much, just told me to sit tight and he'd be there in two hours.

It had only taken an hour and a half.

Enzo arrived at the Buscetta mansion with a small army behind

MILA FINELLI

him, every one of them armed to the teeth. He ordered the guards to
open the gate and let me go. I couldn't hear the whole exchange from
the front door, but it hadn't taken long before the gate swung open and
I ran through it. I got into Enzo's SUV and we sped off.

I knew the guards would inform Giacomo of my departure the
instant I left. So part of me expected to see his sedan speeding after us,
chasing us through the Palermo streets. Or pulling up at the private
airstrip as we boarded Enzo's jet.

But there was no sign of my temporary husband anywhere.

*"Go back to Toronto, Emma. There's no reason for you to stay here
anymore."*

So that was that. It was over. He'd wanted me to leave, so I left.
And now I could return to my life and pretend all of this never
happened.

I could forget that one time I was stupid enough to fall in love with
a mob boss.

The realization came to me in the late hours of the night, long after
he'd gone. Yes, I'd fallen for the man who thought I was dumb and
naive, nothing more than a warm body in his bed.

The man who would never trust me.

Maybe I *was* a silly sheltered mafia princess. After all, in the past
six weeks I hadn't tried to find a way out of this mess. I'd relied on
Giacomo to do it, eager to sleep with him in the meantime. Handed
over my heart on a silver platter. Hardly the actions of a reasonable,
intelligent woman.

It didn't matter. Our marriage was forged in resentment and coer-
cion, distracted by pheromones, and had a zero percent chance of
ending happily.

My sister dropped into the seat next to mine and snagged my hand.
A huge diamond engagement ring flashed on her ring finger. "Okay,
spill. Don't leave anything out, Emma."

"I need your man to hear this, too. We're going to need his help."

"Amore!" She leaned into the aisle and motioned to Enzo, who was
speaking with his brothers in the back. He pushed out of his seat and
walked up the aisle. She pointed to the empty seat across from her. "Sit
down, baby. It's story time."

Enzo sat, then reached for Gia's legs and settled them on his thigh. It was sweet how they were always touching each other.

I drew in a deep breath and tried not to think about how things might have been different in Palermo.

"Start at the beginning, Emmie," Gia ordered.

I rubbed my eyes under my glasses and tried to think of where to start. There was so much. "Papà is dying."

Gia's entire body jolted, her feet falling to the floor with a thud. Her wide gaze studied my face, her mouth slack with shock. "*What?*"

"Prostate cancer, stage four. It's spread all over his body."

Her expression transformed with a flood of emotions, and I let her grapple with the news. "How long?" she finally asked.

"It's hard to say for sure. He just finished with radiation, but they're talking about palliative care."

She blinked several times, then looked over at Enzo. He rubbed her legs soothingly. "Breathe, Gianna."

"Does Frankie know?" Gia turned to ask me.

"No. He asked me not to tell either of you." I stared at my lap and folded my hands. "But I'm tired of secrets. I've seen how destructive they can be. It's time you both knew."

"You've been dealing with this by yourself the whole time?"

"It's only been about five months. He has full-time care to help. Her name is Gloria and she's been a godsend."

"I can't believe he didn't want me to know."

I could hear the hurt in her voice. Her relationship with Papà has always been strained and this was not going to help. "I can't pretend to know his reasons, but when was the last time you tried to call him? When was the last time you came to visit?"

We both knew the answer.

"I would have, if I'd known," she snapped. "He had no right to keep this from me and Frankie. And really, neither did you, no matter what he said. We're *twins*."

"Gianna," Enzo said quietly. "Those are conversations for another time, no? Let your sister continue."

"You can be mad at me, if you want," I said. "I didn't like it, but I would do it all over again. You both have your lives and responsibilities. Neither of you are close to him and I'm still living at home. It made sense for me to honor his wishes, at least for now."

"I don't agree, but let's set that aside for now," Gia said. "Get to the marriage part."

"Do you know a Sicilian named Don Virga?" I asked Enzo.

He inclined his head. "He is the head of the Cosa Nostra, a very powerful man. Stuck in the old ways, as are many of them."

"He came to Toronto and ordered me to pack a bag." I told them of Virga taking me to Palermo, leaving his men behind in Toronto, forcing me to marry Giacomo and imposing the three-month baby deadline.

As I spoke, Gianna stood and began pacing in the aisle, the bracelets on her wrists clicking as she moved. When I got to the baby part, she stopped in her tracks. "If you tell me some Sicilian piece of shit knocked you up, I swear to fucking Christ we are turning this plane around so I can put a bullet in his brain."

"Are you listening?" I said. "I told you, we didn't have a choice. Virga was blackmailing me with Papà and Giacomo with his sister."

"You are related to two of the most dangerous men in Europe!" She gestured at Enzo, as if I didn't know who she was talking about. "We don't get blackmailed, Em. Not you, not me, not Frankie. Not anyone in this family."

"But," Enzo said, his gaze studying my face. "There is a reason you didn't reach out, no? Does this have to do with the sit down between Buscetta and Ravazzani?"

"You knew about that?" I asked.

"I know everything that happens in the 'Ndrangheta—especially when it pertains to your brother-in-law."

"What are you two talking about?" Gia demanded, taking her seat once more.

It was Enzo who answered. "The heads of the Cosa Nostra and 'Ndrangheta tried to bring peace between Ravazzani and Buscetta through marriage. But these days marriage isn't enough. Apparently they also needed a baby."

"Fausto fucking knew about this?" Gia was incensed, her hands gripping the arm rests.

"To his credit, he told them no," Enzo said. "He refused to give Emma over to Buscetta. And Buscetta didn't want the marriage, either. Everyone assumed the matter had been dropped."

"Well, it wasn't fucking dropped." Gia dragged her hands through her long hair. "I hate the goddamn mafia. This is such bullshit."

"You don't hate all of it," Enzo murmured, a small smirk on his face as he regarded his fiancée.

"Shut up. You know what I mean." Closing her eyes, she blew out a long breath. "Okay, keep going. I'm sure this will get worse. Are you going to tell me you're in love with him?"

I didn't want to have that conversation now. Maybe not ever. "We need to deal with the situation in Toronto before Virga realizes I'm not in Palermo any longer and has Papà killed."

"This makes no sense," Gia said. "How are Virga's men allowed on the estate? Papà's security used to be tight."

"It is tight," I said. "Someone is helping Virga."

"Your uncle." Enzo shook his head slowly. "He's learned about the succession plan."

Gia's brows pulled low in confusion. "Succession? You mean when Papà . . . ."

"Dies," I finished. "Yes, that's what he means. I don't know who is inheriting Papà's business afterwards, but apparently it's not Uncle Reggie."

"It's Vito."

We both gaped at Enzo, who was studying the back of the plane. Both of his brothers were back there, talking. Vito, Enzo's consigliere, and Massimo, who was a soldier.

Gia recovered first. "Your brother is taking over Toronto? How long have you known this?"

"Roberto and I came to an agreement six months ago."

That must've been when my father was first diagnosed.

"And you didn't think to tell me this?" Hurt tinged the anger in my twin's voice.

"*Tesorino*," he said with a sigh. "The less you know about my business, the better. We've talked about this many times, no?"

"But this is different. It's my father's empire. Did you also know about the cancer?"

"Roberto said nothing of his health. I assumed this was years away. And I made the deal because I didn't want Raffaele Ravazzani to be named successor instead."

"God, you are literally impossible," Gia said with a dramatic roll of her eyes. "You are damn lucky that I love your competitive ass."

He took her hand and brought it to his mouth. Instead of kissing the back, he flipped it over and pressed his lips to her palm. "Ti amo, micina."

I couldn't take any more of their sappiness. I was too raw, and there was every chance I might break down in tears at any second. "Let's focus, you two. We need to figure out what to do about Uncle Reggie and Don Virga."

Enzo raised his head and called out toward the rear of the plane. "*Venite qui, stronzi!*" Come here, assholes.

Vito and Massimo got up and joined us. "Che cosa?" Vito asked. I could see the outline of a gun under his gray suit jacket. Massimo was a little more direct, wearing a pistol on his belt.

"We have a problem in Toronto that needs to be dealt with imme-diately." Enzo pointed to the seats across the aisle. "Sit down and I'll explain."

My twin grabbed my hand and tugged me from my chair. "You come with me. Let them figure out what to do about Uncle Reggie. I want to talk to you."

I braced myself and allowed her to pull me toward the back of the plane where we settled into plush leather seats. There were two glasses of beer left behind from Vito and Massimo, so Gia grabbed one and took a long swig. "I really hope this was Vito's," she said when she swallowed. "God only knows what kinds of diseases Massimo has, that man slut."

I almost smiled. Only my sister could crack the ice in my chest when I was at my lowest point.

"I notice you aren't drinking." She put the glass down. "Does that mean you're pregnant?"

"I don't know. I could be. But I don't feel like drinking right now anyway."

"Jesus, Emma. Why didn't you call me or Frankie? We could have stopped this."

"Not without putting everyone at risk. I wasn't going to endanger you or Enzo or his family. What about your step kids? Frankie's kids? I wasn't going to start a war over this."

"This? It's your life we're talking about. You're family—and we protect family."

"You know that isn't always possible. Fausto's first wife died in a war. I couldn't live with myself if I was responsible for someone getting hurt."

"So you took it all on your shoulders? That's incredibly stupid—and you know it."

Anger sparked deep in my belly. I was tired of defending myself to my sisters all the time. "I'm not incompetent or stupid. And I'm tired of you and Frankie thinking you know so much more than me, like you have all this life experience that I don't. I've seen people die, Gia. Not on TV or in a theoretical sense, but in real life. I held their hands at the hospital as they took their last breath. I've seen gunshot wounds and stabbings and drug overdoses. I was kidnapped by Russian sex traffickers and kept in a closet for days. I am not some silly stupid child, despite what you and Frankie think. Stop belittling me!"

Her lips parted in surprise. "I don't think you're silly or stupid, Em. But you do put yourself into danger without considering the consequences. Like getting kidnapped by Russian sex traffickers when you flew to Naples to find me."

I knew she was going to throw that back in my face. "And the only reason they found me was because *you* kept calling me!"

She deflated a bit as she regarded me carefully. "I didn't mean to belittle you. I'm sorry if you feel that way. I just . . . feel responsible for you. If something were to happen to you, I would completely lose it."

I reached over and squeezed her arm. "I know, because I'd feel the same. But you can't protect me forever. And you've been gone almost a full year. You can't criticize how I'm dealing with Papà and Toronto anymore. You're not there."

"Fair enough. But I don't like that you've been keeping all this in, dealing with it on your own."

"It seemed easier than asking for help and involving everyone. And isn't that what I always do in our family?"

Gia winced because she knew I was right. "Emma, this isn't like me asking you to take my finals for my junior year. This is marriage to a gross old mobster. Frankie and I never wanted that for you."

"He's not gross. Or old."

Gia's eyes narrowed and she let out an irritated huff. "Oh, I see. Does this mean you actually *like* him?"

I couldn't meet her gaze, so I stared at the glass of beer instead. "I love him."

"What the fuck!" she barked. Enzo shot to his feet, his brow lined with concern as he checked on her, and Massimo's hand flew to his gun. Gia waved at them to sit back down. "Mind your own business, mafiosi. Everything is fine."

"Can you calm down?" I whispered to her. "I'd rather not get accidentally shot today."

"I'm sorry. I sometimes forget how protective they are of me." She adjusted in her seat and drank more beer. After a few seconds, she said, "So, you're in love with Giacomo?"

"Yes, but he doesn't feel the same. We don't need to worry about him coming after me."

"What do you mean, he doesn't feel the same? How can he not love you? You're the sweetest person on the planet."

Giacomo didn't see it that way. *"You think you're smarter than everyone else, but you are just a naive sheltered girl . . ."*

"Well," I said, staring at the bubbles in the beer. "Some people don't want sweet, I guess. Anyway, it doesn't matter. I'll get an annulment and we'll forget it ever happened."

"Can you? What if you're pregnant? He won't let you go, then."

"He already let me go. He doesn't care if I'm pregnant."

"Bullshit. There isn't a mafioso alive who doesn't want his child. They love reproducing and making more mafiosi."

"Enzo doesn't." He had two children from his first marriage, and he told Gia he doesn't care if they have more kids or not. Which was good, because my sister wasn't in a rush to become a mother.

"We'll see about that. Lately he's been dropping hints."

"Really? What are you going to do?"

"I can't think about that right now. Besides, we're talking about you, not me. When was your last period?"

"Um, two weeks ago?"

"So we probably need to wait another week or so before you test. Frankie will know."

At the mention of my older sister, I frowned. Frankie would be so disappointed in me. "We don't need to tell her about this right away, do we?"

"What happened to you being tired of keeping secrets?"

"I mean secrets about other people. I'm fine keeping secrets about *me*."

"Well, I'm not. And she needs to know. Actually, I'd be surprised if Enzo wasn't texting Fausto as we speak."

I craned my neck and saw Enzo typing feverishly on his mobile. "Shoot. I really hope he isn't."

"Relax." Gia patted my arm. "If anyone understands being sent away to get knocked up, it's Frankie. And look how that turned out."

Giacomo and I weren't Frankie and Fausto, though. Not even close.

Gia's mobile buzzed. She lifted it up and checked the screen, then flipped the device around. FRANKIE.

"Oh, great." Leaning on the table, I buried my face in my hands.

"Let's get it over with," Gia said and pressed the button to accept the call.

CHAPTER TWENTY-NINE

Giacomo

The narrow dirt road stretched out in front of the car. We'd been driving since dawn, twisting through the dry mountains beyond the city, because it occurred to me this morning where Viviana might go.

Palermo was my city, my people, and no one—not even a Buscetta—could hide from me there. She was smart enough to know that. We had people at the airport, the docks. No one had reported seeing a young couple fitting Viviana and Federico's descriptions.

But the hills . . . the hills in Sicily were almost impossible to search. This was why my father went there to avoid going to prison and why he'd lasted so long out there.

My father's farmhouse, a mouse hole buried amid kilometers of rock and vegetation, was about two hours from the city. Viv and I had talked about the place over the years, as I'd regaled her with stories about how ridiculous it was to see Don Gero living like a farmer. I told her about the trek there, how hard it was to find the farmhouse. Without a doubt I gave her enough clues to find it on her own, because why would I ever think she'd go there?

Not once had I thought it a possibility. Even if she hadn't been under guard at Mirabella, her feelings about our father meant she normally avoided anything to do with him. Which, I supposed, made it the perfect place for her and Federico to hide from me.

I crushed the steering wheel in my grip. My sister hiding from me? It made me want to tear the entire country apart with my bare hands, then beat Federico to death.

"Where did you sleep last night?" Zani asked me out of nowhere.

I looked over to glare at him, but he was scrolling on his phone. "None of your business."

"The boys said you didn't go home and you were too drunk to drive. So where did you go?"

"If you've already talked to the boys, then you know where I went."

"Yes, but I want to hear you admit it."

I scowled. I didn't need this aggravation today. I was hungover and pissed off. "I slept at Theresa's."

Dead silence.

"I only slept there," I qualified. "I didn't fuck her."

More silence.

Gesù, I hated when Zani acted like this. I already regretted sleeping at Theresa's house, but I hadn't been thinking clearly. "Nothing happened. I passed out on her sofa. You can ask her."

"Oh, I did. Who do you think she called when you showed up at her door?"

Minchia! "Why didn't you come get me?"

"Because you didn't ring me. Which is very telling, no? You knew I would talk you out of going back to your mistress."

"I didn't go *back* to Theresa. I slept on her sofa."

He hummed in his throat, still scrolling on his damn mobile. "Why didn't you go home?"

"Emma and I had a fight," I mumbled. "But I don't want to talk about it."

"Too bad. Have you apologized yet?"

"No, because I have nothing to—"

My phone rang into the car's speakers, interrupting us. Had my men found Viv?

Quickly, I pressed a button. "Pronto."

"Don Buscetta, we have a problem." It was Dino, my head of security at the mansion. He was breathing hard. "Don D'Agostino was just here and he . . ."

My entire body clenched. D'Agostino? In Palermo?

"He, what?" I growled when Dino trailed off. "Spit it out."

"He demanded we let your wife go—"

"What?" Zani shouted. "You told him to fuck off, I hope. Tell me you didn't open the gate, Dino."

But I already knew they had. Emma was gone. I could feel it in my soul.

"We had no choice, Don Buscetta. Mi dispiace. But they had more men than us and more guns. I didn't want to risk—"

Zani reached over and punched the button to disconnect the call, while I slammed my fist into the side of the driver's door. The air in the car turned heavy and I couldn't breathe.

I told her to go. What did I expect?

More time. I'd expected more time before she left me.

I didn't want to imagine that house without her. I wouldn't smell Emma's scent or hear her laughter, never kiss her or hold her. No more boxing lessons or gelato.

All the sweetness and softness? Gone.

But I'd pushed her away, told her to leave, so why would she stay? And she was related to the only two men in the world capable of extracting her after one phone call.

"What should we do?" Zani asked. "Send men to the airport? Stop the plane from taking off? We have to get her back."

"No." My voice sounded strangled, distant, even to my own ears.

"You can't be serious. You're going to let D'Agostino come to Palermo and steal your wife away?"

"He didn't steal her. She called him."

"Che cazzo! Is this because of your fight? What did you do?"

"I told her to leave."

I didn't regret it. After the way I acted it had been the right thing to do. She deserved better than a brute of a husband. Last night showed us both what would happen if she stayed. I wasn't the soft and kindhearted man a woman like Emma needed.

The best thing for her would be to go to Toronto, become a doctor, and forget this ever happened. Build a life that suited her instead of being trapped in mine.

"I want to speak to him," I told Zani. "Ring D'Agostino."

"I hope you're telling him to bring her back."

I thought of Emma, weeping quietly on the bed, curled into a ball. Exactly like my mother all those years ago. "I'll not make her stay. If she wishes to leave, then she can go. I won't stand in her way."

"She's your wife, Mo. She could be carrying your child."

"Call," I barked.

Shaking his head, Zani began dialing on my phone. Ringing soon echoed through the car speakers.

A deep voice answered. "You're too late." I could hear the satisfaction in his tone.

"If anything happens to her," I said softly, deadly. "I will peel the flesh from your bones. Are we clear?"

"That you would dare to question my ability to keep her safe is an insult."

"She's still my wife, D'Agostino."

"Not for long, Buscetta. One way or another this marriage ends very soon. Capisce?"

Did he think I was worried for myself, the coglione? "That favor I asked for, about Virga? Now you know the reason I asked. Have you made any progress?"

"Yes, but I'm not inclined to help you, considering you married my woman's twin without permission."

Fuck this.

I didn't wait to hear anything more. I disconnected and stared through the window, not seeing the rolling hills around us. I could feel my friend's eyes burning into the side of my head.

"I can't believe this," Zani finally said. "Are you willing to let her go so easily?"

"I won't keep her against her will. If I do, I'm no better than Virga or my father."

Zani cursed softly but didn't argue. I flexed my hands and told myself it was for the best.

I was fine before Emma came along and I'll be fine now that she's gone.

Viviana was my family, the only one that mattered. I'd find her and bring her home to stay with me. Then I would redecorate the mansion to remove any traces of our father. Hell, I would tear it down and rebuild it from scratch, if that's what she wanted. Her safety and happiness would never waver again, not for one instant.

And her boyfriend? Federico Chiellini was about to be on the receiving end of every bit of my anger and frustration. I was looking forward to it.

———

We finally arrived at a small turnoff. "We have to get out and walk from here."

"I hope it's not far," Zani muttered as he stepped out of the car. "These shoes cost seven-hundred euros."

We opened the trunk and pulled out our pistols, then I began leading Zani up the path.

For the next thirty minutes we climbed higher and higher. Though the surroundings were slightly more overgrown, they were familiar. My father had insisted both Nino and I learn the route, no one else. That way we could come out and periodically bring him shit. The routine was always the same: I came alone, ensuring I wasn't followed, then for two or three hours my father shouted instructions and berated me, after which I left.

Until Giulio Ravazzani and Alessandro Ricci killed the old man and set me free. It had been the happiest day of my life until—

No use thinking about that now. She was gone.

I swallowed the burn in my throat just as we arrived at the small copse of trees surrounding the farmhouse. Instantly, it was clear that my father's hiding spot was occupied. Laundry hung outside on lines and fresh wood had been chopped. A stranger might've stumbled across the place, but my gut told me it was Viviana and Federico.

Silently, Zani and I edged into the trees and approached the back

of the house. Then laughter—loud feminine laughter—wafted out of
the open windows and I nearly tripped. Che cazzo? Was that Viv? I
hadn't heard her laugh like that before.

This must be someone else.

We took our places near the door, Zani to the side, and me directly
in front. Then I raised my foot and kicked the door in. Wood splin-
tered and then Zani was through first, moving into the farmhouse, me
on his heels.

We both stopped short.

A barefoot Viviana stared at us in horror. She held a glass of wine in
her hand, her long hair swirling around her shoulders, and a young man
was behind her, his arm around her waist. Soft music played from a
phone on the table.

I ignored her, my focus entirely on Federico. "Get your hands off
her or die."

Federico moved slowly, raising his arms up, but Viviana moved to
block him from my view. "Giacomo! What are you doing? Why are you
here?"

"Viv, get out of the way."

"I won't. I don't want you hurting him."

I spared her a dark glance. "Move aside and let me handle this."

"No. You have no right to break down the door and come in here
with guns pointed at us."

I remembered my sister's aversion to guns. Reaching behind me, I
tucked the pistol into my waistband and motioned for Zani to do the
same. I didn't need a gun to kill Federico anyway.

I held up my palms. "There, no guns. Now step away from
Federico."

She set her wineglass down on the table, then put her hands on her
hips. "You're mad that we ran away."

"Yes, I'm fucking mad," I said through clenched teeth. "This
stronzo had no business taking you out of Mirabella."

"This stronzo is my *husband*," she shot back. "So mind your tongue,
fratello."

Husband?

The news hit me like an uppercut to the jaw. What the actual fuck?

My muscles swelled, anger flooding me, as I took a threatening step forward. "You pezzo di merda," I spat at Federico. "You married her without my permission! I will punch your teeth into your throat for that."

Federico opened his mouth to speak, but Viviana beat him to it. "You're not hitting my husband. I love him, Mo."

"When?" I snapped.

"Last night. Blessed by a priest and we signed the paperwork. It's official."

Cazzo madre di dio. My sister was married and I hadn't even been there. Never would I forgive Federico for such an offense. "Married or not, you are not safe out here, unprotected. You need to be under a doctor's care, watched by my guards."

"No, I don't. You want me there to keep me safe, but I don't want to stay. Even if something bad happens."

She wasn't thinking rationally. I needed to speak with her alone. "Zani, take Federico outside."

"No!" Viviana grabbed her husband's arm. "I know what that means. And he stays right here, with me. Alive."

I didn't want her upset, so I held up a hand. "I wish to speak with you privately. I swear it. Federico lives . . . for now."

My sister looked between Zani and me, and the mistrust on her face shredded me. I probably deserved it, as we both knew I preferred to settle things with violence, but I was still her brother. "I've never lied to you, sorellina. And I never will."

Her shoulders relaxed and she let go of Federico, but not before kissing him on the mouth. I tried not to react, but it was fucking hard. They shared a whispered exchange, then Federico followed Zani outside.

When we were alone she picked up her wine. "Would you like some?"

"I want to know what you think you're doing."

"I'm living my life, Mo."

"It's dangerous. You need to be under surveillance. With guards who can protect you."

"Federico can protect me."

I rubbed my eyes. "You can't be serious. He's a baby."

"He's twenty-five and raised in the life. His father—"

"Is Don Chiellini. Yes, I'm aware. That doesn't make him capable of protecting you."

"I don't care. I love him and we're staying together."

"Then come to the mansion. Live there with me. Both of you." I would hate it, but better that than worrying about her every second.

"No."

"So, what? You're going to live under Chiellini's care in Catania?"

She shook her head. "Neither one of us wants anything to do with that life anymore. We're done with the mafia."

The words cut like a razor across my chest. "*I* am that life, Vivi. I am the mafia. What are you saying?"

"No, you aren't, Mo. That was Papà and Nino, not you. Don't you see? We can all be free of it now."

"There is no breaking free for me. Even if I hadn't taken an oath, I accepted the role as Don Buscetta to protect you."

"Me? What did I have to do with it?"

"Because the world thought you were dead and I've tried to keep it that way. But you're a Buscetta. If I'm out of the picture, any son of yours would have a claim to the throne. And many men wouldn't care if you were willing or not, if it helped them secure the crown."

She paled. "You can't possibly think that Federico has designs on taking over. That's not why he married me."

"I don't know shit about Federico at the moment. But what I do know is that I've spent my life keeping you safe, and you disregarded my efforts by running off with the first man who pays you the least bit of attention."

"That's not fair. You make me sound stupid and weak! We love each other, Mo."

"Even if that were true," I said, struggling for patience, "you can't put yourself at risk for this man. He's not worth your life."

She looked at me like I'd started speaking another language. "Yes, he is absolutely worth it. Our love is worth it. My future happiness is worth it. Would you not put yourself at risk for Emma?"

I didn't care to have this conversation. "That's hardly the same and you know it."

"Dai, fratello! You are so hard headed. Come." She took my arm and started pulling me to the sofa. "Sit down and stop growling at me."

We settled next to each other and she gave me a small smile. "Giacomo, you can't keep me under lock and key forever. I'll only come to resent you for it."

"Is that what you think, that I've kept you locked up? You know why I did it, Viv."

Her voice softened. "I do, and I'm so grateful. You've always looked out for me. But you're married now, too. You should be focused on your sweet wife and making babies with her."

"Emma has gone back to Toronto."

The words tumbled from my mouth unbidden. Then I cursed my stupidity. Vivi and I had enough to discuss without bringing my problems into it.

"What? Why?" She narrowed her eyes and frowned at me. "What did you do?"

I clasped my hands in my lap and gave her the truth. "You know how you said you saw him in me? Well, it's true. And Emma reacted the same way Mamma used to."

"Oh, Mo." Her hand landed on my arm. "I never should've said those words that day. You are *not* him. Not even close."

"You didn't hear the things I said, or see her curled up and crying. It was unforgivable, Viv. It's good she left."

"You don't mean that. I could hear in her voice how much she cared about you."

"It doesn't matter. I won't make her stay and terrorize her for the rest of our lives."

"I don't believe it. I don't believe you'd terrorize any woman. You're not like him. You're the complete opposite of him."

"Then maybe I'm becoming him. Maybe I really am—"

"If you say you're cursed again, I'm going to punch you."

I sighed. Vivi loved me, so she was trying to reassure me. But I didn't deserve it.

"Mo," she said. "You said she left. So even if you were awful to her, she didn't just take it. Instead, *she left you*. See the difference? She won't let you turn into Don Gero. And you know what that means?"

I peered over at her. "What?"

"That means you can't let her go. You have to win her back."

Win her back? Impossible. I wouldn't even know how. "I came here to talk about you and Federico, not my marriage."

She lifted her chin. "There's nothing more to discuss about me. You're going to let Federico and I live our lives."

"Are you pregnant?"

She shoved my shoulder. "Dio mio, is that all you got out of what I said? No, I'm not pregnant. We are using condoms."

I frowned. I didn't want to think about my sister having sex. "How will you support yourself?"

"I don't know, but Federico and I will figure it out. Maybe we'll stay here. Maybe we'll move to Paris. Whatever we do, it will be on our own terms."

It wasn't lost on me that Emma had predicted this. *"Maybe she wants a life for herself, one where she isn't locked away."* Except I hadn't listened. And now my sister has married and is moving away from me.

My throat tight, I forced out, "All I have ever wanted was to protect you, sorellina."

Viviana eased forward and wrapped her arms around my neck. "And I'm grateful to you for it. I never would have survived without you." I held her close and we stayed there for a long beat before she said, "It's time to let me go."

What choice did I have? I could drag her back to Mirabella or the mansion and keep her hidden, but she'd never forgive me for it.

For my entire life I always put my sister first, so why would I stop now?

"I don't want to," I said quietly. "But maybe you're right. Maybe you need to choose."

I felt her sag against me, her relief evident. "Grazie, Mo."

I kissed her forehead. "Be happy, Vivi. And you will always be my family."

"I'll contact you once we settle somewhere."

"Ti voglio bene, cara mia."

"Ti voglio bene, fratello."

When she eased back a tear had fallen down her cheek, so I smoothed it away with my thumb. "Can I still punch Federico? Just once?"

She laughed, as I knew she would, and wiped her eyes. "Don't you dare. I happen to like his teeth where they are."

There was nothing left to say. We stood and hugged one more time. My body felt empty, hollow and exhausted. I'd lost the two most important people in my life today. There was no one else.

Viviana grabbed my hand before I left. "Go and get her," she said. "Fight for her forgiveness. Otherwise you'll regret it for the rest of your life."

"I already have so many regrets. What's one more?" I kissed her cheeks, then walked outside. The sun was high and hot, but I felt absolutely nothing.

CHAPTER THIRTY

Emma

I expected the jet to head straight to Toronto.

Instead, we headed for Naples.

I didn't understand. Papà was in danger the instant Don Virga learned I'd left Palermo. The sooner we reached the house, the better. I tried insisting, but no one listened.

My twin, on the other hand, wasn't worried. She expected us to wait in Naples, like good little mafia wives and girlfriends, while Enzo and Vito went to deal with Virga and Uncle Reggie.

I had no intention of letting this happen.

No one knew the house, the routines better than me. I could go places and talk to people that Enzo—or even Gia—couldn't. Uncle Reggie wouldn't be expecting to see me, which gave us the element of surprise. And if he really was working with Virga, we needed all the help we could get.

"How could you lie to us? You lie to men, Emma, not to your sisters."

Frankie's disappointment earlier had lodged like a fist under my ribs. I didn't like upsetting my sisters, but I still believe protecting them and their families had been the right thing to do.

And I was about to do it again.

I waited until Gia went to the lavatory before approaching Enzo and Vito. They were talking quietly in the back of the plane, while Massimo reclined in a seat, his eyes closed.

Enzo glanced up as I came down the aisle and his dark gaze pierced right through me. "Emma. Do you need something?"

"I want to help you."

"We're strategizing right now," Vito said, implying that my help was both unwanted and unnecessary.

"I realize that and I can help with the plan."

"Your sister doesn't want you involved anymore," Enzo said. "And because I love her and need to keep her around, you should retake your seat up front and forget helping."

I wasn't going to back down. Maybe the girl who'd flown to Palermo six weeks ago would be intimidated by these men. But I'd discovered a lot about myself since marrying Giacomo. I was much stronger and more resilient than I'd ever given myself credit for.

I slid into an empty seat. "Virga has men hanging out on the estate. As soon as the three of you show up, my father will be killed."

"We're aware," Vito said. "Which is why we were planning to ambush them."

"Just you three?"

Enzo frowned. "You say this as if we are not enough."

Massimo snorted, his eyelids still closed. "I've seen Enzo kill eight men with only a pencil. He—"

"*Stai zitto!*" Enzo snapped at his youngest brother, then refocused on me. "If you tell us the layout, that would help. Maybe you could draw up a floor plan."

"Yes, I can do that. But none of you can get close to Reggie without causing risk to my father. I won't allow it."

Enzo and Vito exchanged a look, and I could see Vito's lips twitching like he wanted to laugh.

"Emma," Enzo said gently. "You need to trust us. This is what we do."

No, that wouldn't fly with me. Not anymore.

I had trusted that Virga would honor his promise about my father after the wedding.

I had trusted Giacomo to find a way out of marriage.

And then I trusted him again when he said I belonged to him.

No, I was done trusting people. Trusting people had only backfired on me in the last month and a half.

"With all due respect," I said, looking them square in the eyes, "he is my father and I will be the one to protect him."

Instantly, the respectful brother-in-law disappeared, leaving only the powerful mafia don in its place. Enzo leaned in, his voice low. "And with all due respect to you, I won't risk your safety by letting you get involved."

"Let her help, amore."

We all turned toward the front, where Gia was retying her hair in a knot atop her head. She looked exhausted as she walked toward us.

"Gianna," Enzo said. "You're not thinking clearly."

She slid around me and dropped into Enzo's lap. Her eyes met mine in silent agreement. *I'm on your side,* they told me. *Always.* I gave her the smallest smile. *Thanks, Gigi.*

Snuggling into his side, she said, "You don't know Emma, baby. Not only is she smart, she's the only one who has been in the house recently. Let her help you devise a plan."

"I've been thinking about it," I explained. "And I think I have a way to get to Reggie in a way he won't see coming."

Enzo kissed the top of Gia's head, then looked at me. "Oh?"

I took a deep breath and let it out slowly. "Yes, and it also involves me."

CHAPTER THIRTY-ONE

Giacomo

Blood stained my hands and clothing, but I hardly noticed.

Last night we captured two of Virga's men and began leaning on them for information about their boss. It was risky, torturing the men of il capo dei capi, but I didn't care anymore. I wanted to know where the old bastard was hiding.

And if Virga exacted retribution, so be it.

I had nothing left to lose.

Just as I was about to deliver another kidney punch, Zani held up his mobile and called, "Our friend in Siderno. He wants to talk to you."

Hardly a friend. I considered telling Ravazzani to fuck off. It was his fault we were in this mess to begin with. If he hadn't taken away the Sicilian drug trade, my father and brother never would've gone after Giulio Ravazzani. My father and brother would be alive, and I never would've been forced to marry.

"He says it's about your wife," Zani added.

That got my attention. Emma left yesterday morning, and I assumed she was with D'Agostino in Naples, planning on how to deal with her father and traitorous uncle.

Wiping my hands on my jeans, I walked over and took the phone from Zani. We went into the side room and shut the door. "Pronto."

"You stupid motherfucker," the voice growled. "You married her without telling me, without her family knowing. Do you have a death wish, Buscetta?"

"If you know of the marriage, then you also know why. Now, I'm in the middle of something so get to the point."

"I'm offering you a choice."

"Oh? And what's that?"

"Give up your claim to her and any child she might be carrying."

I didn't like to be threatened, even by Emma's brother-in-law. Ravazzani might have all the power in Calabria, but this was Sicily. I wouldn't be cowed by him. "Or?"

His voice lowered until it was a smooth menacing rumble. "Or I kill you. Painfully, slowly. You will beg for death."

"Save your threats. She left me. I've already given up my claim."

"I want the marriage dissolved on paper and filed officially. Then I don't want you anywhere near her ever again."

"I don't have time for this, Ravazzani. Emma wanted to leave and I let her go. Your interference is unwarranted."

"Listen to me, stronzo. I want your word that you will stay out of Emma Mancini's life."

"Buscetta," I snapped, irritation twisting like a vice around my shoulder blades. "Her name is Emma Buscetta."

"Interesting. Because if you gave her up willingly, then you wouldn't give a fuck what last name she uses."

He'd tricked me, the clever motherfucker. "I give you my word that I'm letting her go."

"Your word doesn't mean shit to me. Hear me now: if you try to take her from Toronto, I'm coming after you with everything I have."

My muscles swelled and I was growing angrier by the second. Zani put a hand on my shoulder and mouthed, *Calm down.*

I exhaled slowly and did my best to sound unbothered. "I'm not a man who takes women against their will—or locks them in beach houses," I said, reminding Ravazzani of the way he'd reportedly treated his wife. "I believe women should be allowed to make their own choices."

He was silent for a long beat. I'd obviously hit a nerve. *Good*.

Finally, he said, "Then you shouldn't mind signing whatever paperwork I have drawn up."

Gesù, the dramatics. "Stop talking about it, then, and have the papers sent. I'll sign them."

"The first sensible thing you've said."

I ignored the dig. "You know Virga is working with Reggie Mancini to undermine Roberto, no?"

"Yes, we are aware. It would have been nice to learn of this earlier, however."

"That was Emma's decision to keep it from you, not mine."

"Have you lost your balls, Buscetta? Are you not the man in your house?"

He sounded like my father, always questioning whether I was man enough. Fuck this. I disconnected and stared at the floor. I wondered if Emma knew about the annulment paperwork. Had it been her idea?

My chest drew tight, a familiar strangling sensation returning in the vicinity of my heart.

"You okay?"

I shoved thoughts of Emma, Ravazzani, and an annulment aside and gave the phone to Zani. "Of course. We should get back in there. I want to know where Virga is hiding."

"You didn't ask Ravazzani about Emma."

"I assume she's in Naples with her twin, while D'Agostino decides what to do about Toronto. They have to move quickly. If Virga hears she's left Palermo, Roberto Mancini is a dead man."

"Wonder if Reggie Mancini knows where Virga is hiding."

I had considered this already and discounted it as a waste of time. "Maybe, but it'll be faster to get answers out of Virga's men. Let's get in there."

In the other room the men were dangling from hooks, bloody but conscious. I could tell they'd been talking while we were gone, because they both wore sly smiles. I picked up a claw hammer off the table. "What do you fucks have to be happy about?"

"Because we know something you don't."

"That's why you're here, stronzi. So I can learn where Virga is hiding."

"No," the other man wheezed. I'd broken one of his ribs already. "It's about your wife."

I gripped the handle of the hammer tightly. Were they trying to draw this out and distract me, or did they actually know something? "Your information sounds outdated. She's not my wife."

The first man grinned around bloody teeth. "Then you don't wish to know what Virga discovered about your bride yesterday?"

Were these two bullshitting me? I glanced at Zani and read the uneasiness in my friend's eyes. He was worried they might be telling the truth.

I considered the two men carefully. "You said you didn't know where Virga was hiding, so how would you know shit about what he discovered yesterday?"

"Because the men are talking about it. Word spreads quickly when it concerns Signora Buscetta."

Had something happened in Naples? Had Virga tracked her down?

I switched the hammer out for a knife. Flipping it over in my hand a few times, I walked over and plunged the blade into the thigh of one man. He howled in pain, his back arching as he dangled. I found another knife and did the same to Virga's other man.

When they both quieted I picked up the hammer again. "Whoever tells me first dies quickly. Whoever doesn't will suffer for hours in agonizing pain as I carve you up, letting you finally bleed out onto the floor. Now, what will it be?"

Both of them remained quiet, their eyes closed tight as they battled the pain, so I hit each of them in the kidney with the hammer. "Tell me," I shouted, "before I cut your dicks off!"

The one with the broken ribs was the one to speak up after a few more swings of my hammer.

"Virga learned . . . your wife . . . in Toronto."

A ringing started in my ears, the kind that came after a blow to the head. I gripped the wooden handle in my fingers and tried not to hurl the hammer against the wall. My wife, my sweet little scientist. Why wasn't D'Agostino keeping her in Naples, safe from harm, while he dealt with Reggie Mancini? Why would he take Emma to Toronto while Reggie was still breathing?

There was only one reason. Because they planned to involve her somehow.

Those motherfuckers.

Striding over to Zani, I snatched the pistol from his hand. With one shot I killed the man who'd given me the information. Then I opened the door and strode into the outer room, where two of my soldiers waited. "He dies slowly," I told them. "Make it excruciating."

Zani was right behind me as we exited the building and headed toward the car. "You don't want to see what else they know?"

"I know enough." I unlocked the car and opened the door. "They are using Emma as bait for her uncle."

"Che cazzo? That can't be right," Zani said, frowning as he slid inside the sedan. "Why would they put her at risk like that? D'Agostino wouldn't dare."

"It's the only reason he'd take her to Toronto. Maybe Emma insisted on it, thinking she could help. But whatever the reason, D'Agostino is about to be very fucking sorry." I started the car and put it in drive. "Text the crew at the airport. I want the jet ready in thirty minutes."

"Thank Christ. I'm relieved you are pulling your head out of your ass and going after her." Zani started working on his phone. "Should we call D'Agostino next? Or Ravazzani? We should warn them."

Ravazzani would only threaten me away from Toronto again, and D'Agostino wasn't known for being reasonable. No, I wanted to handle this myself.

Still, I wasn't willing to risk Emma's life for my pride.

I tilted my chin at Zani's mobile. "Tell D'Agostino's brother that Virga knows Emma is back home."

"Toronto isn't her home. Her home is here. With you."

He was wrong, but I didn't argue. Emma belonged in Toronto with her family, freezing her sexy ass off as she finished school. But I wouldn't allow anything bad to happen to her, not while I had breath left in my body. I didn't care if she was in Palermo, Toronto, or in a bunker under the Kremlin. I would come to her rescue. Every. Single. Time.

"There." Zani put his phone down. "I've warned Vito D'Agostino. You know, this could be a trap. Virga wants you there, unprotected."

"I don't give a shit." I peeled around a corner. "Nothing else matters if she dies, Francesco."

"About time you admitted that you love that woman."

I hadn't said anything of the sort. But Emma was *mine*—and I wasn't going to allow anything or anyone to hurt her.

CHAPTER THIRTY-TWO

Emma

Toronto, Canada

The low sound of the television was the only noise in the too-quiet house. It was strange to be home. My father was thinner than before and slept longer stretches. The treatments had taken a toll on him. Soon I needed to meet with his doctor and discuss next steps.

But not today.

I couldn't think about my father and his failing health right now. I needed to concentrate.

A single set of footsteps sounded in the hall. Putting down the book I was pretending to read, I braced myself. No one should be on this floor right now.

A man appeared in the doorway. Uncle Reggie. His gaze swept the room, the bed, then landed on me. "Emma. What a surprise. I didn't realize you'd returned."

Liar. No doubt he received a phone call the instant I walked into the house a few hours ago. "Hi, Uncle Reggie. I got back earlier today."

He took a few steps inside, closer to my father's bed. "Back from Panama."

"Peru," I corrected, even though we both knew I'd been in Palermo.

"Yes. Now I remember." His eyes were flat and hard, hardly the stare of the loving uncle. "You look pale. I thought Peru was sunny. Were you not outside much?"

"I was mostly inside medical tents. There wasn't time for anything else."

"I see." He glanced over at my father's bed. "And how is he doing?"

"Do you really care?"

He cocked his head. "What is that supposed to mean?"

"It means I know you've been working with Don Virga. I know you're the one who let him take me to Palermo."

The moment stretched as he grappled with my revelation, first surprise then resignation settling on his face. "So you've figured it out. I have to say, I hadn't expected you to be the one to put the pieces together. Maybe you're as smart as they say."

Before I could respond, he reached under his jacket and pulled out a pistol. It was black and menacing, the weapon perfectly at home in his large hand. "You should have stayed in Sicily. Married. Quiet. *Alive.*"

Through sheer strength of will, I didn't move. "You can't kill me. You're courting the wrath of both Ravazzani and D'Agostino, if you do."

"Who says I planned to kill you?" Raising the pistol, he aimed it at the lump in my father's bed and squeezed off two rapid shots.

I covered my mouth to keep from screaming. A good thing because Uncle Reggie seemed to forget about me for a few seconds as he stared at the lump under the blankets.

It must have struck him that something was wrong, because he darted toward the bed. "Where is the blood?" With one smooth motion, he yanked the blankets and sheets off and tossed them to the floor.

The plastic dummy we'd placed there stared up at the ceiling, lifeless, two bullet holes in its empty chest. My father was safe in another part of the house, well guarded.

"Motherfucker!" Uncle Reggie shouted, whirling on me.

But it was too late.

The D'Agostino brothers and their men were swarming the room, guns aimed at my uncle. "Killing your own brother?" Enzo sneered. "That is fucked up, even for you, Reggie."

Reggie's surprise faded quickly and he suddenly pointed his pistol at me. I froze and stared at the round hole where a bullet could end my life. Sweat broke out on the back of my neck, but I didn't look away. I knew this was a possibility when we crafted this plan, but knowing it and experiencing it were two totally different things. I struggled to remain calm.

Reggie snarled at Enzo, "How the fuck did you get inside?"

I spoke up. "Did you honestly think three teenage girls didn't figure out how to sneak on and off of the property?"

"Fucking D'Agostinos," Reggie said. "This doesn't concern you. This is Mancini business."

"Wrong," Vito said. "This is soon to be my business, which means it's D'Agostino business."

"And it has been D'Agostino business since I made a deal with Roberto a few months ago," Enzo clarified. "And do you know what D'Agostinos do to traitors, Reggie?"

My uncle's face turned purple as he sputtered, "T-this business is mine every bit as much as it belongs to Roberto. He had no right to make that deal with you!"

Enzo didn't blink. "I don't think he would agree. Should we ask him?"

"He's too sick. He's not in his right mind. Besides, all the men here will follow my lead. They'll never accept some Neapolitan piece of shit."

"This stronzo doesn't wish to leave here alive," Massimo D'Agostino mumbled.

"Uncle Reggie, please," I said. "We know you've been working against my father. Put down your gun and beg for his forgiveness."

"Forgiveness? I'd rather die."

"Don't say that." I clasped my hands tightly in my lap. "This doesn't have to end badly."

"You should listen to her," Enzo said. "Drop your gun."

"I was willing to kill my brother," Reggie said to Enzo, though his eyes were still on me. "Killing my niece isn't nearly as hard. So you will drop your guns instead."

"Reggie!" my father's voice barked from the doorway. "What are you doing?"

I looked at the empty space where the phone was hidden. "Papà! No!"

Reggie's attention switched to the door—and that was all the chance Vito needed. One quick pop to the head and Reggie dropped to the ground, a bullet between his eyes. I didn't need to check to see if he was still alive. I knew a wound like that meant instant death.

I shoved my guilt aside for now. My uncle had tried to murder my father and worked with Virga to force me into marriage. There would never be peace while he still breathed. I knew this, but I wished there had been another way.

"Go round up the others," Enzo ordered his men. "Let's clean house."

"Wait," I called as I rose to my feet. "You aren't going to kill all of them, are you?"

Enzo holstered his gun and came over to me. One of his large hands patted my shoulder awkwardly. "You did well, Emma. The voice recording on the phone worked just as you said it would. Bravissima, bella."

"I'm serious, Enzo. Please tell me you aren't going to slaughter all my father's men."

"We must root out all the men working with Virga and your uncle. It is too dangerous to leave any of them alive. It's how we deal with these things, Emma."

"But not all of them are disloyal to my father."

"That is what we are about to find out. It's the only way I can leave you here and know you are safe. If there's any doubt, your sister will have my balls. Besides, these are Vito's men now. As of today, he's taking over."

"You are telling the men that my father is sick."

He gave a brisk nod. "It's the only way and your father has already agreed. Each man here will pledge loyalty to Vito. Those that refuse earn death."

My goodness, that was harsh.

Enzo gestured toward the door. "Allora, go and see your father. No doubt he's very worried about you."

There'd been no choice but to tell him of Reggie's treachery and our plan to kill his brother. My father was sad, but he understood. He told me he had a suspicion that something wasn't right over the last few months.

I hadn't confessed the part about going to Sicily and marrying Giacomo. I was afraid of what that news would do to my father.

Better not to say anything.

I averted my eyes from my uncle's dead body on the floor and stepped into the hall. Massimo D'Agostino followed me, his gun still in his hand. "You don't need to come with me," I said over my shoulder. "It's not far." We set my father up in Frankie's old room at the other end of the mansion.

"I do." Massimo kept his eyes on our surroundings, hyper vigilant. "Your uncle's men have not all been secured. The threat has not passed."

He was wrong. My uncle was dead, his compatriots being dealt with. In a few hours it would all be over. My father was safe to die in peace, however long that took.

————

I knocked on my father's door. "Gloria, it's me. Everything's okay now."

My father's aide answered the door. Her expression relaxed as soon as we locked eyes, then she threw her arms around me. "Oh, I'm so happy to hear it. We have been so worried."

I squeezed her back. "It's over. I'm okay."

"Let the girl pass, Gloria," my father grumbled behind us. "I want to see her."

Gloria and I parted, but I held onto her shoulder. "Let me speak with him alone for a few minutes."

"Of course. He's eating lunch, so I'll come back in a bit."

Gloria edged around me and left. Massimo stood awkwardly in the bedroom, still holding his gun, then pointed to the hall. "I'll be right outside the door."

My father was sitting up, a tray of mostly uneaten food nearby. He looked tired and worried. As I drew closer, I smiled as best I could, hoping to reassure him that I was okay. "Hello, Papà."

"Come here, *principessa*." He patted the bed and I sat down, careful to keep my weight from shifting him. I leaned in and kissed his paper-thin cheek.

My father didn't mince words. "Is he dead?"

"He is. You don't need to worry any longer. Enzo and his men are dealing with the others."

"Thank God. Your sisters, they have chosen good, strong husbands."

Giacomo was a good man, too. I wished I could tell my father about him, but what was the point? "How are you feeling? Uncle Reggie's betrayal has to be upsetting for you."

My father made a dismissive noise in his throat, then coughed for a few seconds. "He was always jealous, always pushing for more. But I needed him when I got sick. I didn't think he would ever do this to the family."

"You could have brought Vito here sooner. Let him take over."

"Yes, I should have. We always think we have more time, don't we?" He studied my face. "How are you? I know you don't care for violence."

"I'm fine." I could still picture Uncle Reggie's lifeless eyes, staring at nothing. But honestly? I was too numb to process anything right now.

"You don't look fine. You seem sad. Ever since you returned from Peru, these sad eyes. What's going on, principessa?"

"Just a lot going on," I lied. "Don't worry about me."

"But I am worried about you. It's what a father who faces death must do for his children. We worry about what happens when we leave."

A series of small explosions went off in my chest, bursts of pain that I tried to hide from my father. "I want you to get better. I want you to relax and focus on your health."

"Emma, we've both spoken to Dr. Morrissey. We know the inevitable draws closer every day. That's why I want to discuss something with you."

If this was about his funeral arrangements, I might actually start sobbing. I could not handle that conversation right now. "Papà—"

"I want you to marry Vito D'Agostino."

All the air left my lungs in one *whoosh*. "What?"

"Now, listen. I know you aren't interested in marriage, that you think it will interfere with your studies. But Vito is smart. Ruthless. And he isn't one to react rashly or have a temper. I believe this is a good match for you."

But I'm already married.

It was on the tip of my tongue, but I swallowed it back. I couldn't say it and hurt my father like that. Besides, it didn't matter. My marriage would be annulled soon and I would be free to marry again.

But I didn't want to marry Vito. Or anyone else for that matter. Maybe someday, but my next partner wouldn't be in the mafia, that was for certain.

"Absolutely not," I said when my mouth could form words again. "That isn't happening."

"Emma, I let your sisters choose their own men—"

"You tried to marry Frankie off to Giulio Ravazzani."

My father gave a tiny shake of his head. "That is immaterial. She chose Ravazzani in the end. But I want to choose a good husband for you. I don't want you waiting too long to marry."

"Have you talked to Enzo or Vito about this?" I assumed the answer was no. One of them probably would've mentioned that bigamy was outlawed in Canada.

He exhaled heavily, and I knew he was growing tired. I patted his arm. "Let's talk about this later, Papà. I don't think either of us are in a place to make any serious decisions right now."

"You are avoiding the issue, hoping it will go away." He leaned back and closed his eyes. "If you marry him, the business stays in the Mancini family. My grandchildren will still lead this 'ndrina. This is important to me, Emma."

Guilt gnawed in my belly, and I felt like an even bigger disappointment. Not only was I lying to him, I was crushing his dreams of continuing our family legacy. "I'll think about it," I forced out.

"Good. That's all I ask. We'll discuss it more tomorrow."

He didn't open his eyes, and I took that as my cue. I kissed his forehead. "Ti amo, Papà." I took the lunch tray away and reclined his bed so he could rest.

When I opened the door I found Massimo there, eyes alert and gun at the ready. "How much of that did you hear?" I asked quietly in Italian as we walked downstairs.

"None of it. Why?"

"I have to find your brother and talk to him."

"Who, Enzo?"

"Vito. My father wants me to marry your brother. We need to come up with a story to not disappoint him."

"Maybe a story like you are already married to another man?"

"Quiet," I snapped. "I don't want my father knowing about Giacomo."

"He'll find out eventually, bella."

"Not if we're granted an annulment first."

It shouldn't take long. Frankie was having Fausto's lawyers draw up the paperwork at this very moment. Things were slightly more complicated because Giacomo and I were married by a priest, which meant an Ecclesiastical Court needed to pronounce the marriage annulled. But no one said no to Fausto.

Bottom line, I would be single in no time and it would be like the marriage never happened.

"You can't marry Vito," Massimo said. "It would be shameful for him to marry another don's ex-wife, especially one from the Cosa Nostra."

"Hello? You're not listening. I don't want to marry your brother."

"Why not?"

We arrived at the bottom of the stairs. No one was around. "Gloria?" I called, but there was no answer.

We began walking through the house, searching for signs of life on the first floor. Now that my uncle was dead, the house should be filled with D'Agostinos and my father's men. "Where's Gloria? Where did everyone go?"

Massimo grabbed my arm as he moved closer. "Something is wrong."

"What? How do you know?"

"Stay here." He went to the front windows and peeked through the curtains. Then he pulled out his phone and hit a button. It rang and rang.

"Who are you trying to call?"

"Vito. I don't see anyone outside." He marched back to me and took my hand. "Come on. I'm taking you to the panic room."

"Try Enzo."

"He rarely answers his own phone, not unless it's your sister. Come. We're wasting time."

He tugged me along, but I dug in my heels. "I'm not going to the panic room. I'm going up to stay with my father." I'd go crazy in the panic room, alone, wondering what was happening to everyone else.

"Emma—"

I tore my arm out of Massimo's grip. "I'm going to his bedroom. I'll be fine. Go, find out what's happening."

"My orders are to stay with you."

I wasn't going to argue. "Then let's get upstairs to stay with my father." I hurried toward the stairs, desperate to reach my father's room and make sure he was okay.

Massimo trailed me, his footsteps silent on the old floors. I tried to think positively. Enzo and his men were capable, so everything was probably fine. We would laugh about this later, and Enzo and Vito would tease Massimo for overreacting.

When we reached my father's room I pushed open the door. I'd hoped to find Gloria sitting next to my father's bedside.

Instead I found Don Virga.

And he was pointing a gun at Massimo.

Massimo started to lift his gun, but Don Virga was faster. The silencer on the end of the gun muffled the sound to just a puff of air, and Massimo crumpled onto the ground, clutching his abdomen. I gasped and covered my mouth with my hands. Oh, no. Was he dead? Blood pooled on the floor underneath him to stain the carpet dark red. My chest hollowed out and I started to kneel, desperate to help him.

"Don't move," Virga barked. "Or I'll shoot you, as well."

I forced myself to stand perfectly still. My father didn't move. Was he dead? Asleep? "What are you doing here?"

Virga settled deeper into his chair and kept the gun trained on me. It was the second time today I'd been held at gunpoint and I was not a fan. His weathered face broke into a slick grin. "It is nice to see you again, Signora Buscetta."

Massimo moaned on the ground at my feet. Thank god he was alive. "You need to let me help him," I said and gestured to Massimo.

"You should be worried about yourself, Emma. Tell me, why are you not in Palermo?"

"I came for a short visit. To see my father."

Virga shook his head. "Lies. You came to escape your husband, to escape your duty to the Cosa Nostra, no? Did you honestly think I would let you disobey my orders?"

"I didn't escape him. I came here to see my father."

"Is that so?" Virga adjusted his pistol so it was aimed at my father's prone form. "Perhaps I should kill your father to make sure you do as you are told."

"No!" Relieved that my father was still alive, I took a tiny step closer to the bed. "I'm not disobeying your orders. There's no reason for anyone else to get hurt."

"I will decide who else gets hurt from now on, little girl."

Speaking of hurt, why hadn't my father stirred? "What did you do to him? Why isn't he awake?"

Virga gestured to an empty syringe on the hospital tray. "Morphine. He won't be able to help you now."

Shit. I swallowed hard. "The house is crawling with guards, as well as Enzo and his men."

His withered face curled into a pleased smile. "I'm afraid not. They've all been called away on an urgent threat involving your twin."

My heart actually stopped beating in my chest, blood rushing in my ears. I thought I might pass out. Gia was waiting in the hotel suite we'd rented last night to finalize our plans. "What happened to Gia?"

"Nothing, but D'Agostino doesn't know that."

That was a relief, but I still had Virga and Massimo to worry about. Maybe if I kept him talking, I could delay any further violence until Enzo returned. "How did you know I was even here?"

Virga looked at me like I was a fool. "Did you honestly think your father's room was the only place I installed cameras?"

Crap. Yes, I had. We only disabled the single camera in my father's room before laying our trap today. "You don't need to hurt anyone else. I'll come with you."

"That's a good girl." He rose slowly out of his chair. "Your husband made me look like a fool. Did he honestly think I wouldn't find out about him speaking to the other families, trying to turn them against me?"

I had no idea what he was talking about. What mattered was stabilizing Massimo, then getting Virga out of the house before Enzo returned. I couldn't live with myself if Enzo or one of his brothers was killed because of me. My sister would be devastated. "Please, let me quickly help Massimo and then I'll go back to Palermo with you."

"I don't care about that Napoletano pezza di merda. Get moving."

"You have to let me help him. He'll bleed out on the carpet if I don't."

Without waiting for Virga's approval, I bent down to check on Massimo. Blood was everywhere and his skin was alarmingly pale. His eyes were screwed shut, face twisted in extreme pain. "Just hold on," I whispered as I took his hands and placed them over the wound. "Press here as best you can."

I spotted Massimo's gun under his hip. Without thinking about it, I kept my back to Virga and slipped the gun into the pocket of my hoodie. I wasn't sure I could use it, but there was a small amount of comfort in having a weapon on me.

"Go." Virga shoved my shoulder. "Get up and walk toward the stairs."

Crossing my fingers that Virga hadn't noticed me taking the gun, I stood. "I'll come. Just don't hurt anyone else."

"*Amunì, amunì!*" He pushed me from behind. "Hurry. I want to leave before the other D'Agostinos return."

CHAPTER THIRTY-THREE

Giacomo

Cazzo, it was cold here. How could people stand it? My Mediterranean blood weeped for sunshine the second we stepped off the plane in Toronto.

A high stone wall surrounded the large Mancini estate, the entrance gated and well-fortified. Roberto Mancini had taken security seriously, which was a relief. I hoped my journey here proved unnecessary.

But I wouldn't draw a full breath until I saw Emma, unharmed, with my own eyes.

We drove slowly by the main gate. There weren't any guards visible, but several cars were parked in the drive close to the house.

D'Agostino's plane touched down about thirty-six hours ago. They would've come straight here, Emma to see her father and D'Agostino to kill Reggie Mancini as quickly as possible. "She's there."

"Thank fuck we beat Virga here," Zani said. "One less problem to worry about."

Zani's contacts in Toronto hadn't seen or heard of Virga's arrival yet. But that didn't mean anything. Virga was very good at not being found. "I hope that's true. Because I will rip off D'Agostino's balls if he puts my wife in any kind of danger."

Zani parked the car on a side street. Surrounding the Mancini property was the wall Emma had once mentioned. It wasn't terribly high, and I could easily imagine her sisters climbing over it to escape.

"What now?" Zani asked as he shut off the engine. He reached into the glove box and pulled out a pistol.

"We climb over the wall and sneak in."

There were more guns in the trunk, so I got out and began tucking weapons into my clothing. When Zani joined me I pointed at the wall. "She once said they used to sneak out of the house, over this wall. So if Reggie's men are watching, I don't think they'll see us."

"After you," Zani said with a sweep of his hand. "I'm not going first."

"You are supposed to protect me. You took an oath."

"I took a blood oath for the Cosa Nostra, stronzo. Not to climb walls and rescue women you never should have let go in the first place."

We crossed the street. It was after sundown, so we had the added benefit of the darkness for sneaking onto Mancini's estate.

Even in the dim streetlight, it wasn't hard to find the section of the wall Emma told me about because there were obvious foot holds in the stone. I placed my feet inside and pushed up to grab the top edge. Three seconds later I was over, dropping to the ground, with Zani quickly following.

The two of us kept close to the wall as we moved toward the house. I couldn't hear any guards. I glanced back at him and read the concern on his face, as well. Normally, mafiosi are laughing and joking with each other, so this silence meant we needed to be alert.

Lights blazed inside the house and perimeter. A covered pool was surrounded by shrubs, while a circular drive sat up front. I headed for the drive. No one would expect us to walk right in the front door.

I clutched my gun loosely as we edged around the cars, keeping low, our shoes soft on the stone. I told myself there was a good chance we'd walk inside and find Emma safe with the D'Agostinos, Reggie Mancini already dead.

Just as we were about to climb the steps, the door opened and

Emma appeared. She was wearing an oversized hoodie, her head down, but I'd recognize her anywhere. My lungs inflated, relief like a drug in my veins, and I started to smile. *Thank Christ.*

Then a man stepped up behind her, and the second he saw me he grabbed Emma from behind. She stumbled backward, arms flailing, but it was too late.

Virga's gun rested against her temple.

Her startled gaze met mine. "Giacomo! What are you doing here?"

I kept my gun at my side, but Zani had his pistol trained on Virga. Though I wanted to look at Emma, I didn't dare. I needed to keep calm. "Let her go."

Virga shuffled Emma in front of him until they were both on the stoop. "You have saved me a trip to Palermo to kill you, Buscetta. And I get to do it in front of your pretty wife."

"The only one who is dying today is you. Release her and maybe we'll kill you quickly."

Virga gave a soft whistle and four men materialized like ghosts from the side of the house. I recognized them from Virga's yacht, and they each held a Glock on us. "Drop your weapons," Virga ordered. "Or I shoot your wife in the head."

My muscles shook with fury and resentment, mostly at myself. This never should've happened. I never should have let her out of my sight, so this was my fault.

"You won't hurt her," I said. "Ravazzani and D'Agostino will wipe you and your clan off the face of the earth, if you do. Not even you are that stupid."

"It will be a tragedy." Virga's face morphed into an exaggerated expression of mourning. "Bullets were flying everywhere. We have no way of knowing who shot her, though I did my best to protect her from you."

"They will never believe it."

"They will, because they hate you. You married their innocent sister-in-law without their permission, a second son who is nothing more than a dumb ox."

I remembered my call with Ravazzani, his anger at the marriage and insistence I give up any claim to Emma. D'Agostino hadn't been any friendlier. They would shed no tears if Emma were widowed today.

But would they believe her death was an accident? There was a chance Virga could convince them. After all, the whole world thought Emma meant nothing to me because I'd stupidly let her go. I agreed to an annulment. Why would anyone think I'd tried to protect her?

Still, I didn't want to give up. The fighter in me couldn't let that happen. All those years enduring my father's cruelty, all those years taking out my anger and aggression on my opponents in the ring? I never thought I would bend to another man, not while I still had my wits and my strength.

But this was different. This was Emma. I couldn't bear to see her hurt, not if I had the power to prevent it.

Besides, what did my life matter if she died?

"Let them go," I said. "You want me. So, give Zani a car and let him and Emma go. I'll stay."

"I'm not doing it," Zani said quietly. "I'm staying with you."

Despite my best intentions to remain focused, my gaze drifted to Emma's face. She was staring at me, her eyes full of emotion, those lips I loved to kiss trembling with fear. I hadn't seen her so pale before, so terrified. Not even when Virga forced us to marry. She was so brave, mia piccola innocente, and it killed me to see her like this.

I had to keep her safe.

"Get her out of here," I rasped under my breath, my eyes never leaving my wife. "Per favore, Francesco."

"I'm not leaving you."

"This is all very touching," Virga sneered, "but you're hardly in a position to give orders, ragazzetto." He motioned his men forward. "Now, toss your weapons onto the ground. All of them."

CHAPTER THIRTY-FOUR

Emma

I couldn't breathe. My heart was beating too fast, my mind tripping over the horror surrounding me. I didn't want Giacomo to die. Not here, not now.

When I first saw him in my father's driveway, I froze in both surprise and overwhelming relief. Stupid, so stupid. I should have run instead, not let shock root me to the spot. Because of my stupidity, Virga got his hands on me and used me as a human shield to capture my husband.

And now he was forcing Giacomo and Zani to give up their weapons.

"Don't do it," I pleaded, which caused Virga's arm to tighten around me.

"Shut up," the older man growled. "The weapons, stronzi. On the ground. Now."

Giacomo carefully lowered his arm and pitched his gun onto the dirt. Zani did the same. Then the guards rushed forward to pat them down, removing the other weapons they had strapped to their bodies. A small arsenal soon piled up at their feet.

Once they were unarmed, Giacomo and Zani were restrained with plastic ties around their wrists, then forced to their knees. Helpless.

I had to do something before it was too late.

The pistol sat heavy in the pocket of my hoodie. I hadn't forgotten about it, but I wasn't sure what to do. If I took the gun out now, would Virga shoot Giacomo? Was I shooting behind me at Virga? Could I even do that? I'd never fired a gun in my life.

"You are a traitor, Buscetta, trying to turn the other families against me. Now you will see what I do to traitors to the family."

Giacomo didn't flinch. "It wasn't hard. You are not well liked among the families."

I could feel Virga vibrating with anger against my back. His hot breath ghosted my ear as he snapped, "You will regret this, ragazzetto. I will make you suffer."

That didn't phase my husband either. He shook his head. "No, you won't. You have to kill me quickly, before D'Agostino and his men return."

"Maybe I will put you in the trunk and take you somewhere so I can kill you slowly." He shifted and I could feel his eyes on my profile. "Or maybe I will kill your wife in front of you first."

Giacomo puffed up, his bicep and pectoral muscles swelling. His nostrils flared as he inhaled, and he reminded me of a dragon about to spit fire. "If you touch one hair on her head, I will peel the flesh from your withered old bones."

Virga shoved me away from him, then marched down the steps. When I caught my balance I saw he had Giacomo's hair in a fist, their faces close together. "I hardly think you can stop me, ragazzetto. But hear this: after I kill you I will pass your wife around to my men, who will degrade her and humiliate her. When they're done I'm sure the Russians have a brothel where she can live out the rest of her days, someplace Ravazzani and D'Agostino will never find."

A shiver of revulsion, along with a flood of bad memories, went through me at those words. I was kidnapped last year by Russian sex traffickers. It had taken me months of therapy after Enzo rescued me just to sleep in the dark again, and I sometimes still woke up in a cold sweat, dreaming of those few days locked in with a dozen other young women.

No way was I going through that again.

And no fucking way was I allowing Virga to hurt my man.

In a blink I pulled the pistol out of my hoodie and aimed it at Virga. Like I'd done it a hundred times before, I squeezed the trigger. The force of the explosion nearly sent me off my feet, my ears ringing as I struggled to stay upright.

When I looked up, chaos greeted me.

Giacomo and Zani were both on their feet, hands somehow now free, fighting with Virga's guards. Virga was on the ground, unmoving. Had I . . . ? Was he dead?

My stomach twisted and I couldn't pull my eyes away.

I heard other gunshots, but they weren't from me. The pistol, heavy and cold, remained clutched in my hand, my arm dangling at my side. What had I done?

I had no choice, right? He was about to kill Giacomo and send me off to a Russian brothel.

I could feel the edges of my vision start to swim, blackness creeping in along with the guilt. I killed someone. I was a killer, a murderer.

I bent over at the waist and tried to breathe, but the air wouldn't come. My throat closed up, and I knew I was going to suffocate. I dropped to my knees, bracing my hands on the ground.

From far away, I heard a familiar voice. "Amore, amore. Bambina, come here."

Boots appeared in my vision, then gentle hands were pulling me up. Giacomo was kneeling there, his eyes clouded with worry. His palms cradled my face, but I couldn't feel him. I couldn't feel anything.

"Breathe, Emma," he said sharply. "Take a breath."

I tried, but all I could manage was short huffs of air that did no good. I couldn't make my lungs work properly.

I'm having a panic attack.

I knew what was happening, but all the advice, all the ways to alleviate a panic attack eluded me. I couldn't think straight. I shook my head, my free hand clutching Giacomo's shirtfront in desperation.

His fingers tightened on my skin and he looked me square in the eyes. The coffee-colored irises held so much trust and affection, a softness I'd hardly seen from him before. "You can do it," he said quietly. "I promise. You're safe. Everyone is safe. I'm not going to let anything bad happen to you ever again. Just breathe, bambina. Per favore? For me, just breathe."

The vise inside my chest eased a fraction and I was able to suck in a shallow breath.

His lips curled up at the edges and he started taking deep breaths to encourage me. "That's it, amore. Keep going. In and out, like me."

I matched his pace, inhaling and exhaling slowly. My vision cleared and I felt myself return to my body as if coming out of a dream. My knees were on the ground, my hand gripping Giacomo, and his thumbs caressed my jaw. I leaned into his touch, so relieved I could cry.

Leaning in, he pressed a kiss to my forehead. "That's my good girl. So brave. You saved my life, bambina."

"I killed him," I whispered into the hollow of my husband's throat.

"No, Emma. You shot him. I killed him."

That made me feel marginally better, but I didn't like the idea of hurting someone, of being responsible for someone else's death. I wanted to heal people. Was I kidding myself? Maybe someone like me, coming from the world in which I grew up, couldn't escape this evil.

Giacomo wrapped his arms around me and pulled me against his warm chest. "Whatever you are thinking, stop. You're a good person. You aren't cruel or vindictive. But it was his life or mine—and you saved my life."

I nodded. I understood, but I wasn't ready to celebrate it. And Massimo was still hurt on my father's floor. "I need to go inside."

"Zani and I will take care of things out here." He eased back, but didn't let go of me. "Ti amo, mia bella moglie."

Warmth settled inside my chest, thawing me out slightly, but I couldn't say it back. The words were stuck. I had too much swirling in my head, too many emotions warring in my chest. I gave him an attempt at a smile, then kissed his cheek.

When I turned, he put a hand out to stop me. "Wait."

"Giacomo." I sighed in annoyance. "I really need to get inside. Massimo D'Agostino is bleeding out on the floor upstairs."

"Give me the gun, bambina."

I realized he was trying to pry the pistol from my fingertips, but I had a death grip on the handle. "Oh." I released the metal, glad to get rid of the weapon. If I never shot another gun, it was too soon.

"Good girl," he said and kissed my forehead again. "Go and save him, amore."

Taking care not to look at the bodies on the drive, I hurried inside and went upstairs. My feet couldn't move fast enough as I ran the length of the hall. When I reached my father's room I heard someone banging on the closet door. I unlocked it and found Gloria there, sweaty and disheveled.

"Thank god. That man forced me in here and I couldn't get out." She saw the bed. "Oh, no! Roberto!"

"He's been given morphine, but he's okay." I could see the steady rise and fall of his chest under the blankets. "Help me with Massimo."

Gloria worked in an emergency room in Toronto for years, so she sprang into action. She grabbed a pair of gloves from Papà's first aid kit and knelt by Massimo to assess his injury. Taking out her phone, she called my father's private physician and told him we had a gunshot wound and he needed to come right away.

"You made it sound like my father's been shot," I told her as I put pressure on Massimo's wound.

"Which means he'll be quick about it." She dumped a bunch of sealed gauze bandages on the ground next to us. "Your father called once to have a rash looked at and I swear the doctor was here in fifteen minutes flat."

I suppose being a mob boss meant you had the best of care whenever you needed it.

"Let's pack the wound to stop the bleeding," Gloria said. "Though I'm worried about how much blood he's lost."

"Should we call an ambulance?"

"No hospitals," my father's weak voice said from the bed. "Not unless he's about to die."

"Allora, allow me to help." A large figure knelt next to me. "Tell me what to do."

It was Giacomo.

Gloria didn't miss a beat. "Put on gloves and start unwrapping these bandages."

"Who the hell are you?" my father asked as he struggled to sit up.

"I am Emma's husband, Giacomo Buscetta."

"Husband!" I could hear the hurt and disappointment in my father's voice. "Is this true, Emma?"

My insides curdled with dread, but I lifted my hands so that Gloria could pack the wound with the gauze Giacomo was unwrapping. "I'm sorry, Papà," was all I could manage.

"Signore, I will give you all the details once the young D'Agostino is stable. But Emma and I were married in Palermo several weeks ago and you should know that I'm keeping her."

It wasn't romantic per se, but the declaration was such a blunt, to-the-point Giacomo thing to say. If I wasn't so focused on Massimo, I might've swoon.

"I can't feel his pulse," Gloria said, pressing on Massimo's throat with her fingertips. "We should rush him to the hospital."

In a flash Giacomo lifted the unconscious Massimo like he weighed nothing at all, then strode from the room. As we hurried after him, Gloria elbowed me. "You married that hunk of man meat? Nicely done, Emma."

"Emma!" my father called behind me. "I expect you to return with an explanation."

"I will, Papà. I swear!"

And I hoped he would forgive me.

CHAPTER THIRTY-FIVE

Giacomo

I hated hospitals. Thank god Emma was here and knew what to do.

The young D'Agostino was rushed to a treatment room, which left Emma and I alone in the waiting area. Zani stayed back at Mancini's to deal with clean-up, and Gloria returned to look after Roberto.

Emma and I sat side-by-side in uncomfortable chairs, while a sporting event I didn't understand played on the television. It was on ice with brooms and looked fucking freezing. "Why is your country so cold?" I asked my wife.

She bit her lip in the most adorable way. "You're Sicilian. The surface of the sun would seem cold to you."

"You're probably right." I was dying to touch her, but I wasn't sure if I could. So I moved my leg closer, until my thigh met her knee. She didn't move away and I considered this a small victory. Quietly, I said, "I am very happy to see you."

Her gaze flicked up to mine briefly. "I thought you didn't want me anymore."

It gutted me that she believed this. I didn't want to have this conversation in a hospital, surrounded by other people, but Emma deserved the truth. And I knew I wouldn't get her to leave until D'Agostino had been stabilized.

I leaned closer and put my mouth near her ear. "I have never, not once stopped wanting you, amore."

She gave a small shiver, then eased away from me. "Then why did you order me to go?"

As I stared at grown men sweeping ice, I wondered how to put all my thoughts into words. "Because I'm not my father. I won't keep you against your will. I've seen what it does to women in our world, and I couldn't stand to make you unhappy."

"So you told me to leave, then didn't come home all night. Where did you go?"

I wouldn't lie to her. "I drank in my office, then went to Theresa's."

"You slept with Theresa?"

Gasps erupted from some of the women seated around us, and one grandmother-type sent me a disapproving glare. I answered loud enough for everyone to hear. "I passed out on her couch. Nothing happened, *sul mio onore.*"

"Oh." Emma didn't speak for a long moment, like she was thinking this over. "Then why did you even go there in the first place?"

"I couldn't think of someone else who would take me in at that hour."

"Because you didn't want to come home."

"It was a mistake, bambina, and I am sorry for it. I was worried over my sister and took it out on you. Can you forgive me?"

"Is she okay?"

I noticed she skirted the topic of forgiveness. I tried not to take this as a bad sign. "Viviana is married and wants to live her own life. As someone once predicted."

Emma grabbed my arm and squeezed, her expression full of sympathy. "Oh, I'm sorry. That must devastate you."

I wasn't about to lose this chance. Angling toward her, I took her hand in mine and laced our fingers together. I loved touching her, feeling her soft skin against mine. "Her leaving wasn't nearly as bad as yours. It felt like a part of me died when I learned you left—"

"Aww," I heard from one of the women nearby.

Heat burned under my skin and I lowered my voice. "Can we go outside or somewhere private to talk?"

Emma nodded, then stood up and went to the desk. She told the attendant we would be right outside, and to please come get us if there was news on D'Agostino.

I followed her through the automatic doors and a blast of cold air stung my bare arms and face. Long strands of brown hair blew around Emma's face as she stared up at me, so she took a band off her wrist and put her hair up in a bun. It made her look so young and sweet, and my chest expanded with tenderness. She was the sort of woman a man was lucky to find, a rose in the middle of thorns. How had she stayed so perfect, so pure in such an ugly world?

With one finger I smoothed a piece of hair behind her ear. "You are so beautiful," I said quietly.

She rolled her eyes dramatically. "Hardly. I've been held at gunpoint, nearly kidnapped, and shot someone. I'm a literal mess."

"Not to me. I couldn't be more proud of my strong and resilient wife."

Her expression didn't change. In fact, it turned even more skeptical. "You don't have to be so nice to me. I know you agreed to sign the annulment papers. Fausto told Frankie about it."

"As I said earlier, I didn't want to keep you against your will. I thought you should have a choice in your future."

"And now?"

"Now I wrestle with both sides. Part of me wants to keep you in Palermo, even if you don't want to come back."

"What happened to not being like your father?"

I wasn't my father, I knew that now. Emma would always come first with me. Losing her had shown me that her happiness *was* my happiness. I would do anything for her.

I ran my knuckles along the edge of her jaw. "Please, bambina. Come back with me. I'll spend every day at your feet, worshiping the very ground you walk on. I will fight for you, for our children, and I promise to love you harder with each breath I take until the day I die."

She blinked a few times in rapid succession. "But Virga is dead. We don't have to stay married. You can go back to your fuck buddies and your mob boss life. We can both forget this ever happened."

"Is that what you want? To forget me?" I wouldn't blame her if the answer was yes. What had I done to make her want to stay with me? Why would a genuinely decent person like Emma want to be with me, a crude killer who'd never known kindness? I held my breath, waiting for her answer.

"I can't see how it would work," she said, once again avoiding the question. "I want to have a life, a career in medicine. I can't do that as your wife."

"Why not? Your twin has her own career, no?"

"Yes, but it isn't easy. It requires money and security and a lot of patience on Enzo's part."

"Dai, you think I don't have patience or money?" Grabbing her hand, I stroked the soft skin of her inner wrist. "I will make this happen for you, I swear it. Please, choose a life with me, amore. All you have to do is say yes."

Indecision swirled in the depths of her brown gaze. "You said we would never be equals, that I thought I was smarter than everyone else."

I clasped her face in both palms and rested my forehead against hers. "Emmalina, I'm not a perfect man. And I can't promise I won't ever hurt you again or say something stupid. But I love you, and I will apologize over and over until you believe me."

Her fingers wrapped around my wrists, holding me in place. "I have to think about this."

My heart sank to my toes. I hadn't convinced her. Maybe she didn't love me as much as I loved her, or maybe she couldn't forgive me for what I said and did. Or maybe I truly was cursed.

I pushed all my emotions aside, buried them deep. There was nothing more I could say. If my confession hadn't changed her mind, then I had to accept it. I had to let her go.

I started to pull away, but her hands latched onto my shirt. Eyes pleading, she whispered, "Wait, Giacomo. I'm not saying no."

"But you are not saying yes, either."

"I just need time. This all happened so fast and my father is still dying. I don't know what I want or need—"

"Emma! Oh, my god!"

A tall brunette with similar features to my wife launched herself at Emma, breaking our hold. I stepped back and found Enzo D'Agostino and his brother Vito striding toward us. They both wore grave expressions, no doubt worried over their other brother.

"Hey, Gia," Emma said, hugging her sister fiercely. "I'm so glad you're here."

"Where is he?" Enzo barked at us, his brows pulled low.

Emma answered first. "He's being treated. They haven't given us any updates."

"Then I will learn these updates for myself." Enzo moved around us and headed straight for the hospital doors.

"No, wait," Emma called, but Enzo didn't break stride. He disappeared inside the building, Vito right behind him.

"Come on, Em," Gia said, tugging her sister along and pretending I didn't exist. "Let's go find out how Massimo is doing."

Emma let Gia pull her toward the hospital, but I stayed put. I only cared about her, not a Napoletano mafioso, and I wanted to continue our conversation. I wasn't ready to give up. I imagined throwing her over my shoulder and carrying her back to my plane, fighting any man who tried to stop me.

"I just need time."

I wasn't stupid. I knew what that meant. It was what people said when they didn't want to hurt you to your face.

Emma looked over her shoulder at me, and I saw her frown. *Are you okay?* she mouthed.

Not *Come with me*, or *Hurry up*. Not even a promise to talk later. It was clear she didn't want me to follow.

Instead, she was worried she'd hurt me, because that was Emma. She cared about everyone else at the expense of herself. It was one of her most admirable qualities, but I didn't want her concern. I wanted her to fight for us, for me. I wanted our fake marriage to have a real chance.

I wanted her to choose me.

But that obviously wasn't going to happen.

The big industrial-looking building swallowed her up, the electronic doors closing with a *swoosh* then falling silent.

I let out a long breath and steeled myself against the pain rippling through my chest. As a young boy I'd learned that love disappointed and hurt. It allowed others to have power over you. It gave them the ability to rip out your heart and shred it into tiny pieces.

I wouldn't make that mistake again.

Turning on my heel, I left.

CHAPTER THIRTY-SIX

Emma

The house was full again.

Gia was staying here along with Enzo and his brother, and Frankie had flown in from Siderno. Massimo was still in the hospital, but he was going to be released soon.

I should have been happy. I was surrounded by a big chaotic family, just like when we were growing up.

Except I was miserable. Someone was missing.

The Buscetta plane departed two days ago while I was still at the hospital. Giacomo and Zani had disappeared without a word, presumably going back to Palermo. I didn't blame him. He'd poured his heart out and I hadn't been able to give him an answer about how I felt. I'd asked for time, and so he left.

There hadn't been a word since.

I stared into my mug and stirred my tea. Everyone was still asleep, and I was using the quiet time this morning to think. My sisters had avoided the topic of my marriage and my missing husband, but that wouldn't last. There had been too much tragedy to deal with the past few days, but I knew them well. Soon they would demand to hear everything.

I wasn't sure what to tell them.

Did I love Giacomo? Yes, unequivocally.

But love wasn't enough to build a marriage. A real partnership depended on respect and communication, a sharing of values and goals. If I went to Palermo, I was giving up on what I'd worked for—a way out of the world in which I'd been raised. Giacomo might promise things would be different for me, but how could they be? A man in his position couldn't make too many allowances without risking everything. And Sicily was definitely old school in its thinking.

"Ciao, bello. How is my little man this morning?"

My head snapped up at my oldest sister's voice. Mobile at her ear, Frankie breezed into the kitchen wearing fancy red silk pajamas. She always looked beautiful, like a mini-version of our mother, who'd been a world-famous model.

Frankie went to the espresso machine and began fiddling with the controls. "Mamma loves you, Marcello. Yes, I do. Ti amo, ti amo, ti amo."

Marcello was her two-month old son. How she stayed so gorgeous after having three kids so close in age was a mystery. I would undoubtedly be a mess 24-7.

That brought up thoughts of Giacomo and babies.

"You're going to take my big load like a good girl, no? And I'm going to put a baby inside you."

I flushed and shifted on my stool. Those types of memories weren't helpful. This required logic, not emotion.

"Thank you for that," Frankie was saying into the phone, the tone of her voice changing. "And yes, I miss you, too, Paparino."

Whatever Fausto said in return on the other end made my sister blush, so I looked away. I couldn't take another happy couple right now. Enzo and Gia were bad enough.

She brought a demitasse of espresso to the kitchen bar. "I have to go, you dirty old man. My sister is here and you're embarrassing her." She paused. "No, she's moping." Another pause. "I'll tell her. Speak to you later, amore mio. Ciao."

When she disconnected she sipped her espresso. "Fausto says you're better off."

"Why did you say that I'm moping?"

"Because you are. Did you sleep at all last night?"

Barely, but that wasn't the point. "You all need to leave me alone and let me run my own life."

Frankie snorted. "Have you met your two sisters? Have you met your brothers-in-law? Leaving you alone isn't in the cards, Em."

I didn't want to talk about any of this, so I shifted topics. "I heard you sat with Papà for a long time last night." Frankie had been distraught, to say the least, when she learned our father was dying. She was working through the stages of grief rapidly, alternating between grief, anger, and despair since she landed in Toronto.

"Yes, I did," she answered. "And don't change the subject. We're talking about you."

"I don't want to talk about me."

Gia came in. "Oh, good. We're talking about Emma." Her dark hair was a mess, and she was wearing the shirt Enzo had on yesterday, her legs bare. "Let me grab coffee before we start."

"We're not starting anything," I said.

"Yes, we're starting," Frankie said sternly. "So buckle up."

Gia went to the espresso machine. When the drip started she put her hands on the counter, then bent to stretch out her back. Frankie watched her with a critical eye. "You okay over there, G?"

"I think so? Jesus Christ, my man can do damage. It's a good thing I'm in shape. Otherwise I'd never survive his dick."

"That explains your hair," Frankie said.

Gia took a band off her wrist and pulled her hair into a bun. "Don't hate on me because I chose someone younger and better looking than your husband."

Frankie shook her head, a chuckle escaping. "Sure, keep telling yourself that."

My two sisters liked to take digs at each other. Normally, I'd try to play peacemaker, but not today. If they were arguing, then they were ignoring me and my marriage.

"I'm surprised Fausto didn't come with you," Gia said. "Considering

Enzo and his brothers are here." Enzo had kidnapped Frankie once, before he and Gia fell in love, and Fausto wasn't the type to forgive and forget.

"Don't worry," Frankie said. "They had a lengthy conversation before I landed. I believe threats were traded on both sides."

"Figures." Gia picked up her coffee cup and came over to the bar. "Enzo wouldn't tell me what was discussed, only that Fausto was sending men to watch over you."

"I'm not afraid of Enzo." Frankie waved her hand. "He loves you and would never dare do anything to risk losing you."

"Facts," Gia said and sipped her coffee. "Did she tell you what happened?"

"No. You?"

"Nope. So, let's have it Emma. What happened?"

They both stared at me intently, like this was a deposition. Or an inquisition. My sisters were scary when they wanted to be.

I got up off the stool and went to the microwave to warm up my tea. "There's nothing to tell. He came to help when he heard Don Virga was here. When that was over he asked me to return to Palermo, but I told him I needed more time. Then he left."

"Enzo said Giacomo is very protective of you," Gia said. "Like, extremely protective. Sort of how someone in love would act when their partner is in trouble."

"He let me go," I pointed out. "Twice. Neither of your men did that."

Gia and Frankie both gaped at me. My twin recovered first. "Uh, Enzo said some pretty terrible things and kicked me off his yacht. He's lucky I didn't cut his balls off."

"And Fausto? Jesus," Frankie said, shaking her head. "He was awful to me before I was kidnapped. The only reason he didn't kick me out was because I was pregnant with Raffaele."

I'd forgotten this. Because they were all so happy now, it was easy to forget their early struggles. "I don't know. I feel like it's different. We were forced to marry and it all happened so fast."

"Right, because being kidnapped and locked in a cage on a yacht was slow and sensible." Then Gia gestured to Frankie. "And being swooped away and taken to Castle Ravazzani overnight gave you lots of time to prepare, right?"

"Tons," Frankie said dryly. "Come on, Em. What's really going on here? Do you have feelings for him?"

"Duh." Gia answered for me. "Of course she does. Have you seen him, Frankie? He looks like a professional rugby player, totally built and covered in tattoos."

"I haven't seen him," Frankie said. "But I've heard he used to fight professionally."

"Enzo says Buscetta was a beast in the ring."

"Oh, I don't know if I like that." Frankie adopted her protective older sister scowl. "I don't want you with someone violent, Em."

"He's not violent." Other than punching walls, which I didn't approve of. "He would never hurt me."

"How do you know that?"

I thought of how he'd held my face, helping me to breathe during my panic attack. How he'd stroked the inside of my wrist when trying to convince me to give our marriage a chance. He'd refused to take my virginity until I consented. And the way he'd taken punishments for his sister as a boy. Those were not the actions of a cruel man. "I just know. He's very sweet and gentle with me."

"Then what's the problem? He clearly wants you. Was he terrible in bed?"

Only Gia would ask something so personal. "No," I said, my skin turning hot. "That was definitely not it."

"Looks and fucks like a god. Got it," Gia said. "So, why are you acting so broken and sad?"

"Because life is about more than sex," I snapped. "It's about having a career that is more than a mob boss's wife."

"And he won't let you?" Frankie asked. "I know Sicilians are a little behind the times, but—"

"No, he said I can do whatever I like. But . . ."

Gia squinted at me, reading me as only my twin can. "But you don't believe him."

"It's not that, exactly. You both know what I dream of doing, what I've been working toward for years. How can I be a doctor and yet married to a man who kills and tortures for a living? It makes no sense."

"Em," Gia said with a sigh. "Life doesn't always make sense. There are some things that can't be explained, like the popularity of neon or puffy vests. God knows I never thought I'd end up shackled to a mob boss and stepmom to his two kids. But he makes me really happy and I love his kids."

"And I certainly didn't want this," Frankie added. "Nor did I want it for either of you. It's a hard life, one full of danger and risk. But I love Fausto and our family. I wouldn't change any of it, no matter what happens down the road."

"It's not the same. Yes, you're a fashion designer," I said to Gia. "And Fausto let Frankie get her MBA and work for his legitimate businesses. But I want to be a doctor, which is completely against everything the mafia stands for."

Frankie's brow wrinkled as she studied me. "You think I agree with everything Fausto does, how he earns his money? Because I don't, Emma. But I love him and that means accepting him as he is. And I have to live with my choice."

"Well, I don't know if I can live with it," I said honestly.

"You accepted it with Papà," Gia pointed out. "Growing up here, the big house and private school and riding lessons. Not to mention you're the closest to him out of the three of us. You didn't even move out when you had the chance. And Papà is as mobbed up as they come. So why is it okay for him, but not for Giacomo. What's the difference?"

I stared at my cold tea. No good answer came to mind.

"You want logic, Em," Frankie said. "But love isn't logical. Sometimes it happens despite our best intentions. Don't throw it away because it doesn't make sense."

"Right," Gia added. "And you can look at it like you're evening out the cosmic balance sheet. You're out doing good while he's out doing bad. Maybe some of your good deeds will save his soul when the time comes."

I rubbed my eyes with my fingers. "You know I don't believe in any of that stuff."

"Then believe in yourself." Frankie reached over to squeeze my arm. "You're a smart and decent human being, Em. If anyone can balance out the evil in this world, it's you. I think Giacomo needs you even more than you think."

"I will fight for you, for our children, and I promise to love you harder with each breath I take until the day I die."

The conviction in his voice left no doubts, but what did I want? I dragged in a deep breath and let it out slowly. I couldn't deal with this right now. Too much was happening. I had to focus on my father.

"I don't want to talk about this anymore," I said, setting down my mug. "It's a lot right now and I'm still processing."

"Fair enough," Frankie said, "but don't wait too long. These men have their pride, too."

"Oh, God," Gia groaned. "It's true, Em. And once you fuck with his pride, he has to get it back. That's when shit gets ugly."

"Or really, really good," Frankie muttered under her breath, and both my sisters laughed.

I put my mug in the sink and headed for the main stairs. Sometimes my sisters were no help at all.

———

As I approached my father's bedroom the next day, I was surprised to see Enzo coming out. Had they been discussing business?

Enzo didn't smile when he saw me, but I didn't expect it. He only smiled for Gia and his kids. The rest of the time he looked like he was five seconds away from ripping someone's head off.

"Ciao, Enzo," I said. "Come stai?"

I expected him to keep walking, but instead he stopped and folded his arms. "Your sister is worried about you."

This wasn't exactly news. Gia brought it up every time we were in the same room, which was why I started attending my classes in person. I needed to have a routine again, something to take my mind off Giacomo, or I'd go bonkers. "I'm fine. I'm going to sit with my father for a few minutes while he's still awake. Excuse me."

I started to walk past him, but Enzo blocked my path. "Are you talking to Buscetta?"

"No." I hadn't talked to Giacomo since he left over a week ago. "Why?"

"We are wondering why you haven't signed the annulment papers."

I wished I had an answer. All I knew was that I grew sick to my stomach when I thought about putting my signature on that document.

Which made no sense.

"I'll sign them in my own time. And everyone should mind their own business and stop focusing on my disastrous marriage."

"From what I saw this was no disaster. He came to protect you as soon as he heard Virga was in Toronto. He nearly died to save you. And I saw the way he looked at you."

My throat tightened, a ball of emotion lodged right in the center. I swallowed hard. "Yeah, well. I don't see how it could ever work between us."

"Mamma mia." He shook his head. "I never thought I'd meet a woman more stubborn than Gianna."

"Thanks?" I really didn't know what to say. This was the longest exchange I'd ever had with Enzo, and talking about my husband with him was too weird. "I guess I should go visit with my father. See you later."

I started toward Papà's room and opened the door. He was sitting up in bed, looking over some paperwork. He removed his glasses and set the papers aside when he saw me. "There's my baby girl. Come in and sit down. I've missed you."

"Hi! I'm sorry. I meant to stop by before class." But I'd been too busy sulking. I sat on the edge of his bed and moved in to kiss his cheek. "I saw Enzo coming out a second ago."

"He's smart, that D'Agostino. Gia hasn't always made good decisions, but ending up with that man is the best thing she's done."

Though he made it sound like a joke, I knew Gia was sensitive about his opinion of her. "Papà, she's desperate for your approval. Don't tease like that."

He sighed and briefly closed his eyes. "I've been hard on her over the years, but she should know that I'm proud of her. I'm proud of each of my girls."

"Well, she'd like to hear it again, I'm sure."

"Always trying to bring peace to the family. You're like your mother that way." His lips curled into a wistful smile. "I can't wait to tell her about each of you when I see her again."

My eyes began burning, but I didn't want to cry. I'd come to terms with his death months ago. Now I just wanted him to go peacefully, without any suffering. "You're not dying yet."

"Not until you make up with your husband, at least."

The story of my marriage had tumbled out to my father days ago. He was furious over Virga's manipulation and Uncle Reggie's betrayal. I knew he blamed himself. But I also told him all the good things about Giacomo, how happy we'd been for that tiny stretch in Palermo.

Now my father wouldn't let the idea of reconciliation go.

"I'm not moving to Sicily," I said. "I'm going to stay here with you."

"Your place is at your husband's side."

"No, it's here with my ailing father."

"Bull-fucking-shit, Emma."

I blinked. My father rarely cursed in front of us. "You don't want me to stay?"

"I want you to sort things out with Buscetta. A wife should not abandon her husband."

Was he actually blaming *me?* I slid off the bed and lowered myself into the chair. "I didn't abandon him. He's the one who left."

"He asked you to come back with him. Said he wanted a real marriage with you. If he left without an answer, that's on you."

I instantly regretted telling my family everything that happened with Giacomo. "I'm not ready to deal with it, Papà."

"You must, because he won't wait forever, sweetheart. He's Sicilian and Sicilian men have a lot of pride. Rejection won't sit easy."

Pride again. Why was everyone obsessed with Giacomo's feelings of self-worth? What about *my* pride? "I didn't reject him. I asked him to give me time."

"To an Italian man—hell, to any man—it's the same thing."

It was?

The two of us fell silent. I hated disappointing my father, but how could I even think of leaving Toronto? Every moment left with him was a gift, and I wasn't going to squander it. "If he loves me, he'll wait."

My father snorted and that turned into a prolonged coughing fit. When he was able, I helped him take a sip of water and he cleared his throat. "You don't think Giacomo will wait for me?" I asked as my father relaxed into his pillows.

"Why would he? Have you given him any reason to think there might be hope?"

No, I hadn't. Hard to give hope for something I wasn't sure was possible. "There's nothing wrong with an annulment. Or even a divorce, Papà." I forced the words out, even though they stung my throat like acid. "It's okay if it doesn't work out."

His gaze turned shrewd, assessing. He looked exactly like the father of my youth, the one who knew exactly when one of us had been bad. "Emma, this isn't like you to give up so easily. What aren't you telling me?"

I hadn't told him this part. It wasn't easy to tell your father you didn't want to marry a man that was like him. "I'm not certain my vision of the future lines up with Giacomo's. You know, medical school, residency. Practicing medicine. I don't know many mob wives with careers."

"Your sisters both have their own pursuits, though Frankie has put those on hold for now to look after the children. And your mother had her own career. Why can't you?"

"Yeah, but Mama gave up her career when she married you."

"True, but it was her choice. I never asked her to."

"That's not what she told Frankie."

My father's pale skin lost even more of its color and he struggled to sit up. "What?"

"Settle down." Rising, I helped him back onto the pillows. "You'll have another coughing fit."

"Fuck coughing fits. Tell me what your sister said, what Sofia supposedly said."

It wasn't hard to recall. Frankie had been telling us this story ever since I could remember. "Mama said we should have our own lives and never give them up for any man."

"And how is that me forcing her to give up her modeling career?"

"She obviously regretted it. And she never modeled again after we were born."

"True, but she still worked and accepted jobs after we married. I didn't stop her from that." His eyes clouded, unseeing, as he stared at the far wall, lost in a memory. His lips curled into a knowing smile. "To be honest, I loved it. Paparazzi followed her wherever she went and she was invited everywhere. Men all around the world lusted after your mother and she was *mine*. I was so proud. It wasn't until she became pregnant with Frankie that she retired. But that was her decision."

"Then why did she regret quitting? Why insist that we each get a college degree before marriage?"

He paused, like he was gathering his thoughts. "Your mother grew up in a poor town outside of Rome, and in that area the mafia was all they knew. It wasn't like here. It was old school, Emma, where girls were married off at thirteen, fourteen years old. After they married, wives were hardly seen outside the home again. I wouldn't have allowed you to be married so young, but your mother worried just the same. She wanted her girls to be strong, educated, and to be able to stand up to any man you married."

An unbelievable sense of sorrow wrapped around my heart, sharp and painful like thorns. "There is so much I don't know about her, about your life together, and now you're—" It was too hard, too heavy to actually say the word at the moment. I would probably start sobbing if I stopped to think about it.

He reached for my hand, but was too far away, so I laced my fingers with his. "It's okay. You can say it. I'm dying. We both know it's happening, sweetheart."

I shook off the dark cloud. There was no use ruining this with tears. I'd spent months accepting the inevitable. "Soon you won't be here and the connection to both of you will be lost."

"You aren't losing me yet, and we can talk about anything and everything before then. But it's time for you to live your own life, not sit here with me."

"Will you please stop trying to get rid of me?"

He squeezed my hand weakly. "I want to see you happy. Buscetta is a good man."

"You barely met him."

"We chatted briefly before he left for Palermo and I could see that he cares about you very much. And both D'Agostino and Ravazzani speak highly of him, and you know they don't often hand out praise—especially with the Cosa Nostra."

Papà and Giacomo had talked? "What did the two of you talk about?"

"You, mostly."

My eyes grew wide. "Me? Like what, exactly?"

"That is private between your husband and your father. But know that we agree on the most important thing, which is your happiness."

"He said that?"

"You seem surprised. From what I understand, he's promised you the world to get you to come to Sicily."

I couldn't help but picture Giacomo's pleading expression as he said, *"I will give you everything you want and spend every day at your feet, worshiping the very ground you walk on."*

"He's no bullshitter, your husband," my father continued. "I like that. He says what he means."

"Yes, that's definitely true." I let go of his hand and sat back in the chair. "I don't see how we make sense together. A doctor and a mob boss. It would never work."

"Sweetheart, haven't you ever heard that opposites attract? No one thought a famous model and a mob boss would work out, but life isn't always about what's sensible. Sometimes we make our own logic. You just have to be willing to take a risk on it."

CHAPTER THIRTY-SEVEN

Giacomo

One week later

I tightened my hold on the steering wheel, wincing at the resulting jolt of pain in my freshly-scabbed knuckles. It was the only thing I could feel these days. Everything else was blessedly numb.

Over the past few weeks Zani and I had eliminated the remainder of Virga's clan. A new il capo dei capi would be crowned soon, but it wouldn't be anyone from Virga's family. They were all dead.

I didn't care who took over. As long as he stayed out of my way, we'd get along just fine.

"You fighting again tonight?" Zani was staring down at his phone, scrolling on one of the social media apps where girls posted half-naked pictures all the time.

"You have a problem with it?"

"Of course not. I love to watch my closest friend try to taunt someone into killing him in the ring."

I scowled at his sarcasm. "That is not what I am doing."

"Oh, so you're hoping for another concussion? Fingers crossed, then. Maybe it will be the one to finally do permanent damage, no?"

I kept my attention on the road, ignoring him. Zani didn't understand. Fighting was what I knew. It was in my blood, the marrow of my bones. My father made me this way, molded me into an empty shell capable of withstanding incredible pain and agony. An animal reacting on pure instinct with no need for thoughts or emotion. It was good to be that man again.

I didn't want to feel or think. I craved pain—both giving and receiving—because when I was unconscious I couldn't dream.

"Have you tried reaching out to her, because—"

"Do *not*," I snarled, "even bring it up."

He muttered a string of curses under his breath and continued with his phone. When it rang a few minutes later I assumed it was one of his many hookups.

"Pronto," he said, mobile at his ear. "Tutto bene?" He listened for a few more seconds. "You're kidding. No shit? Sì, sì. We're on our way."

"Cosa?" I asked when he disconnected.

"Sal needs you at home."

"What for?"

"An emergency, he said."

This wasn't like Sal. He wasn't one to panic. He'd faced some tough shit in his life. "What emergency?"

"He didn't give me any more information. Said to come right away."

"Any word from the guards?"

"No, nothing."

So it wasn't anything to do with security or the outside perimeter, which meant it wasn't important enough to pull me away from family business. Especially to bring me back to the house, a place I'd mostly avoided since returning from Toronto. Too many memories, too many reminders. She was everywhere I turned and it was fucking torture. And Sal followed me around, like a worried mother hen.

I ground my back teeth together. "If this is about getting me to eat again, I'm taking his other eye."

"You can't blame him for being worried about you," Zani explained calmly. "It's his job."

"His job is to take care of the house, not me."

Zani went back to his phone and the car fell silent for the rest of the way. By the time we arrived at the estate, I was ready to strangle someone. The guard gave me a nod before opening the gate, and we continued along the drive. I slammed the car door shut and stomped to the kitchen door, Zani right behind me.

The smell hit me as soon as I entered the room. *Lemons and sugar. Her.* She was here.

My head swung toward the bar. A small frame was there, perched on a stool, long brown hair swirling down her back, cup in her hand. She angled toward the door, her brown gaze assessing me as I drank in the sight of her.

Zani bumped into me from behind. "Che cazzo?" Then he edged to the side. "Ah. Ciao, signora." His hand clapped me on the shoulder and he pitched his voice low. "Buona fortuna, amico."

Zani gave me a shove and shut the door, leaving me alone with Emma. Sal was nowhere to be found, the traitor. We would have strong words later. A warning that my wife had returned would've been appreciated.

I stood there, silent. My tongue felt thick and useless in my mouth. I didn't know what to say to this woman anymore. I'd poured my heart out until there was nothing left. Has she forgotten something here? Otherwise, why not ring me instead of flying all the way here? Why not sign the annulment papers and mail them back?

Punishments are always best delivered face-to-face.

How could I forget? This was practically the Buscetta family motto, a lesson instilled in me from a very young age.

Fine. She could deliver her bad news and then go. I would not break.

I shoved my shoulders back and started forward. Though my empty stomach churned, I went to the refrigerator and took out a sparkling water. Then I leaned against the counter, crossed my legs and opened the bottle. And waited.

"Hi," she said, her voice rougher than usual. "How have you been?"

Did she honestly care? "I have shit to do, Emma. Say what it is you need to say and let's be done."

She opened her mouth, then closed it. Her eyelids fluttered as she blinked rapidly. "Is that all you have to say to me after almost a month?"

I took a long swig from the bottle, the crisp water tasteless in my mouth. "What would you like me to say?"

"I don't know. I thought—well, I thought you might be happy to see me."

Happy? I didn't even know what that word meant anymore. "More curious than anything else."

"Wow." She gave a dry chuckle as she shook her head. "My sisters and father were right. You're not going to make this easy, are you?"

Why would I? If she planned to stomp on my heart again, then she wouldn't get any fucking help from me.

When I didn't respond, she let out a heavy sigh. "I want to work this out."

"The annulment? I assume you have the paperwork."

She jerked, her back straightening. "I meant our marriage."

I nearly choked on a mouthful of water. It took a few seconds to regain my bearings. "I don't understand. I thought . . ."

"What did you think?" She cocked her head and studied me, confusion causing her eyebrows to dip. "Did you think I came all this way to finalize the annulment?"

Yes, that was exactly what I'd assumed. "Are you saying you want to stay married?"

"I am." She licked her lips. "Unless you've changed your mind."

Hope unfurled in my chest like wings, but I beat it back. There was a lot of shit to wade through before I could allow myself to believe this was happening. "I told you how I felt, but you seemed certain we'd never suit. You said you couldn't see how it would work."

"I know. Sometimes I have a bad habit of relying on logic."

"And?" I asked when she didn't elaborate. "What does this mean?"

She flopped her hands on the counter, adorably flustered. "It means that love isn't always logical. There are pheromones and chemistry and—"

Love. I definitely heard her say it. I hadn't been imagining it.

Before I knew what I was doing, I stalked across the tile and went around the edge of the bar. I took her face into my hands and crushed our mouths together. She tasted like surprise and sweet innocence, and I suddenly couldn't get close enough. Without breaking our connection, I picked her up off the stool and set her on the marble counter, then deepened the kiss until she gave me those breathy little gasps I'd been aching for these last few weeks.

Delicate fingers curled into my hair, her nails stinging my scalp, and she wrapped her legs around my waist. I licked into her mouth to find her tongue, my blood humming with relief and desire. I could stand here for hours, kissing her, soaking in the feel of having this perfect woman back in my arms.

She pulled back and sucked in gulps of air. "Holy smokes, that came out of nowhere."

"You said love isn't logical." I kissed her again, nipping her bottom lip. "Do you love me, bambina?"

I could feel her smile against my mouth. "Yes, Giacomo. I do. Ti amo, amore."

Fuck. Me. I hadn't even allowed myself to imagine that she might return my feelings. It seemed too good to be true, but I knew she meant it. Emma wasn't a liar. "Ti amo, mia bella moglie. Per sempre."

"Per sempre, mio grande marito." Her hands ran over my arms and shoulders. "You feel thinner, though."

"Dai! You sound like Sal." I pressed my face into her neck and inhaled her, then kissed the smooth skin under her jaw. "Are you really here? Is this happening?"

"Yes, it is. I've been miserable without you."

I both hated and loved to hear it. "I've missed you so much. And now that I have you, I'm never letting you go again."

"I'm afraid you'll have to."

The words penetrated my lust-filled brain and I straightened. "No. You are mine and I'm not allowing you out of my sight."

She put her palm on my cheek and brought me closer. "Baby, my father is dying. I want to spend time with him, too."

"Then we'll bring him here."

"It doesn't work like that. He can't travel and it's better to keep him at home, where he's well cared for. I won't be gone long stretches, but I plan to go back and forth to Toronto as much as I can."

I hated this. I wanted to keep her here with me, every second of every day. But I also knew my wife. She had to care for others, especially her family. It was deeply embedded in her personality.

"It's a condition of our marriage," she added, as if I needed an ultimatum to be convinced.

"We are already married," I couldn't help but point out.

"I mean, if you want to *stay* married."

"Then I'll go with you," I blurted, then instantly felt foolish for being so needy. "To ensure that you're safe."

"If that makes you feel better, marito." She kissed my jaw, her lips feathering across my chin. "To keep me safe."

Smart bambina. I rubbed her sides and basked in her gentle affection. "I'm going to make you very happy," I murmured.

"You haven't heard my other conditions, though." Her hands went to the button of my jeans, which she popped open. Then she reached inside my briefs to clasp my semi-hard cock. Cool fingers wrapped around the shaft and pleasure sparked along my spine, causing my eyes to roll back in my head.

"Conditions?" I rasped. "Tell me."

"Medical school and residency. Then I'll practice medicine in Palermo somewhere."

"As long as you give me babies along the way."

"But—"

I thrust up into her grip and kissed her briefly. "Babies, Emmalina. Are you pregnant?"

"No," she whispered. "I had my period in Toronto."

"Were you disappointed?" She was breathing hard now, her fingers pressing into my firm cock. This talk was turning her on. I bet if I checked her pussy, it would be growing wet. "Answer me, bambina."

"No. I mean, maybe. Kind of. A little bit."

The truth sent a jolt through my balls. "I told you—making babies is the best part. I'm going to enjoy trying every second of the day with you."

"That won't leave much time for running your empire."

"I will manage." She tugged harder on my shaft, her fingers pulling on the piercing. It sent rolls of pleasure and a sharp bite of pain through every nerve ending. Minchia! That was too good. If she kept it up I might come here in the kitchen. "We will start right now."

"Right now? But Sal and Zani are around somewhere. It's embarrass– whoa!"

I lifted her clean off the counter and began carrying her out of the kitchen. She wrapped around me like an octopus and buried her face in my throat. I slapped her ass once. "From now on you will wear skirts and no panties in this house. I want you wet and available for me at all times."

"I have one more condition. Don't you want to hear it?"

I was done talking. "Whatever it is, I agree." I started up the stairs, taking them two at a time.

She chuckled and sank her teeth into my earlobe. "You're never allowed to remove your piercing."

"I wouldn't dare, mia sporcacciona e dolce moglie."

EPILOGUE

Giacomo

Toronto, Canada
Three weeks later

It was the night before my wedding.

Or "vow renewal ceremony," as Emma called it. My wife was a stickler for details.

But I considered this our real wedding, one we chose for ourselves.

Unfortunately, I was spending the night before the ceremony with three men I would soon call family: Fausto Ravazzani, Enzo D'Agostino, and Roberto Mancini.

Fucking unbelievable. I couldn't wrap my head around it.

The Ravazzanis flew in this morning from Siderno, while D'Agostino, Gia, and his two children, had been staying here for the past week with us. Emma and Gia had arranged all the wedding details in a surprisingly short amount of time.

Now the four of us, along with Zani and Vito D'Agostino, were settled in Mancini's library with whisky and cigars. While the smoke was hot, the air remained frosty. We all had reasons to dislike and distrust one another.

Mancini was the single cheerful person in the room at the moment. And why wouldn't he be? His three daughters had married the most powerful men in Italy.

I watched my father-in-law take a sip of whisky. "Should you be drinking that?" I asked.

"Absolutely not, so don't tell my daughter."

"Which one?" All three daughters were taking an active role in Roberto's care, now that they knew his situation. Thankfully, my wife didn't need to shoulder this burden alone any longer.

"Any of them," Mancini said. "Don't mention the whisky or the cigar."

I raised my palms and puffed on my own cigar. Mancini deserved a little rebellion in his final months, in my opinion.

We sat in prolonged silence, no one willing to break the ice first. Ravazzani was polished and controlled, relaxed in his leather chair like a king. D'Agostino was the opposite, his leg bouncing with restless energy. I concentrated on my drink and waited. I wasn't the talkative type and this was Mancini's home, so I figured the conversational duties fell to him.

"It's good that we're all here," my father-in-law finally said. "We need to bury the bad blood for the sake of my daughters."

"With all due respect, Roberto," Ravazzani said smoothly. "This is a happy occasion, no? We shouldn't dredge up the past and ruin it."

"And with all due respect to you, Fausto," Mancini said. "You cannot refuse a dying man's wish, especially on his daughter's wedding eve. Now, I need to know the three of you will work together, as a family, after I'm gone."

D'Agostino's mouth twisted in distaste, like he'd tasted a sour lemon. "You ask the impossible. There is too much ugliness between us."

"Nonsense." Mancini stared at each of us intently. "And for the sake of my daughters, you will do this."

No one offered up another protest, because Mancini knew how to hit us the hardest: by mentioning the women we loved.

Ravazzani checked the time on his gold watch, then sipped his drink silently, while D'Agostino's leg began bouncing again.

"I have no issues with Buscetta," D'Agostino offered up unhelpfully.

"I would say the same," I said, "if only you hadn't held my men at gunpoint until they let my wife leave."

"She asked for my help in escaping you. What was I to do?"

"Stay the fuck out of it?"

D'Agostino leaned his head back and sent three perfect smoke rings toward the ceiling. "When my woman's sister calls for help? If you think I can refuse, then you haven't met Gianna Mancini."

"We can all agree," Mancini said a little louder, "that protecting your wives is paramount. If my daughters are mistreated or threatened in any way, then I expect one or more of you to intervene."

"I did not mistreat her, for fuck's sake," I growled.

Ravazzani set his crystal tumbler onto the table with a snap. "You kicked her out. I think this qualifies, Buscetta."

"I let her go—something neither of you were man enough to do when your woman wished to leave." Yes, I knew the history between Ravazzani and his wife, as well as D'Agostino and Gia. These two could try to act like saints, but they were far from it. Both had held the women against their will.

The temperature in the air dropped another twenty degrees. D'Agostino and Ravazzani glared at me, their eyes promising retribution.

"That's enough," Mancini said disapprovingly. "This is what I'm talking about. The three of you need to set aside the past and work together."

"D'Agostino's woman has come to Siderno," Ravazzani said, "and I let my wife travel here to be with her family. I've not kept the sisters apart. I think that is the best we can hope for at this point."

"Cazzata," Mancini said. "Are you three so shortsighted that you can't see what you gain by a strong partnership? If you help each other, you become that much more powerful."

"No offense," D'Agostino said, "but I don't see us going into business with the Cosa Nostra."

"And I need no help from others to remain powerful," Ravazzani added.

Mancini sighed and rubbed his eyes. "Mamma mia, even at a dying man's request, you are unwilling to cooperate."

I thought of Emma and what she'd want from her family after Mancini died. She would want to remain close to her sisters and their families. She wouldn't like animosity between Sicily, Siderno and Naples.

For Emma, I could do this.

"What do you propose?" I asked Mancini.

"Finally, someone willing to hear reason." Mancini leaned back in his chair. "We are businessmen, so let's do business. What do each of you want to settle your debts with one another?"

This was an easy one for me to answer. "The drug trade Ravazzani stole from Palermo."

"No," came Ravazzani's short reply.

"I'm not asking for all of it," I qualified. "Only a portion of what you stole."

"And I have said no," he said. "Why would I strengthen the Cosa Nostra at the expense of my own pockets?"

"Because Buscetta is family." Mancini let this sink in. "The same reason I am passing my empire on to Vito."

"Yes, now that you bring this up." Ravazzani picked his glass up and twisted the crystal in his palms. "I would like to know, why was my son not considered?"

Mancini appeared confused at the question. "Giulio? Because he has Spain."

"No, I meant Raffaele. Your own grandson."

I snorted. "Because he's four."

"Which means," D'Agostino said, "you would run it in his stead and you hardly need more power. My brother is the right choice."

"This is what I am trying to explain," Mancini said. "We cannot have the houses at odds. It's bad for business, and it's bad for my daughters. We need to set the past aside. Tonight."

"What you are asking is for me to concede," Ravazzani said with a dismissive flick of his fingers. "I give up everything and receive nothing in return."

"What do you want?" Mancini asked.

Slowly, Ravazzani cocked his head in D'Agostino's direction. And waited.

D'Agostino grew perfectly still. "Fuck, no."

Ravazzani shrugged, a perfect lift of his shoulders in his suit coat. "Then we have nothing else to discuss here."

"Basta!" Mancini slammed his hand weakly against the armrest of his chair. "I'm your father-in-law, and I am dying. I have made peace with my three daughters. Do not force me to call them in here and see what cowards they have married."

Cowards?

I ground my back molars together. Mancini had balls, calling the three men in this room cowardly. But he knew he could get away with it because we were more scared of our wives than of him. And Emma would never speak to me again if I disappointed her father.

"There's no reason to involve the women in this sort of discussion," Ravazzani said. "My request is not unreasonable. All I want is a percentage of D'Agostino's computer fraud business."

Ah. This was how D'Agostino made his billions, with hackers all over the globe.

"A percentage," D'Agostino said with a roll of his eyes. "You won't be happy until you take control of it."

"Thirty percent," Ravazzani said.

That caused D'Agostino to laugh—a deep, full-on belly laugh. "Keep dreaming, stronzo."

Ravazzani didn't like that one bit. A muscle jumped in his jaw. "And," he said as if D'Agostino hadn't denied him, "I want thirty percent of the Sicilian gun market."

I sat up straight in my chair. Thirty percent? Of my empire? "No fucking way."

"Jesus Mary and Joseph," Mancini said, dragging a hand down his face. "Here is what I propose. Ten percent across the board. Enzo, you give ten percent of the fraud business to Fausto. Giacomo gives ten percent of the guns to Enzo. And Fausto gives ten percent of the drug trade to Giacomo. Everyone wins."

Except it didn't feel like winning. It felt like losing.

"This is not equal," D'Agostino said. "Ten percent of my profits is considerably more than a few pistols and rocket launchers."

Idiota. He had no idea of the volume and scale of the arms business, apparently.

"It doesn't matter," Mancini said. "What matters is that the three of you are invested in each other's success. You'll stop working at cross purposes and work together. For the sake of my daughters."

I didn't like it, but how could I refuse my father-in-law this request the night before my wedding? Emma would want peace and harmony between the family.

Sometimes you had to take a punch or two before emerging victorious.

"This is why you're a great don . . . You're smart, calm, disciplined."

My bambina. For her, I could do this.

"I agree," I said loudly.

Ravazzani stared at the wall, his jawline like granite, not saying a word. After a long beat D'Agostino let out a breath. "Fuck it. I also agree."

"Fausto?" Mancini prompted when the other man remained silent.

Ravazzani rolled the crystal tumbler in his fingers, then brought it to his lips. He downed the liquid in one swallow. "I don't like strengthening the Cosa Nostra. The GDF are all over their ass nowadays. They could bring us down, too."

"You are not strengthening the Cosa Nostra," Mancini explained. "You are working with Buscetta, and only Buscetta. He's the single powerful family left, now that Virga has been killed."

"Which means the GDF will be focusing on him," Ravazzani said.

"They won't find anything," I said. "I work much differently than my father and brother."

Ravazzani stroked his jaw. "Perhaps, but I will pass on the name of my contact there. You can work out a price."

For protection. I nodded once. "Appreciate it."

"Does this mean you agree?" Mancini asked him.

"If I don't," Ravazzani said, "my wife will never let me hear the end of it. So, I have no choice but to say yes."

"Thank Christ." Mancini pulled a switchblade out of his pocket. "Now, the three of you will seal this deal with blood."

———

Emma

I stared at the woman reflected in the mirror, dumbstruck. "Gia, it's . . . Wow. I don't even know what to say."

My twin had designed a wedding dress for me in just three weeks. The result was an off the shoulder silk gown with three-quarter length sleeves that hugged my curves before dropping into an a-line skirt. It was elegant and classy, and absolutely perfect for me.

"Just say it's gorgeous, dummy." She grabbed my hand and squeezed. "Seriously, Em. You look beautiful."

"I love it," Frankie said, coming to stand on my other side. "Gia, how did you manage this so quickly?"

"I based it on Audrey Hepburn's first wedding dress, the one she never wore. It's simple, but I think it suits Emma's personality."

"It does. I love it, Gigi." My sister was so talented. "It's absolutely perfect."

"Turn around," my father said behind us. "Let me see my youngest daughter."

I slowly spun toward the library sofa, where my father was resting before the wedding started. He looked tired, and I suspected the husbands had kept him up late last night. Giacomo wouldn't tell me what they did or said, except that they'd arrived at an agreement that suited all of them. And the bandage on his palm meant they'd signed it in blood.

Papà's face softened and I could see the moisture gathering in his eyes. "Emma, you look beautiful. You all are. I wish your mother were here to see this."

Frankie slipped her hand into mine, so I reached over to grab Gia's, as well, linking the three of us together. "I wish she was here, too," I said.

He smiled, his gaze dragging over each of us. "She'd be so proud of each of you, of how strong and smart you are. Successful and driven. I know I haven't always been the best father, but I love each of you very much."

"We love you, too," Frankie said, her voice tight with emotion. "But you can't make us cry because the makeup team has already left."

It wouldn't matter. I knew I'd spend most of the day in tears. This wedding meant so much to my father, which was why I'd insisted on having it. A happy occasion, surrounded by our family—*all* our family.

The door to the sitting room flew open and two small sets of feet came running in. "Nonno! Nonno!"

We turned to see Raffaele Ravazzani run into the room, his sister Noemi on his heels. Frankie darted toward them, grabbing the kids before they could reach my father. "Slow down," she said. "Nonno is resting. Be careful with him. Remember what I said?"

"That we aren't monkeys and he isn't a tree," Rafe repeated, using his English instead of Italian.

"Come over here," my father said. "Nonno wants to see both of you all dressed up."

Carefully, the kids went over to my father and stood before him on the sofa. "Mamma mia, how nice you look! Who helped you with your tie, Rafe?"

"My Papà." Rafe tugged at the small tie around his neck. "But I hate it. It's too tight."

"No, it isn't," Frankie said. "And don't pull on it. You can take it off after the photos."

My father leaned down and squeezed Rafe's shoulder. "Mine's uncomfortable, too. Later, we'll take them off together, okay?"

"Okay."

"And let me see my beautiful girl," my father said as he focused on Noemi. "You are so pretty it makes my eyes hurt," he said softly, then tickled her ribs. She giggled and crawled up onto the sofa next to him, and he wrapped an arm around her, pulling her close. My father was gentle and sweet with Noemi, much as he'd always been with me, which confused the heck out of Frankie and Gia. They hadn't seen this side of him until recently.

"What time is it?" I asked.

"Almost time," Gia answered. "Are you ready?"

More than ready. I didn't mention how we were already married. This ceremony, surrounded by friends and family, would be the one I'd remember. "Should we go down?"

There was a knock on the door. "Dolcezza?" Fausto said from the hall. "May I come in? Are the kids in there?"

"Pronto!" she called.

My brother-in-law, looking every inch the elegant and handsome Italian older man in his three-piece suit, came into the room, a small baby cradled in his arm. No wonder Frankie's ovaries couldn't keep up with him. Fausto spotted the kids with my father and frowned. "What did I tell you both?"

"Not to run around," Rafe said repeated dutifully, "but—"

"There is no *but*," Fausto said. "You follow my orders, *figlio mio*. Capisce?"

Rafe didn't appear happy at that. "Why am I in trouble and not Noemi?"

"Because you're older," Frankie said, taking Marcello's sleeping form from Fausto. "You're supposed to look out for your sister."

"That's not fair," the boy grumbled. "I don't want to be older."

With a shake of his head, Fausto kissed Frankie on the mouth. "They learn how to argue from you, *piccola monella*."

"Papà likes to kiss Mamma," Noemi whispered to her nonno.

"That's good," my father said. "All husbands should like kissing their wives."

She peeked at me from under her lashes. "Will Zio Mo like kissing Zia Emma once they are married?"

I bit back a grin, while Gia snickered next to me. "If she saw your sex hair this morning," she said, "then she'd know the answer to that question."

"Stop, you two," Frankie admonished, though she was smiling. "Don't corrupt my kids."

"Hello?" Marie, the wedding coordinator, poked her head in. "Are we ready to begin? The guests have all been seated."

"Yes! Thank you, Marie," I said. "We're ready."

Fausto went to help my father get up and settled in a wheelchair. Gia was there, as well, making my father laugh to lighten the moment. Papà didn't like the wheelchair, but there was no other choice. I wanted him to walk me down the aisle. Who cared if he rolled instead?

We assembled at the back of the French doors that would open out onto the patio. The drapes made it impossible to see out, but I knew Giacomo was there, waiting for me. I could feel him, mio grande marito.

Zani, the best man, was standing near the door. Fausto took Marcello from Frankie, then cast a deadly glare at Zani. "Careful of your hands, Zaniolo. She belongs to me."

"Oh, for god's sake." Frankie shoved Fausto toward the doors. "Get out there and sit down, Paparino."

After one more kiss on his wife's mouth, Fausto disappeared through the French doors. I took a deep breath. I wasn't one who craved attention, but I was doing this for my father. For all of us. For the memories this would make.

"Okay," Marie said. "Maid of honor and best man? You're here." She pointed by the doors for Frankie and Zani to line up. "Then we need our ring bearer."

Rafe pushed forward and Marie handed him a pillow with the rings on it. "I won't lose them," my nephew promised.

"I know you won't, ometto mio," Frankie said, turning and smoothing his hair.

"Now the flower girl," Marie said, and helped Noemi get in position with her basket of petals.

Gia and I positioned my father's wheelchair in the back, ready for our cue. Marie texted someone on her phone, and soon the sounds of the orchestra reached our ears. She smiled as she positioned herself by the doors. "You all look beautiful. Breathe. This is the fun part."

The doors opened. The patio had been transformed with twinkling lights and flowers, and heaters were positioned to ward off the chill. Against the gray backdrop of the afternoon Toronto sky, it was perfect.

"It looks like fairies live there," Noemi whispered to Rafe.

"Fairies don't exist," her brother said with complete conviction.

"Yes, they do," Noemi argued. "Mamma, tell Rafe that fairies are real."

"That's enough," Frankie whispered. "We'll talk about this later." Frankie sent one last warning glare over her shoulder before beginning to walk down the aisle with Zani.

Marie sent Rafe next, then Noemi. When the aisle cleared it was our turn, and the small number of guests stood up. That meant it was time. I could see my husband standing at the end of the aisle, so big and handsome. He was a rock, the man who helped me realize that I didn't have to handle everything alone. I didn't have to save the world at the expense of my own happiness. I had nothing to prove to anyone.

And I was going to be a mob wife *and* a doctor.

"Go, go, go," Marie said, waving us forward.

Gia gripped the handles of the wheelchair and I took my father's hand. "Let's do this."

The End

———

Thank you so much for reading!

Want more Giacomo & Emma?

My newsletter subscribers get special "after the wedding" bonus scenes! This includes a peek at what Gia/Enzo, Giacomo/Emma, and Fausto/Frankie are up to after the wedding reception.

Sign up at milafinelli.com!

ACKNOWLEDGMENTS

Thank you so much for reading Mafia Virgin! This series has been a labor of love, and I'm grateful for each and every one of you.

Many hands help make these books shine. Thank you to Jennifer Prokop for her amazing editing and to Letitia at RBA Designs for the sexy covers. Diana Quincy deserves so much credit, because she always reads these books first and helps me sort out my mess.

So many people help with the chaos of my author life that I'd never be able to properly thank all of them here. But Nicole is the queen who keeps things running smoothly, allowing me to focus on writing. I'm very thankful for all she does!

Thank you to the readers who have supported this series. I love all your edits and posts and memes. They always make me smile.

I would be nothing without my very own Paparino, who helps me with these books and dinner and laundry and a thousand other things that make it possible for me to write. Ti amo, baby.

More books coming soon!

xox,

Mila

ABOUT THE AUTHOR

Mila Finelli is the dark contemporary pen name of *USA Today* bestselling historical author Joanna Shupe, who finally decided to write the filthy mafia kings she's been dreaming about for years. She's addicted to coffee, travel, and books with bad men.

For signed books, merch, news & more, visit Mila's website at milafinelli.com.

Join Mila's Famiglia on Facebook!

Want more Fausto?
Sign up for Mila's newsletter and get a FREE Fausto &
Frankie bonus story!

ALSO BY MILA FINELLI

The Kings of Italy Series
MAFIA MISTRESS
MAFIA DARLING
MAFIA MADMAN
MAFIA TARGET
MAFIA VIRGIN

Coming soon!
MAFIA DEVIL

Theo & Nic's story, originally published in the 2023 Pride Not Prejudice
Anthology. Expanded and spruced up for Spring 2024.

———

Start at the beginning with Mafia Mistress
Book 1 in the Kings of Italy series!

MAFIA MISTRESS

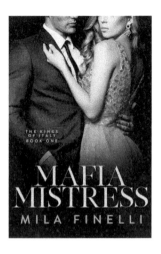

FAUSTO

I am the darkness, the man whose illicit empire stretches around the globe. Not many have the courage for what needs to be done to maintain power . . . but I do.

And I always get what I want.

Including my son's fiancée.

She's mine now, and I'll use Francesca any way I see fit. She's the perfect match to my twisted desires, and I'll keep her close, ready and waiting at my disposal.

Even if she fights me at every turn.

FRANCESCA

I was stolen away and held prisoner in Italy, a bride for a mafia king's only heir.

Except I'm no innocent, and it's the king himself—the man called il Diavolo—who appeals to me in sinful ways I never dreamed. Fausto's wickedness draws me in, his power like a drug. And when the devil decides he wants me, I'm helpless to resist him—even if it means giving myself to him, body and soul.

He may think he can control me, but this king is about to find out who's really the boss.

MAFIA MISTRESS is available in eBook, Print and Audio.